THE ETERNAL RETURN

The Eternal Return
Copyright © 2023 John Kolchak
All rights reserved

Published by Ward Six Press
Pasadena, CA USA
Design by Geraldine Baum

First printing, 2023
ISBN: 978-0-9840130-9-8
wardsixpress.com

THE ETERNAL RETURN

JOHN KOLCHAK

Ward Six Press

Nothing that exists is absolutely worthy of our love, so we must love what does not exist. But this object of love which does not exist is not a fiction. Our fictions cannot be more worthy of love than we who are not.

—Simone Weil

What if, some day or night, a demon were to steal after you into your loneliest loneliness and say to you: "This life, as you now live it and have lived it, you will have to live once more and innumerable times more; and there will be nothing new in it, but every pain and every joy and every thought and sigh… must return to you—all in the same succession and sequence—even this spider and this moonlight between the trees and even this moment and I myself. The eternal hourglass of existence is turned over again and again —and you with it, speck of dust!" Would you not throw yourself down and gnash your teeth and curse the demon who spoke thus? Or have you once experienced a tremendous moment when you would have answered him: "You are a god, and never have I heard anything more divine!" If this thought were to gain possession of you, it would change you as you are, or perhaps crush you. The question in each and every thing, "do you want this once more and innumerable times more?" would lie upon your actions as the greatest weight. How well disposed would you have to become to yourself and to life to crave nothing more fervently than this ultimate eternal confirmation and seal?

—Friedrich Nietzsche, *The Gay Science*

"You see, Alyosha," Grushenka turned to him with a nervous laugh. "I was boasting when I told Rakitin I had given away an onion, but it's not to boast I tell you about it. It's only a story, but it's a nice story. I used to hear it when I was a child from Matryona, my cook, who is still with me. It's like this. Once upon a time there was a peasant woman and a very wicked woman she was. And she died and did not leave a single good deed behind. The devils caught her and plunged her into the lake of fire. So her guardian angel stood and wondered what good deed of hers he could remember to tell to God; 'She once pulled up an onion in her garden,' said he, 'and gave it to a beggar woman.' And God answered: 'You take that onion then, hold it out to her in the lake, and let her take hold and be pulled out. And if you can pull her out of the lake, let her come to Paradise, but if the onion breaks, then the woman must stay where she is.' The angel ran to the woman and held out the onion to her. 'Come,' said he, 'catch hold and I'll pull you out.' And he began cautiously pulling her out. He had just pulled her right out, when the other sinners in the lake, seeing how she was being drawn out, began catching hold of her so as to be pulled out with her. But she was a very wicked woman and she began kicking them. 'I'm to be pulled out, not you. It's my onion, not yours.' As soon as she said that, the onion broke. And the woman fell into the lake and she is burning there to this day. So the angel wept and went away. So that's the story, Alyosha; I know it by heart, for I am that wicked woman myself. I boasted to Rakitin that I had given away an onion, but to you I'll say: 'I've done nothing but give away one onion all my life, that's the only good deed I've done.' So don't praise me, Alyosha, don't think me good, I am bad, I am a wicked woman and you make me ashamed if you praise me. Eh, I must confess everything…"

—Feodor Dostoyevsky, *The Brothers Karamazov*

Part I

LOS ANGELES

THE SITTER

Before any of the following happened I strongly believed that autobiographies were for the most part worthless unless one had lived through exceptional times or was oneself an exceptional individual. I can't claim either. That percentage among us is infinitesimal. Most of our lives, I had come to feel, are utterly pedestrian no matter how alternately "touching" or "tragic" or "funny" they may seem to us, no matter how unique we think we are or were.

For each individual who has survived war, famine, the Holocaust, gulags, or grotesque personal misfortune, there are millions who experienced the same fate but lacked the skill, the ambition and, most importantly, the vanity to actually put pen to paper. And so vanity and a little bit of skill combined to show us the experiences of only a few. Mankind, I firmly believed, was not even the proverbial anthill, but something more akin to a parasitic, self-reproducing fungus, spewing out replacements for ridiculously short lives in an almost paraphilic manner; one would need to set the bar rather high to warrant writing about oneself.

After the following happened, I changed my mind and decided that whatever I wrote would be worthwhile after all; for posterity perhaps, or at the very least as a case study for clinicians. Although the rationale for existence continued to pose a logical problem, I eventually got my mental illness under relative control, and so I broke the promise I made to myself to never compose an autobiography.

So call this what you will: autobiography, confession, case study.

I won't tell you my real name for obvious reasons. Everything has been changed to protect the innocent and the guilty. Call me Lucky. I started using that as a nickname in college as a fatalistic joke based on the quirky "funny" posters one would sometimes see in crappy bars: "Lost Dog: Three legs, blind in left eye, missing right ear, broken tail, recently castrated, answers to the name "Lucky." And the joke stuck until I started using it as a sarcastic badge of pride. But let's start. Names are names or misnomers. And one should never trust a writer anyway, whatever his nickname may be.

We create life knowing that it will grow old, wither, and die. But when we choose to create art, we gamble on whether it will be utterly forgotten or last for years, perhaps hundreds of years. Inside every womb is a casket. I will die soon—or maybe not terribly soon; no one knows when one will die—but by writing down what transpired that summer, that season in hell and bliss, as recommended to me as a form of therapy by my doctors, I have finally found a modicum of bittersweet peace. I am now back in California, my adopted land on the edge of the earth where I have come back to the safety of warm weather and, more importantly, the safety of sitting, which is precisely where and how this story began, when I was The Sitter, several years ago.

Back then, having lived in California for over a decade, I had come to the conclusion that my lot in life was mostly to sit. It is, after all, something I am quite good at, and in this late stage of life it is way too difficult to move my ass towards bigger and better things. This understanding was not provoked by a failed visit to a prostitute, an unsuccessful attempt at assassinating a politician, or humiliation by colleagues or former classmates; it was a gradual process of giving up.

Sitting has many noble qualities. For one, it does no harm—except, perhaps, in extreme cases of prolonged sitting, to yourself vis-à-vis hemorrhoids. Secondly, it puts one in the perfect position to reflect. Reflection is beyond you when you're running. I don't mean physically running, I mean trying to outrun the pack. Consider the Buddha, or Saint Simeon the Stylite who sat on a Greek column in the desert eating leaves from an adjacent tree, shitting green off the side of his Corinthian tower. Did they not both manage not only to achieve enlightenment but also to fight off demons? And all this simply through the process of sitting.

So there, I'll say it once more: inactivity, be it by fate, circumstance, or volition, is itself noble. Or so it seemed to me before I started on this journey.

Certainly the world has its pecking order, but the Hindu castes were not created for putting people down. Rather, they are an extension of the natural order of things. They helped create a Dewey System of cataloguing each according to their particular skill—or vice. Each has its place within the mill, within the anthill, including us sitters, of course. It would be foolish to compare a panther to a snail to see who is more noble, and even more foolish to compare a carrot to a panther, or a turnip to a hippogriff. And thus I, in my personal carotene splendor, also feel that I have at times reached enlightenment, or at least have come close. There is still much more sitting to be done, though sometimes even the vegetables scream when they see how pointless it all is. The words of Maxim Gorky: "Man is destined for happiness the way birds are destined for flight" I paraphrased this according to my own means and experiences as "Man is destined for happiness the way a hippopotamus is destined for flight." And that is why I sometimes dream that I have indeed become a panther, only to wake up in my garden variety garden yet again. After some feeling around in the dirt to make sure I'm here among the worms and the moles I know, I reach for my bottle of liquid pesticide—it helps keep both intruding bugs and unpleasant thoughts away—and begin to contemplate further.

It wasn't always like this, of course. Back in my salad days—oh, pardon the puns, there will be more—as a seedling, I knew nothing, but as I took shape, I'd watch the springs and summers with delight and wish I could grow higher, bud into a sunflower, look straight at the sky or maybe sprout legs and pull myself out into the world. Alas, the limbs I grew were as useless as those of a mandrake and like the mandrake I would scream when fate tripped me up, or pulled me around by the hair. When did I become stone ass? There was a time when I had ambition—misguided, naturally, but looking towards the stars, dammit, not into the dirt in the navel. Let me try to retrace my steps.

The catalyst behind it all was Betty. Poor Betty with an ass made of even heavier stone than mine, for she was immobile. But let me start a bit earlier, back in the smoggy, beer colored glow of Los Angeles, before I embarked on my "sentimental journey" only to return and return and return.

I had thought about calling this book The Book of Regret, but that would not have been accurate. For did Geppetto regret carving his Burattino when all he wanted was a piece of crusty bread and a glass of rotgut, with the unfortunate doll just a by-product of his sodden mind? And did his Pinocchio not get flayed, tortured and hanged by the blind cat and the lame fox only to be reborn again and reunited with his maker? I digress. Let's start from the beginning, or at least somewhere farther back—somewhere we can lay a footprint in the quicksand and try move forward, or backwards, or somewhere, as long as there is movement. Even the sitter— perhaps I should say only the sitter—knows about movement. But again I am getting ahead of myself. Let's start with Los Angeles…

It is difficult to recall when exactly I resigned myself to my throne, though even after the melding was nearly complete I would occasionally entertain dreams of escape, most of which were absurd in light of my age and poor health. I sometimes dreamt of working on an oil rig, or better yet, joining the merchant fleet, watching the endless expanse of oceans in between stops in moist, dark places like Lagos, Lourenço Marques, Nagasaki… Their names were fine fodder for fantasy. And my dreams were always incredibly vivid, both at night and during the day. It was easy for me to slip into a semi-hallucinatory, hypnagogic state. Not to escape reality the way an abused child dreams up living fairy tales in which he slays the evil dragon who represents the abuser, but in a fashion somewhat related. I was able then, and still am, to enter a liminal world at the necessary moment. As much as I still wished to see the baobabs of Morondava and the rooftops of Antananarivo, or even more accessible places like Greece or Japan, I knew that time was running out, and so I became an armchair traveler. I complained too much, it's true. I could have been living in Alaska or Siberia or Tierra del Fuego or any number of horrible places that stain the map. But eventually the oranges of Hieronymus Bosch and the tennis balls that washed up on the sandy beaches of Southern California, or bobbed around in the blue surf, began to bore me to tears and I lost my appreciation for those places to which I had longed to move for so many miserable East Coast winters. Some dark, moist places were undoubtedly staid but many others smelled of the lost idea of possibility, the way clean, bright cities when seen from the ocean gleam with promise, yet almost always turn out to be disappointments.

In my early teens I spent a period of around two weeks in a twilit existence. I was sick with a fever and my mother, who distrusted, feared and hated doctors, naturally did not take me to a physician. I don't think I saw a single doctor in America until I was eighteen or so, and that was a compulsory physical examination prior to my admission to college. Those two weeks were the earliest I remember of living in a pure dream world. It was winter, or perhaps an especially cold and dark early spring, and for a week or two I awoke when the sun had already set. I remember those nights well, the pure bliss of delirium, two weeks of living in darkness. I remember that when I was slightly better we took a taxi to Queens to visit some people, an elderly couple, some kind of artists or literati. From the car window I saw the street lamps and traffic lights streaking by as if in a hallucination, forming horizontal lines as the car drove wildly over the Triborough Bridge. It was around that time, during one of those long hallucinatory, liminal phases, that I composed my first book—something about cosmology; perambulations on the nature of the universe and the idea of infinity. Utter nonsense, but the subject gripped my adolescent mind.

Infinity. I had no idea what I was talking about or what I meant, and I still don't. But there was a certain feeling, or a certain sensation, that would come over me—much stronger back then, of course, than today, when the skies seemed open and life was full of promise—and a wave of exhilaration would pass through me, and like Jansen's tenet that grace can be found anywhere, even in the most depraved of circumstances, so I found infinity in even the smallest scraps of tragedy and the slightest of loves, in sordid stories that nonetheless possessed that indescribable spark somewhere within them that lit the paper lantern. Some of that feeling has survived, though I still have no idea what I was trying then to express.

The inertia, the entropy, that took hold in the years that followed first appeared shortly after we moved—my wife and daughter and I—from Hollywood to Pasadena, a place they call "Connecticut with palm trees." What few friends I had soon stopped visiting. The sitting, which had started in Hollywood, coincided with my decline into alcoholism. The move to a more self-contained city, even though it was only fifteen minutes from my old neighborhood, encouraged more isolation, the isolation encouraged more drinking, and the drinking encouraged more sitting.

My old building was a collection of curiosities, a panopticon, a Kunstkamera that in more talented hands would have made a decent comedic novel, but my misanthropy pulled me away from even attempting to "immortalize" these rather pathetic specimens in any body of work. You can see, I trust, or hope to believe, why I didn't venture far from my throne, and why I stayed the same after our move. I much preferred to sit, and to sit alone.

There are some expressions about certain characters, real or fictional, or even semi-fictional. "He came to such and such a place solely to die" is a popular refrain. I came here to live but chose to sit. Don't get me wrong, I don't live in a jar outside a restaurant, nor do I lack limbs, nor am I paralyzed. The paralysis is neither physical nor mental. On the contrary, it's willed. The mystery is how it all came to be. Despite being glued to the spot, I still yearned to escape, either permanently or perhaps just "to write," or even to finish my life somewhere new, in isolation. Argentina always interested me, partly due to its relative isolation and partly because the plane fares to Buenos Aires are sometimes cheaper than they are even to Europe. I researched these things rather heavily. Flights to Montevideo, Uruguay were even cheaper. I never fancied the old blind librarian Borges. I despise blind people. They remind me of moles. I also hate them because blindness is my biggest fear. Tango and steak. And nice Beaux-arts architecture. Pedestrian dreams, I suppose. Perhaps something else, I don't know what—cheap health care? That would be impetus enough, maybe... The Polish guy who got stranded in Argentina, worked as a bank teller, wrote books, where was the brilliant literati society then when he would literally almost starve and finally in desperation had to knock on a neighbor's door and they gave the poor sod a plate of chicken and rice... This, in the richest country in the world at the time. I hate blind people everywhere. No matter if they live in Buenos Aires or Saskatchewan. "Geographical cure" is a phrase I rather like, but rooted as I am, I do most of my traveling through books and television, and I am aware. I have read that most of the island paradises of the South Pacific are actually hellholes of garbage and prostitution, sex slavery and forced abortions just to name a few. There are other authors to talk about these things, but the point is, I was glued to the throne because I am a sitter. Strangely, just as things turned progressively, almost geometrically stagnant, my perception of time went into warp speed, as if hurtling down a black hole, accelerating with each moment, not just each day. Becoming a new dad in middle-age was supposed to have marked a "personal and spiritual renaissance"—I recall the phrase from some book or other, implying that you will live again, be young through your children—but instead my stagnation and my sitting continued. The West simply became a detour on the way to the cemetery, and that is what happened to Stacy when she moved to California. But more about Stacy later. I am getting ahead of myself once more.

I should say something about myself before we press on. Just a few words—for color. I would say that I am neither utterly pedestrian (owing to my insanity) nor quite unique (owing likewise). The problem with uniqueness is that it was ingrained in my mind by my parents. All my life, until my parents' death, I swallowed a myth that I was more than unique, more than talented (they were obsessed with vacuous superlatives), that I was destined for greatness and a spectacular life—none of which was true and none of which came to pass. This reinforcement contributed much to my present condition (more on that later too), and bred within me the most profound laziness. Instead of soberly addressing what I should be doing with my life in a practical way, I was constantly told that something great was going to happen to me, that it was right around the corner. And so l walked around like a rock star without a band, while the beast in the jungle waited.

Physically, I am not entirely unattractive—or so I eventually decided. Though I have always struggled with relationships, I have never been rejected by women due to my physical appearance. It has, I suspect, been various aspects of my personality that many of my love interests have found difficult. But I have always been able to put on charms, put on airs, often aided by Dutch courage; and the fact that most, if not all, of my inamorata were attractive, confirmed that there wasn't anything terribly wrong with me as a man and a lover, with the possible exception of my predilection for booze, though that was often exaggerated in the mind of my lovers and formed the basis of an excuse for the inevitable separation.

Allow me to jot down some brief biographical notes. I have been living in Los Angeles for twelve years, but I spent most of my life in New York City. I was a real New Yorker, fully acclimated to a frightful and maddening city that is a world in its own. Over the years I rented apartments in every borough except Staten Island. Apart from an ill-fated summer in San Francisco and four years attending college in upstate New York, I hadn't lived anywhere else. But after some time New York became unbearable. I convinced my partner—now my wife—to move with me, and so we sought out smoggier and greener pastures in Los Angeles.

I was born and raised in Europe. "Occupied Europe," shall we say. In its epicenter, no less; the command room of the Evil Empire, Moscow. Not just geographers but most educated folks will agree that Russia, while a transcontinental country, occupies one third of the European continent and culturally falls squarely within the framework of "European civilization." Here in the US, I found and still find to this day Americans who believe that the Eastern Slavs came from a different planet, that we walk around in bearskin coats and the ground is permafrost. The last part is true in the far north, of course… but I digress.

My Russian roots made my assimilation difficult for a long time, and though I loved Russia's culture and its writers and its songs, with no hope of ever returning I tried to embrace not only New York but all of America. But that only deepened my feeling of homelessness, made an absence where a sense of belonging ought to have been. Everywhere I looked I could not find myself, until eventually America—the idea of America, I should say—died for me. Much of Russia is cold, this is true. But if one looks at Russian paintings (the same goes for Scandinavian works, by the way), one sees that the vast majority of them are set in summer. The short, warm season is what gives inspiration to northern Europe. We may be Scythians, but we are not Eskimos. In America my imagination ran wild, searching for something which I could never find, neither on my day trips nor my interstate adventures. America was tinged with sadness from the start, and eventually it drowned me. I sought something in this country—not Karl May westerns but something that I always felt was just below the surface of that long, endless street of grey that stretches from ocean to ocean. I had sought something but I found nothing but a carcass. Over time, as a way to survive, I cultivated a perverse affection for that carcass—but it never lasted, and it was not enough. Even the sordid became tiresome. Even after we quit our jobs, packed our car with essential belongings, and headed for the sham utopia of sunny southern California.

A few years later some friends came to visit us in LA and we drove with them to the Grand Canyon. I had already seen that beast, twice. I could well understand why those first Spanish explorers, dumbstruck on discovering this unreal place, lost their minds. At first I could only look at it for a few minutes and I was done. This time, with our friends, we camped the night next to a man and his son. To me the child seemed kind of slow, but it's possible he was just shy. I don't remember how old he was, perhaps ten or twelve. His dad struck up a conversation with us. He asked about our trip and whether we'd been here before, and I described our cross-country route. "Yeah, we did that trip—me and him and his mom—we camped out around here…" He paused then and looked up at the stars. I wondered if she was dead, or just divorced. This man too sought possibility at one point. And then his cards were taken from him. He must have been only a few years older than me, no more than a decade, and now I'm more than a decade older than he was and I can still see the look of regret on his face as he turned his head away from me, then to his kid, then back to the campfire. Wherever his mother was it didn't matter. Something in this boy's father was dead. *Partir, c'est mourir un peu, mais mourir, c'est partir beaucoup.*

That lonely man with his boy at the campfire has never left me. The way he talked, the way he said so simply, "His mother and I…" I knew and saw regret, defeat. People latch on to certain phrases, episodes. Those philologically inclined perhaps more so. Classical scenes of farewell, or better yet—scenes of regret. There are too many to count and I have ratcheted my own points and continue to do so. My mother was the queen of regrets and farewells, and I will tell you about her later.

Another experience of regret, from when I too was around twelve years of age, has also stayed in my mind. A very banal regret. I was somewhere on the Jersey Shore with my dad, buying fruit at a farmer's market. My favorite band at that age was New York Dolls and I was wearing a t-shirt with their name on it, which the fruit seller commented on. "New York Dolls, I remember them… I partied with them a few times…" She smiled, but bitterly. The smile of regret. Perhaps the smile of a washed-up groupie. It is related to the smile of sorrow that says "I fucked up" but it is a unique smile in its own right. I had no idea how old she was—at that age it is impossible to tell. For me, at least, it still is. Even if she had been twenty-something, as I speculated, she seemed already infinitely older and wiser than me—and more damned. Though

I had no idea about groupiedom and was not even moderately knowledgeable about sex, I sensed something about her: the sense of regret, the sense of defeat, the sense of the end of youth. That girl at the fruit and vegetable market with her bleached hair, holding on to memories of "partying" with the band stayed with me. It is remarkable that I remember it to this day, thirty five years later. But off track. Regret will come back in spades in this narrative, and the full nature of regret only came to me much later when I decided to squash it, strangle it. I began to understand certain things about what happened to me that year in New York by putting pen to paper, by understanding that the process of giving up can be interrupted by one last burst of madness and freedom.

It's actually very easy to recognize when someone fucked up. You see it in their eyes, in their manner of talking, the voice of regret, that obscure feeling that life is elsewhere and has shot passed them. The unassuageable look of loneliness. One would have been tempted to put Betty in that category of unfortunates simply because she was confined to a wheelchair—but that would have been a mistake. Her wheels served her well, she was, to use the cliché "fiercely independent" and had a tremendous amount of interest in things—mostly me and my family for some reason, or so I thought. But she had that constant look that read "I blew it" written all over her face. In short, Betty had a secret. Or secrets. Just how horrible or mild those secrets were was impossible to say. As for her supposed interest in me, perhaps she saw my own regret, a reflection that I too fucked up somewhere along the way.

"How time passes, faster than in the blink of an eye"—that was a recurring line in the one book I managed to finish while living in LA, a story about Christ called "Next Year in Jerusalem," a reworking of the Gospel story in which Christ struggles to define what it is he is preaching. My version eliminated the fantasy and fireworks of the New Testament, and Christ comes to a miserable end one sunny and absurd day. But instead of providing momentum for the next book, finishing that story left me feeling empty, stagnant. As much as I looked forward to fishing tennis balls out of the surf instead of using an ice scraper on my windshield while standing in feet of yellow snow, I had reached a state of permanent torpor. Blue Pacific blues. Blue was supposed to be the color of possibility... When the mail would come and there was nothing there but junk, or if the mail came early, I would feel like the day was now over and there was nothing left to look forward to. Yes, my wife was supporting me, and despite the logistics—that with my being out of work for so long I would have been reduced to working as a Walmart greeter and whatever pittance I made would offset the cost of daycare and babysitting—I still yearned for something from life other than a piece of bread and butter. My wife Charlotte, my dark eyed Sephardic princess, had become so subsumed by her job at a certain fashion magazine that our sex life progressively withered unto atrophy, and at that point in time I write of, we were in a roommate situation—where the roommates despise one other. And that led me to live in a world of imagination. I will not say much about Charlotte in this book. I do not wish to give her more pain than I already did by being a bum. I will leave out our troubles in case she ever reads this book. Let's just say we met in New York, fell in love, and upon my suggestion agreed to move to LA with me. And it turned out somewhat like that son and father in the campground by the Grand Canyon, one of us blew it and that one was me. Whilst Charlotte quickly adjusted to not just the city but found social circles and a profitable job, I continued to dwell in fantasies of "making it" in the film industry without any connections, but mostly without even any plans. It was a recipe for failure straight out of David Lynch's Mulholland Drive but I couldn't see the palm trees for the rats.

It was after the birth of our first and only child that I gradually ceased to exist in Charlotte's mind. So when life gives you lemons, you make vodka and sodas with lemon. When reality is unsatisfying, you can hedge pleasant dreams against nightmares.

After over a decade in LA I started to have the most incredibly vivid dreams of New York, as vivid as dreaming can be, as vivid as the dreams I would have about having a conversation with either of my dead parents. As is often the way in dreams, my physical perception would be different and the geography of New York would change. The skyscrapers lost their height somewhat, and there were fewer people. The sheer height of Manhattan and the density of the crowds interferes with seeing that you are actually there when you are, and so these days it is only in dreams, when New York is bathed in a benign light, that I would actually visit. I tend to believe that was less true in the 1970s when I arrived. Even then it might have been claustrophobic, but it was nothing like it is today.

On waking from these gold and yellow dreams I would keep my eyes closed and remain in bed. I would lay there motionless like some Proustian brat as I fell, up or down (who could say?), from the heaven of my dreams. And yet even as I fell, lost as if I were an invalid confusing twilight and dawn, my eyelids would peel open and the yellow—yes, yellow—light, would peek in through the blinds. I would stay in bed as long as I could stand it, half-believing that I was in that fictitious and at times benign New York that doesn't exist and that most likely never truly did.

How the world spins; how tightly we are all are tied together, especially now.

I could hardly bear to look at photos of New York anymore. New York was my life, my lover, my enemy. I miss it now more than ever, but what I miss is something that is either gone or may not have ever existed. I am putting all of this in the book that I am currently writing. This morning I wrote (from personal feeling) something about how so many people born or raised in New York wish to escape. And New Yorkers who move to California wish nothing more than to "return" but they are not sure where they really yearn to return to.

The yellow evening sun beating against the glass and burglar gates, protecting my childhood safety and my mind, while garbage-strewn alleys were outside instead of guardian angels crashing into airplane pilots, yet my young imagination ran wild; decades before I heard of that Franco-Brazilian aviator, I was my own Alberto Santos-Dumont in my own airship circling around some type of imaginary Eiffel Tower. The airship had now sunk. It had deflated years before.

My life revolved so much around my parents that when it came to forging my own identity my development was rather stunted. I was coddled by my parents; they presented me to others as the perfect child, but I was very far from perfect.

It took me five or six years to start going through my mom's boxes. Among carbon copies of letters sent to relatives abroad and endless Xeroxes of the articles she wrote for the émigré newspapers, there were hidden clues. I realized that I was not the only one who felt like their life was made up of missing pieces.

Of course everyone has secrets. Some of these are utterly naïve and benign, some are a bit murky but ultimately harmless, and some others are pitch black, bitter to the core. The latter ones are rarely, if ever, revealed.

It was not a major revelation to me, as I dug through my mother's papers, that she had kept a "motherload" of letters between me and my old lovers. What freaked me out was that she somehow found and saved the correspondences. It felt like a betrayal of trust. My mother had always been a snoop and an egregious one at that, constantly prying for juicy bits, often brazenly. Going through her boxes—her smell still there; her name, Julia, handwritten on the lid—I wondered at the olfactory reminder: does this mean that matter can neither be created nor destroyed?

That was what came as a stark contrast to her own history. I remember only very few things from her early life, I do not know quite how she and my father met nor even why they decided to get married. Memory is selective and so are histories, which is why everything needs to be written down, so that they will not be forgotten and in some sense, or in some way, our lives will go on forever. I, Herodotus of Halicarnassus, here present my research so that human events do not fade with time.

Going through the suitcases and crates of my mom's life I found an interesting note from her own mother. It described how my mother was born. I found it enthralling. My mother did not know anything about how she was born and why. This is probably more common nowadays but under the hammer and sickle it was not only taboo but a Hester Prynne letter scenario which perhaps never left either the mother or the daughter.

I threw out a great many of the horoscopes she wrote for extra cash, and in which she also believed. She decried religion, and in the depths of her delirium would yell, "I am going to hell and I can't wait!" And yet like all of us she needed to believe, to believe in something. Looking through them I found a note scrawled in a hand I recognized as my grandmother's. It started, "You were born..." but I immediately put it away. I knew my mom was resentful of her mother but here I had found one of many skeleton keys, one that might open a locked door. Even though my mother spent most of her life—no, all of it—with my grandmother, she did not know her own history. And just as her mother would "abandon" her,—so she abandoned me in the same fashion at times. Julia wanted to live unencumbered and I was too young to know how to live, and I still don't. Julia wanted to be unfettered and I unfettered myself from New York only to find a different type of entrapment in LA:

in perpetual unemployment, in marriage, in fatherhood, in age. Each move of us insects is not enough to escape the web of God the Spider.

I had a Day of the Locust one time.

DAY OF THE LOCUST

One day I tried to trap a locust. We had bought our daughter an insect trap, not so much a trap to lure critters in for a specimen collection—although that would have been possible—but more like a tiny pet carrier, basically a plastic box with a couple of little mesh windows to let in air. The locust was impressive, a very large bug, an ugly brute of a cousin to the mechanical genius we call the grasshopper. He was still, resting on my patio door. I didn't think it was possible but in one deft move I slammed the plastic jail over him and lowered the gate. Oh how he moved! Berserk! Thrashing and flailing against this confinement which he had never experienced before. After a few seconds I set him free.

What happened in those seconds? I saw the flutter of life. My world did not split open like that of a Brazilian society woman discovering a giant roach in her Ipanema penthouse who promptly put the bug in her mouth. I did not bite into the locust and taste his primordial ooze that I share with him. Instead apart from his entomic agony I wondered above all, do locusts dream? And if so, what do they dream?

If we assume a priori that there is no god, no spiritual power or purpose of any kind, we are suddenly not so different from our arthropod cousins. We can talk all we want about the difference between us and the other animals, but that argument is nothing more than a dead horse whose carcass we daren't stop flogging. Very well, we have art. Very well, we have memories, civilizations etc. But do not ants and termites also create civilizations, and are they not also made of intricate and elaborate structures built using learned and recalled behaviors? Of course they do, and their anthills and termite mounds are as impressive as our megacities and just as cruel. Now, what separates us from them, these architectural geniuses on a par with Renzo Plano and Rem Koolhas, is that we do not know if they dream.

As the frogs croak, the lemurs howl and the birds chirp, what do they wish to send out into the universe? How are they different than we who accumulate tomes of notes and letters? The grasshopper fills the trunk of his belly with all sorts of sounds and all manner of faiths. But the wiser locust, when I released him, flew straight up towards the sun. He launched skyward like a bird in search of salvation. It reminded me of the end of Andersen's tale about the girl who stepped on a loaf of bread, a scene I had referenced years earlier at the end of my screenplay for Garbage Dump, or the Girl from Below. And as the bird flew back to her nest, so Stacy returned, and returned, and returned to her home in upstate New York and also returned to her nest in my mind until I had finally had enough—or so I thought. And through my own self-loathing I thought of Stacy when I wrote the following poem.

I am the girl who stepped on bread.
I didn't mean to, but I did.
Selfish, treading on the loaf
and disrespecting life, I chose to sin.
And now I bleed while
wingless flies and fierce invertebrates cover my eyes.

I am the girl whose vanity and pride
took hold of me and cast aside
all decency. I pay the price, though
nothing new: self-loathing is and
always has been me.

I am the girl who threw the bun into the mud
and used the heavenly gift of food as just a brick
so that I wouldn't sully dainty shoes,
and now filth rips into my sides and
there is nothing left in hell for me to lose.

But I had never ripped the wings off flies.
I found no pleasure in the suffering of
other creatures. Once, as a child, in fact, I cried
to think that even Stalin, when his fangs weren't
dripping blood, would suck upon a chicken leg
and smile and say a silent prayer of thanks
for simple pleasures simple tastes provide.
He was a priest by training, after all.

So here's my plea to you, oh Lord.
I threw the bread into the mud, it's true,
but is it really one strike and you're out?
The world is not just flawed, it's bitter
and it's brittle. Forget the bread I threw
into the mud, and try to meet me
in the middle.

Los Angeles lacked a spring, and therefore it lacked rebirth. It
was a steady amber-lighted purgatory. Even in the most miserable
of New York winters, in the blackest of Decembers and the most
violent of Marches, one could discover within and without the hope
of springtime, la primavera, the green stalks pushing through the
black, the first hints of sweetness in the air. Whan that Aprille with his
shoures soote. The Zephyr and the night wind, breaking through the
gloom and always signaling, no matter how quixotically, a fresh start.
    I remember sitting at the kitchen table in Queens, bottle

in front of me, staring out onto the black night, listening to a melody that was the harbinger of spring, thinking that once we turn the clocks forward and St. Patrick's Day passes and the first buds appear and the ice melts, etc etc etc, hope will return. But hope is not enough to yield a result. What was that song? Did it even exist? If I could pray, I would have asked, "Please, Lord, take everything but don't let my memories go away, no matter if they're dumb, sordid or painful, let me keep all of them."

In LA it was easier: spring the way I knew her never came and when it did it didn't bloom but brought rain and fog, the opposite of a curtain rising.

I also fancied myself as a writer. I had written screenplays, poems, and a novel which went nowhere. I had, on scraps of paper and in notebooks, and a whole jumbled mess of thoughts and ruminations I hoped one day would find a readership in book form. After I killed off screenwriting or as film and filmmaking killed itself, and after the failure of my first book, I decided that I had to do something with all the sweat and tears I expended on my screenplays, all the emotion and wringing of hands and gnashing of teeth, all the love and hate I had put into my central character Stacy Fox. But there was a problem: a writer's block, an incurable procrastination, a type of paralysis that is hard to describe. Possibly fear of failure as well, and fear of completion. I wanted to put off being depleted, I didn't want to see "The End" flash on the screen. I was petrified of endings.

I was also manipulative. The excuse was always there when I got shit for not finding a job: "Just let me finish this book and then…" but there was no "and then" because the book was not only unfinished, it hadn't been started. I wasted years doing a similar thing in New York with my delusional idea of filmmaking.

Apart from the desire for success, validation and immortality, the basic instinct behind writing a book is to create something—

to give something life. I was heavily pregnant but labor seemed very far away. Before my madness began, just as my mid-life crisis began to percolate, I felt as if my life was a cassette or video tape paused at this exact moment, a tape that I fast forwarded the way one does with porn, except nothing happened, no climax to be seen. And that here I was rewinding the tape until this moment and there was nothing but a dreadful blank and hissing noise that followed. Perhaps a blank slate should sound positive but I could picture rewinding the tape to replay it yet again on my deathbed, knowing that there is no rewind button in life.

I started to recognize that not just the world around me but I myself was settling into the mold of vulgarity and that the fire of things was being extinguished. Dreams were the only things that truly interested me. I began to live for them, and gradually the nocturnal world of fantasy replaced the daytime world as my primary reality. The further I drifted from the real world of people and buildings into that other world of feelings and shadows, the more I felt, in those hollowed out daylight hours, that something might not be right with my head.

Apart from the surreal nature of my existence, founded as it was on memories and a progressively stranger dream life—money was a huge concern. I was not homeless, but I still had no pot to piss in and I was fully dependent on my wife's generosity. She could have kicked me onto the street at any moment. Luckily for me she was not that cruel; I was fed and housed and provided with smokes and a bottle of popskull.

Sometimes I would comfort myself by returning to my amateur studies of Hinduism, physics and multiple universes. That way I could picture that at the same time Tom Hanks, Roman Abramovich and Madonna were living in abandoned latrines, and I had a mansion so big that I could not count the rooms. They were such sweet dreams.

Sure "you can't take it with you" and death is the great equalizer, but for me that was never enough. I yearned for something more. Dreams, daydreams, spiritual meditation, reveries and memories filled the gap reality left open, filled that hole that burned.

What was striking and disturbing—first one, then the other—was how the whole concept changed with age. Yes, there were many times of love; but there was no longer romance. And while I was not ready to have an affair, it frustrated me that I lacked the means to have one. I could not even afford to rent a hotel room or buy my theoretical mistress dinner, not even a single cocktail. I missed so much… the human touch, the excitement, the initial trepidation before a date (even that teenage need to masturbate before the date so you don't cream your jeans). When it comes down to it, a basic human need was missing.

The other things that are not sex but are the trepidation and the prelude to fucking, which might even in and of themselves be more exciting, were certainly erased. Undressing together, the unsnapping of the bra, the way the legs are lifted to remove the panties… And then the climax, ejaculating into warm orifice, those were now distant memories. Loneliness cracks the walls of madness, but sometimes it seals them.

One would think that there were other fish in the pond, but having only a dollar to my name all I could do was look or reminisce, observe buttocks from afar, pine for the human touch, recall good times gone by. Recently there was a bleached blonde at the library, I stared at her ass and the curvature of her hips and thigh. I never got to see her face. Then on the same day, there was a brunette in tight jogging shorts, her buttocks doing a little dance up and down, I followed her down the street as far as I was able, hoping to catch a glimpse of her face, but she kept walking and walking, and faster and faster. Thus I was reduced to nothing but these utterly innocent escapades, if one could even call them escapades—the miniscule pedestrian delights of looking at a young woman's jiggling ass.

At night, before falling asleep or in the waking hours, I found memories and I found regrets. I missed out on gratuitous sex. I had always thought during those times that if I fucked them I would have to date them, and if dated them I would probably end up marrying them. I wanted an ideal of some sort, and thus I deprived myself of just straight up and probably fantastic antics in bed.

I did not squander love, in fact I pined for it, but I certainly squandered many potential trysts. I was always waiting for the "right one" and so I missed out on quite a bit of fun between the sheets. It was my doomed romanticism that made me so superficially selective. Now that it's too late I realize I should have screwed everyone in sight. What made me prudish and horny at the same time? Perhaps I was searching for an ideal woman. A pointless task. Perhaps I feared commitment—equally dumb, for I lived with women who cheated on me, women I despised but whom I could not let go of out of fear of being alone. Even though my cock practically pushed a hole through my pants during the day, I sometimes looked at girls that I wouldn't have minded fucking and saw them as sub-par. They needed to be under the presumption of at least relative innocence. This was also the age when the fear of AIDS stalked each encounter. Thus I would masturbate to the most egregious of porno hookers while weeping over the Marmeladovas. I had come to regret not taking advantage of it all when loneliness would meet loneliness if only for some skin-on-skin contact.

There was a girl in college whom I knew distantly and whom Dick (more about him in a bit) dated solely for sex, the way I should have done. Not particularly attractive, a bit mousy. She also possessed odd angular features, not quite as bad as a Demoiselle d'Avignon but somewhere in that direction. But Dick told me that she was constantly horny, to the point of skipping school and masturbating all day when she did not have a lover. It made my cock hard hearing about it and yet I still did not pursue her. And then I blew it again. I ran into this mousy girl in Manhattan several years after college. It turned out she worked around the corner from me, so we would meet on lunch breaks and smoke breaks. I knew she was waiting for me to ask her out and to fuck her. It was not too difficult to tell. And for reasons that I now, in middle age, find baffling, I ignored the hint. She was not a looker by any means, what with her zits and greasy hair and flat chest, but she did have some saving graces apart from the alleged horniness. She fancied wearing knee high riding boots and tan trench coats, both of which were mild fetishes of mine. I would go out and smoke with her and think about getting in her pants, which were practically already unzipped for me... yet nothing happened. The office moved to a different part of town and I forgot about her. We could have had fun.

Back to LA. As I said, my love life was suffering immensely. My only consolation was a fantasy world filled with a harem of imaginary lovers. It wasn't a bad life. I could do anything without being, as it were, unfaithful. I never "cheated" except in dreams; and yet how frustrating it was, as the king-size bed became wider and wider, and the divide between us grew. Though the trope that one can never "really possess a woman" had always seemed true enough, it only hit home once physical contact between us became obsolete, and after a solitary morning wank I would bang my fists and wonder why I could not have that woman's embrace. Meanwhile, helicopters with yellow beams twirling like fireflies through the International Yves Klein Blue of twilight reminded me that I was still in California.

When it wasn't sex dreams, it was vivid, technicolor images of New York, but ones that only existed in faded memories—a mythical past that might have never existed. Or if it did, then only through a child's eye. A past that was seen through a particular prism of youth and time. As the dream ended I would struggle to return back to earth, and most importantly to return to Los Angeles. It would take me a long time to ascertain where exactly I was, and squinting I would look at the space between the blinds to make sure that I was seeing palm trees instead of New York's brown brick.

Living across from the old folks' home was a curse. I had originally thought it would be quiet; it was not. Sirens would wake me in the middle of the night; big red ambulances, impressive enough to delight a child, would be waiting to take away the next patient to pump him or her up full of life just for a little a while and then dump them back into the facility. My next-door neighbor glowed in the ecstasy of that twilight, pushing her poor devil of a husband who in turn was pushing a century of life back and forth between hospital rooms and ambulances, shuffling between death and twilight. A necrophilic love.

Yellow is the color of jaundice, of twilight, of submission, perhaps also of jealousy. New York used to oscillate between yellow and blue. San Francisco shifted back and forth between blue and white. Yellow and blue, blue and white, white and nothing. New York, San Francisco, LA.

When you see a city on the horizon you feel like something spectacular is going on, as if approaching an endless party but it never works that way, at least not here in California. The white buildings up on the hills are there but once you reach them there are no people on the street and there is no life. A façade. A very American façade.

Blue is the color of possibility. Brown is the color of shit and comfort.

Around the start of my madness I would have the most incredibly vivid dreams of New York—the boroughs and burrows baked in that specific New York light so vivid and so present that

I would struggle to make out just where exactly I was waking, and it would take me many minutes to make out where I was as I tried to push my eyelids open. For minutes, up to half hours I would let the bed spin until I found precisely where I was. Los Angeles too in that liminal state would be a dream world, verdant and rainy— isolated of course, as isolated as it is—but in the twilight feeling it felt quite magical. And then harsh reality would gradually drag my body out of slumber. Sometimes I would write poems like "Dream Travels." And they rang true.

The airlines have reduced their prices
But still too much for me to pay
Cheap means so little,
when you have little or none.
Lucky for me, deep sleep
allows me cheapest travel
all around the globe
with lots of leg room
on my king sized mattress,
in the black night when day is done.

Sometimes I dream I live in England
Its moist green magic in the mist,
And Jack in the Green hiding
right behind each oak tree,
Pointing out strangest marvels,
Like underground rivers of London
and other wonders there for me to see

My atelier in Mayfair's in a mews house,
I'm famous and well off, a painter or
Perhaps even a writer, believe it or not!
The future's never seemed so bright

Then I awake

Sometimes I dream I live in Italy again,
This time not in the cemetery known as Rome
But on some sunny isle, Sicily or Sardinia
In between swims I meditate on when
Aeneas or St. Paul got stranded in a storm
And crashed on these same shores.
I sit on the white terrace and rack brains,
Trying to find a rhyme for orange

Rarely I dream that I'm back where I came from,
Where under necks the swans are cut
A place quite famous for its progeny:
some of the biggest cunts and charlatans
the world has ever seen:
In other words, people like me

On sweetest nights I dream I live in California
And I'm on set, making a film
I watch the actors speak my words
And animate the actions I saw
in my mind,
I watch my writing come to life
As I imagined it, but satisfaction
Comes to rude awakening
when sun begins to bang
against the blinds.

Life's not just short but it gets shorter by the second,
I rub my eyes and think of all the places
I would like to visit, while staring at LA's brown sky

Solution is reality.
No need for boarding pass or ticket
No need to scrimp and save.

In padded casket's when I'll finally
fly out of this thicket,
while yellow palm trees
sway over my grave.

Why did I come to this schizophrenic state of alternating between hate and love for the city I left behind? I partly came out to LA to make films. For years I was obsessed with film and filmmaking—but that possibility popped and sighed out. All dreams fade upon waking and it doesn't worry us. What worries us is when waking dreams are shattered. In New York I managed to give it one final go and made a film, whose self-fulfilling title was My First and Last Film. But here in LA and elsewhere the filmmaking industry became nothing but bullshit—a bunch of cartoon characters and men in tights and computer-generated effects. This was not the cinema I grew up with, nor the one I wished to participate it, and so a major part of my life, ambition and identity was amputated. I witnessed the complete degradation and eventual demise of an entire art form. And thus, stagnation became progressive. Having given up on film I tried to adapt my screenplays into prose, but fear and trembling would quickly set in. First, it is a tedious job; and second, what is the point? My nihilistic thoughts would spiral further and further down a lagomorph hole.

Things changed when my daughter was born. As a man obsessed with death, my own and others, I would wonder—no, worry—what I could leave her. I was a Sitter, developing hemorrhoids in static comfort—I had nothing to leave. My parents left me nothing but memories. Often, in the night time agony of thoughts and meditations, I would consider writing down my life for her but would only make brief sketches. Like my father, I played Scheherazade with myself—"fear of failure" to those who seek a simple answer to everything; but for me, not truly hypochondriacal but actually suffering from certain ailments. I felt that I could keel over any minute—and yet, I did not wish my life to be completely over just yet even though I often felt that it was indeed finished. I kept looking at the California blue, the blue Pacific blue, and kept wondering: what happened? What had I done with my life? Years had passed in Brooklyn and Queens in which I did absolutely nothing!

But back to the sham utopia. The yellow snow balls with rocks hidden inside had been replaced by tennis balls washing up in the cold Pacific surf; but strangely, the California associated with the hackneyed "fresh start" began to seem more like a new detour toward the cemetery. I wrote a poem about it, titled "The Man in the Seersucker Suit."

I have a brand-new lover now.
He's bald, young, and pink.
Polite but with disdainful scowl
He has an ocean for a pool in which
all swimming is VERBOTEN!
his way of getting back at others.

I touch his heart and yet he too
is just as cruel as past romances.
I'd like to offer him my all
but his love isn't true.
He has much bigger fish to fry,
has money on his mind and
wears a fancy gold and white
seersucker suit.

I know he's only teasing and
that I should just exclaim, if not "Oh, what a joke"
then at least, "Oh, what a pain."
Finding myself again
in an embrace of geographic cure,
which is again debunked,
geography might change but still manure
is manure, and why does every bright new place
so full of hope and promise
always have to leave a space
under the table for a fat iguana?

He left me but he hasn't kicked me out,
I don't know where to go just now,
and where is he?
Why did he leave me?

I've searched and think I've found the place
where that young man resides, but
I'm confused and wonder why he chose a slum!
Disgraceful but he sits atop an old Masonic Lodge,
down by MacArthur Park.

Questions pop up, here's two or one:
for starters, is he really young?
And will he speak Hungarian and imitate
my Mother's tongue or
sprinkle holy water on my
burning eyes until all is revealed and
I am pushed and break my
neck falling down steps in Echo Park?
I can't see clearly now. My head's a mess.
And far from me to be the one
who'll find out what he thinks,

but I confess, I find his presence
comforting, yet at the same time I dread
and fear this fine young chap, I'll call him
Pink for now, so I will christen him in homage
to his baby cheeks.

He is a nice young lad with
shirts pressed by most talented
of foreign tailors: hardly a crease,
but that is outward, the fact is that
he spreads disease, I've learned.
I've heard reports of him stumbling around
all neighborhoods in town, and in the gloaming
Pink's shirts appeared quite sullied, dredged with mire,
but he's still roaming, in my dreams, and those of
newcomers, offering riches in exchange for
very unprotected love.

How he taunts me! Such a cruel love!
I weep and soon after I fall asleep,
then the nightmares wake me and I scream.
My Lord, this man just will not stop!
All your demands I'd heed but now my man is gone,
I sound like a teenage hustler in need!
Where is he when I need him?

Seersuckers at just fifteen bucks in the
back pages of the Readers Digest rip
themselves right up from ads and breaking
free, fold paper into airplanes, pinions,
and even follow me to San Francisco:
old sailor's town of winos and opinions

I don't care much for hippies, fog and hookers,
or seals and buffalos looking as dazed as
homeless lunatics in the Panhandle of
Rotten Gate Park
The views are great, I'll give you that
but I still fear the dark and
that damn suit.

The Angel of Apocalypse stands
fast, feet firmly planted on the earth,
and delegates his delegates as needed.
They've got their work cut out
but Pink has got a cushy job, for suckers are so many!

It's his realm here as well, and all he needs is just
a little lolly, one that he dangles by your tongue
and laughs while hanging to the trolley
and waits for the right time to push you off.

Why should we care about decay?
It is our nature to start rotting once we're born.
But in this land of screenplays, palms, cosmetic dentistry,
agents, fantasies, riches and all the things you've
dreamt of back in greyer pastures, the medicine
goes down like syrup. We swallow and we play
on railroad tracks.

The views, don't let's forget about the views!
Pink knows much better than the Californians.
That ocean vistas and Pacific sun
will still be here forever when we're gone.

"Now would you like a sucker, sucker?" He grins with
bright new teeth, the filthy little fucker,

pulls up a chair and glass, and guiding burnt
out eyes towards the horizon, murmurs, snot-nosed,
"Look and see! No better place
on Earth for you" and, hissing, adds "or me!"

We lift up sunglasses and squint
and struggle to believe Pink's lies that
this is actually our home and listen
to his old used car salesman's technique
while he assures us that the ocean's warm.

How long did this descent into stagnation last and when did
it begin? It started perhaps a decade ago, and gradually settled
into a more or less molten mass… just the odd bubble of protest
popping and sighing from the surface. Granted the world is a swan
dive out of the cunt into the grave, but the stagnation was another
issue altogether. For not only did the days turn into nights, and
the weeks into months and the months into years, it was after this
"morassic" period that I began to truly experience regret. It is
better to regret something you've done than something you haven't
and I kept regretting more and more that there were things I had
never done. Some of them quite appropriately regretful like finding
a profession and sticking to it, some of them base and perverse,
mostly sexual. And some of them purely philosophical. One of the
ironies of life is that as you grow old you finally begin to gain some
knowledge, some self-awareness, an understanding of this loaded
deck of cards we call life—but by the time one does, it is too late.
The knowledge is squandered on old age the way that ignorant bliss
is squandered on youth. Childhood bliss is one thing—the bliss of
childhood magic. The bliss of old age is the bliss of forgetting. There
is no such thing as the bliss of middle age, instead it is the age of
a bloodsucking insect constantly stuck to your person reminding
you of all the things you could have done but didn't, and telling you

that all the wisdom you have gained during these decades on Earth are for naught—for you can't go back and live your life a different way after you have become older and wiser. For a fool, no matter how much he learns later, may die a wise man but his youth was still wasted and foolish. Thus in deepest darkest hours I would let despair cover me with her dark wings, as I sobbed pathetically in the proverbial pillow thinking "Why didn't I know this before?! Why, God, why?" It was as though I had lost the past ten years in the blink of an eye, and ended up with no skills, no profession, no job—nothing. No security, no living relatives left, not much human contact left. Not to mention no health. It began to seem as if my existence now rested on memories and dreams—dreams of the past, dreams of regret, and only very infrequent dreams about any type of future. Yes, I wished to see certain places before I expired, mostly in Europe again, to bathe my boots in the warm waters of the Tyrrhenian and possibly to keep walking straight in, submerging myself, never to return. Suicidal thoughts became prominent. If one could not physically travel, there was the magic of the internet now though, traveling through ready-made images in the worst-case scenario. Soon enough there was only futility and frustration. Even the act of sex, which by that point I had mostly abandoned, seemed mechanized and pointless, nothing but the friction between a vulgar appendage and a bizarre orifice to produce a momentary distraction from daily horrors and fear of death. I am distracted again. Whither Europe? Europe withered.

With no plan, no career path, no idea what I was going to do, merely waiting for something glorious to happen to me, I somehow managed to find work at an advertising agency, while still walking around with my head and my cock in the clouds.

That was the year I met Brandy March.

ARBEIT MACHT FREI

Winter 1996. The previous six months were spent unemployed and I was freezing to death in an unheated Brooklyn apartment. Oh, that winter of my discontent, sleeping in my coat with a fur hat on my head, unsuccessfully searching for work, staring out at the fanciful Dutch Gabled brownstones across the street and imagining I was elsewhere. And life was elsewhere. And it seemed like it would never stop snowing.

When spring came and the snow finally started to melt in Prospect Park, I got a call back from an advertising shingle that I sent my (mostly fictional) resume and cover letter to in response to their want ad for an "office assistant" which turned out be mostly janitorial work. When I met with the boss he told me my duties would include making sure that the toilet paper rolls were fresh in the bathroom, etc, and I heartily agreed to any and all job responsibilities, even toilet-wise. To my surprise I was refused this lowly position, but was offered instead an "actual" job—that of "account executive," a phrase that meant nothing to me. The boss thought I was above the ass paper and took enough pity on me to offer an opportunity.

Two weeks into this suit-and-tie pointless and low paid charade I left work one evening and started walking crosstown to the west side for no reason at all until I stumbled into a hotel bar and ordered a martini and said to myself categorically, "I hate my job." Outside the rain was horizontal, smearing the lights of the billboards and streetlamps and taxis. By the time I had finished two martinis my job felt like something from the distant past and I decided to look for something else.

"Stop right there. Let's start over, you need to brush up on your interview skills," said the (not unattractive) fat blonde interviewing me for a position in the lower reaches of the marketing department at Mercedes Benz. The fat blonde was probably thirty, if that, and I was nary a few years younger, but as I spewed out the obligatory answers to her questions my mind was focused solely on fucking her fat ass right over the goddamn desk with that beautiful view from her office in the Lipstick Building. Nothing came to pass and I knew that when she playfully scolded me over my lack of "interview skills" I tried to believe that we both for a split second shared a fantasy of me shoving my cock as deep down her throat as humanly possible, for all to see—a little elicit show for those who could catch a glimpse from the parallel of another building which reached up to at least that devilish thirty fifth floor.

Alas, fantasies remained fantasies, and as this interview was on an unseasonably cold spring afternoon, it was quite easy for me to walk off (and freeze off) my erection the minute I exited onto Lexington Avenue during one of those blizzards that send chills down your back and make you question New York.

All would have been a pointless frustration were it not for the appearance of Brandy March later that year. Oh Brandy, Brandy, how we would fuck in alleyways, standing up, on subway platforms, how you would suck me in cabs, in toilets; no place was off limits when we were young and my cock was hard and your panties were practically dripping in anticipation.

My fear of life's brevity and ultimate termination was always pronounced but nowhere near so much as it had become now, as I entered the third phase of my life. And when this fear would take over me on those sweaty summer nights, I would close my eyes and Betty would come to me, spreading her dark wings, sitting on my chest like a succubus, like a night "mare," and would whisper to me "Life is long, long..." And in a second I would imagine penetrating her was akin to entering a cave of ice. What else could it be, now frozen from paralysis?

But what interested me more than her ice cave was the truly frozen ice in her soul, as if she was permanently living frozen in one particular moment—and while it would be logical to pinpoint that moment to the time of her accident, somehow I felt that it started earlier, as if she was born in a cemetery. And then when I would see her, all would be forgotten on my end, and the crooked fairy tale continued as long as the summer was still present. I will get to Betty, shortly, for Betty is the entire point of this book.

The horrible feeling that "time was running out" became more and more pronounced, and dug into my heart each night; I had become accustomed to the feeling that life was ridiculously short and it was imperative for me to finally finish something—but what?

It is a well-known fact that the older you get, the faster time flies. As silly as it may sound, time started flying when I was in my late twenties. Though I thought that life had potential torpor would set in. In my thirties the desperation accelerated and by the time I was forty it was a struggle to go on. I was stuck in an endless autumn.

How I wish to see New York again through a prism of 110 film, through Agfacolor. To see again the novelty of me and my mom eating a Burger King sandwich or walking down Central Park South or lingering in the record shop Colonie where I would be entranced by the art and would buy the records based on their covers, like books, anticipating magic within. Or the Apple Jack diner on 7th Avenue—or was it Broadway?—where my parents would go sometimes because it served hard liquor… or that brilliant yellow and orange light that blasted its way through the east-west cross streets not giving a damn and illuminating everything, a light that is found nowhere else on the planet…

And with my dad, the city of Pittsburgh in the humid summers and the rolling hills of Pennsylvania became the landscape of Moldavia, Hungary, Romania... My father and I imagined Vermont to be Russia, when we would go cross country skiing, not by the landscape but by the sheer number of birches. In this way I imagined the places that I never knew. And the birch idyll would be blasted out of my mind the minute we went back to the yellow snow surrounding the anthills of New York.

Dreams and dream visions would bring me back to a Europe that was ceasing to exist. Just like life, just like history, just like time and just like death, Europe was becoming undone and gradually erased. And what does it matter? If the Germans razed Warsaw, the Americans Dresden, the Russians most of their own cities—what does it matter when the whole planet will be erased in time? Is it worth pining for Onion Domes when there will be nothing left in the end anyway? Ozzy man dies and don't call me a Sissy Phus.

Charlie don't surf. It has come to pass that nothing much matters anymore—and that is why I pined for the Cold War and wrote about my "saudade."

I MISS THE COLD WAR

I miss the black and white.
I miss Apartheid and Pol Pot,
Communism and genocide.
I miss living under the threat of
mutually assured destruction.
It was exciting—
romantic, one could say.

I pine for the days when
Unter den Linden and Friedrichstrasse and
Alexanderplatz were off limits.
And for the days when poetry could
land you in prison.

I long for a walled city in the twenty-first century.
I wish there were more poets in jail.
I miss the concept of the revolving
restaurant on top of Strijdom Tower where
one could spin around, chewing on impala while
men landed on their heads at the bottom of
John Vorster Square.

I miss the cities without billboards.
I miss dreaming about steamy, humid nights in
Lourenco Marques, Luanda,
or Nova Lisboa.

I miss imagining the sounds of bullets in the night
and the sounds of people screaming.
I miss not being one of the poor sods waiting on
Avenida Quatro de Fevreiro for a steamer to Portugal
with wife, baby, and refrigerator in tow.

Back in Europe it wasn't that exciting,
we had our noses stuck in cabbage, we'd given up.
But Asia, Africa, America, oh my! Cowboys and
Indians and rodeos! And good guys, and bad!

Noses and toes in cabbage, we watched the bad guys
on black-and-white screens and thanked our luck.
And we were proud we weren't "oppressing the blacks."

I miss the bleeding and I miss the proxy wars.
I miss the blood and sand and, in the end,
I miss that history's remembrance is fleeting.
I miss conviction and convictions, one way
or another. And when I look at all of it today,

I miss the black and red more than I miss
the current grey.

Meanwhile I kept obsessing that Europe was committing
suicide. Europe had been replacing itself by a festering ethnic stew,
and I missed the Cold War the way I missed my youth. The way
I missed good and evil. Whatever you have in childhood, be it
in Auschwitz or Holmby Hills, there is a magic that can never be
recreated. One can try, of course, to relive it in writing, in children,
in travel, but it is always gone… long, long, gone.

In my mind, in at least part of my daily life, interrupting my
omnipresent sense of loss and fear of death or aging, I would try to
come back to that empty rabbit hole.

THE WARREN

We're thrust into the world as blind as rabbits,
as meek and tiny creature struggling to see.
Not like leverets that pop out of the womb
with open eyes, wide-eyed and screaming: "What the shit?"
We're more akin to rabbits than intrepid hares.
Hell, even Hitler suckled on his mommy's tit,
or so I'd like to think.
I'll give him benefit of doubt.

Most any parents, even monsters, will try
to build a home, however feeble it may be.
A nest that comforts tiny offspring with the warmth
of straw or hay or fur.
What happens to the nest when parents die?
Was all the comfort just a lie?

Do frail and gentle creatures always hunted
dream of a return?

Tall, tough and stupid humans like myself
certainly do, in times of pain, yearn to come back
to nest or even womb. At least for a look and see,
but what is it we seek?
To know what's happened to the warren?
It overgrew with moss because security was
trumped by instinct to be free.

God blessed and cursed us with the melancholy of reflection.
Memories blaze with whispers of eternity and stasis.
They also leave us shivering outside
a burrow that's been overgrown with weeds.

The entrance to the hole's closed up with dirt,
and deep inside a family of rats
is busy chewing the foundation which the rabbits built
and laying nests in place
for their own filthy young
which multiply in spades
and give fuckall about your house
or your remains.

In vain we sit outside the tunnel to the warren of our minds
and wish that we could be within its warmth just one more time.
But warren's been abandoned,
now there's nothing there but rats,
and all that we are left with is yearning for the past.

Any attempt at reviving the architecture of the mind is futile. It
is impossible to recreate, no matter what the climate (Los Angeles
certainly does not remind one of Russia, but even some place
close to Russia would be lacking in authenticity with a KFC and
McDonalds on each corner). Here in LA, on my bookshelves,

countless dead souls stood like memorials to fallen soldiers. Tombstones not just from Moscow or Petrograd (though a few from St. Petersburg) but the majority exiles, wherever the Slavs blasted out of Europe like birdshot. Places of publication: Paris, Belgrade, Harbin, Florianópolis, Sydney, San Francisco, Buenos Aires, Berlin, Montevideo… skeletons rotting in the moist earth of New South Wales or the delta of Río de la Plata, their thoughts and lives stood at attention, at drumroll on my shelves, soldiers who refused to bow down to the enemies of time and death. I wished to join them in their ranks, among this army of lives who defied oblivion at least for a little while, some of them generals, some NCOs, some even petty officers or privates. I was nary a cadet at this point for I hadn't written anything of value, and yet how I wished, so desperately desired, to join that standing army even for a spell, even through a tiny little book a miniscule achievement that would allow me to stand guard with them at least for a little while after I died. But what magic, I have to say again, exists in childhood, and what a bleak and utterly grey area sets in before you can blink. No attempt at going back will succeed, except perhaps in dream travels or hallucinations, if one is inclined to have them. I am fairly certain that I was able to hallucinate as a child. Once in Moscow I was convinced that I was able to fly, and coming to America I had visions of levitation again. Looking back, I believe it was probably fever-based and yet it felt more real than anything.

Later, again in a fever, I spent several weeks in a perfect nocturnal existence. The night-time world made me even more prone to a liminal way of being. I started writing this a few pages back but got distracted with thoughts of infinity. Anyway, during that illness, I would wake when it was already dark and I did not see the sun for days except for a tiny sliver through shut eyes. The world had turned black and my imagination flourished since I knew not what was real and what was a dream. I did not leave the house during that time except once with my mother to visit some friends of hers in Queens, and in the cab ride over the bridge I felt as if I was hurtling through space like an astronaut, the streetlights stars and constellations, a swish of light from blurry eyes a comet, the illumination of the Triborough Bridge a Kuiper Belt, stellar winds outside the Dunkin Donuts on Queens Boulevard, solar flares in front of a 7-11.

With the end of the illness and resumption of daytime activity I would feel that proverbial joie de vivre that comes after leaving the sick bed, especially when accompanied by the first breath of spring. And yet, with my mind's heliograph on hiatus till my next illness, I missed those dark nights of interstellar travel.

My Mom's apartment in Moscow and then in New York was packed to the gills with books as is mine now—an attempt at recollection, preservation, mystery and comfort all at the same time, to recreate the past within the present. Even in the thicket of palm trees and smog, it is possible to hallucinate Northeastern Europe; and though my wife continued to complain about the fact that the house was groaning with "my mom's stuff" I only parted with the books when pressured and when we were low on funds and high on bills. But I kept and held on to those most sentimental vestiges of bygone times, immortalized in the written word. Thus my soldiers, my ragged army, my stalwart dead souls stood guard throughout the bookshelves, the corridors, the closets... Many of them memoirs, many written during the most turbulent times, written in exile in places far from home. Dead souls everywhere which nonetheless served as comfort, perhaps even protection from oblivion.

There is nothing like a book to keep you alive, and so I was comforted by ghosts who still managed to speak from beyond the grave. The physical aspect of having these souls around was also a testament to their resilience... their journeys, like my mom's final journey on the green velvet couch:

SURVIVAL

I do not wish just to survive,
but rest and travel come at a price
and I am broke and always have been,
not to mention tired.

Diseases and addictions take their toll,
but bell will toll for one and all.
You're sickened by the fly that's
drowning in your glass
yet our lives last just slightly longer,
and end a bit more meaningful,
than those of insects. And this too, shall pass.

Technology to boot has not been kind,
And any twit or git can… pardon me,
I meant no insult and
sticking to myself, I'll travel
on the internet in mindless abandon.

Poets will play their organs in the towers
long and hard while we, the others,
live in basements and journey where we can
through our minds: it costs naught, as I've said.
Or not more than a pen and piece of bread.

Some fuck the most expensive whores
on huge four-poster beds
and others do it standing up
in phone booths with some ditch bitch.

Some go from rags to riches
while others from riches to rags,

and you can brag but
we will not feel sorry
for we are not dogs.
In times like these we
do not give a damn, is all.

Who gives a damn, then?
I start to see method in the madness
of someone oh so dear to me,
immobilized and dreaming
on an old green velvet couch,
one made in Yugoslavia,
purchased in Moscow, shipped
through Trieste, through Italia
and finally years later simply dumped on
piss-soaked streets of old
New York. So much territory covered
just to be discarded. Sound familiar
in regard to all I wrote?
I hope you'd get the point:
you'll be disposed of too.
Is it that hard to live with
dreams so unfulfilled?
You be the judge, you
read the verse, upon some more reflection
you might just get the drill.

I was reminded too of the lost writer Konstantin Vaginov and
that a writer is an undertaker by trade, not a maker of cribs or prams.
It was at my mother's apartment, which was filled not just top to
bottom but also side to side with books, that I was magnetically
drawn to a weird title, an otherwise nondescript cover bearing the
words "The Goat Song." I was not much of a reader at the time and

I had no idea what the book was about but I was nonetheless able to discern and appreciate something poignant when I read it, and there it was on the very first page a line that haunted me forever: *"A writer is a coffin maker by trade, not a maker of baby carriages."*

Vaginov, born Wagenheim, a Russian of German ethnicity, saw the Bolshevik Revolution and the collapse of the monarchy akin to the fall of Rome. And in his surreal, elegiac and melancholy prose he described men who still held on to the notion of bygone times while everything changed and crumbled. And his characters walked like me through extreme ugliness, cynicism and vulgarity, pining for a glorified and partly imagined past. I tried to translate him numerous times but each attempt came to naught.

He was an aesthete who saw the world engulfed in ugliness and retreated to his (literal attic or garret) tower, absorbed in works and days. One of my attempts at translation went as follows: "A writer is a coffin maker by trade, not a master of baby carriages. Show the author a casket—one tap on the side—and he'll immediately know the type of materials used in construction: when it was built and how, which laborers helped put it together. With another knock of the knuckles he'll even identify the parents of the deceased. At the moment, the writer is preparing a little coffin for the past twenty-seven years of his life. He is terribly busy. But please don't think that he has a goal in mind while he's setting up his next little grave—it's just a passion of his. He sniffs around, and when he smells a corpse that's when he decides that a coffin is needed. And he loves his dead and walks among them even while they're still alive. He greets them daily, presses his hands into theirs, speaks and engages in palaver whilst secretively ordering wood, nails, even lace for the occasion." I knew of no one other than myself who thought of death so obsessively and ceaselessly. Later in life, the death of my parents accelerated the obsession and the absurdity of the process of life and its cessation that cast a veil over much of my existence and which I numbed or dispelled with alcohol. I had "inherited" from my mother, not just grief and heartache but what remained of her library—or rather, the portion of it that was not stolen by her "friends" when she was immobile, for she became the ultimate Sitter at the end of her life, and I told that story to Betty.

So many of the books were memoirs, autobiographies; Russians fleeing the civil war or WW2, scurrying and hurrying to put down their histories and experiences on paper, writing frantically from places outside of Russia like Paris, Berlin or Madrid and sometimes far away from Europe in places I have already mentioned like Harbin, Rio de Janeiro, San Francisco, Sao Paolo, and Sydney. And maudlin poetry, nostalgia, Sehnsucht, saudade... Were they even aware of their quests? Were all these people, writing in vain, unaware that their lives were actually not that unique? And was my life not unique either? Perhaps that's why I always abstained from writing about it, and ignored the mantra "write what you know"— perhaps that's why I discarded this idea and aspired for something different, something greater. How could I write what I know when I knew so little? Instead of a catalogue of one's life's comings and goings—there are countless such examples in Roman letters—I wished to frame it differently, to write something completely irrelevant to my life because I had recognized that my life was not all that interesting. Certainly it would be interesting—if the manuscript survived—to a scholar, say, two thousand years hence, but only in the way that an utterly banal correspondence between two ancient Romans is interesting.

No, that was not what I wished to do or what I set out to do. In my book The Girl from Below, I wished to bottle consciousness. I wished to distill a feeling. I wanted to create a time capsule and put a message in a bottle—but it was a futile task, for everyone smells spring differently and every loss of virginity is unique.

In my own case, I lost my virginity to a girl I "lured" to a fake "uncle's" apartment only a few blocks north of where I would later be having my "writer's retreat." Wendy Novak. And after we fucked the first words she said to me were, "Harvey's going to kill me." That pretty much ruined women for me for at least a decade. And it is part of why I considered my book worthless, and why I could not finish it. I wonder if I had ever been in love at all anytime throughout my life.

Returning to the matter at hand: by now I felt as if my endeavor to write was even more miserable and shortsighted than these poor Russians scattered throughout the globe. And that like these phantoms on my bookshelves and in my closets—there were too many books to have out in our Los Angeles flat, and we had just reduced our storage space—these memoirs, when stacked upright, were indeed tombstones. Which in itself was great. I had an idea to invent some type of interactive device for cemeteries where you could press a button and hear the voice of the deceased.

The voices of the deceased lay in tomes and volumes here in our house. Oddly these tomes did not include my mother or my father, who went to the next world without leaving their histories behind. Which is why when I tried to tell Betty about the interesting bits I always wanted to go home to write them down but instead they formed part of the "oral tradition" yet again. Defeated, I would wonder: would I end up as one of those scraggly paperbacks on my bookshelves back in Pasadena—would whatever I thought my "magnum opus" end up as something utterly pedestrian, a curiosity on eBay at best, as a collection at a library for unknown authors at second best or, more realistically, as the proverbial canary cage liner? Thus in fear of these potential scenarios I would sit, sit, and sit... and nothing would come.

Around that time my wife told me about an article she had read about decluttering one's house, that it is essential to keep the things around you that make you happy, and discard the ones that do not. But for people like myself that is impossible—in the idea of the eternal return, one has to accept it all, the good and the foul—and as far as keeping memories is concerned, so much can be delved into further. A love letter full of shit, full of mendacity, one from a dreadful relationship that brought one to tears can still be put away in a cardboard box, like a wedding ring or gold tooth extracted in Auschwitz might make its way into a strongbox in Bariloche or Asuncion. Memories matter to us all; victims still pine for their tormentors as much as sadists miss their guilty pleasures. Everything had shattered, or perhaps crumbled, then simply degenerated or rotted or fallen into premature obscurity. "Ah, youth..." and Onhava regained... Some girls would reappear, and other girls would be "sucked out of a finger" i.e. plucked from thin air, in my dreams as the Russian saying goes. And the dreams, oh the dreams, the sweeter they turned the more acidic and acerbic and sour and astringent the daily existence with my wife became. So many girls would come to me in dreams, so many... One night it was a petite blonde with piercing steel-blue eyes. Cold as a razorblade, cold as Tippi Hedren, and with a dubious past, yet not as cold and not as shady as Emily Vainonen who I will introduce soon. This blonde, despite her shady past (I don't know how I knew that she had a shady one) was remarkable because she was genuinely concerned for me in whatever it was that happened in the dream, something I have not experienced in a long time in my family situation. And so I embraced this blonde and held her close, squeezed her as tightly as I could—but I never took the next step of having dream sex with her. Each night a new girl would appear, too many to remember. Some were based on real lovers from my past but most were entirely fictional. The other day, prior to the blonde, it was a Chinese girl, gloriously dressed in one of those gorgeous Oriental silk suits, flashing her hairy pussy to me and shoving her tongue down my throat. The day before, it was a gorgeous "pleasantly plump" brunette, smothering me almost maternally in her gigantic breasts. Unfortunately, very few of these dream romances were consummated; they tended to be limited to kisses, embraces, squeezes, the possibility of something greater and stronger—the way one feels on a first date when the heart flutters. What I lacked in real physical intimacy I made up for in the frequency of these demon lovers who came to me almost nightly, in the variety of their looks and shapes, outfits and bodies and personalities, each one unique, all these nocturnal paramours I found myself involved with. To hold a woman—to hold her by the waist, to push her forward to embrace her, to kiss, slobber, to stick your tongue down her throat and hope for an ever more powerful tongue to dart into your own mouth, to press her closer, to kiss again, to push her up against the wall and stick your hand down her panties... And yes, sometimes these dream women would actually ask me about what I was writing down, and sometimes even say "I believe in you!" And then I would wake up. At the very least, these dreams confirmed a depressing yet solid notion—the impossibility of owning a woman, of truly possessing a partner beyond the initial passionate embraces which fade faster than one could imagine.

Sometimes it was worse, more complicated. I would fall asleep midday and dream of the imaginary blonde but the only sweat is my own and I awake covered in Californian moisture with no blonde in sight. I would grasp around in the twilight of my dream, hoping to find just the right sweaty, sleeping blonde. As suddenly as she appeared, she vanished. The minute she turned around to embrace me, I awakened. I never got to see her face.

There is something wrong with making the bed in the morning or the afternoon with the sole purpose of waiting to lie down in said bed ten or twelve hours later. The day is just an intermission in sleep, and sleep a blissful interlude between rising and falling into a dream world. Sometimes, after dreaming, I would often wake in a glorious mood, as if I had found the fountain of youth. As if I did exist, in a parallel universe, as a young man with his arm around a young woman, laughing and enthralled in the bliss of early love. Everything would come to life once again, the dead would rise, my parents would still be there, I would walk down Manhattan streets on summer nights, and all of my screenplays were films. Or rather, they too existed in yet another parallel universe in which my characters were real people with real lives and real deaths. But sometimes, when things seemed bleaker and I felt closer to oblivion, I felt more like Henry Spencer finally embracing the lady in the radiator.

All cities hide ghosts, but it was the little ghosts that would get under my skin. Not the gargantuan horrors of Moscow, Berlin, or Rome, but the little, little roaches stabbing little, little loves. At one point I couldn't even stand to look at porn because it meant looking at other people having sex. The little deaths, faked or not, were missing in my life.

My passive existence was not without the occasional aggressive outburst—like the time I broke my hand by punching the refrigerator—but mostly I was a bored, detached observer of other lives. I would start each morning by watching other people have sex, thanks to the glorious powers of the information superhighway. Often the interest in pornography would ebb, but there wasn't much else to replace it. And yet, how repetitive it all began to seem. Intercourse looked more and more like some animalistic frottage, the climax a kind of evacuation. With my dream lovers I began to feel as if I was losing my marbles, especially when each night a new one appeared. Some of them came so brilliantly, one right after the other, and each one was different and each one offered me this accursed sympathy that I felt I could never find. Not all of them were sex dreams, but they were all about longing. Sometimes it was about a woman who would take me in after a car accident where I broke both of my legs and would let me rest and rest her head on my chest and feed me chicken.

How I yearned for something like that—a type of love without any hairs, without requisites… I started making a list, jotting down the description of each female phantom that offered me imaginary affection during my sleep. But soon I stopped the senseless and depressing cataloguing. Making these lists became tedious and repetitive, and even the hints at sex in the dreams was gradually disappearing.

So many dreams faded. That feeling of being able to start all over, in any fashion, was an impossibility now. With the hope of a spring eternally dashed, I needed to embrace the only autumn I had ever known and all the fallen leaves. If only we believed that death meant sleeping and dreaming eternally we would no longer fear it.

I was not blind to the absurdity of my situation; on the contrary, the absurdity had become a kind of survival mechanism, creating more lucid fantasies. It felt like a teenage pop song from the 50s in constant rotation: "In Dreams," "Dream Lover," "All I Have to do is Dream," etc, etc. Yet not all of my dreams were dreams of sexual or romantic longing. At least half were a longing for the past. One night I dreamt about the playground in Van Cortland Park, in the Bronx where we first lived after coming to the US. The dream was so vivid, so close and dear, that upon awakening the first thing I did was to Google images of the park. And there it was, unchanged—one of the few places in New York to have been left untouched. In 1977 it was a relatively idyllic place to grow up, far away enough from the nightmares plaguing the other boroughs and much of the Bronx, but my mom insisted she needed a Manhattan address and so we moved to a shit part of town called Washington Heights, which is where my early descent began. But more on that later.

I imagined taking a long cross-country road trip with my

daughter to show her where I had lived, where I had been, where I had traveled with my dad (I never traveled with my mom). We'd visit the playground in Van Cortland Park, she'd play there like I had years before—but she would be older then, "too old for playgrounds." It was a loose fantasy. Perhaps as a teenager, I thought, I would take her on the many road trips I took with my dad.

Showing your offspring architectural and geographic memory is ill-fated and pointless. In theory it could work, but for how many generations? Perhaps two at most. The fruit rots to make earth. If I belonged to a family of royals whose hereditary home—in Spain, let's say—is preserved for hundreds of years... but I do not. I had only this simple and sordid playground in which to house my past. And soon, I knew, that too would be gone. the anthill, the beehive: replace, replace, replace is how the world spins... I gradually became convinced that it is only in the written word that a life can be preserved.

In the gaps between dreams, I daydreamed. My daydreams felt almost like screenplay scenarios; the further removed they were from reality, the more I enjoyed them. The strange thing is that most of these girls felt like they were already dead—born dead, born in a cemetery. The graveyard as maternity ward.

One night I dreamed I saw Earth from outer space. Unlike my other dreams, this one seemed not to have been rooted in reality. And yet, looking back, I recall that as a teenager I met an astronaut and spent a day with him. He was a friend of my mom's boyfriend. Though the he didn't go into much detail, he told me that he and his colleagues never recovered from seeing our planet from afar. It was the most amazing, life changing experience one could imagine, he said, and life was never the same afterwards. In my dream, I stared at the blue earth, marveling, waiting for that life-changing experience when something strange happened. A hole in the globe of the Earth opened up, opened like a door in the Earth, and out

ARBEIT MACHT FREI   67

of it peered a blue-skinned devil. He stuck his head out, peeked around and then shut the "door" again, as if he was making sure that everything was alright with the world—or, I suppose, to make sure that everything was not alright and that, in fact, all was going according to plan. He closed the door and disappeared.

In another dream, I was standing in line to go see a movie with my blonde girlfriend. It was chilly and she was wearing a warm coat with a fur collar. She was taller than me—I don't know why I remember this detail... ah, yes, it was because I was able to rest my head on her fur collar. I was wearing a threadbare coat, a thin skinny cotton suit. She let me put my head on her shoulder and wrapped me up a bit inside her thick and fancy wool coat, and smiled. I wish I remembered or even knew what film we were queueing to see. That would have been interesting, and a nice clue about what the fuck was going on in my brain.

It was brilliant dream after brilliant dream. Very often, I was young. Quite young. In my early twenties. Somehow I was friends with an extremely wealthy Park Avenue matron. Perhaps she was one of the widows who would volunteer at the information desk at the Metropolitan Museum of Art. She had a daughter she wanted to introduce me to. And then I saw the girl—a blonde in her early twenties, perfectly coiffed, with a bit of an air of mystery about her but what struck me the most was that her mom wanted to introduce me to her. The girl was down visiting her mom on Park or Fifth during a break from school. I had never felt such joy, so much appreciation, for just being myself. It was incredible. I was bursting with enthusiasm to see this girl at her Upper East Side penthouse with the full approval of her mother. Then, as usual, the dream shattered. Like Proust, it took me close to an hour to descend from the dream world to living life. I did not want to leave. I would grasp the bed sheets as if I was in turbulence on a trans-oceanic flight holding up the airplane by my wrists. And then of course the turbulence would pass and I would awake in brown and dirty USA. But with this last one, there was a darkness hidden at the top of the stairs on Sutton Place/York Avenue/Fill in the Blank Avenue of riches. I awoke thinking that the mom was somehow pimping her daughter out to me, a classier version of retired porn actor's descent into hell with the peasant woman and her daughter in A Serbian Film. Birth is of course a creation, so what better way to degrade your creation than by selling it and disposing of it to horrible whims of strangers? That was not a good morning, that dream left me shivering. But then another dream lover was sure to come over the following evening, and so I would make the bed and wait for evening for another flight with eros and chaos. There were still many unfinished Spanish castles that needed to be completed.

Like a starving beggar salivating in front of a grocery store window, I would look at newspaper ads that advertised a whole new life via a new career. Or like a nineteenth century "Gymnasiast" in one of the more sordid stories, a la Notes from Underground, fishing around in his pocket to pay for a whore, salivating like that beggar but for pussy instead of bread.

I read that in middle age, memories of past times become more and more important as one gets older, and soon they make up the majority of thought. I have always been occupied by memories, to the point that I could witness the memory being formed as the event happened. I would be able to predict just how I would remember a particular episode in the future—with joy, or with a lilting sorrow, or with horror. By now my obsession with memory had become acute.

The brown sky at an airplane's take off, the green carpet of soggy England upon landing when I visited London. Random memories that stuck while others withered away.

I have always found it difficult to imagine my parents witnessing things that are alien to us now—communism, world war, etc., but now I see that I too have seen whole worlds disappear—the worlds of the 1970s, the 1980s, even the 1990s. Or, for instance: how does one go from Auschwitz to having a condo in Tel Aviv on the bright blue Mediterranean Sea, with washer and dryer, 24 hour supermarkets, etc? People adapt to both extremes.

And then, sometimes, another poignant and malformed thought would enter my brain: how I wished not just to hold her but to put my arm around her waist, the way couples do, the way I had done with my wife, the way I did with girlfriends, to put my arm quite around that curve between the ribcage and the hipbone that makes a woman, and walk like a couple—it tormented me that I would never be able to do that with Betty, even if she herself had consigned herself to that fate. For me it was a stabbing, teeth-grinding regret. She would forever be pushing herself on wheels, always shorter than me, her waistline, her hips, her feminine architecture always out of my natural reach. Unless, perhaps, we managed to get out of that wheelchair and if not fly upwards then to lie down on the sweaty bed and embrace laterally. But still I wished to have that promenade with my arm around that female curve, one that more talented men than me had blown their brains out over in despair. I remembered my fling with Brandy March—one of the most unequivocally stupid women I had ever known. She was taken, so there was no question of us having a "relationship" but mostly, with Brandy and other girls as well, it was that process and experience of putting my hand around the waist that knew no higher equivalent of romantic excitement. This is what I pined for with Betty and it was obviously impossible. Romance may begin with holding hands, but it is putting your arm around a girl's waist that leads to the bedroom. Now NYC reminds me of the painting "The Suicide of Dorothy Hale" by Frida Kahlo and the Blondie song "Honey Here's Looking at You."

Several days in succession I had dreams about Brandy, who I

will talk about shortly. The dreams were mostly about holding her around the waist as if we were a couple; the beauty of it all was that we were not a couple and that she always had her ridiculous boyfriend to go home to. But it was all positive and joyous for strange reasons, for in real life, twenty five years ago, it was a given, so to speak, that we would never be a real "couple" and that after a night of rapturous, sweaty intimacy she would always have to go back to her geeky cuckolded fiancé who she would kiss goodnight with the taste of my sperm on her lips. But that wasn't my desire, to cuckold this hairy boring grey portly idiot. That was never my desire. Brandy, the proverbial brain surgeon that she was, actually set up a date with three of us, with Ollie (real name Oleg: he was a Ukrainian Jew) the cuckold sitting there both bovine and frightened looking at me with the distinct fear that I might have just fucked his fiancée in the ass.

What was funny is that I did not wish Ollie any harm. He was, as I mentioned, an utterly grey individual who was, sadly, cuckolded. I did not know if he knew how many cocks went in and out of Brandy's ass when he was turning a blind eye but as a grotesque, utterly hairy fool who looked like a troll from under the moss, he had no choice but to accept this arrangement for she was beautiful. If I looked like him I wouldn't blame her either. He somehow ended up with Brandy—an idiot, of course, but a beautiful one. The most beautiful girl he could have dreamed of ever having. As for me, it was much simpler. I found no satisfaction in making "Ollie" miserable even though when I would ejaculate inside her I would see stars and we would embrace in a sweaty apotheosis which cannot be described in words. But shooting in her and kissing her afterwards was not the highlight, it was something else—it was holding her waist as we walked together as a couple both of us knowing full well that we could not be a couple, she always having to go back to that slug Ollie and me back to my lonely flat, back to masturbation and dreams of success. And now, twenty years later, with Brandy officially married to that Ukrainian cuckold, I do still dream of her—not of sex but of her waist, putting my arm around her waist. I remembered she used to like wearing leopard pattern panties.

All these people… it was as if it was yesterday, but I felt an odd combination of yearning and disgust for them. The size queen's husband who liked to watch me fuck his wife in her hairy cunt. Emily Vainonen, who was born in a cemetery. Shelly Farrington, who came from the same moss covered maternity ward. So many people who were born dead. And being dead must be dreadfully cold, so their bony fingers and skeletal frames tried to drag me in for some warmth or comfort, or even just a pointless screw. And I, naïve and filled with romantic longing, did too many times—more than I wish to remember—allow myself to be dragged into those little caskets.

Most weren't even tragic. They were "pathetic" in a Chekhovian way. And in some Chekhovian style some were almost comic, like Andrea Easton, with her puppy eyes who wanted to "discuss" our relationship otherwise she would call it quits when in fact we had no relationship to discuss—sexual or otherwise. What ties poor, pathetic Andrea to the others is a sense of self-importance. I suppose even living corpses must need something like that in order to stay afloat in the world. But none of this mattered to me anymore. I had mostly forgotten about these people. What I wanted to do that summer in hell, which this book is about, was to hold Betty by the waist, spin her around and kiss her deeply. Before I started writing this, I only held women by the waist in my dreams.

And each night when I was in Brooklyn in the summer that I am getting to, during those days I would return to my sublet and try to write and nothing, absolutely nothing, would come out. Even a forceful struggle to put down a line or two of The Girl

From Below yielded no result. And as much as I wished to create something, I was much more intrigued by what, if anything, my so-called relationship with Betty would bring about. I knew there was a mystery in there, far deeper than just the mystery of how she lost her legs, but I had no clue as to how to pursue it or unlock even the first door to this labyrinth.

I had seen things. I had seen things on videotape. I had seen a hairy-assed, hairy-backed Jew travel through all the wonderful cathedral-spired and onion-domed capitals of Eastern Europe to shove his cock up some eighteen year old's asshole and ejaculate on her face so she cannot just buy herself a plate of potato soup but also get some lipstick and stockings in the process. And when seeing these Slavic or Hungarian little girls, their asses stretched out with hairy Semitic cock, opening up their mouths to receive the sacrament of that pitiful little drizzle of sperm, turning to the camera while an ancient whore off-camera yells in Czech or Ukrainian "Smile, honey! Smile, keep your eyes open!"— when I had seen all that I always wondered how much the girl actually enjoyed what she was doing, the tangible sensations on the nerve endings aside (I have heard in truth that even rape can be enjoyable to the recipient)—how much did these sluts enjoy it all? And Stacy, in my book, seemed to enjoy it.

What happened to all these girls from videos made in 1996, 1997? Had they become matrons, housewives in Brno, Minsk, Debrecen, Lwów, making potato dumplings for Ivan or Istvan? Or did they suffer? Did any of them end up in a wheelchair? And the navel on the porno hooker, pierced or not, could not distract from that she came out of a mother, who back in Brno, Minsk, Debrecen or Lwów would nurse her, and warm up some milk for her for breakfast, and see her grow... into this... There is nothing wrong with sex, not too much wrong with debauchery either. But there is a lot wrong with debasement, and yet I was drawn to it.

THE WAIST AND OTHER THOUGHTS

Waist not, want not. As the waist expands, the penis shrivels. But it wasn't just the physical waist that expanded but the space between the hand and the small of the back became wider and wider, psychologically, mentally... The space increased, the distance became wider and wider, and thus I entered a period of extensive self-pleasure that came hand in hand and hand on appendage with my fantasy life.

Because of my heavy reliance on pornography, particularly the type of porn where it is apparent that the scenario cannot be replicated in real life, I began to wonder: is it possible to live in a life of pure fantasy and still find some satisfaction? Seeking refuge in art to shelter from horror, or using art to stave off insanity—there have been many cases. But those cases that I read about did not talk at all about what to do when the fantasy is a by-product of the strongest urge for not just emotional but physical love. "This demon-haunted world," one character in some book I can't remember used to like repeating that phrase. But demons do haunt us, and when I dream about my mother, years dead now, it is always back in her apartment, always returning. I would meet her there, in my dreams, and she would stand there, yes, like a ghost or demon looking at me intently, staring with the expression that said not just "Get out of my house" but also "Get out of my dream." I was hoping that the dead dream too.

"My boyfriend..." No one in porn says "my boyfriend," but that phrase was always enough to make my little conqueror worm shrink away when I was the other man. And yet it was endearing, in a perverse way. Somehow I would wish that I too had a chance to be a boyfriend. The problem was that I was never quite certain how much I wished to be a boyfriend. And as idiotic as this may sound, it's the same way I never quite wanted to have a job. On the few occasions that a girl has referred to me as "my boyfriend" I was flattered beyond belief, and yet the statement would also fill me with trepidation, not due to a fear of responsibility, but to a fear of failure and finality. The very term was loaded with a feeling that it was temporary.

Here in LA, I read an article about a planned construction project: the capping of the Hollywood Freeway to create a green space and park. One reader left a comment suggesting that they include a cemetery in the park because everyone reading this will be dead by the time of its completion. It is something I have often thought back to, and the thought had been on my mind a lot of late. Man is less than an anthill, we are a bacteria, constantly multiplying, producing new generations, keeping the race alive while individually, in our brief lives, we simply peek through a keyhole for brief moment and then the light goes out.

Life is a journey—or so the cliché goes. But sometimes one wishes to paddle back and park the car or anchor the boat, to return to simpler and more pleasant times. And at any given moment one can say "the ship has sailed." Life is a skydive out of a cunt, into the grave as the Soviet actress Faina Ranevskaya stated.

The world is built on memories. If only instead of eternal oblivion, one could sleep with one's memories after death. The eternal return, the heaviest of burdens?

Thus I embarked on what I already knew, or thought I knew, would be my swan song, the final journey of my life. But I had not guessed what would eventually happen, for there was no way to tell. Life is utterly random.

How I wished to travel back in time, at least just back to the 1970s or 80s.

How I squandered my life with this idea about "film" which barely exists anymore, at least not in the way that I knew it. How I wished I had followed my father's advice that in order to write one needs only pen and paper and the power of observation. I only came to understand that much later, after I had wasted my life enamored by the moving image. I had stories to tell but I saw them as pictures, moving pictures. Ironically "many pictures moving" is how he described the ballets he produced.

In essence, I lost participation in two fundamental aspects of not just society but the Homo Sapiens existence: work and sex.

All things started to become topsy-turvy not so soon after moving to California. "There is a bridge outside my window, but I have nowhere to drive to." This sentence I created bothered and haunted me for decades. Where did it come from? I did have a bridge outside my window in Manhattan, and in Queens, and there was indeed nowhere to go for a long, long time—and though the journey is long, the arrival is always filled with disappointment. Down to even the basic concepts of work and supporting oneself and one's family—the concept of work lost all meaning to me and I admitted my parasitical situation. Yet I could not let go of the thought that most work was meaningless in our post-industrial society. I would have gladly sought employment that had some type of meaning, if not as a skilled laborer (it was too late for that, and the unions etc) then at least as, say, a house painter or a brick layer—but even those options seemed closed to me. And so I chose to sit.

Self-induced pressure to create something, to finish something—to fight against the necrophobia that was consuming me. Shiva's dance, the endless and pointless process of creation and destruction, infuriated me to the core.

Blue is the color of possibility. Yellow is the color of fate. And New York is the unfortunate combination of the two. In LA I would have the most vivid dreams of New York—the blue skies baking in that yellow light. So much so that I would struggle to get out of bed for minutes, half-hours, hours… so much so that I would struggle to make out where I was, and wondered whether I was in fact back in New York.

What would be the ultimate level of degradation one could inflict on oneself, I wondered? Whatever it is, one would need to be guilty of enjoying it, sinking to the basest desires to make it truly perverse and repugnant.

One night it was another plump blonde—I have been waiting for this one to return for a while now. I knew it was only a matter of time. Nothing sexual happened but there was flirtation, holding hands, my arm around her waist, even a little close sort of dancing at times. All this while she worked at the museum, supervising an installation while I was her assistant and photographer. I was nervous and shaky with the camera but very confident with her, bold even, considering she was my employer in this dream. And when I grabbed her hand she did not pull it away and when our fingers touched, she touched me back… I don't remember when I walked hand in hand with my wife… And when she held my hand and I held hers, I felt the electricity of human contact, which was cut short by a massive leg cramp, most likely caused by dehydration. I woke up howling in pain.

What was striking about these dreams is the recurring symbolism of the museum and the photograph. The museum is a repository for memories. According to my Watkins dream book, Mario Reading wrote the following on Museums: "They are what we inherit from the past and they can either enrich us or weigh us down…" Of photographs: "the further into the digital age we venture, the more we tend to define ourselves by images and not by our physical presence. We have already discussed the onanistic elements inherent in the internet, and it is inevitable that our symbolic concentration on images as against the written (and therefore "considered") word will increasingly invest and fuel our dreams. Digital photographs in this context become the reality, acting as a rectifiable resource around which to contrive the narratives of our would-be lives."

So, there I was yet again in that dream stuck between the museum of memories and the quotidian arousals of a would-be life. And yes, each night I would lie down and wait for a new dream lover.

On yet another night I had another poignant dream. There was a girl—not sure who she was or where we were, but in the dream I worked with her. There was definite sexual tension between us, and the more we flirted the more I agonized: shall I have an affair? I asked friends, who all discouraged me, but at the end I decided to hell with everything and wooed her with a song. The song was "Dancing with Tears in My Eyes ('Cause the Girl in My Arms Isn't You)." But who was the girl that I wished to dance with? Betty or my wife? Or this dream girl du jour? And how could I dance with Betty, confined as she was to her throne? And who wasn't in my arms that I wished to hold? For better or worse, the half-life of dreams is very short. By noon this mystery woman had vanished and would have vanished forever had I not written it down. Then what?

ONANISM

One of the odd side effects of living through your memories is that masturbation takes a new, bittersweet turn. It becomes less pornographic as you reach into your pocket of old memories about past loves and lovers. The initial kiss and embrace, the first jumping into bed, the arm around the waist. (Youth! When we still had waists!) The fantasies become not what could happen but what did. Sometimes with a different twist—easily accomplished by the fact that the initial instance has now become latticework in the brain. The days, however, were empty. I need to create a fugue, to make reality different the way lunatics do. Or even like the elderly Odessites looking at the dirty Brighton Beach imagine themselves to be back by the warm waters of the Black Sea, dreaming of the good herring and halvah they had back home.

Every morning I would wake up and after checking my Facebook and email would spend at least an hour or two looking at porn and it rarely, only rarely, led to any type of arousal and the subsequent manual satisfaction. Pornography has its own uneasy place in many, if not most, men's lives. Being the doomed romantic that I was, I found it sad that there was no tragedy left in porn. I was not only a consumer but a creator of sorts. Some time back I spent a dreadful winter in isolation in Brooklyn, in a freezing apartment surround by retarded cats. I was starving, surviving on tallboys of Budweiser and greasy hamburgers and most of the winter was spent in a snowstorm. Around the time that spring began to break through my winter of blackness, spent staring out at the gables of the wonderful Park Slope buildings and hallucinating that I was in

Holland or Flanders, or pacing my cold apartment in a fur hat and typing with frozen fingers a translation of a German play which would never see the light of day, listening to the ghoulish Leonard Cohen and seeking employment through the newspapers, I came across an ad for the ye olde pedestrian admin job which required "must be okay with adult content." A fax and a phone call later I ascended the elevator in the Empire State Building to the twentieth, fortieth, perhaps the sixtieth floor—I do not remember.

"That job has been filled" said the fat, middle-aged Jewess, who quickly followed up with, "Do you know how to write?"

"I do," I stumbled, and before I could say anything further she went on. "I knew you were a writer. I could tell right away. Do you want a writing job? It doesn't pay much." That was the first and only time I had an actual writing job and what a plum job it was. For $300 per article I could write the most egregious lunacy I could think of: "I Was a Gay Male Escort," "The Inside Scoop on Brighton Beach Brothels," "Inside the Shantytown of the Shemales" were some of the titles of my porn oeuvre. The shemale one was actually based on reality, back when New York was still completely insane there existed an actual settlement of transsexuals by the West Side Highway living in tents and teepees.

But back to Los Angeles, when sex between Charlotte and I ceased to exist, I salivated over every female behind that passed me by. Eight to eighty, black crippled or crazy as my friend Jim used to joke. In my case it was more serious, and more cause for concern. The female rump was on my radar the minute I stepped out of the house. There was a woman who walked her dog around the block who reminded me of Sandra Kellogg. She was probably around sixty, and she would wear a short skirt with knee-high leather boots even in the height of summer and we would exchange pleasantries and then I would have to return to my desk and google "mature"+ "blonde" + "boots" and sometimes "black boots," but the results were never satisfactory. At the local supermarket there was a delicious-looking black girl who looked straight out of a sixties girl group. She looked better than every member of the Shirelles, the Chiffons, the Supremes, and anything else black that was all girls and ended in an "s". My pants bulged from my hardon but all I could do was flirt. Millions of blood cells rushed to the penis, the zipper buckled, the buckle strained, and yet what could I do? Back home in a few minutes, back to the grind and thus the organ would drop its furor and desire and my teen Diana Ross, actually someone even more beautiful than Ross, would be erased from memory at least until I saw her again when I returned to the shop to buy cheap wine. So I would go home and wonder plaintively if she shaved her pussy or not and if she did, was it curly like black people's hair, and I would fall asleep in a confusion of pointless thoughts. I would also wonder if she had a boyfriend, if he was black or white, or whatever, whatever, whatever, but the thought of this beautiful girl kept fading as I would fall asleep—until I saw her again.

At home, the routine of cock and pussy was, like I said, mostly based on fantasy. At this point, Charlotte and I had not had sex for almost three years. The bedroom was bleak and dead and I did not foresee any resolution. But the black girl at the shop would look at me with what I imagined to be genuine kindness when she asked "Paper or plastic" whereas at home, a spoon out of place was enough to warrant the silent treatment for four to five days. I was getting old, and there was no way I would be able to entice the black girl into the sack. That much was obvious, but the slightest flirtation would restore my will to live... Perhaps someone would want to have sex with me again. And even more than that, I wished to hold a female hand again, to walk side-by-side with a woman... to put my arm around her waist. In the meantime it was my hand and porn, and while I usually found nothing wrong with porn—in fact it had given me hours and days and weeks and months and years and decades of pleasure—it was beginning to lose its purpose: arousal. As I began to come to grips with the fact that my sex life was non-existent, I started to become repulsed not only by the endless pneumatic motion, but also by the actors. My masturbatory climax was piddling. It was rarely exciting and became more and more akin to evacuation than satisfaction, more a feeling of distance than of connection. The latter made sense, naturally, for there was no human intimacy, only me and my hand and my fantasy.

What is the worst thing in the world? That is the brilliance of Room 101—that everyone has their own terror.

I would lie down waiting for another dream lover to appear. Was this a normal way to dream? Was this a normal way to live? What would be the ultimate degradation? What is the lowest one could possibly sink?

I personally always tried to stay afloat and not to sink but I had seen so many sunken ships around me that fascinated me and repelled me at the same time. My mother always had a perverse fascination with things egregiously tragic—bathetic even—and I tried to avoid those same feelings, yet they would come up again when I would create my characters and stories. But to be fair, horror can take many shapes and many incarnations. This isn't relativism. Christ's suffering is one form, wings off flies is another, Belzec and Chelmno one, solitary confinement another, and an inferno from Dante can compete with the poignancy of a five dollar blowjob, one from a Sonia Marmeladova type perhaps, but as long as Sonia does not actually enjoy it. Then of course, much of that poignancy has been obliterated to a certain extent today.

I myself had never sought out personal degradation. The concept was exciting, of course, but apart from my mid-to-high grade alcoholism I did maintain a self-preservation gene of some sorts, although that was starting to disappear. I was starving for a human's touch… not only the physical act of inserting my penis into someone, but something bigger too. At a party one night, after being told to leave, I stumbled over to a wino bar, and when fully sloshed began to talk to some bar whore and before leaving, actually stuck my tongue in her putrid mouth to which she responded vigorously. What surprised me was how despite her decrepitude the tongue was firm and strong as it swished Old Crow or some other swill and her spit inside my mouth. I ran out in disgust and wanted to wash my mouth out but I was not allowed back into the house and so I slept in the car in self-loathing and shame.

When I woke up I felt remorse for my behavior and my weakness, and soon the following recurring thought returned to me: We wish to preserve—through statues, mausoleums, mummies; from King Tut to Lenin… But we also wish to preserve through books… Yet what a bizarre situation this—us constantly replacing each other and only overlapping. Instead of awful drunken encounters, I needed to write. I had hoped for the curtain of illusion to be lifted but like the old grey hen I pecked around while life shoved me here and there with a broom and nothing had been accomplished.

Thus as life continued to pass me by, I continued to build castles in Spain—be it with my yet-to-be-written book or one of the many potential but definitely unattainable lovers. Like the ebony checkout girl, for instance.

In the early mornings, sleepy and erect, searching for these women in my mind would turn futile and I would try to focus on an imaginary scene of something utterly peaceful. I tried to imagine an island—Sardinia or Corsica or Mallorca, just as I pictured them in the story that Monica Vitti tells her son in Deserto Rosso—but that too was frustrating, as frustrating as the viridian Pacific Ocean, which looks spectacular from afar but is unfit to swim in.

It takes only one tiny detail to remind us that we are all human, that we are who we are, warts and all, blackheads and clap-ridden twats to boot. We live in prisons where we oscillate between pain and sleep, and during waking hours we ignore just how terribly sad it all is. Even the process of eating stabbed me with melancholy. I had written a poem about a similar feeling called "The Sorrow of Food."

Hot, delicious pizza!

Individual pastry, 99 cents!

Don't forget the bread and milk!

Eggs on sale, $1.99 a dozen.
Welfare allots four fresh bananas for the baby
per month in California.

And "Nutrition Guide for New Mothers on
Raising a Healthy Infant" (Moscow, 1968),
discovered in 2008.
Food, glorious food.
We break bread, make friends.
Without nourishment we'd be dead
but we're all dying anyway.
Even the famous fan, Freddie Exley, on his
deathbed, asked not for alcohol but for
"fresh strawberry yogurt."

The innocence of eating is that
everyone must eat and
we'll do anything for it.
We'll steal the last stolen potato squirreled
in our bunk mate's striped pajamas
before he gets to snort some Zyklon B.

Come on, the old refrain is better him than me.

Meanwhile, for me, the innocence is lost.
No longer anything that can be called
a simple pleasure, so I look wistfully at
subway ads for food banks, at the hobos
picking out hairy crusts, at notices
for the assistance programs to
make the poor healthy so they can have
a healthy child .

I fill my guts, I don't break bread.
I have no final supper planned.
I am too filthy to be fed.
I'm way too bitter and too trenchant
to accept a Sacrament
and subway cars still pass me by
and carry on.
Starving, I suffocate.
I don't mean entombed in cork
with cookie crumbs in my moustache,
reminiscing about Swanns…

I mean, we starve and
thirst, because we are the ones!

What seals the terrifying sympathy is the desire to live, and the need to eat. The poignancy of Tralala who exists in a fetid, amoral circle of hell is not the self-inflicted gang rape and swan dive into degradation-as-redemption but where she stops by a cafeteria, splashes some water on her face and orders a coffee and a bun. Even with Betty, I never wanted to hurt her, even a woman who abused me I always thought of as vulnerable, even the strangulation of Nurse Ratched evoked compassion.

But here was the question: was Betty a Tralala, who lived to survive? Who was she exactly? Excuse me, I am getting ahead of myself again… I will explain Betty in time, for I am still alive for now and have a modicum of energy to write down what happened that summer. I am just diverging as I recount all the mixed-up melodies of wasted youth.

Now that we're done with the crass reality of cabbages and hardons, it's time to discuss some of those girls I mentioned.

SOME GIRLS or
THE PROCESS OF GIVING UP

The more my life became routine and was coming to a standstill, the more rich and varied my love life became— in my dreams. A new lover or merely sexual partner would come to me in slumber almost every night. And what variety! Blondes, brunettes, tall and thin or pleasantly plump. Ebony Nubian goddesses and Aryan Valkyries, exotic Hindus and Osakan geishas, the sheer scope was astounding. So vivid it all was that I was surprised that I wasn't roused from my sleep by an adolescent nocturnal emission. Alas, these creatures would fade away within the first thirty minutes of waking life, leaving me cold and heartbroken but with the comforting thought that another incarnation would come the following night. Of course there was no smell of female much less scent of a woman, and certainly not even the faintest recollection of what it's like to insert one's throbbing gristle, one's vulgar appendage into the orifice of one's choice but it was better than nothing, for I had nothing for over two years now. Porn would sometimes inspire dreams. Sometimes maybe a Romanian, a daughter of the Danube… now degraded to the point of her eyes sealed shut with semen, her asshole stretched out…. The end of Communism, of dictatorship begets freedom. And so we dove into orgies, and tubercular wheezing and AIDS and heroin… The myths of the Vltava maiden, the braids in her hair, the peasant wedding so spectacularly present in music… Oh to see a maiden, virgin or not, riding on a Przewalski horse like an absurd vision…

But what would I do with you, my love, my dirty whore who would shove imported black dicks in your ass so you can afford mamaliga and a piece of bread?

And so it went, and eventually, the interest in porn ebbed in light of the depressing aspects. And yet I still tried to find a bit of humanity lodged somewhere deep inside the degradation.

It was all magical, these dreams, like living women except they would only come to me when eyes were wide shut. And someone wrote that in dreams begin responsibilities...

Despair it was. I would often awake, or fall asleep, or daydream in the day of what it felt like to undress a woman—or to get naked together. It had now become years since there was any excitement over the concept of undressing—even when one is completely familiar with one another and each other's bodies, undressing should have had a tiny bit of meaning and titillation. But that was buried. Though they went on, even the fantasies were becoming stillborn.

I retained a vision of a girl I barely knew from high school—Gigi Lexington—whom I had a minor crush on. She ended up going to Albany and I couldn't wait to see her there and ask her out.

I had barely arrived in Albany when my father took me to the mall to buy some new clothes. We both agreed on a fancy floral cowboy shirt—and when my dad dropped me off I was standing by the fountain on campus and there she was—Gigi, my potential new girlfriend, my potential new true fine love... I courted her briefly.

Then I met a witch named Melanie LaBonne.

"She was hot for me! She was wet for me" I yelled at LaBonne during a screaming match, and she found poor Gigi in the campus directory and repeated to her what I yelled. Lonely as I was, I would have vastly preferred Gigi to this cow, but now I had no choice. And so I tried to become used to being happy with her.

Sometimes, sometimes I get a good feeling...

This LaBonne thing happened back in Albany... Albany was awful, so why did I keep on dreaming about it so idyllically in LA? It was a dream of youth, of the oblivion of the past.

The spring of Albany, the digging oneself out of the merciless winter, was as powerful as the fall in Albany, which came in with fangs of the snow demons, relentless, punishing, leading you to the sick, brown snow-covered boulevard of American horror.

A dream: I am driving with my dad, somewhere in California, somewhere in the desert, perhaps going toward Palm Springs when suddenly we make a turn and there is vegetation, the landscape turns green, I can smell grass and trees (California doesn't smell like anything I've noticed, especially LA), and we are now somewhere in what I recognize or guess is upstate New York... I want to get out of the car and stay there in this boring but familiar place, where I can at least smell the dewy flowers, despite the bad reminiscences, despite everything of the past, but I awake... Sometimes the past is exactly what it is—the past, the bygone times. It can be resurrected by being filled with hot air, or written about in memoirs, but to physically go back is always a massive disappointment. This I would learn, this I would most definitely learn that fateful summer that I decided to spend in New York. There is no escape from exile and there is never a homecoming.

White cities, empty cities: Albany was a prime candidate. The four years I lived there were nauseous and entrancing both. The utter emptiness of the streets, the desire to stay there somehow, the push and pull of an empty place, the summer silence... the neighborhoods one wishes to make one's own and, like with woman, cannot. The Sunday smiles. The cities that did not exist.

Eventually, in some ways, all cities cease to exist, not just physically. New York is not the same... Los Angeles, well when was it anything? And the cemetery of Europe, well it's precisely that. The world is its own punishment, little gets littler via modernity and progress. My parents, their friends, their acquaintances, when they lived in these cities, talked, discussed, they were passionate about art, about history, and now the world appears innocuous despite that horror still persists. We just don't care much about it anything anymore. It is as banal as the Auschwitz orchestra greeting new arrivals with a rousing rendition of "El Choclo" as the cattle cars are emptied and Sophie has to make her choice.

Perhaps within the "European" context of New York, despite its malevolent abyss, people were still able to continue—yes, Castles in Spain or whatnot, there was a charm, a familiarity within the density of the anthill. The buses, the leaves, the avenues, even the idea of a short flight over the Atlantic. Something held the lost Europeans together. In LA there is nothing to hold us together, there is no center for us to hold so there is nothing left to fall apart. But how gloriously New York fell apart, glorious in the banality of it all, pedestrian, lackluster. I had to get out.

Ah, the winters of my discontent. The ones in Albany were just a grey streak striking through the heart. The purple fantasies of my idea of a screenplay or book: "The Girl from Below," inspiring, heavily pregnant. And the worst was the stillborn one in Park Slope… A winter spent in delirium. I thought it would never stop snowing… It felt like it would never stop snowing… And then spring came, one of the few true springs when things seemed to miraculously start looking up again. The dreadful thing about California is that the spring is actually a winter, and there is no sense of rebirth.

The end of winter is as biological as the appreciation for health that comes after a long illness. And then there was Albany, the Albany which seemed to have followed me my entire life.

Oh Albany, with your gold and yellow leaves in the fall, your snow banks rising above first-story windows in the winter. Your black springs. The black snow melting in April… I spent the bulk of my time in Albany trying to get laid and I learned nothing there at university and the only lesson I excelled in was heartbreak. So many phantoms from back then… those who were so utterly unattainable for some reason or another.

The Albany springs were green and black. Black because the days were still short but the green of the new leaves on the trees shone through the twilight, through the brake lights, through the tail lights, through the window lights, under the big black sun. "I'm here," spring would whisper, but just as fleeting as a one-night romance she would turn cold the next day and send winds and rain, only to resurrect herself again. A Botticelli in a mini skirt and ripped stockings, smoking a cigarette on Central Avenue. And just like Sandro destroying his work in religious fervor, each wet waste of an Albany slut would destroy that part of her life and return to Long Island to raise a family. Not blameworthy if, for our country's sake, mountains are needed more than meteors.

Yet it was that spark of a meteor, a shooting star, a comet, that intrigued me the most.

"Look!" Emily Vainonen grabbed my hand as we were driving through the Nevada desert. "A shooting star!"

It was the desert, and a shooting star was indeed just that—a flash of something spectacular; but I suppose for the majority of the Albany girls, that shooting star was one sordid, distant episode.

Oh, the things I imagined in Albany. The greatest and most recurring theme was escape. A Led Zeppelin poster with the dirigible made me think only of the power of flight. New York, too, would always push me further and further away, and escape was nowhere to be found—except perhaps in the ocean. And here I was now in California, on the edge of the continent, and again there was no escape.

Albany was the start of the run, the endless marathon, from New York to somewhere, anywhere else, until finally at the edge of the Blue Pacific Blue, I decided to run back to New York, even for a minute, the way a child who whilst scolded and sporting a red butt from a dour and frustrated matron would run back and try to hide under the familiar petticoat reeking of cunt and stale piss.

But underneath the florid tapestry of New York's underpants, beneath the amber light of her evening sun, in the crevasses between her jungle of buildings "tall and frightening," despite the vague idea of potential the place was lousy with worms, invertebrates that would burrow deep into the heart and eat your insides. And that is why, in time, New York became much more of a graveyard to me than California. At least the graves are fresher here.

There is nothing wrong with graveyards—as long as they aren't active. And that to me was what New York had become, a genuinely active cemetery, a Treblinka on the Hudson for those who were not able to either fight it or accept it.

Those moist spring nights that took me to an even hotter, more melting Manhattan, passing through the towns of sweet despair, the towns of fleeting shadows, shooting arrows, all those towns melded together to form the squalid odyssey of Stacy Fox, the heroine of my screenplays.

The airplanes over the roof came later.

Oh Albany, Albany... You were not the rat embrace of New York, your embrace was the grey. Despite the green shoots in spring and the glorious red and yellow of your Indian Summer, you were a time and place for the most depressing of finalities, a place that one returns to die, and when I left you, I found myself in a sailor's graveyard called San Francisco. But that is another story, which I shall come back to. That was the beginning of The New World Symphony—or at least the part that is called "scherzo." But back in Albany, my head was in the clouds, and the cloud was in my trousers.

It was in Albany that I met and fell in love with the Saddest Girl in the World—Wendy Novak. And it was in Brooklyn, on Ocean Parkway almost thirty years ago that we consummated our flirtation. "Harvey's going to kill me." Those were the words she said when I finished inside her, after she took my virginity. And that was when the future of my affairs for many years were sealed with despair.

Harvey was her on-and-off boyfriend. A snotty Jew whose major pickup line was, "Hey babe, I'm looking for a hole." And Wendy, not being the sharpest crayon in the pack, fell for it. There was no doubt that Wendy was stupid, but I was drawn to her for some reason, possibly because of her sadness.

Like a board game, like Life or Candyland or even Monopoly depending on what the devil throws you, certain moves by your piece determine further outcomes, and those moves are dependent on the dice roll. The places you visit on the board of memory stay and haunt you. "Harvey's going to kill me" was the opening of the game of women for me. There were other previous ones in Candyland—the chicken soup incident for one—but the further back one goes the fuzzier the nature of the move is. And so there are these pins on the game board of life that despite the further movement of the play piece still retains its labyrinthine and ultimately repetitive and pointless nature.

But I found myself back in Brooklyn, that terrible summer about which I write now. There I was back again on that same street, returning to the scene of the crime rom where began my maturity (if one can call it that), so many years back.

I suppose there is nothing wrong with admitting that I am—or was—insane, or that I lost my mind, however you wish to put it. The question is, among the other so many unsolved questions within this book: when exactly did my illness start?

Perhaps it was when I decided that I refused to believe that death exists, or that people die, or that anything really exists in the first place. I could not fathom the fact that once there was a person, and then the next moment he is gone. It simply stopped making sense, but instead of bringing comfort it only aggravated my own personal thanatophobia.

Religion is supposed to a band aid on these thoughts but I was never religious nor inquisitive. The inevitable, fatal process of decay burdened my waking hours and I was beginning to find solace mostly in sleep. How I pined for the yellow mornings of childhood, back when New York was a magical place due to my own imagination, and the endless potential I thought it held. And for the blue haze of summer, and the moist white haze of early fall.

The endless expanse of the ocean, the depths of the Mariana Trench, the heights of the stratosphere all became nothing at all compared to the concept of light years, of photographs of nebulas from the Hubble Telescope, compared to this endless, endless anthill. It was an anthill of sentient ants—that was the real problem, that was what maddened me to no end.

And the frustrating back and forth between two edges of the continent. How idyllic I used to consider the Pacific coast, where instead of trash and rats, freezing cold winters and suffocating summers, I would picture myself safe and warm in my California home. Instead I ended up laying here sweating and staring at LA's brown sky, reminiscing about the blue haze of New York and the melting tar of her summer. "As I Lay Sweating" would have been a good title for that chapter in my life.

And so I sent mental postcards back and forth, from the warm waters of Jones Beach to the freezing cold Pacific until I was finally stuck: physically feet firmly planted on the earth with nothing between me but China, Japan and Vladivostok, mentally something entirely different, a place of limbo where even oranges and golf balls were not really "on the ball" so to speak.

Oh Albany. It was you who set the wheels in motion for me to fiddle the summers away, Mr. Grasshopper, B.A.—and it is you whom I periodically think of now in the autumn of my life. It was you, the Central Avenue of every city and town, in the snow and freezing rain and the black and grey skies, that showed me an endless street of nothing but grey and bleak and ugliness. It was you whom I decided I needed to escape from at any cost.

I escaped, for that was my only mission, to leave; and though I left you so many years ago, I have sometimes pined for you, but only because I pine for my youth, warts and all. Everything else is ravaged by time; whatever transpired there is only in my brain and when I am dead, you too will disappear.

Oh, you were not without your charms, your brilliant colors, your autumns. The couple of misdirected little loves; the first breath of spring signaling the end of the frozen nightmare; even the short, stifling summers... But mostly you helped me squander not just my four years there but a subsequent decade. What then shall I make of you now? Shall I preserve you in a few paragraphs here in this book?

No, I learned nothing from you. Nothing but a constant desire to run, to run far away and keep running. And thus I also continued the tradition I started in that town—the tradition of pointless days and weary nights. It wasn't in Albany that Stacy Fox was born, but it was there that the seed of her existence was planted in my brain, ready to sprout and bear an ugly fruit years later.

Back then I did not know where to run. I tried to make myself fall in love with the New World instead but it was a disastrous affair, now a divorce and a hangover that persist into middle age. If only I had embraced Europe back then instead of pulling a Pepé Le Pew to this new land.

That long, grey, interminable Central Avenue—ubiquitous and telling for there is the same opaque, filmy Central Avenue in every city in this country—that was what always pushed me to run, to escape... I had never seen the desert in real life, and thanks to films and TV shows I imagined that you could actually swim in the Pacific Ocean, and that the banality of the banal evil of every Central Avenue in every city and town in North America would be replaced by sand, palms and possibilities instead of dead, raped children stuffed into a cooler left on the side of the West Side

Highway, or guidos dredged up from the Hudson River wearing their classic and most fashionable "cement shoes." I burned with a desire for something clean and new.

How foolish I was. In some ways I substituted hell for purgatory. But purgatory implied, at least according to Dante, pleasant company and fine discourse and conversation, things utterly absent in this new, safe Californian home. That was when and where I truly became The Sitter. But there was yet another decade before California where I had to digest and regurgitate Central Avenue and all the spokes that spread out from that center of misery in various turns including the most sordid of side alleys branching away from the secondary arteries.

Just as tickle torture might be worse for some than the rack, so for me it was impossible to delve into purgatory, and perhaps because of that sin of insolence I found myself transported back to hell that summer in Brooklyn. Perhaps, in another book, when older and wiser, I will be able to describe the underworld scum of endless Central Avenue, but this story, which I haven't yet started to tell, takes place in Brooklyn. And before I can tell it, I must finish this detour into Albany.

LABONNE

Ah, LaBonne, the little town flirt (the Del Shannon song of that name would bring me to tears thinking about her), the whore from Cortland, NY as she called herself, another one dead in the water. *La symphonie pathétique*, really because truth be told she wasn't all that attractive. And her unhealthy relationship to sex probably also contributed to my lack of psychological wellbeing during my own spring awakening. I am however, perversely grateful to her for contributing to the character amalgam of the doomed female protagonists that I started to create in my still unproduced screenplays.

Oh Melanie LaBonne, what a deliciously disgusting entry into the world of sex and relationships you gave me. Neither a hooker with a heart of gold nor a princess with a heart of snot, I fell for you—I am not sure why. And how you tortured me. You refused to suck my cock because your ex-boyfriend had a dick so big that it hurt your throat and you were forever scarred by that experience. Did you have any idea of what you were saying?

Or how about the time you fucked that "little shit" at a party, out of spite when you were spurned, or when you woke up with your face all scratched up by beard burns from the guy three times your age who fucked you in the park?

Yeah, LaBonne, you made it into the screenplay and you have an honorable mention in this book as well. Your attempt at poignancy was naught but an attempt to elevate yourself over a garden variety existence; in fact you probably weren't even much of a slut but you screamed to me in desperation, "I'm just a whore from Cortland!"

And then you fucked me over again. Emily Vainonen—now there was a true whore. But more about her in a bit.

A whore from Cortland, she cried when I confronted her with only the tiniest of indiscretions in retrospect but which meant life or death to my near-virgin mind at that point. LaBonne's tactic of self-loathing and sadism mixed together was something that took a long time for me to grasp.

LaBonne was white trailer trash masquerading as someone striving to improve her lot in life. The Rotary club sent her and her sister abroad—her to Norway and her sister to Zimbabwe—and vis-a-vis said trip they both pretended to be more worldly. Melanie even continued to dutifully study the ridiculous Norwegian language with a private tutor. It wasn't offered in university and she had no need for it but it helped her with building her image as someone cosmopolitan to disguise her trailer park origins.

If only I had had more self-confidence back then, I would have sent her flying. Across the room, or back to stupid Norway, or better yet, Cortland.

But then there were other things, other tiny sins, sins which should be easily forgiven considering one's youth and inexperience, but when the other party, in this case myself, was even more inexperienced and sensitive, I had no tolerance and no pity. That said, I would and could think of her with Dostoevskian "terrible sympathy," even though I wanted to kick her in the cunt. I had a tremendous maudlin pity for the women who wronged me because they were wronged themselves.

Then she told me about the several times she had VD, or STD as you now call it. For a Plain Jane with a page boy haircut and red hair, I now wonder if she perversely found it a badge of honor. For me it was a devil's arrow in the heart, not cupid's.

I tolerated an amazing amount, being so young and innocent. And I pretended that I was in love with her. Truth be told, I was in love with having a girlfriend—I needed someone, I needed sex no matter how lame or psychologically degrading it was to me, I needed companionship… And now, thinking about it, I needed fodder for my obsession over a tragic female character, my very own Carmen.

The nadir was the time we walked hand-in-hand down a snowy, windswept December street. A group of frat boys, drunk, were stumbling our way. Suddenly and swiftly she grabbed me by the arm and pushed us into the foyer of the nearest apartment building and burst out crying. I had no idea what was happening. "It's him! That little shit! That little shit!"

My heart and cock were both still borderline virgins and they dropped in utter fear. I had no idea what she was talking about. On this freezing street, this black street was black enough, what does she want to tell me now?

Through tears she told me about the time she was spurned by a boyfriend at a party, how she went upstairs and fucked this "little shit" out of spite, and how she woke up full of regret the next morning. She obviously wanted to make it all the more dramatic for it seemed rather pedestrian to me now—but at the unripe age of eighteen it traumatized me enough. Madonna/whore etc, whatever you want to call it—the bitch could have kept silent but she wanted to cultivate a story, give her more depth than she actually had perhaps. And that is why she unwittingly became part of the mental sculpture I created named Stacy, and part of The New World Symphony.

"I was at a party, and this guy came and I went upstairs and he fucked me and…"

And now, thirty years later, I don't remember exactly what the horror was about that particular "Little Shit," perhaps I erased it from my mind in the name of self-preservation. Whatever happens at parties stays at parties, unless the party girl volunteers the information.

Is the cruel platitude "once a whore, always a whore" true? I don't know. I would try to erase quite a bit of the whoredom from my mind. I recall one episode although I don't recall exactly which indiscretion (or infidelity) she was guilty of that time, but to atone for it she invited me to a simple dinner of chicken and broccoli stir-fry. "Eat. It's good food..." she said gently. I saw she was a human just like anyone and that was the germ of my future oil and water of hatred and sympathy.

Oh and how she lied to me over one summer when I was back in New York, and disappeared when I decided to take a bus up to godforsaken Cortland to surprise her but discovered that she was out fucking a friend. Like a true coward I capitulated. I went up there and unknowingly fucked sloppy seconds, but that was after a night in agony sitting up late with her white trash mother in her white trash house, drinking whiskey, waiting for her to come home. In the end I gave up and went to sleep. I can smell infidelity from a mile away but chose to close my eyes. The next day I, the cuckold, walked with her hand-in-hand to the blood bank as she was volunteering to donate blood. She told me to wait outside. Innocent and naïve and dumb, it took me days, weeks, months to realize why she didn't want me to be present—because they would ask if she recently had unprotected sex or had any STDs.

My suspicion was aroused, and with that suspicion came revelation. I finally confronted her, and yelled: "Did you fuck Sam?"

"Yes! I did!" She finally broke down and I kicked her filthy ass on the freezing street. But within just a few days she was back on her psychological merry-go-round.

She stood outside my house the next day when I came home from class, cutting her hand with a shard of a cocktail glass, sobbing and wailing. I felt sorry for her. And the next day, somehow, I took her back. I needed sex and the company of a woman, and a woman's touch, though she had become repulsive to me psychologically.

I had no attachment to her anymore though we were nominally still together, so I could do what the hell I wanted. Thus, after a party I brought home a girl and fucked the living daylights out of her. Somehow LaBonne found out, and that was the end for us as far as I was concerned. But she came over for sex again the next night and, idiot that I was, I apologized.

LaBonne was livid, as if we even had a relationship any more, but in order to hold on to a woman, any woman, I allowed myself to be broken, crushed against the wheel. "How many times did you fuck her?" she screamed. "Three," I admitted (back in my youth I was able to do such a thing), and indeed I had fucked that girl three times.

"Fuck me three times," LaBonne screamed and I proceeded to oblige but she could not stop, like a Tralala before I even read the book. Sperm dripping out of her pussy, she kept yelling: "Fuck me four times! Fuck me five times! Fuck me more than you fucked her! Fuck me twice as many times as you fucked her!"

So I fucked her to five but couldn't make it to six. And I never wanted to see her ever again. Last I heard, she has a vineyard in Washington. Horticulture. Whore to culture. Whore from Cortland to viticulture.

But certain nasty and most romantic perversions stayed with me for years—the "man in the park" for instance, the way LaBonne got her first case of the clap. She made vague references to someone named "the Man in the Park" and he was the one who gave her her first STD. Surely a teenage indiscretion but the way she described it—and she simply should have kept her mouth shut when it comes down to it—was filth, filth and more filth. And yet I thank her for it, for it gave me much fodder for The New World Symphony. I pictured her, rejected by a potential new boyfriend after a one night stand, grabbing onto anyone, fucking anything that moves: a petite little strumpet. And thus my sordid fantasies started to take shape.

LaBonne or whoever, borderline drinking age, getting drunk out of her mind and through her tears, the lamps above the bar shatter like amethysts, shatter like crystal chandeliers falling and dropping through the film of the retina.

While that scene existed only in my mind's eye, it expanded further and would be recreated in my New World Symphony— through the character I christened Stacy Fox, but more on that in a bit.

How many LaBonnes and others came to form the zygote of Stacy Fox? Hard to say. Not too many, really. Neither a lothario nor a player, neither a cuckold nor a thief, neither a lover nor a fighter, the one thing I sorely wanted was a girlfriend a lover, a woman…

And so it was that LaBonne became the first drop in the nauseating cocktail of tears, whoredom, and semen that formed my world view of women until I got over it almost ten years later.

Stacy. Why did I pick the name Stacy? A porn actress perhaps? There was also a girl named Stacy who would hang out in the park when I was in high school. A RuJew. Pretty. Short hair. Seemed like a pass-around girl. I overhead her flirting with some boys once, teasing her by asking if she spits or swallows. Coy, she answered something akin to "depends on the situation or the guy," and I was instantly enthralled, I hardly knew her but I sought her out. I found out she worked at a pastry shop on 72nd Street and Columbus— and so, one late afternoon I came over there and spied on her. As she was serving cream puffs and chocolate eclairs my cock was about to burst in my underwear knowing that she sucks cocks and sometimes she spits and sometimes she swallows and I didn't care which outcome was mine as long as my dick somehow landed in her mouth.

In the end, nothing happened. Paralyzed by virginal fear I stood outside the confectioner, my hardon visible through my thin trousers, making an arch from my balls to my belt, and I never went inside that Jewish bakery on 72nd Street where Stacy doled out confectionary delights by day and other sticky pleasures with her hand or mouth by night. For me, chaste and frustrated, it was only the name that was sticky and thus it stuck. "Stacy."

But that was way before the mythology and tragicomedy of Stacy Fox snowballed.

Oh, how LaBonne cut herself with a broken glass in front of me. So dramatic.

But I have neglected to add one telling tale. Once, in the dorms, after some dreadful night of fighting—perhaps over some other nasty revelation ("Little shit! Little shit!"—which sounded almost like "Shrimp! Shrimp!" as the henpecked Faulkner character hears from his fat cunt of a wife, walking down the sweaty sidewalks of a Mississippi town to bring her a bucket of greasy shrimp)— LaBonne demanded that I fuck her whilst she lay there basically panting like a lizard. I rolled over, covered in sweat and frustration. I was sick of fruitlessly trying the old "in-out" with her. Instead of sympathy or understanding that we may have both been too tired, she started furiously dressing. The dorm that she lived in had a high proportion of so-called "underprivileged students" who were becoming infamous for getting into trouble. There were numerous cases of sexual harassment and even one case of actual rape that happened outside. This was the eighties and everyone was racist. Everyone is still racist but we hide behind the veneer of glossy political correctness; back then, though, I could not control myself and yelled, "You're not going out there with all the spics and niggers outside!" She turned and replied in a tone I find it impossible to describe: "Oh yeah? What are they going to do to me? Fuck me until I come?" and slammed the door.

How lonely I was, how I tried to imagine that these little tarts were something of great importance, something that can turn into a bright future. "I want to go to Machu Picchu with you!" I said to

LaBonne as I gifted her a book of poetry that had the famous peak on the cover—"Starting from San Francisco" by Ferlinghetti. What folly. My "love" for her was another act of imagination. There would be no San Francisco, much less Peru. But part of imagination is the belief that anything can happen. The thing is, you don't know what that "anything" will be.

All the little loves were small fry in retrospect, but they can still fuck up an impressionable young man. And like birds gotta fly, fish gotta fry. So let's fry up few more.

HARVEY'S GOING TO KILL ME!

Before LaBonne there was Wendy. She probably set my mind and my balls rolling. The petty sadism of the fairer/weaker sex was exploited by most of these some girls but usually unconsciously. No, "Harvey's going to kill me" was not just stupid, it was demeaning and heartbreaking. This was my introduction to relationships and intimacy and sex? It could have been worse, I suppose. Dick, The Gardener (as we called him, in reality he worked for the NYC Parks Department), whose death I will describe shortly, I was told through gossip, or maybe via his own disclosure, lost his virginity under duress to a 300 lb whore. His patriarchal father arranged the tryst. Perhaps it was that initial tryst that led to him becoming a closeted homosexual? Who knew or who knows.

Wendy was the first nail in the coffin of my infernal plight with girls. The Saddest Girl in the World is how I christened her much later.

TO WENDY NOVAK FROM STATEN ISLAND

Hard to define time. Everything seems
as if it was just yesterday and I can't remember
what I had for breakfast, though I remember
now when I was too afraid to eat a peach.

Another aspect of it all is that some
are born quite old, some born too young,
some born too soon, and some were born
in cemetery too.

The last one, I don't know how true, sometimes
I too feel stillborn, but I do know I've done
more than a bit of squandering time on tears
and nicotine and ethanol
and it continues yet.

But looking back I recall vivid as
the nightfall of the boozy haze of yesterday,
a snowstorm we were snowed in, me looking at your
panties with a drop of blood, the way
you spoke just of regret. Too much to bear,
too much to hold, when one's in cemetery born.

You may have been the saddest girl I ever met
and made me sadder still,
a dead-end start to life and sex,
and the romantic thrill.

"And when my mother dies, I will plant
sunflowers on her grave, they
turn their heads towards the sun…"

The saddest flower which the saddest girl in all the
world offers her mother, passing
one generation down to next.

"The only place outside New York that I had
been to was Quebec.
We took a boat across the St. Lawrence River
and bought wild strawberries."

I do not know if sadness still persists for you.
I have a feeling that it does. I see you now,
returning back home to your flat on
crosstown bus,

(you looked like Betsy and inside I was pure Travis),
and looking out at the falling autumn in New York,
I wonder if you ever will recall
just how you fell or chose to fall, or how
everything became so damned fucked up,
just when you struggled to stand up.

I ordered a slice of apple pie with a
piece of American cheese melted on top.

You could have had anything you wanted.

"Harvey's going to kill me:" those were the first words I heard
after I lost my virginity to Wendy and the first thing I wanted to do
was to stab myself in the throat. It was on Ocean Parkway, where
I am going to retrace my steps soon enough in this book. What
was special about Wendy other than that she looked like Nastassja
Kinski? Not much, except perhaps her sadness, and I was interested
in both looks and sadness, and Wendy was only my first in a
series of girls who were born dead. Born in a cemetery, as I later
termed this condition. After months of trying to woo her, I finally
succeeded in practically "luring" her to my "uncle's" apartment in
Brooklyn. He wasn't my uncle but my mom's alcoholic boyfriend
who volunteered me his keys in case I got lucky. After a Russian
dinner on Coney Island Avenue, accompanied by plenty of vodka,
Wendy was easily convinced that going back to Staten Island that
night would be folly given that my uncle was out of town and had
left me his keys. And thus I first inserted my penis into a vagina. It
lasted only a few seconds, but that was enough for me.

The next morning, despite the horrible words, I walked down
with her to get breakfast. As stupid as it sounds, I felt like a man.
As if something had changed, but not in the way I was hoping.
Perhaps it was the feeling of a man who had experienced dire

disappointment for the first time, not a man who made a conquest.

And thus the stillborn start would repeat, though not eternally. It led me to Las Vegas and to Emily. Whatever Emily and I had was something utterly false, utterly fictitious. It was neither love nor desire (the sex was completely dull). Looking back on it, I have no idea what it was. Emily was a cold bitch; her icy blonde appearance held some sort of fascination for me, but I am not sure why. The appearance matched the personality (the carpet matches the drapes). Emily Vainonen was the cynical, abortion-weary, sexless but beautiful slut who lacked all joy, and even screwing her was flogging a dead horse. But we did have a brief Las Vegas Story.

America, perhaps by twisting my own arm, became an object of fascination—and since I was here already, instead of the elusive and possibly lost Occupied Europe, I began to fantasize and act upon this Bad America of Moonlight Motels and explored it first in my mind, creating my own mythology, and then acted it out on various cross-country travels. Graceland, New Orleans, the Continental Divide… fill in the blank. For decades it was fascinating. Driving through the Blue Ridge Mountains with my dad as a child, I heard Flatt & Scruggs before I ever heard any other bluegrass music…. Purple and pink trees blossoming like pom-poms in Appalachia… Las Vegas before it became a theme park. Then things turned browner as I repeatedly returned to New York.

Old, brown New York—where I found myself again for the last time, and what this book is about—was the catalyst for all things turning grey: that long grey avenue stretching across a continent. In time, the romance of America became bathetic. There were few, if any things left to explore… But my last return to New York was different. It was a final intense attempt to reclaim the past. Let's skip back to Vegas now.

THE LAS VEGAS STORY

The Las Vegas Story begins when I went with my friend George on a cross-country road trip. George and I couldn't have been more different: he a posh, whitebread suburban kid known for his rude attitude, me a mongrel Mongol from the inner city. About all we had in common was that we both liked to drink a lot and had a deranged sense of humor—which was actually kind of a lot really, relative to my current isolation. In theory we were looking for a place to move, in practice we were goofing off. Both of us were interested in film, so the only possible place to move was Los Angeles, but we managed to extend this "exploratory" journey to include Vancouver, Seattle and San Francisco. Our goals differed as well; whereas I had some grand, misguided vision, George simply wished to be on the set of a film or television show. Twenty-five years later my grand vision remains a buried dream while George is living a comfortable existence as a television producer.

Our pointless journey had finished and we were on our way back east when George suggested we stop off in Las Vegas where a certain female friend of a friend was living and working as a stripper.

I had always been attracted to this particular female friend, and I was also fascinated by the concept of Las Vegas: an emerald city sprouting out of the desert. And approaching it from the highway was indeed spectacular. The reality not so much until three days later. Her name was Vainonen. Emily Vainonen.

Life is completely random, that is what makes it horrible at times. Fortuna can dole both good luck and bad, and like life and death, romance is ultimately a spin of the wheel. I knew Vainonen from back in Albany. I had heard various nasty and perverse stories about her, the very frequent visits to the abortion clinic, the bisexual heroin-addicted boyfriend who would fuck men and tranny hookers, a few other things that I had intentionally erased from my mind back then and which luckily I would not even be able to recall today. And back in Albany I didn't even know her very well at all. George and I just wanted to stop over and visit anyone we knew who had moved. I called her from the road and she told us we could stay with her in Las Vegas. She had moved there to work as a stripper. (It was probably much worse than that but I didn't know at the time nor for a year afterwards.) Thus George and I arrived in town and Emily showed us around and "entertained" us. After a few days of the obligatory breakfast buffets, slot machines, 99 cent shrimp cocktails and $4.99 prime rib dinners, all of which used to be part of the draw of Vegas back in the day, it was time for us to head back east and before I knew what was happening, Emily was packing her bags and telling us she was coming with us. I was noticing that there was a connection brewing between me and her. She laughed too much at my jokes and looked too much into my eyes. An impulsive decision like that should have been a warning sign but we hadn't even held hands or kissed yet and still when we got into the car I had a pretty clear picture that Emily and I would end up being lovers. Which we did a week or so later, in a motel just into the Kansas border. Soon enough, to my mother's horror, we were in New York. The city was turning black and purple with winter. She quickly found a job stripping and was able to get a room at an SRO because my mother couldn't stand her line of work, yet we continued. On some of our dates she would tell me stories which made me uncomfortable. About how she ran away from home and hitchhiked to San Diego, or how she spent a summer homeless in New York, sleeping on the roof of a building in Queens by LaGuardia Airport, waking up to the sound of airplanes landing. She stirred up romanticism and mixed it with sin and dread. Yet I went on, just like with LaBonne. I was always dreadfully afraid of being alone without a female companion and I turned a blind eye to the things that disgusted and frightened me.

Looking back, I wonder whether I was ever really in love with anyone, and whether anyone was ever really in love with me. I suppose I had some moments. "Two days of love," says Tunino to Tripolina in the film Love and Anarchy, "is more than most people get in their lives." I suppose there was a semblance of romance in my Las Vegas Story. I think it was some kind of love. (I apologize for the digressions. I am writing and singing my life. I have little else left).

The picture-postcard tour of America was a tremendous source of mystery and inspiration, but I was never able to form a concrete story to match those very vague emotions. Stuck in the New York cold, I listened to Spaghetti Western music, put a cactus next to my writing space and tried to hammer out the plot, but the story simply would not form. I tried in vain to grow flowers by candlelight…

I had been fascinated by the desert and the American West, and here I was finally embracing it. And the perverse romance of Las Vegas was powerful the minute I stepped foot in town and saw it for the first time. This was before it became the symbol of utter vulgarity, the Donald Trump of cities. And yet in 1992 it retained some type of romance for me. And as I drove through the West, the near-hallucinations came easy.

It is possible that my attraction to Emily rested precisely on a tug-of-war within my own emotions—that she held a deep, sordid secret somewhere inside her, which later was going to set my mind and heart ablaze with horror. It was in San Francisco two years later that that horror was revealed to me: she used to be a whore. It explained the blandness of the sex. At the impressionable age of twenty-one, whoredom presented itself as horror cloaked in the romantic notions of the forgotten and the downtrodden, the humiliated and insulted. Nowadays whoredom means little—in fact, something to aspire to in pop culture, but back then it was still enough to devastate, and when it was revealed, devastate it did.

That year in New York with Emily was actually quite boring, with her going to "work" at a strip joint called Flash Dancers which she jokingly called Flesh Peddlers. A strip joint is a strip joint, right? College girls working to pay off their tuition? Or is that a myth and there is something else that goes on behind the velvet curtains? Oh, there most definitely is. Emily regaled me with these stories and I had to control myself not to end her life because I had no way of knowing if she was part of these stories. The time she met Chuck Traynor, director of Dogfucker and Dog-a-Rama starring Linda Lovelace. Or the time an undercover cop asked for a blowjob in the "champagne room" and handcuffed the slut while she was going down on him and then the other cops raided the joint. Of course she only "heard" about it or saw it from afar, but how was I to know? The one episode she told me about which involved her directly was when a big tipper, an older guy, asked her if she would go to Atlantic City with him and stay with him at the poker table for good luck. "I thought about it," she told me, "but I knew you'd get mad." No shit, Sherlock. I was mad that she even considered it and that she told me about it. And yet we continued to live together in a Queens basement for some time.

Perversely, I could not let go of her. I was enamored of her for reasons I still don't understand. In the case of her sex work, my attitude wasn't mawkish. Looking back, I truly did not understand what I was doing. Winter turned to spring and we decided to move out of New York and go to California. Like most women, she did not have a verbal filter and she would hint at things she did in the past without revealing the entire story.

We made plans to move to San Francisco together but left in separate cars, her a few weeks before me. I had to help my dad out with a few things and tie up some loose ends with the move. By the time I arrived, that two-week window was enough for her to find a new lover—an older, wealthy businessman from Berkeley.

I only learned this later, for she refused to see me for at least a week after I got to town. She did not explain to me why she could not see me. I was pulling my hair out—I had just traveled three thousand miles to meet her and she was nowhere to be seen. "I'm busy," or "I have some plans," and finally, ten days or so later, she came to see the apartment I was staying with my friend Dave in the Western Addition, a horrible punk rock/hippie place that housed twelve people in three bedrooms. This was supposed to be temporary and Emily and I were supposed to have gotten a flat together, but it was impossible for me to reach out to her, impossible to make a date, impossible to understand what on earth was actually happening. Days and nights were spent in agony. How could this be happening—and what exactly was happening?

And then that dark secret was revealed to me over the phone by her friend Felicity, who was back in New York. I called her in desperation.

"She met some guy on the road, Lucky" Felicity told me. "I shouldn't be telling you this… or maybe I should be. It's in her personality. It's just the way she is." What the fuck was that supposed to mean?

My ears lost their function. Whatever Felicity said afterwards I did not hear, until I heard her say, "She worked for an escort agency. You didn't know that?"

No, I did not know about her past whoredom. And my mind sank deeper and deeper into hell. Sometimes tragedy is the tragedy of banality. As much as I wished for Vainonen to be obliterated like a great whore, I recently found thirty years later that she became the highly pedestrian "hotwife," sucking off black guys while her Neo-Nazi husband pleasured himself in fear and loathing. A perfectly depressing denouement to her life.

What possible other atrocities did she engage in? I did not go so deep as to think she ate shit or fucked farm animals, this was before I knew of Bodil Joensen. But as is correctly stated, the things you don't know are infinitely more frightening than those you do. When one gets older, of course, these fears become degraded as one learns and accepts man's capacity for the basest depravity, but at that age, I was destroyed by this disclosure. Nowadays, one would have to sink one's teeth into the crimes of the Nazis or the Soviets or, say, child rape or cannibalism to truly be frightened, for we have become hardened and inured. Horror like Room 101, however, for most people resides in the imagination.

I called Emily and told her "I'll see you next time I'm in town, which will probably be never" and hung up. This was a lie, for I would return to San Francisco many times. Yet my disgust was so severe, the betrayal so painful, that I genuinely wished that she would die, and so she melded in my fiction into an amalgam of LaBonne the "whore from Cortland," the teenage hooker from Staten Island from a Village Voice article I read, accompanied by a Dvořák soundtrack (a song of lilting pain) and Stacy Fox, and this plaster mold became the protagonist of The New World Symphony—a continuation of Garbage Dump aka The Girl from Below. In a week I was gone, and sped right back to New York; doing 90 mph with two crackheads and with only piss and hamburger breaks. We left San Francisco at noon on Monday and made it to Manhattan at midnight Wednesday. I was back in the sweat of New York yet again, my West Coast dreams shattered.

Once I returned to New York, I began to make more vague sketches for a book, a story, a poem, but most of all it was a screenplay I wanted to complete because that was when film was still alive and I burned with a passion to make my own film somehow. Yet my story was malformed and rather skeletal—it all centered on this wretched girl who ruined my life, but who was it? And how would I write it?

Although I have so far called it many different things, today, for now, let's call it The Girl from Below. For that is what she was, a creature that I could not define except by her tragedy, her tragic nature. Not a grand tragedy, nothing Shakespearean, nothing operatic; the tragedy was that of a little love, or a series of many little loves. And in a way it was her sordid, small-time insignificance and her many sordid dips into something that really stunk that made her poignant. Or so it seemed to me as I wrote the story. It was subconscious, the title, for it was only much later that I realized that by "below" I was referring to hell.

Much of it was based on my own ignorance, my childhood immaturity, and especially my fear of sex and women. I had always idealized both. Coming from the other side of the Atlantic, thoroughly unfamiliar with the American mores and aesthetics, I was unprepared for American vulgarity. Sure, there is no shortage of whores in the world, tragic or otherwise, but this was quite a few years before whoredom and porn began to be celebrated and appreciated in mainstream culture. Yet during this period of my youth The Girl from Below began to form. An amalgam of various types, but one who always was pathetic, like a guttersnipe version of some Chekhovian expression.

And thus my Girl from Below incubated as I sat in my room in Brooklyn until she was almost finally fully formed and deformed. Every dirty little secret a girl has was added on to her until she became almost a collection of ruinous misdeeds. In retrospect this was, as I said before, juvenile folly, for who am I to judge? And yet this character continued to be nebulous as she continued to haunt me and warranted several unproduced screenplays.

As much as I lusted, I also wanted romantic love and in that period of my youth the two seemed oddly incompatible. Perhaps that first encounter with Wendy and her pronouncement that "Harvey's going to kill me" ruined me much more than I thought. Or perhaps it was the succession of these not so unique women, which I nonetheless found unique, that helped create this dismal archetype. Perhaps it was just my shitty luck. All of them, it seemed, from heiress to gutter trash, trailer park ditch bitch to millionaire slut, all of them were pathetic and doomed. And thus they eventually melted and melded into one ridiculous character whom I christened Stacy Fox.

Stacy's journey began in upstate New York, where my formative years with women began. Later on, Stacey's voyage began to take on epic proportions. Sometimes I would think of her as a metaphor for America, and the whole thing came to be the film that I envisioned, which by now I was calling The New World Symphony. I knew that the last movement would be a scherzo, but I had yet to invent what that final sick joke was going to be.

The first movement was an allegro. And it began in a small town in upstate New York. These too were Stacy's salad days, starting in high school. I don't know how much Taxi Driver influenced me. Stacy was older than Iris in my depressing fantasy. And like a spring awakening, this was Stacy's awakening to the dark. Her dark awakening.

Decades on, never having found success at getting the screenplays produced, I decided to at least make a record of it and convert them into prose. This was the book, so to speak, that my wife was pushing me to finish. And so ostensibly this was my mission when I decided to spend that summer in hell—that summer in New York.

But let me start again. Let's start with the first chapter in the life of the Girl from Below. All of this is rather tame in these times where the passion of sex and fear has been truncated and bowdlerized. Or even worse, declawed of passion and terror.

A warm and green spring night. The long winter is over. Small town. Upstate New York. And so poor little Stacy cheats on her boyfriend. Big deal, right? Everyone cheats. But in my mind, and in the story of Stacy, my "Girl from Below," this is the start of her swan dive into the gutter.

Stuck in a suburban life of manicured lawns, dogs playing in sprinklers, and boyfriends who beat her up both physically and emotionally, she does what every red-blooded American kid would do: run away from home. So she takes the next Greyhound to New York—not today's New York but New York back when it was a slum full of possibility and excitement. But wait, let me go back a little bit. You see, Stacy had a little afterschool job at a diner, and one day there was a new guy, handsome as fuck. Little did she know, the diner staff had taken bets on whether "Romeo" would "score" with Stacy. One night they did fuck, on top of a garbage can in the alley. Stacy wiped the sperm off her stomach, dried her thighs, then went to see her boyfriend as she had promised.

Ah but it's such a small town, word got around so fast. Stacy gets a black eye from her boyfriend and the new guy loses his dishwashing job at the diner. And so the two hapless lovers meet at the Greyhound station and make their way downstate to Manhattan. Jerry has a friend who works for the city, who told him he could hook him up with a job as a garbage man.

So they check into a hotel, and while Jerry's busy trying to get that job Stacy is bored. She would like to earn a bit of money of her own, and so she starts to ply the oldest trade, until Jerry finds out and beats her to a bloody pulp outside of the Port Authority bus station. He is arrested, pulled away from his teenage whore whose teeth he knocked out, who keeps screaming "Don't take him away from me" spitting out bits of tooth.

Soon enough she's on her way back to Cortland or Del Mar or Glens Falls, and walks into her room to recover. And then she thinks of Hans Christian Andersen, the girl who stepped on the loaf, and masturbates furiously over her dive into squalor during this summer "experiment."

All this was supposed to have been accompanied by Dvořák's "American" string quartet.

But the next phase is more profound. It takes Stacy all the way to San Francisco. There she dives deeper and deeper into the scum pond until she establishes herself as a businesswoman, but then some god or devil trips her up yet again.

Stacy is not that much older when the next movement, a scherzo begins. But she wants love. Or sex. Or both. Like myself at that station in my life. And she gets drunk, and she has too many one-night stands to mention. And she has boyfriends. And they find out about her trysts and about each other. She gets beaten up yet again. Until finally, on the day of her graduation from school, she decides to run away once more. Hitching a ride with a truck driver, she leaves New York state for the wild West. Raped repeatedly by the trucker, she eventually escapes in the middle of night while he craps his pants in his sleep in a fleabag motel next to the truckstop. In the truckstop diner she meets a guy named Gus, who is hitchhiking to California. He hides her in his room after she tells him about the constant rapes from the trucker and they watch the trucker hung over stumbling towards his semi from the windows of their smelly motel room, cigarette smoke and mildew and laugh and fall on the bed and make love.

The next morning they're on the road, hitching rides, and in a week reach sunny California. But Gus is a heroin and methamphetamine addict. He has some ideas of his own, but Stacy does too. And once again she wants to make a little money of her own, so soon enough she signs up for a porno shoot. And once again the cat is out of the bag soon enough, and Stacy ends up narrowly avoiding a broken jaw but sporting yet another black eye.

Stacy decides to leave Gus, so she boards the bus for San Francisco not knowing what that town holds in store for her. Fast forward ten or fifteen years: Stacy is well established. She has a fine job and makes decent money, perhaps in finance, and yet the gutter calls. At night she drinks in bars and finds random strangers for random sex. Often black guys. She also has a younger on-and-off lover who is jealous as hell. He finds out and does something to her... but I'm getting ahead of myself yet again.

At one point she moonlights as a dominatrix, not for the money as she's financially comfortable working at the bank, but for kicks. She has a favorite client, a black guy named Gabriel who likes it when she puts her stiletto heels on his balls and makes him writhe in pain; but the most powerful part of their sessions is when Gabriel is tied up and asks her to "say the word," and she does: "Nigger." Then he ejaculates immediately.

So what else happens to dear old Stacy in San Francisco? She starts dating a younger guy—a self-proclaimed poet and writer, and soon enough he finds out about her past and present. And when he does, he waits for her as she's coming out of a fleabag whore hotel on O'Farrell street because Stacy at this point has become an unabashed Belle du Jour and he wants to grab her by the neck and strangle her, to destroy the little breaths of life that keep this cunt alive, this fucking cunt for hire. But he can't do it, so he grabs the end of her scarf and pulls it hard, throwing her into the traffic, and the last thing he says is...

"See you in the next world, bitch!" as he sends her flying into traffic. She could have made it, oh but she was wearing a pretty scarf to help against the San Francisco chill. Long Scarf Syndrome. Stacy could have walked again but I decided to make her paralyzed. She was my creation and I thought it would be a fitting end to her adventures.

But she recovered, and in the physical therapy room screamed, "Who is God?! I asked God what he held in store for me. He never answered! He bullshitted me! He wanted to surprise me!" Then she wheeled herself out of hospital to the nearest bar.

"Her internal organs must work" then the finance bros chuckled to each other, and yet again on a bet she went upstairs with one of them.

"Moist, moist… why does the bed feel moist?" she said as he lifted her onto the bed and as she saw the world spin, from Van Ness, from Pacific heights, from California from America and out into the sky and the blue earth going out from San Francisco from California from the north America from the planet earth and out into space as the blue ball spins and all of it is insignificant.

And that is where I stopped writing. I did not complete "The Girl from Below" either. It was going nowhere, and the point of the book eluded me. What was the meaning behind yet another sordid tale? What was the purpose?

And there were so very many variations on just the right way to end it—but the final one I had imagined was Jerry beating the living crap of Stacy on the sidewalk on 42nd Street, outside the Port Authority Bus Terminal, him getting arrested and thrown into the clink and Stacy returning home to Upstate New York with nary a thought of the consequences—of what they meant for herself or anyone else. And the steam from the Greyhound spilled out and formed a color symphony of white and red against the background of the brake lights of the bus, and her parents rushed over to her in ecstasy, that the prodigal daughter had come home.

My ambition was grossly misdirected. There was no market for such a film and the screenplay itself was vague and malformed, a strange type of violent melodrama. By the time I moved to LA any possibility to actually shoot these scripts were dead in the water. I was not "good for the coast"—I never was, and my aspirations were extraordinary folly.

Once I realized that this was the current status, I started to try to somehow salvage these ideas into a prose novel, decades after they were conceived, but the slogging proved punishing and onerous.

I tried. But I did not finish the book.

Something was preventing me.

My father was the master of unfinished projects. He had, I think, a kind of intellectual stage fright. He would often repeat a mantra blaming the "New World," and insisted that no one who emigrated here from Europe was ever able to accomplish anything significant. He was egregiously defeatist. It was the excuse he needed to not follow up on his ambitions. Now I was stuck in a mire that I recognized as his. My inheritance, so to speak. Some things were too painful to write about while others were too pedestrian to discuss. There was no maudlin and sordid Sonia Marmeladova in the first decade of the twenty-first century. Sex was now glamourized, scrubbed clean of pain, an admirable way to make a living. But blurring the line between good and evil, sin and forgiveness, right and wrong, does not address the issue of pain, and a cure for pain is what I sought. Gradually I realized that I would not find it by finishing the book that I had started as a sex-frightened juvenile, when young women still seemed like keys to better worlds, brighter futures.

In just a few days after I came to the realization that the book did not say anything new, I stopped work on it. Although there was a sequel to the book, which may have been more appropriate, and which resurfaced late in this venture, and which….

When you reach forty, or better yet fifty, the sensation that "time is running out" goes into overdrive.

I suppose it was appropriate that I met Betty, after my long experience with girls who were born in a graveyard. Sad girls who were filled with regret before they were mature and who colored my opinion of women for two decades. Oh Betty, my sad and false true love.

Oddly, these women and girls had done nothing so drastic for them to become martyrs or holy sluts, though they did obsess me precisely in that fashion. In the long run, sucking a stranger's cock in the bar bathroom will not determine whether you go to heaven, whether you will have a meaningful relationship later in life, whether you will become a devoted mother. But in my youth it did—there was the taint of a particular human stain... I thought these women unique in some way, unique in their sadness, their sluttiness, their search for something, misguided as it may be... And thus I wrote about the fictional Stacy, an amalgam of so many girls I had known who called themselves whores or sluts—and not proudly, not in a liberated feminist way. They were indeed ashamed, despite the fact that whatever sexual anti-escapades they participated in were really small fry; and even the concept of the "used and abandoned" did not cut muster—they were all solidly middle class. Perhaps that's where whoredom now originates. For excitement? I touched on that in The Girl from Below as well...

But here, oh my Lord—Betty was handed to me on a silver platter, and I knew that there were dark, sordid secrets lurking beneath, she was solely waiting not to reveal them, this I knew, she waited like Gretchen on the spinning wheel, but she was also Mephistopheles herself.

La vie est dure... ET sans confiture...

Is it possible to fall in love with a fictional character, Pygmalion and Galatea aside? Since by now the waist was not just elusive but totally absent, I imagined my arm around an imaginary waist. In dreams and daydreams, I had a lover. A very vague fiction but real enough to satisfy some needs—an imaginary friend, if you will, one who differed with nights and days but was real enough. For three weeks straight it was a short-haired blonde who for some reason was always wearing a purple miniskirt and leopard print underwear. Before that it was a tall brunette with small tits and a huge ass. That one stuck around for some time. Before that I think it was a short blonde, but she has disappeared somewhere in my murky memory.

All of these girls were probably based on some type of residual memory of past flings—but when it came from art? Is it possible? It worked for Hinckley and Foster via film. But with the written word everything is up to the imagination, isn't it?

Sonia Marmeladova was always intriguing though she was taken, so were Grushenka and Nastassia Filippovna, Sadie Thompson, even the miserable bitch Mildred Rogers had some appeal on a hatefuck level, as did cute, stupid Candy, whose naivete reminded me of Brandy March. Even the pathetic ones were candidates— like Tralala, ordering coffee and a bun before being gang raped to presumed death, which was what gave her humanity and my love and pity, or poor toothless Sophie. But it was my own invention, Stacy Fox, that I kept returning to and falling for despite her utterly sordid and depraved trajectory. And sitting in Brooklyn I would sometimes begin to wonder why on earth this was the book that I supposedly needed to finish.

THE YOGURT GIRL AND ENDLESS AUTUMN

It's a terrible thing to feel that your life is over. But I had experienced the sensation that "it was over" too many times, even as a child, and yet for whatever reason my life kept going. The ones I remember most were San Francisco with its cold white skies at the edge of the continent, and Manhattan with its cold late-summer wind that signaled the start of the season of frost and death, which for me meant death before I was even truly familiar with Her. There is something foreboding about the streets and subways of Manhattan and Brooklyn just before the leaves turn. The first signs of autumn come in August in New York, sometimes as early as late July, and when they do one cannot help but hear summer whimper: "it will all be over soon, it will all be over soon…"

I was the only person I knew or could think of who was not in the final stages of dying from a terminal disease who thought about death so obsessively and incessantly. I had my health issues, of course, but my real problem was work—something I opposed philosophically—the absence of which reduced me to the parasitic part of an economic equation. Were I to die suddenly, I would think, it would probably only benefit my family. One less expense.

Following my Las Vegas Story, I was fortunate enough to find a job at the Metropolitan Museum of Art. Without a doubt one of the great art museum of the world, it also holds special tragicomic memories for me from when I worked there at the information desk and briefly even as a security guard, after graduating from college with no skills. I was selling tickets and guiding visitors. There could have been worse jobs for me at the time, yet I was scraped.

Scraped by loneliness and a fatalistic sense that my life was over. Absurd for someone in his early twenties, but that's how I felt. How wrong I was, and how much now in middle age I would like to have a job like that—surrounded by art, by interesting people (for the most part) and a panopticon of crazy characters waltzing in each day.

There was much hilarity at the Met, much more than at any other place I have worked. For starters there was FGB, or Fat Gay Bob, a morbidly obese homosexual who ruled the info desk as his personal fiefdom; there was the panoply of old Italian guards who could barely speak English and hadn't a clue about art; there were the snotty Lords and Ladies working in admin and curatorial; but above all there was the bevy of interns, fresh-faced youngsters in their final year at Chapin or Nightingale, or their first year as art history majors at Barnard. Which is how I met Arditti.

Where to begin with Chloe Arditti, the yogurt queen (her massive inheritance came from her family's dairy business) of Manhattan? She was not so much a hooker with a heart of gold as a rich bitch with a heart of shit, a sexless but depraved version of Dorothy Malone in Written on the Wind, seeking out filth in gas station toilets without even orgasming. She embodied the unfortunate and unholy combination of nymphomania and frigidity—unfortunate for her, exasperating for me.

Much of it was borne out of both stupidity and trendiness—an inspired celibacy ideation or something ridiculous like that. But the less sex we had, the more I suspected a deeper and more frightening past filled with depravity, one I was neither part of nor would ever truly be let in on. A Queen in Yellow, she wore a mask and yet she wore no mask.

Driving from Brooklyn to see Chloe, there was always a sense that we were all but finished, that our future was empty, our relationship doomed. That my ambitions for a spectacular life were shot, aborted. That the possibilities were buried.

New York acquired for me over those long few years an air of "Endless Autumn." Then came a few years of seemingly endless winter. And then, eventually, exile—from where I now write.

Once we are out of our infant and toddler years, when we have mostly stopped screaming and shitting our pants, we become children, then pre-teens, then teenagers; and throughout these years, which are horribly painful, adults remind us that these are "the best years of our lives." We do not heed those words and turn back self-absorbed into our petty little problems and think we are the only ones who have the right to rage against torment. To look back over those years, which were promised to us as the best of our lives, and to still feel so much anguish and regret... it begs the question: if you could do it all over again, would you?

The winds of autumn, the first sign that summer is coming to an end, reach New York in mid-August. Then comes a one or two week cold spell, the first chill of fall, a harbinger of what's to come. They would always send me spiraling into the deepest depression. It was around that time that I courted Arditti. She, like many of the others, was a living reminder of that recognition that things are over. Nothing gives so strong a sense of infinity as stupidity, and the winds of stupidity blow very hard over the Upper West Side of Manhattan.

How can life be over for a seventeen-year old? Oh, it is certainly possible, especially among the privileged. The poor want to leave, for the most part; the rich want to stay in the gilded stable.

Ah, the Met. In retrospect, the Met was a hoot. Part of our problem as humans, dumb apes that we are, is that we don't appreciate what we have while we have it. As babies and toddlers we scream and shit our pants even when we have everything we need taken care of. As teenagers we hate school and hate our parents. And in adulthood we begin to miss the days of high school and college and when our parents die we miss them as well.

So it was with me at the Met; though I hated it, it was probably the greatest job I ever had.

In the Flemish hall, I would be spellbound by the monumental painting of Rubens with his wife and child. It was not exactly like Las Meninas which I could stare at all day every day for the rest of my life, but both pointed to that saudade of a Golden Age when the Spaniards decided—or understood—that la vida is indeed un sueño. The Low Countries too had their Golden Age, and their own Heimwee. And what was supposed to have been my golden age was filled with longing and mental debris.

My stay at the Met didn't last as long as it should have. I could have easily become the heir to FGB. But I decided I could earn slightly more money working as a security guard. On my first week at the job I was working as an elevator-button presser and I saw a graffito on the inside doors of the lift: "Artist-Ambition=Guard for Life."

After a few months I quit. The endless autumn phased into an endless winter. After Arditti and I parted ways, I moved into my friend Jaime's place at the southern end of Park Slope where I spent the winter freezing staring at the Dutch looking houses (The Golden Age frozen in snow?) outside my window and drinking Jim Beam. I thought it would never stop snowing.

And then came the first breath of spring and I met Sandra…

SANDRA

Let us now consider Sandra Kellogg, who repeatedly threw me under the proverbial bus. "My wilted rose" I called her, for there were ten years and thus ten years of experience between us. She liked to say she was part royalty and part trash—which turned out to be much like a very dry martini—ten parts trash of gin to one part royalty vermouth, or perhaps no royalty at all in fact.

Sandra had a son from a previous marriage but at least she didn't feed him a fatal dose of heroin like the lovely Anne Beverley did to her lovely boy Sid Vicious. In many ways, Sandra was "kind," though unconditional kindness does not exist. It may exist among saints and martyrs, liars and lunatics, but not among ordinary folk. And yet there's female "kindness"—much of it borne out of a true maternal instinct, which makes it both saccharine and sorry.

This reminds me—forgive the digression, I'll keep it short—of a phrase of LaBonne's: "It's good food, eat!" She said it to me as she served me some type of bland chicken stir-fry after confessing that she was lying to me all summer, sucking off strangers in bars and in parks after dark, and I swallowed her goddamn chicken while I wished to slice both of our throats. The pity that LaBonne expressed over the chicken and vegetable stir-fry she made for me as an atonement for her fucking around with yet another guy: "It's good food, eat!" while the bird chunks stuck in my own craw. I could not swallow after she had cheated on me, no matter how tasty or nutritious her dinner was.

She emailed me a few years ago—thirty years later—with a hint of apology, and the only thing I wanted to do was to choke her to death with her goddamn chicken. But that is the pathos of women. The way they leave a cigarette for you in the morning when they're going to work, or buy you a pair of socks or underpants for no reason other than kindness.

But getting back to Sandra. Often she would burst out into tears for no reason, or she would alternate between holding my hand and pushing me away. One time we were in a taxi on our way to have drinks at the Rainbow Room—Sandra had an expense account during her gig at the time, which afforded us expensive dates that she could write off on the client account—and in the middle of the ten minute cab ride she collapsed into a fit of bawling so hard that I was afraid she would retch. We made it inside, but I honestly thought that when the elevator doors opened she would drop to her knees and vomit. By the time we reached the top of Rockefeller Center she had managed to compose herself enough to order us cocktails. We drank together on the terrace as we watched the New York skyline turn a warm crimson, before the curtain dropped and the night filled with yellow lights, at which she only stared and stared and, relieved of her initial fit, gently sobbed.

I had no idea what was going through Sandra's head. I still don't. And I still have no idea what went through Betty's mind when she would gently hold my hand and push herself closer despite the mechanism that allowed her to ambulate, and I felt that "touch of a woman," and even more basically the touch of a person— something that my mother in her delirium said that she missed most of all and whose absence destroyed her will to live.

My relationship with Sandra didn't last much longer. A few months later I met her in a bar and she handed me all the clothes and possessions I kept in her flat. But that evening at the Rainbow Bar was actually the moment when I realized it was over. There are moments like that when you realize your heart will be broken and until it's made official you only wade through mud awaiting the inevitable.

Years later I understood where the sobbing came from. They were the same sobs that came from my mom the last time I saw her. Emaciated on the green velvet couch built in Hungary, bought in Moscow, shipped to Trieste, and now finally to New York, that couch had accompanied my mother's journey from Occupied Europe to the New World. Though she claimed that she cried because she was happy to see me, I understood. These were tears of regret and if I could read her mind I would wager the one phrase going through her brain during that sobbing was the one I knew all too well: "I fucked up."

FARRINGTON THE WORTHLESS

Arguably the greatest vulgarian of them was Shelly Farrington. I'll start with the fact that the gigantic tribal tattoo on her ass was actually a cover-up of some guy's name. "I was so fucking drunk," she giggled while I was deciding whether to kill her or myself. This one was a true case of madness on my own part, for she was worthless.

Dating Farrington was so pointless from the beginning and became moribund so quickly that soon enough it was akin to dating a corpse. I suppose on the upside was the fact that she was constantly horny. On the other hand, sex with her was brutal and chafing. There was neither love nor much of any type of emotion; yes there was passion and orgasms, but it was more like starting a fire by rubbing a stick. Whereas Brandy would melt in femininity, fucking Farrington was more like wrestling. She too, it seemed, was born in a cemetery. In some ways, she felt like the logical (and rather sorry) conclusion to my string of half-baked romances.

A pathological liar and cheater, Farrington devised an utterly bizarre technique to exculpate herself from my accusations and suspicions—the "Two Robs"—an astronomical, geometric ascent/descent into the basest self-delusion. The basic premise, as insane as it is was actually moderately brilliant in self-deception: Farrington had two friends named Rob. One was a semi-gay Jewish guy from France who was her neighbor. The other was her former (and, unbeknownst to me at the time, still on-and-off) boyfriend who would fuck her ass and whose sperm she would drink and then come over to me for sloppy seconds. In a sordid universe of free love this may have been acceptable. What made it not just disgusting but also terrifying was the psychology behind it. Farrington would tell me "I'm going to see Rob," leaving me to guess which Rob, since the first semen-depositing Rob was supposedly out of the picture entirely. However, in this lunatic woman's mind, the ambiguity of which Rob she was going to see was a perfect alibi not just for her relationship with me but even her relationship with herself. If she said she was going to see Rob, that meant she told the truth, never mind which Rob it was, and therefore in her mind she was cleared of any wrongdoing. In her stupidity she actually believed that confessing 10% of her sins would absolve her of the other 90%. Telling a half-truth would offer her innocence.

Foolish I was, or blind perhaps, willfully or not, but the prospect of the offers of sex any time are enough to make a man blind at least for a bit—my folly was continuing it for as long as I did.

The bleakness was that there was no fascination. Yes, it felt dreadful to be in one way or another cuckolded, but on the other hand there was always a cunt to stick my dick in. Even then, it was all so very grey. A cemetery fuck, a type of living necrophilia. And yet, foolish as I was in my relative youth to accept what passed for love, I would still screw her, even when she would ring the bell, come into my house, take off her socks that she borrowed from "Rob" (your guess is as good as mine which Rob's socks they were, or why she had red spots on her knees) and lie down naked on the bed.

Finally I could not take it anymore. It ended with a broken guitar, a framed Sex Pistols poster cracked over her head, plenty of blood and tears and screams and one final slammed door.

True to her lunacy, Farrington sought me out in LA and admitted to having "stalked" me for years. and in even truer fashion sent me condolences when my father died and, immediately afterward, started emailing pictures of her tits whilst I was in the midst of my hour of grief.

Sensitive as I am (or so I've been told, and so I find myself more often than not), there is at least a modicum of pity for these delusional Farringtons and all their ilk, genuinely crafted from a sperm/egg combination that is at the end entirely random. And yet there is a fine line between pity and forgiveness, and a starker line between sympathy and wanting to strangle the fucking living daylights out of someone for being a liar, a slut, a cheater, an unrepentant, manipulative, self-serving whore. "Disease? Oh, I had a few. I forget the names of which ones exactly…"

I'd gone a few years—praise the lord—without hearing from Farrington before this journey began. And I pray that I will never hear from her again.

To be fair, there were moments of tenderness—pedestrian ones, like letting me sleep late, and leaving a pack of cigarettes on the table for me for the morning. And then there were moments of hatred, too many to list. And of pity. And of sadness.

The Farrington bollocks ended rather strangely. She decided to not only go back to college but even to live in the dorms. And the more I think about how odd it was, the more it diminishes what other people, like my parents, went through. Here I was, waxing and whining and crying and pining over some chick who had a huge tattoo on her ass which covered up her ex's name. I had never even believed that such a thing was possible except in the deepest and darkest (pun intended) of ghettos—but what blew my mind more was her explicit confession—"I had my boyfriend's name tattooed on my ass"—which left me wondering which was worse, this dumb bitch or the equally idiotic abortion addict Vainonen, who had a black widow spider tattooed on her mons.

All of which was a cakewalk until I met and truly figured out just who Betty was. But we are only just beginning that story.

BRANDY MARCH

One of the kinder women I knew was a lobotomy-eyed, big-boned, corn-fed breeder from Ohio named Brandy March. An utter innocent in many ways, one who was utterly harmless in her alleged naïveté. Although in retrospect I have sometimes wished we'd been a "real" couple, I can't fully fathom what her boyfriend, Ollie, was going through, as I'm sure he knew that when Brandy would tell him she's going out with girlfriends from work I was actually screwing her to oblivion. But it was not a relationship that was meant to last, and, in further retrospect, that was for the best.

But twenty years later I reconnected with Brandy via the internet. And, considering my lackluster (to put it mildly) love life, it gave me a queer sense of hope and excitement. The talk itself was innocuous and a rendezvous was probably never going to happen—which is what made it somewhat innocent.

"I think we are both raging against the dying of the light," she once wrote to me. She was mostly right. As the correspondence continued, we talked about a fantasy meeting somewhere exactly equidistant between Cleveland and Los Angeles—for convenience's sake. Kansas City? Meet me in St. Louis? My lust was fueled by this fantasy. I was the Beast in the Jungle and Brandy's cunt, mouth and ass was the Altar of the Dead. I could never stand that fucker Ollie, but at that point, were I to meet her somewhere in Omaha or Denver or St. Louis, I would have stuck my tongue as deep down her throat as possible even if she just sucked him off and her mouth was still glazed with his semen. I did not care. I wanted to kiss her so hard as to almost vacuum the life out of her.

None of this happened, of course. If it had, I'm certain Brandy and I would have gotten sick of one another after a couple of days, although we would have been fucked out. But how long does being fucked out last? We would have left our motel, taken a taxi to the airport, then what? We would both be horny again on the plane ride back, me west, her east, but we would both acknowledge that being together as a couple was an impossibility. Being fucked out was simply a band-aid on a deeper thirst, the way I thirsted for her mouth, for her pussy, the way I wanted to shove myself so deep inside her that my cock would not just tickle her intestines but somehow reach right to her inner core. And yes, at times it felt like love.

Does love breed lust? It can. Rarely does lust breed love. As I write this I think of the execrable Farrington, who thought that lust bred love when in fact it was neither one nor the other.

And for Emily Vainonen, for whom neither love nor lust existed, and who contributed so generously (unbeknownst to her) to the character of Stacy Fox, the runaway who met a poignant fate after a series of vulgar, sordid misadventures, it was something else entirely. I still recall her phrases:

"I remember seeing the airplanes flying over as I slept outside on the roof, landing at LaGuardia airport."

"To me, sex is just a physical activity, like playing volleyball or something."

"Whenever I would run away, I would call my parents and say I wanted to come home and they would tell me 'I'm not spending a red cent on you until you come home'—that made a lot of sense. And so I spent the rest of the summer in New York, living on rooftops and getting by as I could"

"And how would you get by?" I asked.

And Vainonen would tease me gently and say "I got by" and sometimes say "There are certain things about me you don't want to know. It's the same for everyone, not just you. Some things just open up a can of worms…"

One episode with Brandy was unforgettable—the level of lust, it stays with me to this day. Almost like "Dirty," the heroine of Bataille's Bleu de Ciel, the first time I grasped Brandy was at the Christmas Party. It was obvious that I had been eyeing her, eyeing everything—her eyes, her face, her hair, her tits, her fantastic ass. From her very first day, months earlier, when she set herself up in the cubicle next to mine, I knew that I would eventually fuck her. It was an unusual thought for me. At the time I was in a relationship with Sandra which was rapidly turning sour. Brandy and I exchanged knowing glances. I was and always had been a flirt, and my girlfriends mostly found it charming unless I were to act on it, but I never did. And I had no idea that Brandy and I would act on it either—until she vomited in my mouth. I wanted to nickname her Dirty. Later we would walk around like girlfriend and boyfriend, with my arm around that infernal waist that people would die for...

A pudgy girl who worked as a copywriter at the ad agency where Brandy and I shuffled papers appeared to have a crush on me. I suppose if I was tremendously drunk we could have had a nice fuck, but there were two things that prevented our coupling: her Cyrano nose and her bulging stomach. In retrospect she was probably dying for a hard fuck, but it was Brandy that I had my sights on, and whilst I knew she had a boyfriend there was enough unspoken chemistry between us that I knew eventually something would happen.

And then it happened, at the holiday party: we were both drunk as skunks but I, being a seasoned boozer at the ripe old age of twenty-eight, could hold my liquor much better than Brandy. Two drinks led to another and before long it was time to say "let's go"—the issue of Brandy's boyfriend did not come up. Cyrano, however, kept tagging along, and as we all piled into a cab Brandy began to vomit and once she stopped I grabbed her face with my hands and tongue kissed her, embracing all her scum and bile and spit, swishing around it with our tongues. It was not a fetish, no emetophilia—I wanted to penetrate her as deep as possible, and I had to wait to get her knickers off so I had to do with her vomit filled mouth. I didn't care.

The dumb Pakistani driver seemed unperturbed by the debauchery going on in the back of his cab, and Cyrano pretended that it wasn't happening. But the seat was covered in puke—there was vomit on Brandy's miniskirt, on my shirt, on my lips, on our fingers and on our mouths. I cleaned us up as best I could with a napkin while the Proboscis watched on, practically exploding with disgust and jealousy. The cab driver said nothing about the state of his car and we went upstairs to another party.

Brandy's mouth tasted better by now, the sour taste was gone and she was mostly clean thanks to a few dabs with a wet towel at the other party. She did not brush her teeth—I suppose that would have been uncouth and/or unsanitary to use a random stranger's toothbrush, but it didn't matter and with the right squeeze of the palm and a quick whisper of "Let's go" Brandy and I left the party and hopped in yet another cab and headed towards Queens.

I took her to an all-night diner. Neither one of us was terribly hungry but I thought she needed to eat. Less than halfway through our meal she volunteered. It was strange because she was sober now and I certainly didn't want to come across as trying to "take advantage" of her. But then she said the magic words, "I want to see your place," and at that point I guessed it was mostly a done deal.

We walked, hand-in-hand, sometimes arm around waist, down the shit-strewn Queens streets two blocks down to my dirty apartment. We both knew that there was nothing to see upstairs. We entered and sat on the couch for a second then I stuck my tongue in her mouth again. She didn't mind. A minute later she said, "I should really be going," and then I lifted her skirt and saw that she was wearing some type of above-the-knee tights and I stuck my fingers deep inside her cunt and she moaned and kissed me again and then I walked her down the stairs.

The next time it was easier. No vomit and no "I should be going." Another holiday party just a few days later. Brandy and I left early and again took a cab back to my flat in Astoria. My flat was poorly insulated, despite being the typical New York City overheated apartment. I had taped up all my windows in my bedroom but the freezing wind still permeated through and through so I had taken to sleeping on my fold-out couch in the living room. It was there that we finally consummated our physical relationship and our relationship manqué. And it would go on and on from there.

"Millions of unwanted pregnancies will be the result of corporate holiday parties," read the headline on a paper called The Weekly World News. Brandy and I flirted with that possibility on our first encounter, but in the end the sex was safe and there was no "accident."

I knew she had a boyfriend, and he may have known or may have been too stupid or perhaps willing to ignore what Brandy was doing, but either way I didn't care. Nor did she. Brandy and I would fuck, screw, suck and blow, anywhere we would find a chance to before she had to go back to the other guy. What type of person was this other guy, I kept wondering.

The most spectacularly desperate passion apart from the vomit kissing was the time that I fucked her on the subway platform, on the E train going back to Queens from Manhattan while people in the passing subway cars were watching. I might be imagining it now but I remember that we briefly even fucked inside a train.... Those are all memories now, of course, the memories of an aging masturbator, but better to possess memories than not to have any to speak of.

Eventually it was time for Brandy to return to her boyfriend, and so she did, and soon enough they both returned to Iowa, when Brandy, I am guessing, clicked her heels and said, "there's no place like home." Thankfully, we fucked one last time before she left.

Decades later, in my season in hell, I fell in love with Betty. But what does falling in love truly mean, anyway? Is it the constant state of anticipation, the yearning, heart aflutter, butterflies in the stomach and all the other clichés? Is it the painful erection that you don't know what to do with at work while waiting to see the other person? The anticipation of licking her sweat, of being naked and embracing? Even anticipating the somewhat sad denouement to the orgasm, that feeling that everyone has experienced but no one described—the still sadness of the embrace after climax. The fear that you will never truly have her, and yet you love her, somehow you love her.

That's how it went with Brandy March, who came across as the most innocent, blonde-haired, blue-eyed Midwestern gal. Except that she would let me fuck her to high heaven and then she'd return to her boyfriend the same evening and probably cuddle with him. The truly strange thing about this relationship with me and Brandy was though it started off as pure lust, soon enough—too soon, really—I had fallen in love with her. And just as my lust started morphing into tenderness, Brandy started to become more distant. She had to return to her boyfriend and marry him, and move back to Ohio. On an intellectual level I understood that that was what she needed to do, that our relationship was based on fucking and that she, in turn, would never understand me intellectually, psychologically, etc. To put it plainly, Brandy was stupid. Sometimes outrageously so. But she was so utterly endearing in so many ways— the way we fucked, the way we walked hand-in-hand, the way— again that goddamned waist—the way we simply pretended to be boyfriend and girlfriend even though she would generally have to go home to her real boyfriend late at night after we spent ourselves in sweaty skin-on-skin. She always had a unique innocence—yes, innocence—despite the cheating. She was not in an abusive relationship with this pudgy, hairy little hedgehog of a boyfriend of hers, nor was she trying to get out of it because of boredom. She simply liked fucking me and spending time with me. As if I offered her a parallel world which she knew was solely fantasy, like the way I screwed her on the E train platform in Queens or how she didn't know how to explain the red marks all over her ass after I spanked the living daylights out of her. Brandy and I were playing. We were not playing with each other, that is what real couples do. We did not have a chess match, we played no games, instead we were like children, constructing a fantasy world of two lovers in an alternate universe of sorts. We built castles, we played Candyland and we both knew that it would only ever be that: playtime. I knew she would need to go back to Ollie / Oleg and that she would marry him. And I, in my own arrogant way, felt that I could not seriously date her for too long because I felt she did not understand my "Sturm und Drang" or whatever you wish to call my bullshit. So we played this way, played for close to a year if I remember correctly. And I remember feeling proud when I would walk into a party with my arm around her waist as if she was indeed my girlfriend, knowing full well that she was not and would never be.

This was how I started feeling about Betty later. I felt that any moment now I would relive the same experience as I did with Brandy. Of course the tables would now be turned. I was single during my "affair" with Brandy, while she was not. Here I was, married and with a child, while Betty seemed to be single (although it was impossible to tell what things she was keeping secret).

Weeks, a month, getting closer to two months that summer and I still had no idea who Betty really was. As with Brandy, I wished to have her as near to me as possible but I also acknowledged that this would never happen, that it was all a dream, a fantasy, a play date.

"But Betty has no boyfriend!" my mind would scream. And besides, Brandy was so long ago, and we had no idea what we were doing! I am not young anymore! And I could not even tell how old Betty was.

BROWN SUGAR

Finally, there was the ebony checkout girl, a young Mary Wells or Gladys Horton with her Motor City hairdo. She had a sweet but slightly haughty attitude and looked as if she belonged in another time and era, like she'd just stepped off stage from singing with the Chiffons, the Shirelles, the Marvelettes. Brown sugar, how come you taste so good? But I could only imagine. And indeed fantasies abounded during my little trips to the shop.

"Do you have a boyfriend?" I imagined myself saying. She'd glance knowingly at my wedding ring and smile and say "No." Then I'd meet her outside after she gets off work and we'd have coffee and go back to her room. "Her room" because she's young and works in a supermarket, maybe goes to community college, has roommates. I'd undress her and suck and pinch her soft brown nipples and then stick my hand down her panties and she'd say "Whoah!" as if I was going too fast but it was only feigned, tinged with more than a small dose of encouragement. And then we'd undress and drop our clothes on the floor. Her black, black skin… A moment of silence, an uncomfortable silence as we stand facing each other in our birthday suits—uncomfortable for a second or two and then she'd grab my prick and go down to suck on it for a minute and then guide it deep into her pink cunt, the treasure cave hidden by her black body.

Then I'd return to reality.

That was the day daylight version. But there was also a night or dawn version:

"When do you get off?" I would ask her again in my dreams.

"Seven," she would reply and wink. And when I'd pick her up after she had left work I would actually hold her hand, and we would go get coffee and as we were waiting for the coffee she would stick her tongue in my mouth and say, "Forget about the coffee, come…"

And I would follow her to her single room in the flat she shared with a friend. We'd try to be quiet but would not be able to stop giggling as she pulled me toward her, dragging me into her room. Then she'd pull me down onto her single bed and undress me, and I would undress her, and I would her hold her tight. Holding her was in many ways so much more important than penetration. But eventually, after licking her pink-on-black cunt (a wonderful color combination, like Elvis' suit and socks), and I would penetrate and stick my cock inside her and climax in two seconds and she would hold my head and kiss me on the cheek and pat me on the back and say "Shh… It's okay… It's all right…" and I would breathe deeply and possibly tears would form and I would lie on top of her sweating as she stroked my head and then…

And then it was all a dream. But it's dreams that helped produce this tears-and-sperm-soaked manuscript, which took quite a bit of effort to produce. Luckily my loneliness took me on a journey.

Brown Sugar faded away before I even made the trip. Something happened. I started to avoid the aisle where she was working. Somewhere in the brain's labyrinth that fantasy just left. I would wave and wink to her and she too responded kindly, but it was over, and I was grateful for it… I had accepted the futility. I wore a wedding ring and I could barely afford to buy her a Starbucks coffee.

One evening, in the supermarket parking lot, I cried over Brown Sugar, alone in the parked car. I got inside, started the engine, and immediately started sobbing. All my fantasies, I saw, were to remain just that. Brown Sugar was just a kid. The next time

I saw her, no hardon arose. Instead I only wanted to bury my head in her lap and cry. And then to punch myself, punch anything and scream: Why was I being denied intimacy?

A WOMAN'S TOUCH

The immoral Propoetides dared to deny that Venus was the goddess. For this, because of her divine anger, they are said to have been the first to prostitute their bodies and their reputations in public, and, losing all sense of shame, they lost the power to blush, as the blood hardened in their cheeks, and only a small change turned them into hard flints.

Was it my disgust at these Propoetides that made me build a woman in my own mind, or was it just my mental illness? I still do not know. But enough about these little loves, if you can even call them that. Let's return to the story, of how the following happened and how I came to write this book rather than the books I wanted to write or the films I wanted to make.

At one point, during a spell of impotence, I was almost pleased to no longer need to orgasm when my dreams of these mystery women turned more romantic. There was one dream that was semi-recurring. A woman who reminded me of someone so intensely and yet I couldn't place exactly who it was. I would rack my brains trying to think of what the inspiration for this fantasy person. I went through all sorts of compartments in my mind—high school, college, work, friends, porn, but still continued to draw a blank. And the face, though remarkably familiar, would vanish like all the others, and I would wait in anticipation and fear for her next appearance. I only remember her dark hair, pale skin and deep blue eyes.

My dreams about New York were becoming so frequent and so vivid, including the Proustian helical descent to waking life that I felt I was under a spell and something was beckoning me to return for a visit. And that was when an opportunity arose. The New York of my dreams was of course, just that—a dream. The weather was always pleasant, the buildings were not as tall, and the tsunami of people was generally absent. It was a dreamy, benign vision of a mythical past—mythical because it most likely never existed, except perhaps through a child's eyes.

And then, just as I was wearing myself down into a stickier and muddier rut, two things happened—fortuitously or not. Both involved death, the great equalizer.

One vegetative spring day, just as I ventured onto the faux parapet of my faux chateau, just as I was in the middle of some ruminations and trying to focus my failing eyes on the neon sign of what is now a retirement home, I was rudely interrupted from my sitting (I was standing, but metaphysically I sit 24/7) when I received news of the unexpected death of a friend—someone I had not seen in several years, with whom I had had a bit of a falling out but had been close to in college. His name was Dick Guerra and he flaunted the name "Dick" as if to flaunt with the ambiguity of the fact that he could come across as an asshole and that he may have been sexually ambiguous. The cause of Dick's death was unstated and after several phone calls to other acquaintances, rumors ranged widely from West Nile Virus to a stroke to autoerotic asphyxiation.

Despite my admiration for all things sedentary and the passivity I have embraced as my lot, I am not incapable of the occasional brash move. I do pull myself out of my garden by my greying stalk of hair once in a while. I did not care about Dick much anymore but there was something intriguing about the whole thing. More phone calls: will I be coming to the wake? Do I need a place to stay? etc. After some deliberation I decided to say yes to both. I don't like to leave the garden, but it was too tempting. I had not been to New York in years. Sometimes I felt pangs of fear, palms sweating even going as far away from my garden as Malibu or San Diego. I am rooted, damn it! A true root vegetable, una verdadera verdure—the carrot doesn't go far from the patch. I also did not wish to be too long away from my lovely wife who tends the garden, keeps the moles away, showers me with love and with the rolling pin and lovingly combs my stalk after leaving me memories of her devotion. I promised I would not stay more than just under a week.

And then, on the heels of Dick's tragicomic news, came another surprise just a few hours later. My wife received news that she had inherited a decent amount of money from her estranged uncle. Her reaction to his death was utterly dispassionate. By all accounts he was a complete asshole and they had not spoken in decades. However the windfall of cash actually lifted her mood and she came to me with a modest proposal—that I should go to New York for Dick's funeral not just for a few days but actually stay there if I want to, to finish my book, no matter how long it would take. She admitted it wasn't so much out of interest in my unfinished project or of my desire to bid farewell to Dick (I had none), but rather to have a benign trial separation for a while in the interest of somehow keeping our marriage intact.

I could not believe my ears when she said, "Why don't you stay in New York for a while... You can give me a bit of a break and maybe you can finally finish your book. It takes place in New York, doesn't it?" "Yes" I nodded. "Then go there, finish it and come back. And then you can get a job."

My heart jumped at the offer but my tongue and brain were slower. Despite our issues, I did not actually want to be apart from my wife and daughter, but how could I refuse the offer? And so, I RSVPd that I would be attending Dick's funeral, booked a flight and told Charlotte that I would let her know if I decided to stay longer than needed.

I decided to pack just two books for my trip to New York: the

Bible (which I had very little use for at this point) and Burton's Anatomy of Melancholy, which, despite being what seems like the work of a madman, I thought might offer some succor in its own deranged way. Hovering over the suitcase, I opened to a random page. After skimming a section on the meat of hares and red deer, which were both deemed to induce melancholy of the highest order, I checked the index and looked at the section on romantic love and marriage. I found little insight.

Melancholy: much has been written on the subject, but the melancholy I felt was somehow different. Perhaps because it was so unrelenting. I recall reading about a medieval author, Dutch or Flemish perhaps, whose encyclopedia entry stated that not much is known about a long period in his life when he was stricken with a major spell of melancholy around the time he turned thirty— lasting until I'm not sure when. Mine definitely started before I turned thirty, but after thirty it got progressively worse. I had an acute awareness that certain things were now gone forever, certain times and people and feelings, whose existence now was confined to reverie. But I was also haunted by the knowledge that "starting over" (that odd, throwaway term) was impossible. And I knew that eventually I would have to return to California. On the next smoggy morning Charlotte drove me to Burbank airport, not-so-secretly pleased that she will be away from me and my annoyance, perhaps using the time to paint the flat or just have some time alone.

The flight from LA to New York is rather painless: traversing the flyover zone, making that odd u-turn over Santa Monica Bay then over some absolutely desolate territory with some flicker of Las Vegas down below, you finally reach your cruising altitude, the flight is made bearable by mini bottles of whiskey, and if you can achieve oblivion for just an hour or so, pretty soon you're on the ground in old brown New York. Whenever the captain announces that we have begun our final descent into Kennedy, I can already taste that nauseating peanuty smell of the terminal, the airline workers who are too pissed off that they're manning the fort instead of the redcaps who make it well known that they will crush your baggage if you don't tip them, cousins of the humorless demons at passport control when flying overseas—the ones who don't have much of an excuse to get a tip or charge a bribe. In the end, I arrived walking out into the inhalable moisture of the airport.

I had arrived. I had returned somewhere... Somewhere that was, if not home, at least now an orphanage.

Part II

NEW YORK

ARRIVAL

My old college friend Mike was waiting for me. Mike was one of the few people I had kept in contact with despite the fact that by his own admission he was basically a straight laced meathead. For whatever reasons we immediately bonded decades ago and the bond still remained. He had graciously offered to get me from the airport and let me crash on his couch. I got into his jeep and we were on our way through the melting night which was only slightly ameliorated by the open top.

I always hated coming back to New York ever since first arriving there in 1977. The TWA flight was circling around JFK airport for hours. I was vomiting. When we finally landed and walked out in the rain. I had never been so afraid in my life.

I wept in fear of buildings tall and frightening
and people small as ants
who scurried to and fro—
Dystopia before I knew that word, and
world was lit by lightning.

As a child, each time I returned to New York from holiday breaks I would break down in tears. I never wanted to go back to that place, and yet I would return whether by volition or circumstance. Only briefly, following my "Las Vegas and San Francisco Story," did I feel a glimmer of hope about New York, especially Brooklyn. Returning from California along the I-95, it was the first time I came back to New York thinking I would make a fresh start. I settled in Brooklyn, where I had never lived prior. There was something different, something refreshing about it, and Park Slope, before it became inundated with yuppies with dogs and babies, felt like a little town. Perhaps that was what I wished for all my life—a little town, a little community—but it wouldn't do. I appreciated the local pubs and the diner on 7th Avenue and of course the wonderful architecture, but I could sense that depravity was only a stone's thought and throw away. Instead of appreciating the brownstones and limestones, Montgomery Clift's grave in the Quaker Cemetery, the grand old boulevards of Prospect Park West and Eastern Parkway, I was not content. I wanted to either move West, very far west as in California, or were I to be here for some time, to go deeper into filth, crime, ugliness, because just a block or two from my house it was happening in spades. A city built on desperation and violence. Nothing romantic, just skeletons. And so I pined yet again to escape New York, but not until I had tried to eviscerate its mnemonic graveyards. But here I was again, graveyard shovel in hand and nothing to show for it. The city had changed beyond recognition and even my sordid Travis Bickle dreams were now left to oblivion.

What makes childhood memories so special? "As a child I played with bottles," my mom said. "I'm just keeping up the tradition."

I felt as if I came to New York to find my first love again. But who or what is one's first love? It is not a girl but youth itself that is one's first love and the one that can never be found again after she leaves forever. And all waiting and forlorn standing on the beach, on the edge of the sea of bygone times is in vain. The ship has sailed too soon, it always does, and does so in the blink of an eye... we do not even notice when it left the dock and went adrift toward the dimming horizon.

I was lucky that the ostensible reason I came to New York was for the funeral. For a while now, years probably, I had stopped paying attention to my appearance. I would for days, sometimes a week, without showering or shaving. Most of my clothes had holes and stains on them. But I did retain the "funeral suit" I wore when I buried my mother, then my father, and now Dick.

I brought my only good footwear, a fancy pair of buckled shoes I had bought in Italy on the Via dei Corso many years ago and which I rarely wore. They were extremely uncomfortable and seemed designed solely to walk a few meters from the plush carpet in one's villa to a chauffeured Maserati. The suit was too hot and the shoes too painful to wear daily and I had forgotten to bring some of my casual rags, so the next day after settling in Brooklyn, I took the train back to Manhattan and bought an inexpensive but reasonably fashionable summer wardrobe at H&M. To feel good, or at least feel better, I decided to try to dress a little sharper. No white shoes, though. Those would only serve as a daily reminder of failure and of buried teenage dreams.

New York brought memories rushing to the surface: those warm autumn nights many moons ago when I had one of my first sensations of feeling that "it's all over," listening to Johnny Cash, taking pulls of a pint of whiskey, overcome with a terrible sadness. Twenty-something, I was way too young to harbor such feelings, but now I realized I've had those feeling all my life, even as a child and in my early teens I felt heartbroken that everything must end, often sooner than one hopes. Now officially in middle-age, that feeling birthed a parasitic twin: How much time do I have left? What will I still be able to see, to do? Which books will I have time to read? These thoughts gave the task of finishing my book all the greater urgency.

The night before the wake, Mike and I were walking up the stairs to his Greenpoint apartment. Mike had moved there years ago with the bright possibility of having thousands of gorgeous Polish girls at his disposal, forgetting that for every Bozena there were several Mareks, Wojciechs and Tadeks pursuing her with better results.

Nonetheless, he stayed in his garret-like flat and it seemed he had no plans to leave despite the rising rent and the disrepair of the place. He opened a bottle of Japanese scotch and we began to reminisce. Mike, too, had blown it many ways. He never married, never had kids, and was not comfortable in his bachelor existence. I remember him making grand plans to turn his life around—to move somewhere exotic, start a business, complete a professional degree, even work on an oil rig off the coast of West Africa—but all these flights of fancy came to naught.

Mike loved talking about himself almost as much as he fancied gossiping about other people, and so that night over a bottle of scotch, we went through the whole roster of friends past and present, making an inventory of their faults and accomplishments, the former plentiful, the latter scarce. "X is kind of a pointless friend" or "Y, I don't understand that guy, or what his problem is" or "Z is all fucked up" without once acknowledging his own faults but sometimes throwing around vague hints that he too fucked up along the way. I in turn, stifled my desire to express my own feelings of inadequacy and regret so as not to turn the scene into an episode of Grumpy Old Men. Periodically I would tune out to his bloviating and look down at my hands, which only brought back thoughts of how useless they are compared to those of a carpenter, a painter, a musician, and then I would look up and tune back in to Mike's rather depressing drivel and chime in to be polite. So it went until we finished the better half of the bottle and called it a night. I closed my eyes on the airbed and fell into a dreamless slumber.

Morning came in what felt like minutes. I was staying in the spare room, which was mostly used as a storage space and lacked curtains. Mike had gone to the gym and then to check in at the office at a new job he hated as usual so I took my time drinking coffee and smoking cigarettes, procrastinating until finally, felled by boredom, I decided to put on my suit and spend a few hours

wandering around Manhattan before it was time for the wake to
start. I was to meet Mike at the funeral home at 6 p.m.

THE WAKE

I arrived at the wake early, a little after the doors opened, so as to leave early. As I entered the hushed waiting hall, a perverse thought entered my head: "Women look good at funerals." I surveyed around to see which, if any, of Dick's former girlfriends were here, and how many of them I had slept with (I only noticed one, but it was still early). The presence of at least a few pretty women at the wake reminded me that I could still look good when I chose to. There is much flirting that goes on during wakes and funerals and probably casual sex afterwards as well. Sometimes among the bereaved, sometimes among strangers; the former to fuck the pain away, the latter as a matter of simple opportunism.

Mike grabbed me by the arm, his eyes alight with contained laughter, and dragged me over to a memorial board decorated with various snapshots of Dick. However, this was not the Dick we remembered. At least half of the photos were apparently given by his Florida friends and there he was, shirtless, wearing short tennis shorts straight out of the Boys Sportswear section at Sports Authority. In one egregiously flamboyant snapshot he stood sandwiched between two mustachioed men, both of whom looked like Tom Selleck or the Brawny paper towel guy.

The wake was tragicomic and the comedy aspect came mostly from the previously unseen photos of Dick, shirtless and in tight shorts, during one of his sojourns down to Key West.

The circumstances of his passing were speculative. All that was stated was that he died in Florida and the official cause of death was heart attack. Dick was of Caribbean descent and had many relatives in that state, so the geography made sense. Slightly more suspect was the fact that the photos were in the funeral parlor during the wake.

Rumors that Dick was gay were always present, but at the wake they were almost completely confirmed. There was not a single photo of him together with his wife and so the rumors spread further. The one that held fast and spread fastest was that Dick, after a particularly vigorous ménage à trois, was famished and ordered a Cuban sandwich from the restaurant downstairs. Shortly after biting into his post-coital midnight snack, the bread and meat stuck in his throat and one of his partners, when trying to perform the Heimlich maneuver, became aroused again and instead of calling an ambulance proceeded to once more penetrate the choking victim while a previously delicious mélange of ham, pork, Swiss cheese, pickles and Challah bread continued blocking the windpipe and the hapless civil servant left this earth prematurely.

I half expected the obituary to read, "Dick will be missed by his wife, possible daughter and José, John, Carl, Mike, Mad Mike, Mike's twin brother Mike, Steve, the guy everyone knew as 'Slave', Rico, "Panzer", Luke, Kelly, Jeffrey, Stu, Stewart, Rob, Ronald, Donald, Michael and Francis, Gerald Fitzpatrick and Patrick Fitzgerald."

Before things got too awkward among the mourners—some of whom were oblivious, some of whom found nothing unusual about the display, though some were at least mildly perplexed—Mike and I decided to make our exit and cabbed it back to his house for more Yamazaki whiskey and an endless chain of cigarettes. The wake gave Mike more fodder to bloviate again and thus we gossiped and exchanged various theories about Dick's sex life until it became tedious again and we went to our separate bedrooms without giving our dead friend any more dues.

BROOKLYN

Back in my youth I entertained three distinct fantasies about the future.

The first one was exceptionally banal. I had been looking forward to purchasing a pair of white shoes. This must have been in the midst of a slushy winter and a period of penury but the fantasy consisted of an extremely mundane scenario—buying said pair of white shoes, then sitting at an outdoor café, drinking, at the first fresh breath of spring.

I have yet to own white shoes.

The second fantasy involved a distant future (or what seemed distant to me when I was in my early twenties). I pictured myself finding success as a film director. With fame would come drug and alcohol addictions and other struggles and I pictured a photo of me published in a national magazine, looking addled, sunglasses shielding my eyes from the Mediterranean sun, my arms around a woman of dubious reputation, standing on the Croisette in Cannes, where my latest and most controversial film was being screened. Needless to say, this didn't happen and I have nailed all my aspirations for progress in that industry firmly in the coffin of youthful fancy.

The third one was the vaguest. It involved me spending a summer in Brooklyn, perhaps more than a summer, living in one of the high-rise buildings on Ocean Parkway. I had always been interested in cities bereft of activity. The Sunday solitude of certain places evokes a wide range of emotions, some frustrating like here in Los Angeles, some that have a particular and strange appeal.

That stretch of Brooklyn through which Ocean Parkway stretches always brought an odd longing mixed with serenity. Perhaps in my subconscious I thought of the long and rather empty boulevards of suburban Moscow in the 1970s. Free from advertising billboards, free from distractions, it would always bring about a feeling of peace, melancholy peace perhaps, whenever I would drive down that road with my dad as we would head to Brighton Beach for dinner, which we did once or twice a year for many years.

It was on Ocean Parkway that my third fantasy would take place. In this version of the future—not distant like the one in Cannes but not as immediate as the white shoes—I would rent an apartment on that boulevard where I would seclude myself and attend to the task of writing my novel. My "great novel," if you like. In this scenario I would awake each summer morning (it was always summer) in the heat and humidity and take the subway a few stops down to Coney Island or Brighton Beach. There I would wash off my hangover with a brisk swim in the ocean, then have lunch (shashlik, lavash, and vodka shots) at one of the Georgian restaurants, then return to my flat and write my book. Perhaps I would meet a lady friend somewhere along the way but mostly it would be a time for contemplation and assiduous work. Unfortunately, there was a hole in this plot. I had no idea what the book I was planning to write would be. In fact, I hadn't even an inkling of a story, a germ of an idea. Nothing. The idea was that I would write, but what I wrote didn't concern me.

I began to realize the reason for my writer's block was that the book was too long in the making. Things change, people change. Was it worth it to go on and continue, when I had become such a different person at this point, so much less obsessed with whoredom, petty or grand? When I had grown out of my trepidation before the fairer sex? Perhaps I didn't—that too is possible—because Betty would indeed frighten me. Her mystery frightened me.

It is the things that we cannot see that are the most terrifying.

A screenplay is like a woman lying around naked waiting to be fucked, whereas a novel is a fully fucked out one. So I set about my New World trilogy (or rather diptych, for the third one was but a vague germ of an idea in which I finally killed off Stacy). I never finished the third one, which should have followed The Girl from Below and The New World Symphony, and so Stacy lived, and I decided to turn the diptych of two scripts into a novel so that, unlike a screenplay, it would exist forever—or at least some version of forever.

The first working title was St. Stacy of Rivington Street. Then I tried others: Garbage Dump, It's Hard to be Young in the New World, and other variations on theme. This was the peak of my interest in the "tragic slut," before or perhaps after I read Last Exit to Brooklyn. And yet, romantic that I am and was, I held on to misery because it was my misery. Now that porn was ubiquitous and glamorized, those feelings eventually left… Inured or jaded, all things like Stacy or perhaps a later inspiration in Mieze from Berlin Alexanderplatz did hold power over me for years, and most likely to the detriment of my own psychological and sexual wellbeing. Eventually I settled on The Girl from Below, because it could be interpreted in several different fashions: the below of the girl in the flat below, or the girl from the basest thoughts and fears, or perhaps from below this earth where demons dwell and torment is eternal and a dwelling place where there is no light or hope.

Stacy started off in upstate New York and went downhill to Rivington—which was in the 1980s one of the most horrible and sordid places in Manhattan. The sequel would take Stacy to San Francisco with its cold shimmering light, but the story mostly took place in New York, where the indefatigable purple of the cold and black spring graced my fictional lover's life and story.

As a child I entertained many fantasies. One of them, almost ripped straight out of Hans Christian Andersen's bathos, involved me finding a shivering waif on the doorstep of our apartment building then bringing her in and bathing her and putting her in clean pajamas and letting her stay in the warmth and the comfort. This before I even reached puberty, believe it or not. But it was consistent motif in my dreams and daydreams. I would always try to "rescue" a pretty girl from something or other.

And so perhaps by leaving the trilogy unfinished I tried to "rescue" my heroine, Stacy, from her fate. I also knew that I could never save her one bit, and so I let her go on in the most vulgar and filthy scenarios.

A few years after this fantasy became entrenched in my brain I moved to Brooklyn—not to a Moscow boulevard manqué but to Park Slope, which a friend of mine had described as a cross between Lesbianville and El Río del Welfare. At least that's what it was like in the early 1990s.

But on this visit, New York didn't seem so bad and so I went with Charlotte's offer of an extended stay. A perfunctory internet search landed me on a listing for a summer sublet right on Ocean Parkway. It was also fortuitously one of the more affordable sublets I could find in all of New York. If Cannes was out of the picture and white shoes were pedestrian, perhaps I could give this third fantasy a try. Soon I would be settling into my one bedroom flat on the Hebraic Champs Elysees that I so perversely admired twenty or more years before.

The subway ride from Manhattan to the deepest end of Brooklyn seemed interminable, and with my hangover hardon firmly in place I dozed off and thought about some girls, about how pointless those flings were and at the same time how much I missed them. I woke up just before arriving at my stop on the Q train. My initial nervousness that the flat would smell of herring and borscht was abated when Ludmilla the landlady opened the door.

Although she was still quite the Brighton Beach matron—overweight, gold teeth sparkling through the crimson lipstick, a terrible red-hair dye job and a too tight t-shirt emblazoned with the Chanel logo—the apartment itself did not looked lived in at all, and if anyone ever cooked kielbasa or opened smoked fish in the kitchen, the smell was long gone. The flat itself was furnished as tastefully as one can get in that part of Brooklyn. The décor was what one would see in shops that advertise and sell "Fine Italian Furniture," always found in Eastern European parts of town: heavy on gold and white, plenty of faux marble and mirrors… The balcony door was wide open and a faint sea smell permeated the premises.

The minute she was gone I was overcome by a wave of exhaustion. The morning air had given way to sticky moisture and I closed the balcony doors, shuttered the blinds and fell asleep in my clothes on the king-sized mattress. I awoke a few hours later with a smile on my face. Though I didn't remember what I dreamt about, a faint residue, some type of pixie dust, remained behind my eyelids—perhaps a fictional or idealized memory from childhood, perhaps laughing with my parents, all bathed in a gorgeous light of summer memories.

"Bliss," I thought. As the first hint of evening came through the windows and flooded the flat with a gentle yellow light, I thought to myself, "I could work here… and I will. It's solitary, but that's what I need."—I reminisced about my mother and how she would entertain guests and talk of literature in between cabbages and dictators. That too was a time that I had never appreciated until now. Those soirees, for lack of a better word, how magical they actually were in retrospect of course but even as they happened, though I mostly wished to get out and get away and start my own life, which while not entirely stillborn did not get off to a good start. And things had gotten greyer, and my lack of friends prevented me making a world like my mother's, where people would gather, drink, eat and discuss art.

All of my new conversations were about pre-school and day care, retirement, vacations, home improvement, car troubles and what latest trash is playing at the multiplex. The magic had evaporated. And those people gathered around my mom's table—they weren't old, now that I think about it. Grownups always look older to children, people in their forties or fifties probably looked ancient to me. And they probably looked like they knew what they were doing, but it was a great delusion. No one knows what they're doing. No one. Not at any stage of the game called life. I certainly don't, even still.

In so many ways it was easier during the Cold War. Certainly for art and literature—adversity and suffering create a dialectic which produces something. The birth of tragedy. And the period between the two world wars, when everyone waited for the apocalypse to come, did it not swell with fecundity? What do we have left? Memories and memoirs, but what happened is relegated to the deep past, which no one cares to remember.

That first evening alone in New York, I was enveloped by the embrace of the steaming night but more than anything else I wanted to hold a female body and envelop her in my own right, with my vodka and cigarette breath and my overarching hardon pressing against her ass, with me tasting her sweat and holding her as we drift off to different galaxies in our sleep, wondering if she will dream of me.

Though I was several miles from the beach, I imagined I heard the crashing waves in the first breath of black night, only to interrupt them with other melancholy colors of yellow and blue. I lay in bed and imagined the old Russian Jews shuffling along the boardwalk, greeting one another with such wry neologisms as "How are you? Pensioneering tonight again?" which I had heard when walking down that depressing boardwalk with my dad years ago. (I remembered that I thought that new expression "pensioneering" was quite clever.) Then again, blue and yellow would come and I thought of places that I had only visited in my mind, places like Yalta and Odessa, Sochi and Feodosia… And then came sleep. Dreamless sleep as black as the Black Sea. Or as my dad would joke, reciting a silly Russian saying, "Darker than the inside of a Negro's stomach."

In the morning I awoke with dread. The page was blank. The page remained blank. The dreaded blank page, the catalyst of all masterpieces and the end all of all failures stayed blank the whole day. Between checking the news and social media (where it's so easy to play God with a point and a click) and gentle boozing I managed to piss the time away with zero effort.

As the blue and white haze of summer daylight dispersed and Brooklyn turned the grey leather of evening, I began to think of colors, and my reverie turned back several decades to the Brooklyn of old in which I lived and which I have promised to describe.

I do not suffer (if suffer is the word) from synesthesia, but colors are my Madeleine cookies and I am sensitive to the memories associated with the sky in various geographies: the soft auburn light of Manhattan at summer's twilight; the cold white and blue of San Francisco; the warm white and blue of Brooklyn or Jersey. As I pondered Brooklyn's sky my mind drifted back to 1992 and my first black winter and dark spring in Park Slope, to New York's black and purple atmosphere with the inky blood drop of an always elusive sun setting somewhere on the horizon, waiting for a spring that came too late and which, when it arrived, was cold and bristly. It was during that winter that I began to feel an overwhelming and persistent sensation of pain mixed with a bleak optimism about the coming of milder weather. This wasn't the pain of pain, the pain of grief or loss, the pain of horror; it was the pain of an ant slowly burning under the heat of a magnifying glass, and it was present everywhere and especially in the seediest parts of New York. In 1992, New York was no longer the realm of Taxi Driver but it was very far from the New York in which I had decided to spend this middle-aged summer. The drugs were rampant, muggings and hijackings the same, and there were still many parts of the city that one wouldn't dare to venture in without risking life and limb. Red Hook, East New York, South Bronx, Avenue D, Rivington Street, the far West Side: all places of vice and crime. It was no longer the New York of Travis Bickle, which was being slowly removed and replaced, but there remained countless pockets of hell. It was, let's say, the New York of Hubert Selby where corpuscles of depravity thrived alongside the middle class. Ultimately it was Selby that won in the dogged live-without-hope way of the inhabitants of these places while Abrahams slept. Taxi Driver maintained a romanticism that was born out of "The Forgotten and Downtrodden" while I saw only the most brutal romanticism, for even Iris went back happily to Pittsburgh and Travis got his hack license back.

In my vague story, which I tried to form at that time, the ant would eventually self-destruct in an orgy of pain, a napalm bomb in miniature. These ideas were very vague and I had to find at least an inkling of an idea before I could start on my book or my screenplay (I was still undecided about which of the two forms it would take). The brutality needed a starting point or at least a starting character. Most of all, it needed degradation for I was drawn to suffering for reasons unknown to me. Without understanding an ounce of what I wanted to say or why I wished to write about it I sought to write something genuinely horrific but which would also somehow bring forth transcendence. But first it needed tragedy and before tragedy, degradation. The degradation of the fictional Tralala or the real life Bodil Joensen, the bestiality star of Danish porn. Soon enough I found two characters who kept searching for an author. Joensen commented in a 1980 interview:

Things went completely out of hand when Spot died. I started taking sedatives. But when someone referred to them as "loony-smarties" I threw them in the fireplace. Instead I started drinking and eating excessively. I gained 30 kilos. Doesn't look well on something that was going downhill anyway. Spot was a real German shepherd that I got from an animal hospital 10 years ago. She had been beaten. She never became anything but a little, weak dog. I've never been able to talk to other girls. I've always been with men. Spot was my female friend. She understood what I said. Was happy when I was happy. Was sad when I was. When we were alone in the house without light and heat we went to bed together. Shared a biscuit. And then we talked, until we fell asleep. Spot is the only living creature that has loved me for being just me. She didn't expect to get anything back. She soothed me when I was ill. I've experienced a lot with Lassie, and like him a lot. But it'll never be the same as with Spot. Lassie has been unfaithful to me. He's an every-girls-dog. Spot was mine. Completely mine. That's why I had such a shock when she died. And started drinking, and eating myself fat in no time. I live with my man for 10 years and my eight-year-old daughter. Still I feel like the loneliest human being now that Spot is dead. In those days I earned easy money in a tough line of work. I fell and fell. "When will I reach the bottom?" I often ask myself those days.

Joensen became an alcoholic, and was at one point imprisoned for bestiality. Her animals died and she turned to prostitution, exchanging sex for alcohol and tranquilizers. In her final interview she said that, "in my position it is hard to turn down anything, no matter how disgusting... for me, staying alive in the hooking business is hell."

I sought out prostitution as a theme not because of any highfalutin idea about mercantilism or exploitation. I sought it out and settled on it solely for these vague notions of pain and degradation. The problem with prostitution and writing about it is its long history of sentimentalism. A millennium before Sonia Marmeladova we had re-invented Mary Magdalene as a repentant whore.

My interest was in a non-repentant whore, not one of today's whores who makes millions but a common dirty little strumpet who takes a nose dive into filth. The whoredom of today is vastly different, it lacks all poignancy and sentimentality or even horror. But back in that first year in Park Slope when sleaze was still sleaze there were poignant streetwalkers all around the city. Apart from the sleaze of the city, I was still recovering from an ill-fated romance with a woman who was essentially a streetwalker at heart. I will explain more about Emily later as I get to the origin of my mental illness which prompted me to write my Symphony but first I must finish explaining my fascination with pain.

Why was I compelled to write that book, or make a film of it? It wasn't autobiographical, it had no moral or judgment, it offered little in the way of either philosophical discourse or a cautionary tale. Yet I obsessed about it as if I had lived it, or was going to live it one day—a waking dream that haunted me and would not loosen its grip. The catalyst for the book, which then became a screenplay and then... (I will get to the "and then" later) was an article in the Village Voice about a teenage whore. This particular unfortunate, from what I recall of the piece, lived in a housing project with her crack dealer boyfriend surrounded by his tied-up pit bulls... and other ghastly details I can no longer remember.

Back in those days I was possessed by a bizarre and ridiculous hubris which I still can't explain to this day. I was a prize winning writer before I had written anything, a rock star who never had a band, and the recipient of the Palme d'Or before I'd made a film. In dreams begin responsibilities, but it is daydreams that destroy all responsibility. All that will be addressed further on, but first I need to explain the Staten Island whorror story and a bit about Emily.

The night wind carried sea air in from the coast, covering Brooklyn in a fine mist. Coming in through my window, the moist, warm wind brought with it phantasmagoric dreams of dark, humid places I have never been to and probably never will—Nagasaki, Lagos, Saigon, Luanda, Sakhalin… My mind drifted back and forth between imaginary places, some inspired by book covers or magazine articles from the 1970s.

"Partir, c'est mourir un peu," my mom liked to quote, and given her obsession with death it makes sense that this quote would hold special meaning. For me, I had always found a tremendous excitement in places of departure, in airports, ferry terminals, railway stations… All emblems of possibility, or at least change—change that one would hope would be for the better, though this is an absurd idea. Few would have been so naïve or romantic to consider a train station in certain parts of Europe in the early 1940s a gateway to better place.

Now the train station seemed closed to me. I don't know if it was during my dream or not or whether it was a realization that my life is half over or worse, coming to a close. There was now something about departure that only seemed like a vague memory. As I sweated in a fitful sleep, moving in and out of dreams, fragmented memories burst and died like fireworks. The supersonic change of the past fifty years in the history of the world and the US and Europe in particular made the mind reel, and when I awoke I had a greasy layer of random words on my tongue: Brooklyn Queens Expressway, Circle in the Square, Stars of the Bolshoi, Listopad, Union City Blue, Hands Across America, "white cities." For some reason the term "white cities" haunted me the most.

I awoke way too early, sweating, and wondered if I had made a terrible mistake revisiting New York, especially this new New York. The problem with the new New York was that it had retained some of the memories but demolished the old ones; but what wasn't demolished? Mnemonic castles build up their own impressive fortifications—up to a point.

My dreams all seemed to be set in the 1970s. Though I had never been to the "Dark Continent," oftentimes they were set

in Africa, and I was would assume various characters: a Merina
Malay cooking an omelet in the spring in Antananarivo, a negro
drinking Horlicks in Monrovia, a Portuguese retornado loading
my possession onto an ocean liner in Luanda, bound for Lisbon.
Why this continent I do not know. Perhaps because, never having
been there, it was a type of terra nullius. I always liked blank slates.

But the majority of my dreams were about women—and
what sweet dreams they were. Since I had forgotten what it's like
to have a girlfriend, a lover, and I tried in vain to recall if I ever
even experienced it. Specifically, I pined for some semblance of the
feeling of "young love." But the dreamed silhouette of two lovers
was precisely that—a silhouette, a shadow.

Even the place names in New York would dig pinpricks into
my mind, so loaded were they with memories, good and bad. I
experienced this feeling with all place names from my past.
Haymarket Square, Berlin Alexanderplatz, Pacific Coast Highway,
Pacific Heights, Brooklyn Heights, Circle in the Square, Sheridan
Square, Brooklyn Queens Expressway, West Side Highway, East
River, Patriarch's Ponds, The Vyborg Side, Hudson Valley, Moscow
River, Theater on Taganka… And here I was on the equally evocative
Ocean Parkway, searching not for what rhymes with orange but
simply how to begin this elusive book, much less finish it. Perhaps
the atmosphere inside my head was too distracting. I had not visited
this part of Brooklyn in so long, a flood of memories was pulling
me under. I kept thinking of my mother and her apartment when
it was still magical. It was impossible to find that magic again, to
recreate it. The child's wonder had evaporated, and the people too
were vaporized. And though we forget people just like we forget
the common cold, vague ciphers tugged at my sleeve.

The memories grew kaleidoscopic. Any random hint
of something from my past would bring up a swell of vivid
recollections, transporting me back across the decades—an apple,

a whiff of spring, cigarette ash. Thus I, in documenting this summer of my madness, am finally trying to give those memories some kind of place—a book, a megabyte, a coffin, a cenotaph.

A writer is a coffin maker by trade, not a master of baby carriages. Show the author a casket—one tap on the side—and he'll immediately know the type of materials used in its construction: when it was built and how, which workers helped put it together. With another knock of the knuckles he'll even identify the parents of the deceased...

Even now, a whiff of something while out walking will set off visions, both remembered and imagined. A flash of spring sunshine on a white building in Antananarivo transported me to the highlands of Merina; a winter storm would take me to Haida Gwaii or Vancouver Island, the morning fog to Sitka or Valparaíso, Punta Arenas or Ushuaia. The earth existed in my head, all the globe was mine—I was the king of infinite space and I did suffer bad dreams.

But how glorious the good dreams were, the stuff of pure bliss, often of childhood innocence or an alternate present for me in my own middle age.

Blue is the color of possibility. Yellow the is the color of endings. And yet how much I liked the yellow of New York as much as the blue, the sunny mornings, mother making cheese omelet with paprika in the kitchen. The yellow eggs, the yellow pies my grandmother would bake. The yellow candles my mom loved to leave burning through the evening hours. The yellow slices of lemon floating in strong Russian tea. The yellow just dying to burst its way through the burglar bars on the windows and forming a zebra pattern on the floor and on my sheets.

And then there was the piercing yellow of early August when she broke down in tears. It was the last time I saw her, and all I could I could sense from that breakdown was her silently saying to herself, "I fucked up..."

Mom would threaten suicide at the drop of a hat, would actually stick her body halfway out the window over a trifle. It took many years for me to understand and recognize that it was a form of psychological abuse, albeit inflicted by someone who was herself in pain. Of course, eventually she succeeded, but the process was long and horrific.

Then my dad died, and then my friends started dying off in the sense that they stopped talking to me. I wept so hard when friends "divorced" me, when Sandra dropped me; they were corpses to me now, as bitter and brittle as the bones of my ancestors, slowly turning to ash.

On the other hand, it could have been infinitely worse. The memoirs of Dr Destouches described a woman whose daughter was dying and who spent the entire moribund agony by her bed, masturbating furiously, one orgasm after another while her child was in agonizing final throes—there is perhaps a reason that orgasms can still be had in pain, more as an escape than perversion. Even certain sections of the Lodz Ghetto under the stewardship of the avuncular and demonic Chaim Rumkowski were rumored to have become infamous for orgies—not just alimentary via smuggled food but also sexual bacchanalia in the midst of extermination. And yet it all makes vulgar sense, for we the living perform it on a daily basis, every fuck and every orgasm is one little death to distract us from the inevitable end in the charnel house we call planet Earth.

And yet, when I would lie down sweating after seeing Betty, despite the millions of blood cells rushing to the penis, I could not use my hand for so-called self-pleasure because I was and was not listening to "El Choclo" on the platform at Birkenau, was and was not hearing a tubercular "Tosca" in the barracks of the condemned. Because I wanted to hear Betty and all I heard was the muted sound of midnight buses passing laboriously and exhaling deeply, to my annoyance, right beneath my balcony.

And in the morning, after a sweaty and fitful night, I would awake with blue. For some reason, the yellow had departed—but the blue stayed almost the same. It was still summer, after all.

At some point things started to seem dirty to me in LA. The precise reasons were unclear, but there were several suspects. The boozing made me feel dirty. Writing porn copy, at first a rather humorous exercise of how to describe a blowjob in one million different ways, became tedious and mind numbing—though it was a very easy way to keep myself in smokes. And not working, other than on porn, also weighed heavy on my sense of mental hygiene. I blamed the rapidly changing (or deranging) world, and I do still stand by some of those theses. Work, honest work, was not anathema to me, but where to find it? The only honest work I could imagine was manual labor, but in my forties I had no idea how to join that workforce. Plumbing, driving, construction, forklift operation, house painting... I was either too old, too physically unfit, or not Mexican enough. Working in an office, creating nothing remotely practical, useful or productive, and talking bollocks for a living made me cringe, similar to my aversion to the practical realities of "George and Martha and Honey" academia.

When remembering my early youth, and my mom and her library, I thought of the émigré author Natalia Kodryanskaya, sipping tea in her Paris apartment in the glow of the evening sun and creating wonderful, phantasmagorical stories, some poignant, some whimsical like that of airplane pilot who crashes into his own guardian angel. Innocent is not the right word, but it was something cleaner than what I felt had befallen me.

When did things become ugly? I am not at all certain, but something happened and I felt sticky, with little to no chance for redemption. "Do not fear death, it is the only way to be cleansed" (to paraphrase the California poet) no longer passed muster, for I did fear death, and still do.

Natalia would hang out with a bizarre compatriot in exile, Alexei Remizov, who would venture into dream states and preferred to spend his life dreaming, and who eventually decided, to the consternation of other exiles, to return to Bolshevik Russia. As ugly as it was, I reckoned, he wanted to die at home. The return, the eternal return... And Natalia, another exile fell into the world of writing fairy tales, perhaps out of genuine affinity for the form, perhaps to hide from the quotidian pangs of exile. And then there was the issue with the moon and the moles...

GLASHA THE MOLE

My mother had a book of Natalia Kodryanskaya's fairy tales, and the one that I remembered best, the one that made me weep more than the others, was the sorrowful story of Glasha the Mole.

Glasha the mole wore a fur coat that felt like velvet., silvery when you brushed your hand against it. When her grandmother wished to compliment her, she would tell her that at the market a pelt like that would fetch at least fifteen kopecks.

Neither grandma nor Glasha knew what fifteen kopecks were and they envisioned this prize in different ways: Glasha saw it as ruddy-faced, freshly baked buttered roll. Grandma saw is it as a whole mole estate, house and land and all. Both of them respected and were in awe of these fifteen kopecks and feared this money in silence; feared, for fifteen kopecks was the price of a mole pelt in the market.

The moles lived underground, shuttered from everyone. Bars on the windows, gates locked, fences high so that the sun would never accidentally come past them and shine a light through the shutters, so the doors wouldn't open, so that darkness would not be swept away by a golden broom.

The moles' trade was hunting and banditry. Rarely did they venture above ground for anything but their evil crafts.

Glasha was called a holy fool, a simpleton among the moles. All day long she would dream about the day that the sun, the golden wanderer, would visit the land of the moles and that they would then start to live like the rest of God's beasts.

Each year, when spring came, Glasha would venture outside and, blinded by the sun, would walk out into the fields.

She would touch every little blade of grass, every flower, every leaf with her little paws. She would know when the poppies were blooming. And she would move her clumsy paws against the silk skirts of the poppy flowers and steal mementos of the summer— their tiny black buttons. And she marveled at how her mother and stepmother would gather up in their little golden cups the morning dew and how they would water them with sweet water, and give water to the yellow bee, and whatever flies and bugs and insects came their way.

Every little flower, every bush, knew Glasha and called her lovingly by her name. In the dry summer, she saw the bells of the flowers shrink from the heat and she called on the sky to bring rain to the earth, and in her wishes and dreams, the wings of blue butterflies lifted her up to the heavens.

Birds would sing, and through the rustling of insects and the perfume of new grass came the chirps of grasshoppers, and Glasha loved them all the more for their consistent, dedicated noise, and she thought that without them her world would be completely empty.

The bumblebee hummed, scurried around the meadow, drank thirstily from each flower and all seemed not enough for him, this insatiable one. Oh, how many flowers he stomped on, how many he ruined in the course of a day! The bumblebee was the top dog in his family. Glasha feared him the most. Feared him more than fire. And the bumblebee didn't know that there was a Glasha and her fur coat was like a rock to him. And truly, Glasha would pretend to turn to stone when she saw the bumblebee in the meadow.

All things underground lost her interest, and all subterranean concerns became hideous: the moles' cruelty, the darkness, the cold. Here on earth, where from morning to night birds sang, crickets chirped, and the grass grew—was all a beautiful song to her.

In the twilight, before shuffling home, Glasha would sometimes lean against a rock by the country road. Ants would be hurrying home and she would try to exchange a word but they were too much in a rush: "How much news the ants must accumulate," she thought, "moving so fast throughout the day, and how excited they must be to hurry home to tell everyone what has happened in the world." So she would watch the ants return home and tell everyone the news.

And it was only when night spread out her dark skirt, and there was no longer a spot of sun left... Only then would Glasha return home.

Once she sat on her little rock and saw a black beetle walking down the road, his suit all covered in dust. Surely a traveler from afar, she thought, and smiled.

Sometimes Glasha would venture to a different part of the meadow, one that was grey with dandelion leaves. And she would blow on the dandelions herself until the whole meadow was covered in grey flames of lace petals and the dandelion puffs looked like clouds. These were Glasha's clouds. Wind walked upon the fields, taking away the butterflies and the flowers, and threw the dandelions down to earth.

And Glasha wondered, "Where does Wind live? His house has no windows." She would ponder. "And how cold, how cold it must be for him, Wind, the poor thing."

And she saw on the floor a rug, knitted from grass and flowers and buds, that she wanted to gift to Wind.

"Birds never sing in his house, ever," Glasha sighed. She went headlong toward Wind, bowing her head.

Silently she made him a promise: "Wind, I will make you a fur coat for the winter, so you can keep warm..."

And though Glasha knew that she had nothing with which to make a coat for Wind, she still wished to comfort him somehow, and so she went down into her hole and threw out her favorite toys—dried leaves and acorns—and instead started to make a coat for Wind out of flower petals to keep Wind warm.

Apart from Wind, Glasha really loved the Sun, the deadly sin of the moles. "I love the Sun!" Glasha would say to herself and quietly laugh from joy. Meekly and silently she would give praise to the Sun, for she feared that Grandmother might hear because to love the sun in the Mole World was a mortal sin.

And the moon—that one she was never able to see. Moles sleep when the moon is out, and most of them have never even heard of such a thing. And when Glasha finally was able to see the moon it became a fickle enchantress, for this rock in space helped the cruel mole bandit Onofri steal her away from her home. While all the moles slept, the moon shined a light and Onofri was able to enter her mole village. And that is how he stole Glasha in the middle of the night and took her to be his wife.

Onofri would not let Glasha walk in the meadow, nor sit on the rock and marvel at the twilight. The cruel mole locked her in a dark chamber and forced her to mend his boots.

Glasha cried. Her hot and bitter tears seeped through the ground, and made their way through to the river.

The frogs saw Glasha's tears floating on the surface of the water, and they understood. The ducks heard Glasha's tears, which spoke to them, and they understood.

"Poor, poor Glasha!" cried the frogs. "Her husband Onofri is just a mole by day but at night he's a bloodthirsty wasp. All day he's out hunting, but when he comes home, he files his claws, sharpens his teeth, makes sure his mouth is intact. Before eating his own brothers, he skins them, takes them to the market to sell their skins. He hides the bones of his brothers, picked clean and sucked to the bone, under his bed. Might he be building a little dollhouse out of mole bones?"

"What horror," said the ducks, "to build a house out of the bones of your kin!"

And that very evening the ducks sent a petition to the Cat King to find and question the criminal Onofri the mole.

The Cat King washed himself, asked his cobbler to shod him and off he went to the meadow. And on his way who did he meet but Onofri. Squinting from the sun, Onofri showed the Cat King the satchel on his back—in the satchel were a dozen field mice.

The Cat King was furious.

"It's not enough for you to eat your brothers, now you're after my own goods? Eat your own moles, mole. You can give me the mice, and we're settled."

Onofri's head started to spin. "How much can I get for a cat skin at the market?" he wondered. "Fifteen kopecks? Yes, perhaps fifteen kopecks..."

Onofri killed the Cat King with a swift blow and skinned him, and then took the cat's skin to the market.

When the folks saw the mole carrying the hide of the poor cat, they wailed and jumped on the bastard, then they grabbed him and put him in the docks.

After Onofri was executed, the now blind Glasha went outside and to her freedom. She had lost her sight not from the sun but from the eternal darkness of the world below, her eyes had now failed. And now poking around in the dark she was no longer afraid of the bumblebee, for not only could she not see but her heart had turned to stone. Yet she still managed to crawl onto her rock on occasion, and speak to passersby who would listen to her, and she would tell the same stories to whoever would listen, about the cruel mole Onofri, her former husband, and the sad fate that moles endure, and how the moon, unaware of what she was doing, destroyed her life.

Why this story stuck with me I do not know, but how I pitied her, poor Glasha. Pity: that accursed, Russian, Christian, maudlin feeling of pity that continued to rear its pitiful head even as I became older and more hardened. A trait I was unable to ditch.

The insidious statement that everything happens for a reason is patently false. Indeed, it is the utter randomness of life that makes it so sinister at times. And yet looking back at my life through a rear-view mirror I couldn't help but think that something brought me here. I wouldn't say it was predestined, but there was something about those little loves and greater betrayals that somehow, almost, fit into place. The word "karmic" is sometimes used to describe these feelings, but "karmic" implies errors. I say errors because the Hindus believe, as far as I know, that evil comes from ignorance instead of malice—and that is why I afford them the most favorable of opinions.

UNCANNY VALLEY or A CONEY ISLAND OF LOST SOULS

The first few nights and days in New York I was an emotional wreck as feelings and memories swelled, but soon enough I accepted that this is where I was and that this will be my home and writing retreat for the next two months. Once I had settled in, I started going to the Russian-Georgian restaurant "Primorski" each day. Not solely out of nostalgia—my dad and I would go there once in a while when he was in town—but because their fare was genuinely tasty. The owner, Khota Kochaveli—a six-foot seven giant with a severe limp—would strut around periodically to make sure all was in order. Rumor had it that Khota the Georgian narrowly missed a mob hit and his bum leg was a sign of pride. Other rumors supported that it was a much more pedestrian (literally) accident. Much like the rest of his nation, whose most famous son was the genocidal cretin Iosif Vissarionovich Dzhugashvili, better known as Josef Stalin, the Georgians, stuck in their no man's land in the mountains between Europe and Asia clinging to every far-fetched accomplishment they could dig out of their soft kidskin boots. Having found naught but lint they resorted to rehabilitating "Koba" as the true example of macho swagger. Khota followed that tradition if in nothing else than pride in his height, girth and wounded leg. It would have been a comical sight if it wasn't a tiny bit frightening, but the Georgian and Russian and Jewish mobs in the bowel of Brooklyn mostly preyed on their own, and the cooking was delicious, much better than eggplant parmigiana at Gemini Lounge—and at least I was fairly sure that there weren't refrigerators filled with corpses as there were in Bensonhurst. Soon, I would tell Betty how my dad lived in Georgia and escaped the war, but that was in due time.

As I Lay Sweating: that could have been the title for my book, for it seemed like each time Betty did one of her disappearing tricks the AC would stop functioning. It was on one of those sweaty nights as I lay thinking about the ending of The New World Symphony ("Moist, moist, why does the bed feel moist?") that I remembered a striking phrase. I don't know who said it. It went something like, "Nothing that exists is truly worthy of love, so we must love that which does not exist." This poignant phrase ended up being particularly fitting by the time this carnival was over, when the leaves turned brown and the night wind came. And yet I will continue to love Betty until I die. We will meet again, one day, despite what the doctors say. Most likely in the next world.

To say that my nights were "filled with pain" would be a misnomer. Alcohol dulled the pain in the evening—it was the mornings that were the worst. I would wake up with a desire both to fuck Betty and to kill her, to put her out of her misery and me out of mine.

How I sweated in the night, how I tried to kill demons who would immediately reappear the way sidewalks formed asphalt again when they looked like they were melting just minutes ago. How painful and horrible were the mornings when Betty was gone and I had no idea where she was. I will explain all of this. Give me a minute while I relate how I met her.

Every day I would go to Primorski restaurant for lunch and order the same thing—lamb shashlik, pickled cabbage, a small carafe of vodka and a bottle of mineral water. Primorski was always nearly empty at lunch, and this day was no different. The few other patrons were elderly Jewish and Georgian couples, all sporting enough gold teeth that if melted down would be enough for a Golden Calf. On the first fateful day, it was particularly hot and I could feel a bit of sun stroke coming on. I ordered a cold beer, downed it, and headed over to the men's room—which is when I noticed her.

A young woman eating alone, also drinking vodka, in shots, the Russian way. A brunette, with bangs, she looked a bit like a young Bettie Page.

She looked out of place there, somehow. She did not have the look of someone from the former USSR which I can identify straight away. She looked like an "Amerikanka," but a brunette.

(Side note: I have fond memories of eating lunch at the Metropole Hotel in Moscow. My dad would take me there sometimes. One day there was a blonde lady with dark glasses at the adjacent table, having lunch by herself. I fell instantly in love with her. I will never forget that moment when my nether regions quivered for the first time. It wasn't the fact that she was a blonde, they're a ruble a dozen in Russia; it was her sunglasses, and the way she was smoking her cigarette. My dad said, "Go ahead, say hi", and I walked up to her and said something, I don't recall what. It did turn out she was a foreigner, perhaps French or Canadian or German... I don't remember what I said or what she said in return but she was my first crush. The blonde with dark glasses. I think she gave me a stick of chewing gum).

This girl in Primorski was extremely good looking, one of those girls you see sometimes and say to yourself that they're too good to be true. It was when I was walking back to my table that I noticed she was in a wheelchair. Not one of the hospital ones you get after breaking a leg but one that would be used for life. I understood that she was paralyzed.

Her condition when combined with her beauty made her look all the more tragic. As much as I wished to talk to her I didn't know what to say. I ordered double the amount of vodka I usually drank at 3 p.m., munched on my kebab and left to go home to wonder if I would ever see her again and how to devise a strategy in case I did. I thought about taking out a "missed connections" ad, but even that was problematic for it would not have solved the question of how to start a conversation. And what about my wife and family? What if Charlotte found out and cut me off entirely? I was not ready for an affair. And what kind of an affair could I have with her, I wondered? It was a frightening question.

The next day I timed my routine to make sure that I would arrive at the same time. While on the beach I was hoping, praying that she would be there, while at the same time knowing that I would chicken out of talking to her. When I entered Primorski, there she was. Again I was filled with trepidation, so I repeated the previous day—ordered double the vodka and hardly ate my shashlik. I went home and finished another bottle of vodka, fell asleep and woke up at dawn. This must be a dream, I kept saying.

Ever since I saw her, I could not concentrate. A blank sheet of paper stared me right in the eye and I became utterly unable to write. My dreams were plagued by thoughts of my parents while my waking hours were filled with dread about the idea that I had somehow "abandoned" my family. I was cheating on my wife in my mind whenever I thought about this mystery woman. I was drawn to the misery of her circumstances. A morbid curiosity, most likely inherited from my mother, who also almost relished talking about things she found repugnant or frightening or both. Very much a Russian trait.

On occasion I imagined that I could try to hold the door for her as she wheeled herself out when exiting, but each time the "doorman"—a caricature of a polite brute with epaulets straight out of a nineteenth century novel—would beat me to it. A few times I considered following her outside as she pushed herself down Coney Island Avenue to at least guess the direction of her journey home, but fear of being accused of stalking held me back, and I remained a beast in the jungle.

After another night of fitful self-doubt, I resolved to approach her at the next opportunity. In the meantime, the self-doubt was like an imp tapping on my shoulder, reminding me that I had squandered so many opportunities, that I was rootless, jobless, and getting old. I felt as if my life was over and there was no reset button. My hands were worthless, they were not the talented hands of a surgeon, musician or painter—they shook too much and I had little patience for painstaking work. Did I already harp on my lack of talent? My body was not cut out for athletics or sports or dance. And my mind was always in a semi-delirium, easily distracted. Architecture would have made a fine profession, the art of building something that lasts, but I lacked the math skills; and now I found myself obsessed with a pathetic task of trying to build something lasting by writing a book, but the book was not coming along at all. My book, my house of stone. Thus I remembered a poem I once wrote about never owning a house, which will most likely be the case. It originated from a childhood memory but was compounded by the disassociation I was experiencing from Charlotte and the way she way she had thrown herself into her work for her geriatric boss, who I readily admit was much more talented than me. And I resented both Charlotte and myself for having these thoughts.

> We'll never own a house, this
> I know is true, just
> how my Mom laughed at me sadly and said
> the same thing. Mind you, I was
> ten years old and still it scalds just like
> the cup of chicken broth
> I burned my hands with on the bus from Philadelphia.
> She laughed, and yet your thoughts
> are much like hers, and that means thoughts are
> elsewhere yet again.

My mother humored me and then,
in the blink of an eye, destroyed my dreams.
Perhaps correct and true, perhaps too cruel but
think, for ten years old, my bourgeois dreams were
quite precocious and thus easily destroyed.
Imagine that, to buy a house, how
rooted we all were in misery back then, and
ended life with misery again,
of course she thought
it was a joke.

Nevertheless, American philosophy after
some thirty years turns
quite contagious, no longer is outrageous,
the desire for a nest, especially when that
old habitat has been destroyed by rats.

I want to be, or have, or do, and fear that it's too late
for number three or two, but just
to be is not enough for me.

We'll never own a house, and Mom was right:
it's might that in the end makes right.
I'll write more rubbish destined for the bin and gather
crumbs to stick into my cheeks for nourishment and for
some droppings I can chew on in between the
Holy Mass, the joke is who's the one who will
first pass? Not you, but you know who.
I've made a fine fool of myself, have I not?

The future: that's where I'd like to steer your gaze
but you've a telescope aimed at the sleeping stars
while a sinkhole opens up under your feet.

I'll be the first to admit that I'm a lout. It doesn't
help me much, I'll take the crumbs. And yet
when there's a halo being polished day in day out,
a swarm of feelings will awake and slither all around.
We'll never own a house and never travel, never move.
I'll never see my continent again.
I'll never write my book, or make a film,
make music worth two bits,
and most of those ambitions, well, they're over anyway.
Now what about you?
What about kids? Unless you
take a break from polishing the halo,
while life is shooting past us like an arrow
can you rely on what the future brings just based
on Mr Zen?
Perhaps on my end, I'll have time for bathroom breaks
when I'm a civil servant once again.

You are not Trouble, which for rhyming would mean wife,
I think you'd know I wouldn't write one bit of verse
if I wasn't so in love.
The matter's plain so try to see my point,
It's hard for me to swallow half a life.

As I drifted off into another vodka haze, I decided to lie down
and close my eyes but sleep did not come. All I kept seeing were
visions of the woman in the restaurant. Some nights I stayed too
long on the boardwalk, watching ships in the distance, mostly
freighters coming in from god knows where and going god knows
where in turn.

Where is Europe now, I wondered again... Whither Europe?
Wither Europe? Across the black of the ocean... Everything
has changed. Random thoughts of regret dashed into my mind

and collided in a jumble. Great love was gone, but the idea of some little loves remained. Little loves imply futility or doom, with just a little burst of joy somewhere in between.

I recalled how the bleak yellow light of the New Yorker Hotel bounced against my yellow beer I was drinking waiting for my Greyhound, about to return to the grey Central Avenue of Albany and all Central Avenues across the country and how I realized that something was wrong and that something had to change. "I will go to Macchu Picchu" with you I told the "Cortland slut." LaBonne. Now pushing fifty, I again had nowhere to drive to or fly to...

Life is gruesomely, pitifully short, and at no time in one's life is this so apparent as when you hit the halfway or two thirds mark. After many a summer dies the swan... the question is, how many summers?

Brandy appeared in a dream, coming over in nothing but an apron, and I was wearing nothing but a t-shirt, and when I realized that my wife would be coming over any minute, I ran to the bedroom to grab some underwear but all my shorts and socks were in the wash and then I woke up. It is fine that actual human generations disappear, but cultural generations are another thing. Now that the Cold War is over there is an actual generation of Russians in New York who are gone. Who were these people in Brighton Beach now? Who will be the next? Nothing lasts forever, but how quickly things disappear.

My morning swims became rarer and rarer until they ceased altogether. My nightly routine was a series of heavy dreams and my morning ritual consisted in nothing but "gentle" boozing until the time came that I would see the mystery woman again—same time, same place—though I still lacked the courage to approach her. What would I do? What would I say? I was tormented by thoughts of her each waking hour.

Enough was enough. I was alone, my family on the other end of the continent and here was this mystery woman, and being in a wheelchair she was harmless—that is, there was no chance I thought, no chance for a romantic encounter, and I could no longer take it. The next day, at the usual time, I tripled the vodka and finally with enough Dutch courage decided to go up to her. I walked over to her table like a man walking to the gallows or the firing squad. She was working on her kebab but when I was almost next to her and was about to speak, her eyes darted up with a sniper's precision to meet mine in the sights of her pupils and simply said "Betty. My name is Betty. What took you so long?"

My first thought was "Thank God she isn't Russian." A Yank. If she had been Russian, there would have been no chance of romance between us. It was a relief. Sex with Slavic women always seemed oedipal to me. I composed myself as much as possible and after swallowing air for thirty seconds in order not to stammer, I blurted, "I didn't know what to say."

"Well, now you've said it. The ice is broken." She forked the final piece of lamb into her mouth. The last chunk turned out gristly and after an attempt to chew she gave up and spat the meat into her napkin.

"Excuse me," she said with no embarrassment. "So… Did you want to talk to me because of how I look or did you want to ask me about my legs?" she said. "Because I won't talk to you about them. I've had too many people do so and they always had something else in mind. I'm a person. I wasn't invented by Hans Christian fucking Anderson. So what is it?"

I had no idea what to say. "I think you are beautiful." It was a cretinous thing to say. So I quickly followed up with "I wanted to ask if you're Russian, and…" (As if that was a valid pickup line. Perhaps it could have been, but she beat me to it.)

"No. I'm not Russian. Are you?"

I told her "Sort of. I'm Tatar."

"What's that?" she asked and smirked. "Like the steak? Come, do you want to go for a walk? Let me pay for this. I want to smoke.

If you want we can get a coffee."

Two things immediately took me aback. The first—that she said "go for a walk," but I quickly realized that people confined to wheelchairs still call moving about "walking." I suppose the reason it struck me is because I wanted her to walk. The second was how she immediately asked me to go for a smoke and a coffee. It seemed kind of brazen, even un-ladylike. What could I do? Of course I said yes, and within minutes we were heading toward the sordid boardwalk of Brighton Beach, where old Odessa Jews were "pensioneering" and walking up and down to look at the orange and purple twilight in the twilight of their own years.

We lit cigarettes and though she struggled to push herself and smoke at the same time she did not allow me to help. I was terrified, but she was a natural when it came to small talk. In just a few short minutes I was completely at ease. We made chit chat as if we were neighbors at the very least, if not friends…

When we reached the top of the ramp she had to stop to catch her breath, but soon she bit into the filter of the cigarette with her teeth and said "So, seriously. Tell me, what is this Tatar?"

TARTARY

My father would often say, rather pompously, "I had a rich life. A very rich life. I wish that everyone could have just a small fragment of the life I had." However, this was quite true. The things he lived through, how fate threw him around, how he avoided death so many times, are enough to fill a book or two. Of course, there were certain things that he would never talk about.

And so I started telling her about my old man. I did not tell her everything, but I tried to give her snippets and a type of condensed chronology. How he regaled me with his "tales of bygone times." But the full story, holes and all, was much more intricate...

It's the things that can't be seen that are the most frightening. And that is how people lived in the USSR especially during Stalin—with one eye closed and the other a slit which only allowed a little bit of light and a little bit of horror to enter. For the gas vans were disguised as bread trucks, and when you woke up and your neighbor was gone you went about your daily life as if nothing happened. For those who survived, if they did, would not talk about the horrors they lived through. Life had become happier, life had become better, comrades.

We in the twenty-first century have become inured to horror in our own way. But the monstrosity of the twentieth century, the orgy of violence and mutual destruction, was handled in a similar fashion. And just like the death of millions is a statistic and the death of one is a tragedy, so we continue to select, consciously or not, what will affect us and what will end up as background noise. And yet whatever we choose not to look at will still be lurking in the shadows, no matter how we wish to sweep away with our eyelashes all the demonology of the world. Though my father liked to talk a lot about his life, he too, like everyone else, knew and acted in accordance with the fact that some things should never be spoken of. Perhaps that is what kept preventing him from writing down his life story despite how many times I nudged him and pleaded with him to put it down on paper or at least audio or video. My mother too kept many things hidden, and would only give hints about certain other events or people, like mysterious Aunt Maria and the black sheep cousin Julek. I knew they existed once and that something truly terrible happened to them but I was afraid to find out and so I never asked.

My dad was born in a town called Zlatoust. The first time I "saw" Zlatoust was in an image by the early photographer Prokudin-Gorskii, who was commissioned by the Tsar to document the Russian Empire; in retrospect in its twilight. A railroad town in the Ural Mountains, it was probably as depressed and depressing back in 1910 as it is now and as much a portrait of a lost world as the world we lose each year on our journey to a brave new one.

On my first Christmas in America
I saw through the vitrines
and how innocuous it seemed even while stepping
over homeless dregs so rank with filth
and bestial, hiding in a snowbank
poised to rape, all of the sights
formed a reality more real against the whirligigs of
Altman's sweet displays.
This back in nineteen hundred seventy-seven.

Is this Dickensian toss a better bet?
Back in Moscow you would have had

way more respect if you had wept.
Where there was talk of clementines
strung on strings around the tree
the angels would come down and see
and sing, and people wept for times most
only knew from novels of times past.
These were forbidden terms, of course, and with
informers everywhere
my parents whispered things into my ear which
in retrospect sound like Eastern Europe's
Altman's window dressings
And who blessed wonder
on a dead fir tree

Then there's The Nutcracker,
the final coda with some choral singing
feels like the swan song of a family
in celebration: chestnuts, oranges
and healthy fires burning in the hearth
while right below their windows
a crowd is sharpening their knives.

Zlatoust means "golden mouth," why the name I have no idea.
There was no glorious Golden Horn on the Bosphorus in this
backwater. My father did not remember anything of his childhood
there. The civil war had just ended when he was born, and the
family relocated to Ufa, 300 kilometers west, in the Republic of
Bashkiria. They lived outside of town in a settlement called "Gypsy
Meadow," and I recall him saying they were the only Tatar people
there, and that their neighbors were Gypsies. Though the family
had very little, his mother would sometimes bring the neighbors
food when they had nothing to eat.

There were six of them: my father, his parents, and his three sisters—Fatima, Fatiha and Fagilya. They owned a horse which kept them in fermented mare's milk, which my father almost overdosed on—kumiss, as it is called, made him drunk and dizzy. I picture those years in monochrome. White snow and black soot from the chimney, from the factory smokestacks, the metallurgical works. A few fleeting moments did stay with him—running away from the Mullah when he was about to be circumcised and running through the village pantless... Winter ice floes on the White River, skiing on homemade skis, boots stuffed with newspaper for insulation, the horse, the prayer... until tragedy struck.

He did not tell me much about his father—perhaps he didn't remember or perhaps there were things he didn't wish to recall. All I know is that he was an "invalid"—perhaps he had been in the Civil War and that was what forced them to flee Zlatoust, but I don't know whether he was on the side of the Reds or the Whites. His mother was a cleaning lady, a charwoman. How they fed their kids I haven't a clue. Grandfather also drank—a lot—and one drunken night in the heat of an argument with my grandmother he stuck a knife in her and she bled to death.

I assume that my grandfather was jailed, for the family was broken up and my dad and his three sisters were all sent to different orphanages. Why they were separated, I don't know. The sisters ended up in Uzbekistan, Central Asia, the desert of dust and the valleys of melons and figs. What happened to my father at the orphanage I do not know—he seemed not to have remembered it well—or did not say much about it. But one day, all changed again, this time for the better.

"If it wasn't for them, I would have ended up a factory worker or a train conductor..." He would remind himself of that fortuitous event when a group of talent scouts came into town looking to diversify the ethnic makeup of the Kirov Theater—an early experiment with "diversity" and "political correctness." And so he was saved from his fate, snatched from the land of kumis and honey and poverty and taken to a real city. It was there, in Leningrad, that my father's world was formed, where one would sleep with one eye open, that just as much as how the Tsar's children played ball while outside a crowd was forming, sharpening their knives, that there is another layer to life, not always seen except through a periodic peek through the curtain, or through the Veil of Maya.

"We lived as in a dream, a fairy tale. We knew there were terrifying things all around us, but in the theatre, we were able to shut the doors to our minds..."

How I wish I could have written an entire book about him—but all he left were fragments, which I suppose is better than nothing at all, and more than most people get.

One would think that with ballet being the last of the oral traditions, he would have wanted to leave something more substantial behind but I see, albeit vaguely, that being firmly ensconced in the theatre, the process of creation and destruction, the fleeting nature of performance, a masochistic and ultimately perhaps unsatisfying one, or at least ephemeral—for when the performance run is over, it is over, and one has to begin again—that in spite, or perhaps because of that cycle it came naturally to him to let it disappear, to drown in the lake of time.

Tatars, Tartary, Tatarstan... all bring to the Russian and European mind a certain Orientalism. The reality was much more banal before it turned from banal to wicked to a perverse orgy of self-destruction spanning the entire Eurasian continent and beyond. But everyone knows that history, at least the war, is still remembered. Not so much the details, or what went on behind Stalin's curtain. Somehow, some of the arts were spared obliteration. And so my dad was sent to St. Petersburg, then Leningrad, to study at the State Choreographic Institute, now named the Vaganova Academy.

Thus began the fairy tale, which would be interrupted by war soon enough. Like all fairy tales there was privation and misery offset by magic and enchantment. The theater survived, sometimes bowdlerized, sometimes intact, but outside the theater doors black wings enveloped the cities, the countryside, the virgin lands... no speck of ground was spared. And just as in pre-revolutionary times, there were those outside sharpening their knives, except now those were the ones in power. Petersburg itself is a place out of time and out of space, a warts-and-all fairyland both enchanting and sinister. The magic of those early days of my father's life was broken when the war began. Being kids, my father and many of his classmates treated the war like a game at first, not yet recognizing the gravity of what was happening.

"Where didn't my life throw me around?" he used to say, and it was true. And how I envied him and continued to when I realized how little my own life threw me around—table tennis compared to the Paris Open.

Memories bounce around as well, no one tells their story in a linear fashion, and so those years which he told me about so many times are a kaleidoscope, a mosaic. When the Germans began bombing, he and his schoolmates were sent up to the rooftop to throw off unexploded shells.

Soon enough he lucked out again. As a student in performing arts school, he was one of the lucky ones who were evacuated from the city before the siege. Then it was back to Ufa, then somehow to Tashkent, Uzbekistan. Persimmons and melons of Central Asia where his sisters, my aunts, got lost in the desert... Siberia, then Outer Mongolia, where a bottle of vodka saved his life. Then back to Leningrad when the war ended. The city was awash with vodka but there was still nothing to eat. Then to Georgia, then Moscow. Artistic success, tours abroad, and then after retirement I was conceived and born. All this before we settled in the New World.

I had read somewhere that a true biography needs to be full of holes and mysteries. In my father's case it was certainly more than true. Always on the verge of accomplishing something, he would invariably pull back, sometimes even sabotage himself. Perhaps some of it was a type of stage fright, perhaps some of it fear of failure. What was it that he was holding back and why did he rein himself in?

One of his unrealized dreams was to stage a ballet to Mussorgsky's Pictures at an Exhibition. A brilliant idea that no one had done and which he could easily have pulled off but never did. There was always something, some excuse for not going forward. In class, he would often quote the early choreographer Jean-Georges Noverre that ballet is "many pictures moving." And I too was obsessed with moving pictures—motion pictures—until I had to bury that dream under the mantle of idiocy and mediocrity which had befallen that medium. There was no going back to cinema ever being an art form again. But life—well, life is more like flash frames, not moving pictures. There are always holes and broken lengths of film strip, and censors both outside and within.

Clive James said that "Arrogance is the natural condition of a mind in exile." I tended to follow his example. Though for a long time I identified as American and found myself enthralled, fascinated by this country, at last the cup ran dry and at the time of writing this, and for quite a few years before, I had lost practically all interest in my adopted (not by my choice) land. Dropping the arrogance, the new world was for us a disappointment.

My father seemed to be open but I knew that he too, like everyone, had memories that no one wanted to know. While he became more open with me as I got older, it was on holidays that I would notice more and more that he was tortured by something he couldn't reveal. It was as if when he had time away from work and distraction, away from creative composition (he was always composing ballets in his mind and always thinking about music), he was forced to reflect and the reflection made him sink into a hole of what I imagined were dark thoughts. Whether on a ski trip through New England (he loved Vermont and upstate New York and the birch trees that so reminded him of Russia), driving through the fog after sundown and seeing the church steeples white against the black but starry night, or on some sunny Caribbean isle, waist deep in the bathwater of the sea, his gaze was always turned elsewhere and his mind was not in the present. Even on the brightest and happiest of days he would talk about Stalin. Palm trees and bathwater temperature ocean did little to ease his obsession with past horrors.

When my dad would drop me off in rancid New York after our summer holiday, he would go around the block in his car to make sure I was entering the building. I would wait for him, though, and he would beep a few times and I would go inside and he would drive away... And I felt so alone and would weep not just because I missed him immediately but because I sensed his loneliness too and I would weep for how alone he was, from childhood on. Before I was able to even formulate such a thought, I wept from the nebulous emotion, but now I see it was the emotion of how truly alone we all are at the end. And my dad was probably the same age I am now during those episodes of abandonment. How I wished to understand... Now that I am the same age there is nothing to understand, nothing at all. We are all dreadfully alone.

"On a toute mélange." The green forests and meadows of Tartary, the blinding light of the Uzbek desert, the tugboat captain drunk on the way to Kronstadt when the war ended. The stories were endless, fascinating, and yet my dad adamantly refused to write them down so all I have are snippets and flashes. Everyone in that country had something to hide, something to ignore, something to sweep under the rug.

My mother seemed to have even more things to hide than

my father. Or maybe I just never asked. Or maybe it wasn't that interesting, but she never regaled me with adventures the way my father did. Of course, she was much younger than him. But there were various unsolved mysteries that would pop up, certain names: Julek (don't know if he was a cousin or an uncle, probably a suicide), Maria (an aunt, I believe; an alcoholic who met some type of gruesome fate that no one discussed). A few others. And that is why I vaguely understood Betty when she would start saying, "There are certain things one should never talk about, Lucky…"

But this was America. What kind of terrible secret could she be hiding, I wondered? What was it that she didn't want to talk about, especially when I wasn't even prying. My dad's life and death were still very much on my mind, and I missed him tremendously. But along with the grief there was frustration and a cautionary tale, for he never finished the book he was planning to write, a book about his experiences which were infinitely richer than mine, yet here I was trying to finish something that didn't even have anything to do with my life—or so I thought at that moment.

There were too many random reminiscences of his that would pop up in my brain. Too many to list, and as my brain fades and the memories fade so do the details and the stories themselves. "In Tbilisi, when the rains came down and flooded the hilly streets, we used to roll up our pants, take off our shoes and walk wherever we were heading—to work, to see girlfriends, to the theater, to lunch, to the pub. Sometimes, at the invite of a Georgian patriarch, we would rise at dawn, travel up into the mountains until the road was no longer asphalted, switch to donkeys, and then take the mountain track up to the top. There we'd watch the men slaughter the lambs and kids and toast with grape brandy."

To me it sounded surreal, an unimaginable orientalism and flight of fancy. I believed every word, of course—there was no reason for my father to lie. In these days when every Trustafarian has been to the most exotic of places and those places aren't all that exotic anymore, my wonder will sound exaggerated, but in the 1970s and 80s it wasn't. Apart from Georgia, Senior also spoke fondly of the Balkans, mostly Bulgaria, where he danced the Hora with dictator Zhivkov at the Russian embassy, where again he was taken as a tourist at the crack of dawn to visit a monastery of hermits, who for some reason escaped state atheist persecution.

Then there was the time that vodka saved my dad's life. Sure, alcohol had "saved my life" many times when I drowned my sorrows over a girl, or my parents' madness, or any number of things that I simply could not handle. But my father's vodka story was different. Somewhere in the steppes when life was throwing him around as a youth, before he even drank much, if at all, someone gave him a small vial of vodka, perhaps the equivalent of a double shot, and told him to keep it safe as it might save his life. And soon enough, somewhere in the steppes, the train he was on (where was he going?) was commandeered by the army, just like in Dr Zhivago minus the dead baby (not to say that there were no dead babies after that night). My father ran as the train pulled away and managed to jump and hold onto a metal rail just outside the door between cars. Soon his fingers started to freeze so he alternated hands, holding on as the snow whipped up off the tracks. He started banging, unable to bear it anymore, but nothing could be heard over the sound of the tracks. Finally the train slowed down and a bearded mug swung open the door: "Whadaya want?" The kid now almost frozen doesn't say anything but reaches into his shirt and produces the little flacon of vodka and shows it to the mug, as in "Here, take!" The mug pushed the boy inside and my dad cheated death yet again.

"I spent half my life in a prison and the rest in New Africa, he would say in jest. He did not say it to be racist—by Africa he meant an utter lack of culture, lack of civilization. For older European men of his generation, before everything was deemed to be at most "different" but never better or worse, the New World, compared to his experience with art and culture, was indeed as primitive as Africa. And while I tried to convince him about the fecundity of American culture especially in the twentieth century, in many ways he was correct. Ah, the brave New World—where did Huxley get the name for his book? I forget. A world so promising and so treacherous, a world I made a highly uncomfortable peace with, here on the edge of the continent. The point is that he didn't leave behind the one thing he wanted to leave behind—a book. So after he died, his whole world ceased to exist. I was terrified of that happening to me.

I became so wrapped up in telling his story to Betty that I not only lost track of time but didn't ask Betty anything about herself. Maybe her paralysis made me fearful and put me into a nervous ramble, but I didn't ask for even any basic details from this mysterious stranger. Or perhaps I was also nervous because in the back of my mind was Wendy Novak, the Saddest Girl in the World, with whom I dined at Primorski thirty years ago and who took my virginity that night on Ocean Parkway at my uncle's apartment.

"That is a fascinating story, Lucky," she said when I was finished. I had lost all track of time and had no idea how long I had talked for. "But I have to get going. If you want, you can walk me to the bus."

"The bus!" I thought with the marzipan sympathy of the downtrodden and the humiliated. How does this "poor creature"—yes, I even said the phrase "poor creature" in my mind, in recollection of a bad Victorian translation of Dostoyevsky that probably was "Bednyazhka" in Russian, which would sound better as a neologism akin to "an unfortunate" or something—make love? I would have to be exceptionally sensitive to even broaching the topic were it ever even to come to that... And again I wondered if she was incontinent and whether that would be something I could deal with, again were it even in the stars that we would ever end up naked in the same bed together. A friend of mine had an easier time. He dated a woman with an amputated leg who wore a prosthesis and when it was time for coitus she asked him point blank: "Do you want the leg on or off?" He shuddered and that was the end of their attempt at faire l'amour.

But pressingly I had to decide and I told Betty "No, no bus. We'll get a cab." She thanked me and for some unexplained reason, in light of my hatred of NYC cab drivers, the taxi man was nice enough and was able to help her into the cab and folded her chair and put it in the trunk in two minutes flat.

The cab ride took less than ten minutes, and at one point she took my hand and squeezed it—hard. As if we had known each other forever. I hoped that she felt the same way I did. And then it was time to part. The cabbie let her out and put her in her chair.

"How can I see you again?" I stammered. The evening was magical—truly magical, as if invented by a sorcerer, as if she was a frog princess or a sleeping beauty who would magically walk again once I kissed her. The kiss was a peck on the cheek and she said, "Meet me tomorrow at the restaurant." Then she wheeled herself away. And as the cab door closed the sweat on my back turned to ice, for it looked like the same building where I lost my virginity to Wendy.

It felt like the chair, her chariot, had driven over my brain. For whatever reason, I found it infinitely more tragic for a woman to be condemned to such a fate than a man. I wrote a poem once about a beautiful girl I saw who was as disabled as Betty. At the Velaslavasay Panorama in Los Angeles.

You spoke in dreadful monotone yet with enthusiasm,
    describing marvels not just in the collection but outside too,

what lies and stands on the surrounding streets,
remnant of time smoggy LA preserves by university campus.
And then I asked about the rabbits
who live as pets in the museum garden. You answered
that they moved too quickly to see up close
now that you lived in a wheelchair—
something I hadn't noticed till you said those words.

I'm married. My pet name for my wife is Bunny.
Hence irony. I'm sad that since the rabbit
dwelling changed outside and up the steps,
you can't often see the big bunny and his wife who live
out in the garden. I didn't even realize
that you were partly paralyzed.

I know that whether or not someone lifts you and
carries you up the spiral staircase that you can
still see lagomorphs and Arctic panoramas,
and human miniatures and human docudramas
and monotone and boring intonation cast aside,
I know you stand up straight as any human if not more.
I mean no pity, please don't get me wrong.
Although, to be honest, I'd work on monotone.
Actually, scratch that: I find it charming.

You remind me of a friend, one who also travels
on wheels and stands on phantom heels and yells out
to the heavens. I picture him happy, Sisyphean,
though angrier than you, and that's a major difference.

I saw in you a beauty, in and out, and strength hard to explain.
I do not wish for you to think I write with pity, quite opposite

I saw affinity, for I know weirdness
of both fate and life begins with birth.
Such is the price of living on this earth.

I remembered my wife and child and decided not to think about them tonight. After Betty left I went to a ridiculous Russian supermarket where all the shop girls were dressed in purple shirts with the Chanel logo silkscreened over the tits, bought two bottles of cheap wine and hailed a taxi home.

Overjoyed by the promise of another tryst, I did not even finish the first glass. Usually, so excited, I would not have been able to sleep, but that night I crashed on the bed and slept like a baby.

In the morning I awoke with the enthusiasm for a woman that one only has when one is young, and again I was distracted from my "work." Heart aflutter, I started the day with cold white wine. I skipped the beach, and spent the day doing what I do best—sitting. Until it was time to leave. I made sure I arrived early, but when I opened the door to Primorski she was already there.

"Hello."

"Hello."

Smiles. What did we talk about on that next rendezvous? It's hard for me to remember. I was mesmerized by her dark hair and bright blue eyes, a contrast I had never truly seen before, or so it felt.

She hadn't asked much about me the day before, nor was she particularly curious this second evening, but after some small talk she finally asked, "What do you do?"

It was hard to mouth this one but I sheepishly and disingenuously said "I'm a writer."

"I wish I could be a writer. I always wanted to write," she said. "But I think I prefer to leave the writing to someone else."

"Anyone can be a writer," I said. "Well, maybe not anyone—

you need a certain amount of skill, but everyone has a story, don't you think?"

"Oh, everyone has a story alright. More than one. I've got plenty, enough for a novel for sure, maybe even a movie or two."

Just as I was about to start talking bollocks, perhaps augmenting my current lot in life as essentially a middle-aged bum, she interrupted me.

"Oh, did you know—the circus is in town! And this is the last year that they walk the elephants through the midtown tunnel! Maybe we can go. I think it's tonight. I don't know how hard it would be for me because... because of my chair. Anyway, it starts much later. Go on."

I found something to grab onto to work the conversation.

"My mom was in the circus. Well, she studied in circus school. There is such a thing in Russia. And my grandmother, she basically ran away with the circus like the old cliché goes."

Her eyes lit up.

"Now that's something I want to hear! Tell me more, please. It sounds fascinating."

I ordered vodka and zakuski and started to tell her about my grandmother and my mother and their life journeys but did not go much into detail. In turn, I learned that she was from upstate New York, that she lived in California for a while, and that she had only recently moved to Brooklyn when her aunt died and left her the apartment in her will.

What did she look like? Like everyone and no one. A woman with, if not a million, then at least a dozen faces. She reminded me of someone different each time she turned her head slightly. It was hard to guess her height for she was sitting down, and always would be, but I guessed she was medium to tall. Her brown hair fell just below her shoulders and her forehead was capped by choppy bangs. I do not pay much attention to people's eyes but I noticed that hers were dark, very dark. Though it was early summer, and we were one block away from the beach, her style of dress was conservative, almost Presbyterian—a smart brown skirt suit which glared in contrast to the fake Versace blouses and Adidas track suits donned by the rest of the clientele, the unofficial national costumes of much of Eastern Europe.

It was also impossible to tell her age. With each motion she would alternate between twenty and forty or even fifty. Her skin exhibited a mild pallor, though it was not unhealthy—more like the pallor of a woman consumed by grief, dressed in her best sober clothes at a funeral. Even her shoes, which in her state were reduced to solely a fashionable bangle, were perfectly chosen to match the rest of her dress. In a way, she was morbidly perfect, especially with the tragic wheels.

She ate neutrally, dispassionately, and would always seem engrossed in some thought or another, never in her surroundings. How I liked to visualize a thought balloon over her head, a way to peer into her mind; yet she remained opaque. One could that say she was "pretty," but what is pretty? As I wrote in my book about Jesus, Pilate questions the bumbling Yeshua Bar-Yosef "What is good? Does God like it because it is good? Or is it good because God likes it?" In the avian world and most of the mammalian, the males do the peacock dance, the lion's mane, the strut of the cock and the pageantry of the cockscomb. Yet here, among us hairless primates, the females run the show and strut to attract the most disgusting of men, for a myriad of reasons. Does the Slavic peasant girl Olga, dolled up in rouge, her hair braided, or Svetlana in her Kokoshnik want to look pretty? Yes. But for who? God? God seems to prefer nun's habits and burqas and hijabs.

No. Olga or Svetlana is looking pretty in order to get fucked by Ivan, or Mykola or Drazenko. Pretty is only pretty among innocent children, admiring patterns and colors. One morning, when

I was helping my young daughter get dressed, she liked the outfit I picked out and said "Papa, it's so pretty." That is God's "pretty," the pretty of the truly innocent, for those who are not yet familiar with the other side. The pretty of the swan whose bright white feathers never touch the muck and mud of the pond but float above the dirty bottom in their bright white feathers.

The other pretty, for those who have reached sexual maturity, is for erotic attraction. The porno hooker takes as much time and effort on her makeup as the Hollywood actress and for both the idea is for you to imagine ripping her clothes off and smudging her mascara all over her eyelids in a fit of lust. Pretty for adults is not the same as pretty for kids.

So I will let you decide how pretty Betty really was and imagine what she looked like, other than the fact that she was a brunette, and that there was something harsh about her. Not angular features, no intimidating nose, no particularly off-putting lesbian chin. It was in her eyes, a darting, piercing look which given her circumstances was understandable. She was, no doubt, attractive, but I had to wonder about the word "pretty."

There is only one woman in the world, she just has different faces. Was it Kazantzakis' Devil who said that? It doesn't matter. It was a brilliant thing to say.

So many fantasies would arise, mostly in the early hours of the morning. Blanket above my head, I would wait for either another chance at sleep or a hardon to raise its ugly head—most often neither would happen and I would toss and turn until I realized that I would neither be able to go back to sleep nor to return to the world of fantasy. In this liminal state I would hear everything that was going on outside—my wife getting dressed, slamming drawers and doors, my daughter screaming—but I would force myself to keep my eyes shut and dream, and the dreams sometime did come for a few minutes at least. Sometimes they were sex dreams but most of the time I was simply holding a woman around her waist, walking somewhere with her, on a first or second date.

SUMMER NIGHTS

So it began. It felt so fresh, so warm and vernal, and I felt so young that I began to wonder if I had ever actually been in love before, or whether I had only imagined it and pretended, or whether anyone ever loved me either. But now I could sense that Betty cared for me somehow. Betty, my crooked Venus, popped out of her clamshell among the sea foam, wheels and all. I imagined that she loved me indeed.

And yet during that invincible summer I kept returning to my endless falls, the warm zephyrs interrupted by colder autumnal winds. Many nights and hungover mornings I would wrap my legs around a pillow and squeeze as hard as I could, trying to imagine that I had wrapped myself around Betty's misshapen body. I would imagine a scene in which she awoke, morning breath and sand in her eyes, and I pushed apart her useless legs and stuck my head between her thighs and my tongue in her fur and I would make her feel the little pleasure that God, despite his sadism, had granted us.

As the summer went on and thoughts of Betty filled more and more of my time, I spoke to Charlotte less and less often. She didn't ask and I didn't tell, and vice versa. Soon enough it became a routine. She and I both assumed that I would be coming home eventually, perhaps sooner than later. What was happening during our hiatus was never discussed, it was an unspoken arrangement. The one thing which did sting my heart periodically was my daughter. What was I doing here, trying to write a book—was that something I was doing with the intention of "leaving her something?" In a perverse way it was, but it was precisely that—perverse. I knew that

I wasn't going to leave her a house, or an inheritance, or anything material whatsoever. I could leave her my life story, which wasn't particularly interesting, or I could leave her a filthy book that I had written. In either case it was better than leaving her with nothing. When it became clear that my life orbited around regret, what made the realization worse was knowing how commonplace it made me. Too many men dance with regret throughout their entire adulthood and this was certainly my case. As the summer progressed and all I did was just occasionally touch Betty's arm or hand, I started to feel dirty. Filthy. At first I thought it was just guilt for being unfaithful—at least emotionally—to my wife, but there was also a creeping sensation that something was foul, physically unpleasant, but I could not put my finger on it. I had no problems with corpses. I had buried my parents—my mother embalmed, my dad au naturel but after a proper Muslim wash. My mother looked like a grotesque made-up doll in the open casket; my father looked like he was just sleeping. I had never experienced the true olfactory assaults of putrefaction and death, but there was something grimly nauseating about Betty. Her hands weren't clammy, her skin and visage were pale but not moribund; it was a free-floating sense of something that is finished, over and done with.

Betty and I liked to pensioneer along the seafront as much as the Brightoners. I used the word in jest, but in fact we were close to being there, Betty and I, me with my fear of ageing and her, an invalid. For a long time everything was fine, I cherished every moment I had with her and did not ask questions. It would have been suicidal to ask questions at the time that I was enraptured. One time, she even stopped my train of thought as if she knew what was on my mind and said, without looking at me, "Don't ask me too many questions, Lucky. The answers will come. They will, eventually. Let's just enjoy our time together for now…" and so we'd promenade down by the seaside.

The dates were frustrating when she didn't want to talk. And that was often, and often enough that she would seem like a Coppélia or a RealDoll and no matter how I tried to engage, her eyes remained opaque and focused on the distance, always looking toward the horizon, the roof of the sky, yearning for another, different life. I would interrupt her stare and ask, "Are you okay?" and she would get sore and raise her voice and say "Yes, I'm okay, why do you keep asking me that? I'm just thinking..."

"A fox has seventy-seven thoughts," my mother used to say without explaining what she meant. I still don't.

I would hold Betty's hand but her pupils were focused on the darkening sea and the twilight when the stars would start to twinkle, and if I tried to talk she would pull my hand away and grip the arms of her chariot and then gently, I would try to take her hand in mine again and she would let me hold it and I knew not to press my luck further. As a result, many dates were spent in quiet confusion and frustrating bliss, and as I became gradually accustomed to this eccentric state of affairs I began to accept it, though the loneliness and heartache persisted.

I grew up in the wrong time, ill-equipped to deal with the rapid transformations taking place in the world around me. Even if I had been blessed with talent, it's hard to say whether it would have done me any good. It's enough to be good at one thing and I didn't have one thing. My father was very, very good at two things, actually: his character dance—which will soon be forgotten, not just his but the art form itself—and teaching. Perhaps he did not want to rock the boat by adding a third or a fourth, like actually finishing something, and that was part of his fear of failure. For me, fear of failure became a self-fulfilling prophecy as I realized I was not good at even one thing.

As we walked and talked and I told Betty about my dad, I couldn't help thinking that I was approaching the age my dad was when

I first became conscious of his existence—sometime in his fifties, as my infant mind matured and was starting to form memories. And though by that age my dad was full of energy and hopes and plans, he mostly prided himself on his past, something he knew he would not be able to recreate or supersede. I, on the other hand, had no past to equal his life story even remotely. This was a source of deep despair, it conflicted with my pride about his extremely interesting life and my envy that he managed to live through such hard and crazy times and had a story (even if he refused to write it down). It was on one of these walks with Betty, talking about the old man and reciting his story by rote, that I paused and blurted out:

"Soon I will be the same age as my dad was, when I first remember him from."

"Age is nothing" she smiled. "You never asked me my age, by the way."

I had tried guessing her age. I felt she was younger than me, for sure, but how much younger was hard to tell. Her raven hair might have been dyed but it was hard to tell. She had no wrinkles, he skin was perfect. There were no signs of ageing except sometimes in her attitude, which was a result of her accident, of course—the accident which she had not yet told me about. Given how much time we spent together it seemed absurd that I hadn't yet asked her about the accident, never mind her age. Though I hesitated at first and thought of a way to deflect the question, I threw caution to the wind and asked, making sure to do it half-jokingly.

"Okay. How old are you, anyway?"

She smiled at first and then her smile turned into a grin that I am yet to decipher.

"A girl never tells her age, And never tells her thoughts!" And then she pulled me by my shirt down closer and bent my head down to her mouth and whispered, "I'm immortal!" and laughing maniacally pushed me away and grabbed the wheels of her chair in each hand and rolled away furiously, pushing herself down the street with amazing strength. She wanted me to catch her, of course, to play tag; on paper she was no match for my speed, and yet I had a hard time catching up to her, for it felt as if she was flying, going so fast, as if trying to reach a velocity from which she would ascend from the dirty pavement and up into the purple sky. It took me some time to catch up and the effort left me winded. She spun the wheelchair around and, out of breath and wheezing, laughed like a child.

We spent our summer nights in timid romance and innocence, as if we were an underage couple in the DDR holding hands in the Pinguin Milchbar. But in truth it was more like the poet Khodasevich, describing the mutilé de guerre accompanying his lady to the cinema. My mom was very fond of that poem, as she was fond of everything grotesque, everything both brutal and pathetic; it enthralled her and repelled her at the same time. But here, who was the mutilated and who was intact? What was she mutilated from, not just physically? I was enchanted by her but deep down I was also vexed. Not only because my book was not being written but also because there remained so much I did not know about her. I did most of the talking. She offered only occasional snippets about her past. I didn't wish to push it, but I was grinding my teeth waiting for the reveal. She said something about sunflowers, their being her mom's favorite. At "sunflowers" I lost her and zoned out, recalling a line from that poem about Wendy Novak from Staten Island.

> And when my mother dies, I will plant
> sunflowers on her grave, they
> turn their heads towards the sun...

"I had a difficult relationship with my mother," she admitted. I had missed everything else she'd said for the last five minutes.

"How about you? Is your mom around?"

"No," I told her. "She's been gone a few years now."

"What was she like?"

I hesitated.

"Do you not want to talk about it?"

"No, I can," I told her.

"Tell me about her. You only told me a little."

"Why?"

"I'm just wondering," she smiled. And so I began to speak about my other parent.

MUSCOVY

It is tempting to tell my mom's story back to front. That horrid end in June, in the sweat of Manhattan, the yellow light breaking through the windows to illuminate decay, the natural end of things. "You making haste on decay: not blameworthy." Perhaps. It ended in a hospital room, something she always wanted to avoid—and not blameworthy for that.

The first time my wife left me alone with our daughter for ten days to go to New York, our child, then three years of age or so, would wake up every morning and ask, "Mama's coming tomorrow? Okay?" to which I would reply "Yes, of course," and my daughter would yell out a triumphant "OKAY!"

Sometimes this catechism went on for hours.

"Mama's coming tomorrow? Okay?"

"Yes."

"OKAY!"

"Mama's coming tomorrow? Okay?"

"Yes. All right."

"ALL RIGHT!"

On the one hand, it was a relief that my girl at least postponed the issue of Mama's return till tomorrow, instead of asking if she was coming back today. But it also brought back memories of my grandmother Antonina—Tonya for short—who outlived my mom and who, in her demented state, probably asked the same question in her nineties. Why doesn't her daughter visit anymore? Why doesn't she write? It made my heart contract. She never did know why her daughter stopped visiting her. Perhaps it was that vain hope that helped her live to almost one hundred, nourished by the faint possibility of seeing her only child once more.

Before my mother's descent into madness, or rather on the cusp of her swan dive into self-destruction, she showed me a letter she wrote to her mother, my grandmother, from summer camp. It ended with "Dear Mummy, I really miss you and if you don't come and get me soon, then I will most definitely throw myself in the pond and drown myself." Suicide ideation ran in the family. I wasn't sure I was ready yet to tell Betty everything about my mom.

"My mom was an interesting person," I said. "Very interesting. I wish I knew more about the details of her life. So many things were hidden and so many things were not discussed. This was a Soviet mentality, of course. People had to keep certain things secret."

"I understand," Betty replied. "There are certain things that no one should ever talk about. Do you want to talk about something else?"

There was a pause in the conversation.

"Whatever your pain, Lucky," she added, "I have a feeling that her life was very interesting. We only have one life and everyone should have a story."

That phrase, "everyone should have a story," frightened me. It reminded me of something that I had written in my screenplay The Girl from Below. Stacy's boyfriend manqué asks her, "So what's your story?" and she replies, "I don't have one yet."

Betty definitely had a story, but she was withholding it from me. A swell of emotions rose up in my breast, a nauseating cocktail of confusion and sadness. Not quite the combination of fury and arousal that one experiences on learning of a partner's infidelity, but coming from the same place.

Seven years after my mother died, I would still dream about her flat. For years and to this day, I suffer from PTSD and have recurring nightmares about which was indeed a nightmare scenario. The mind reels from even a basic recollection of Julia's decline and descent.

But sometimes there is that dream that reappears from time to time, and it is always a variation on the same theme. Somehow, I find myself in her apartment in Manhattan and I am still clearing out the clutter when she suddenly walks in. Walks, yes. She is always walking in the dreams. When she enters I find I should be happy but instead I am frightened. And she in turn is not particularly happy to see me. Apprehensively I try to find out where she was and how she is still alive. She stops me before I can finish my sentence and says "Don't ask me where I was. I can't tell you about where I was or who I was with." I assume that she was in the "other" place and I would awake shivering in a cold sweat.

Just like my mom's mother would "abandon" her, so my mom would abandon me. The most egregious instance was when she sent me and my grandmother in Atlantic City in the 1970s, the murder and rape capitol of America at the time—a perfectly idyllic place for a child to spend the summer. The sea in New Jersey that summer was snot green and I refused to set foot in the water. I watched cartoons all day took a walk down the boardwalk in the evening, dodging junkies, cripples and lunatics, watching an armless and legless man rolling a cigarette and playing a Casio only to come back to our rental apartment and watch more cartoons. For my mom it was convenient—she could come down every weekend on the casino bus and spend her time gambling. And yet, even after that sad and cruel summer I still cried coming back to New York.

Another time I came home from school and she was not there. I bawled like crazy and my deaf grandmother, who was living with us, made me dumplings. She too had no idea where Julia had gone. I ran out onto the street and waited for her to show up—she had done this many times before, but she always showed up eventually, after putting me through hell, after my grandmother and I would sit and I would ask her, truly believing her to be a magician, to "wish" that mom's would be the next car. "Aren't you a magician?"

I would ask her, and she would say, "Yes of course I am. Now wait and count the cars, and the fifth car will be your mom's." The fifth car was never, ever my mom's. But I still believed, tears in my eyes, in her magic and in a fortuitous, beneficent faith.

After a few hours of this my grandmother and I would give up and go back inside, the old lady never letting go of her spell on me. "Maybe the spirits aren't working with me tonight," she would say, or "the spirits seem to be off this evening." And then I would lie in my bed with my eyes open until my mother finally arrived home, six hours later, drunk and delirious. But that one time in the spring I ran away. I headed towards the bridge because bridges always gave me hope, and as I ran I could hear the sound of Madame Butterfly, which had been playing on the radio, grow fainter and fainter. Bad weather was rolling in, a gentle thunderstorm with pink twilit clouds and warm rain swelling with fate. Looking down at the cars from the overpass on the Cross Bronx Expressway, I had the feeling that the bridge was heaven and the freeway the underworld. A few hours passed. There could have been no easier place to jump than right there, with "Un Bel Dì" playing faintly between my ears. Instead I threw my cigarette (I started smoking early) and headed back home. I imagined my mother dead, and wondered what would be the next step. Then she called. She was in Florida with a boyfriend I had never heard of.

When the thunderstorms broke over the George Washington Bridge and I cried my eyes out over my missing mom, the following thought struck me: women can appear and disappear at whim. And so the fear of abandonment was handed down from generation to generation. It is what made me accept women who were insane or disingenuous—anything but more abandonment. And that is partly why I ruined my own life, by sticking with these freaks, whores and junkies, solely to avoid being alone. It was a pattern. I was helpless to the endless repetition, to the eternal return.

Perhaps deeper still, I feared that I had abandoned New York, abandoned my past.

There is a song my mother sang for me almost daily for a time. It was only years later that I found out the author and the rest of the lyrics. It was not something one would sing to a child unless in Victorian or even medieval times. Why instill the sense of hopelessness in a developing mind? And how apropos was the part about a big black roach scurrying under the couch. It was called "Lullaby" by an émigré writer named Sasha Czerny, and it went something like this—my translation from memory:

> Mother went away to Paris
> So don't bother, sleep my son,
> Go to sleep, my only one.
> Nothing happens without means.
> Go to sleep now, please be still.
>
> Slick and black old cock-a-roach
> Proudly crawls under the couch
> And his wife will never leave
> She'll not flee to gay Paree.
>
> It's so dull with us, mom's right.
> The new one's slick and such a sight
> Slick and rich just like a roach
> Never boring, not at all.
>
> Now come on, son, turn off light.
> See the fire burn through the night.
> See how snow windows adorns.
> Sleep, my rabbit; sleep, my kid.
> All the world's a bitter treat.

Once upon a time there lived
two moles.
Oh, stop playing with your toes.
Sleep, my bunny; sleep, my kid.
Mother left us for Paree.

Who are you, are you my kid?
Mine or his? Is this defeat?
Sleep now, child, it's all right.
Please don't stare into my eyes.

Once a time there lived two goats,
One a Nanny, one with horns.
Roach dragged Nanny to Paree.

Sleep, my kitten, sleep my kid.
In a year your Mom you'll see.

Belly large when she returns,
She'll embrace you, back from France.

I supposed that Betty was somehow abandoned at one point. But
when? In San Francisco, like me? But that made no sense because it
was I who abandoned San Francisco for the equally filthy comforts
of New York. I didn't tell her too many of these thoughts. I suppose
we were both in our "own little worlds" in some ways. I still knew
hardly anything about her. And she was still mostly silent when
I encouraged her to tell me more about herself. To put it plainly,
she wanted to know a lot about me. And though I wanted to know
more about her, I was afraid to insist. In the end I went along and
told her more about my mom.

JULIA'S STORY

My mother suffered from an unfortunate combination of optimism and fatalism. This sad blend of thoughts was something I derided her for as her mental illness progressed. Even on her death bed I called her out on her bullshit way of thinking, something she had passed down to me and which I fought all my life, just as I fought the inability to finish things which I inherited from my dad. Julia, for that was her name and that is what I shall call her from now on, always believed that something wonderful would happen any minute while at the same time she was resolved to a deep and dark acceptance of life's tragic finality. The first time I saw this (and later Betty would remind me of this depressing combination of emotions) was when I was probably about ten, in what I have since dubbed "the chicken broth incident."

It was only a few years after we moved to America that Julia's drinking began to accelerate. My father had not really abandoned us but it was close to abandonment and as a child I was mostly unaware of whatever was going on between my parents. Alcohol is the great comforter, and Julia already had her own abandonment issues with her own mother who was always on tour back in the Soviet Union and would leave her young daughter at various summer camps or relatives while she traveled.

After my father was no longer living with us, Julia would generally wake up at three or four in the afternoon. I did not know what she was up to at night and I did not understand why she slept so late. I realized much later that they must have been excruciating hangovers. One day, surprisingly for her during those times, she decided to arrange a family trip—the family then consisting of me, her and my grandmother—to Philadelphia to see some history of this new country we were trying to understand. Because of her inability to rise even before noon, we arrived in Philly on the Greyhound on a Sunday evening at around 6 p.m. and almost everything was closed. We walked around an empty city for a bit and soon it was time to get back on the bus as twilight set in and the abandoned streets began to look menacing. I had not eaten anything and was also coming down with a summer cold. Inside the bus terminal, which was as uneasy as the streets outside, there was a vending machine which sold, from the same spout, a selection of coffee, tea and (surprisingly) chicken broth. A huge novelty for us. The Soviet vending machines were also automatic but they rather than disposable paper cups they used one glass mug, and one had to finish one's drink in place under pressure from the queue behind and then replace the same germ-rimmed mug for the next person in line. Julia was enthralled by this machine that served bouillon and ordered me a serving, but when I reached for the paper cup it was too thin and the broth much too hot and as I pulled the steaming beverage out from the dispensing nook the chicken broth went all over my hand, scalding me. And then it was time to board the bus back to New York.

As I nursed my swollen, scalded hand on the bus, with tears rolling down my face, my mother nonchalantly observed the Philadelphia suburbs. Then she turned to me, pointed at the landscape of suburban America, and said: "Would you be able to live in a place like this? I wouldn't." I wanted to tell her that I would have very much wanted to live in a place like that, away from New York's rats, mice and roaches, away from the danger and garbage, away from a city that was probably exciting to a woman in her thirties but which was terrifying her young son, to live in a place where I wasn't constantly frightened… but the burn on my hand was so painful that instead of simply answering "yes, I would" I screamed, "Right now I can't live anywhere! I don't want to live anywhere! I don't want to live!" She looked at me calmly, shook her head and did not speak to me for the remainder of the ninety minute ride to Manhattan.

Perhaps I am making too much of it, but I believe this was the first flower of a long-cultivated defeatism which I am only now beginning to understanding, now that it is too late. The other day I dreamt that I was celebrating with my dad that I had gotten into film school at NYU. I had never been accepted to NYU or film school and now it is far too late to even entertain the idea of going back to any type of school. That ship has sailed—but it was only one in a large fleet of ships that have been sailing regularly throughout my life. Of course, I did not tell Betty everything, but I did think about everything whenever I told her something about myself.

There was another moment on a bus ride home, a few years later, which was equally formative. I had spotted a very beautiful house out of the window, whose beauty contrasted so starkly with the rats and roaches and muggers and rapists of New York City. It was not a mansion or castle, there was just something about the house that seemed normal, clean, and safe, like a house from a dream. Julia smiled bitterly and instead of saying even something throwaway like "If you work hard you can buy a house and raise a family there" she said "Come on, son. You know we'll never be able to have a house like that." And so unwittingly or not she stabbed a dream in the heart.

I screamed at her when her joints gave up and she decided to stop walking. "What the fuck are you hoping for? That Jesus will climb through the window and make you walk again?" She said yes, and laughed.

The last words I spoke to her, over the phone while she was in hospital, dying from self-imposed malnutrition, were,

"Can you at least try to eat a cheese sandwich." She proudly answered "I can!" But she didn't, and two hours later she was dead.

It is neither fair nor clean to speak poorly about the dead, but what I told Betty that night was more than simply blaming my issues on my mother. In speaking about it, I felt as if I could finally "confess" just how much Julia had influenced me in both good and bad ways, and explain my natural inclination towards tragedy. Betty's curiosity reminded me of how Julia would pry and hover in social situations, how she would ask the most importune questions of guests, at dinner parties, at receptions. And the gnawing, inquisitive stare that accompanied her questions reminded just slightly of Betty herself.

Julia reveled in bathos. Another thing I took from her. In stereotypical Russian fashion she nurtured and reveled in feelings of sadness and poignancy. I remember, before I even knew what it was, her referring to a "five dollar hooker" when we lived in Italy, not as an insult directed at someone we knew but an actual unfortunate prostitute. I remember flipping through an art book of paintings by The Wanderers, a nineteenth-century collective of Russian realist and impressionist painters. We would often stop at a painting called The Sick Husband by Maximov, and she would point out the suffering of the family as the breadwinner was laid low by illness. "Look," she would say, pointing out the obvious, "Husband is sick, can't work, the wife is praying for him to recover, the kids are probably hungry." I knew it, I understood and I wept but I did not need to have it beaten over my head. She reveled in both suffering and pity but it was also mixed with a macabre fascination with misery. When I was a teenager we walked together down a disgusting street and saw a homeless guy picking through the rubbish outside a McDonald's. Julia stopped and grabbed my hand and watched in fascination. "Look, he's hungry," she said to me enthralled, as if to reveal something that I would not have understood without her commentary.

One of the first, most striking things I found in my mother's house as I was clearing it was a photograph of her as a little girl, who already possessed that look of despair. It was something described in Osamu Dazai's book "No Longer Human." It was an uncanny valley. And during her final days, it was as if we both, her from her stubborn madness and me for my lack of compassion, had ceased to be human. In self-imposed exile onto a dark planet of her own making, confident that everyone had abandoned her, Julia literally decided to stop walking. She decided to sit and reign from her filthy Yugoslavian green velvet couch, the one we had in Moscow that was shipped to Trieste and then to New York—the couch's journey of decay paralleling the corruption of her own body and mind. In time, by remaining motionless, she actually lost the ability to walk. In my own grotesquery, inherited from her, I wondered if they needed to break her legs and knees in order to fit her into the casket. She surrounded herself with neighbors, greasy fat Dominican women who would give her take-out mofongo and rice and change her diapers (she had refused a home nurse for fear of losing her freedom and destroyed her own freedom in the process). The Caribbean women would steal from her, emptying out her little stashes of greenbacks that she had squirreled away in tins throughout the flat. Julia knew she was being exploited, that these good Samaritans were only waiting for her to die so they could somehow get her apartment—a three bedroom in even a shit neighborhood like Washington Heights was still a lucrative prize. She knew it and accepted it with the fatalistic part of her brain. And yet how wonderful that apartment was at times when she was younger and held court with writers and poets, many of them douchebags or charlatans but some of them rather interesting. I believe she could not fully understand mortality, as much as she claimed wisdom, and reveling in misery did not make her wiser. In the decline and fall she would call me and say things that I knew were put on to elicit the basest pity. "I have no one, son. No one. I am so lonely. I went down to the laundry room today and saw a stray cat that I thought of bringing upstairs but the thing screeched at me. It was a disgusting cat, scrawny and mean. White fur but so ugly and dirty. I thought why not... But so filthy, so dirty... should I take the creature upstairs? It's so disgusting, dirty, filthy..." and I was reminded of the five dollar hooker in Rome and I knew that this was her idea of pulling at the heartstrings, and I could not and would not let it get to me.

Of course, madness breeds madness and each mad person feeds off the other. Julia was often capable of unspeakable kindness and sympathy. I remember calling her once when I was in a dark delirium of my own, sobbing. She said something like, "Son, of course I care about you. I am concerned that you're lonely, that you drink too much, that you feel unappreciated, that you eat hamburgers for dinner instead of a home cooked meal." I also remember her, around that time, bringing me a sandwich and mineral water after I was working on my tomfoolery of "casting" for a short film I was trying to make. But it was downhill from then on, a dive into darkness that enveloped her faster than I had thought possible.

Towards the end, when she was firmly glued to the Yugoslavian couch and in full delirium, I visited her in the early stages of her self-induced paralysis. She was on her bed/couch smoking, drinking and crying but still reigning over her atrocious abode, and on the coffee table betwixt her makeup and cognac and coffee was a photo of herself in her twenties. And I felt resentful that it was a photo of her instead of one of me. She could not let go of youth, of bygone times. What I first saw as vanity I began to see later as a nostalgia for times that are gone forever.

The last time—was it the last time?—that I saw my mother. Her face and her head utterly drenched in tears and sweat. A suffocating

New York summer. Her body wasted, the cripple was surrounded by photos of herself—not me, not family.

When in hospital again, over the phone I begged: "Can you at least eat a piece of bread and cheese?"

Proudly, almost defiantly she said "I can!" And those were the last words we exchanged. Two hours later, when the nurse stepped out, my mom gathered all her remaining strength to yank out the respirator and life support and thus ended her life. She finally drowned herself in the pond.

I told Betty most of this, the story of my mother and her illness. But I left out the reasons (fear and PTSD) why I fled New York for California. It was like being in AA and leaving out the part about drinking. So I offered Betty a sanitized version of the story, focusing much more on the good and the positive—of which, to be fair, there was much. Julia's "salons," her drinking and dining parties where I watched from afar as adults discussed literature and politics and the state of the world.

The people, the emigres, held constant company, as we stewed in our Harlem baths reminiscing, discussing. There were constant get-togethers, forget about the free-flowing vodka and vodka snacks and copious amounts of "cognac" which was actually Armenian brandy; delicious Russian potato salad, Olivier salad, herring, all matter of smoked fish, sausages, dumplings, caviar… But it wasn't the food it was the gathering and in the gathering people talked and discussed, they didn't flap their lips—though some did—people talked about politics, art, music and gossip was only a small part of the talk. They talked about the beaten to death at that point subjects of the Cold War, about which priest worked for the KGB, about who was on the payroll of either the CIA or the Soviets. And it was exciting. And surrounded by "adults" made it doubly exciting even though I had very little clue as to what they were talking about most of the time. But the surprising thing is, as little as we knew, the adults didn't know much either. We looked up to them, some of them were wise and interesting and introduced us to books, but some of these people were in their thirties, forties, not even in their fifties and were not the wise old elders we imagined them to be, with no grey locks or eyebrows that drooped to their stomachs as you see in medieval Japanese paintings. It had taken me until now, in middle age to understand that our parents know nothing, that they are as clueless as teenagers, all of them, and that their so-called wisdom was nothing but trial and error, and even then it was faulty, reached more by groping in the darkness than seeing the light. I write this as a parent myself. My daughter looks up to me—or so I hope. I can help her with language and I can introduce her to art and music, I can tell her about histories both benign and atrocious but at the end of the day, no one is wise and no one really knows anything.

So I told Betty more about the yellow light coming through the windows of my youth; I spoke about her kindness, her humor, her work as a journalist and as a social worker working with refugees. I told her how interesting she was, how she was a great conversationalist and a very funny lady. I gave her all of that but tried to eschew the demonic bits.

JULIA'S WHEELCHAIR

It must have been during one of the first "horrors" as I called them, that when Julia was in and out of hospital and when I had to go to New York and figure out what to do. Like me she had a tremendous fear of confinement. It took root in Soviet times, when everyone suffered the same fear, and I inherited it. But this was the beginning of letting go of the levers toward her final death wish.

Patients had a right to refuse treatment, no one made the choice for her. She asked for the wheelchair. She didn't need one, if she only tried walking—but she had given up, precisely for the ideal she had always wanted: a tragic sense of life. And then it was as if the devil wrote the screenplay and she gave Satan a kiss for his wonderful plot point.

"It is my birthday, you know?" she told the ambulance driver who had driven her home in her brand-new wheelchair. And it was true, she turned 65 that day. And everything fit in perfectly for her: "It is my birthday and for my birthday I get a wheelchair." It was all so completely perverse, for there was no need for her to have a wheelchair in the first place if she made the effort. Besides, her Washington Heights apartment was completely wheelchair inaccessible. "It's your birthday?" asked the ambulance guy. It was too perfect, like something from a Douglas Sirk melodrama. It fit right in with her tragic sense of life. Was it Russian melodrama? Mental illness? Both? Or something hidden to boot? Whatever was hidden, I would realize later, was something I would never know.

And so she plopped down on the green velvet couch shipped over from Trieste and didn't leave it for another four years until she died.

As my mother's madness progressed, it took turns toward truly arcane and bizarre scenarios, not out of place from the most grotesque of Russian and German literature. She progressively went from not leaving the house to not leaving the couch. She willingly decided to stop walking and in Kafka or Canetti fashion found a succession of imbecilic grotesque caretakers to attend to her. In some ways I understand—she adamantly refused to leave her castle, the very thought of a "facility" i.e. nursing home or rehab place made her shudder, and she would always scream at me as if I was at fault, insisting that it was I who wanted to have her confined or committed. Were I wiser, and more patient, I would have sympathized with her fear, for I too have a tremendous fear of confinement. But the panopticon of demons which she contracted to take care of her were like characters from a absurd Viennese novel from the 1920s, with goblins lurking behind every heavy velvet curtain and imps scratching the down blanket.

My mom always hated Ukrainians and yet for some reason she chose them out as friends her whole life and as caretakers in her twilight. There was Oksana Derevenko, a self-styled gypsy from Ukraine via Brazil. And then toward the end of her yellow and green delirium (yellow for that ubiquitous yellow light that always came through the windows of her Manhattan apartment was always coupled with the green velvet couch, the green velvet chairs, etc) she hired some lunatic named Mykolka to stay in my old room, a boarder. No sooner had this Mykola moved in that he began to complain about my mom's smoking (she went to the grave biting a Capri 120 between her teeth). "Honey," she would telephone me, "This asshole Mykola said he's bothered by my smoking so he offered to construct a canopy over my couch where I could just sit and smoke in peace—a canopy! A smoke screen, as he called it! Can you believe it?"

What was there to believe? If she had invited a goblin into her house then of course, all was believable. And yet this was the most bizarre one yet. One day that goblin took me aside and showed me what he was "working on"—the charts and graphs of a crazy person, some type of "nuclear secrets" according to Mykola that he was planning on selling to the government. Lunacy, like the canopy he wanted to encase my mother's bed in. A sarcophagus with a tube connected to the window to let out her cigarette smoke.

One day, like all these types, Mykola left. He took with him a bunch of my mother's cash. Mykola, Mykolka, I tried to remember why I always hated that name, even though it was nothing more than a dialectic version of "Nicholas." Then I recalled. Mykola was the drunk peasant in Raskolnikov's dream, the one who whipped and beat his horse to death because it was his "property." Oh, the dreams and nightmares that my mother left me with, enough for many Dostoevsky novels and tenfold more dark dreams.

There is a photograph of my mother, which I can't now find, but whose image is indelibly etched in my mind. She is at the top of the World Trade Center, on the observatory deck. Her head is in profile and she gestures, arm outstretched with a feeling that reads "Fuck it all." There is, from what one can detect given the angle, a bittersweet smile on her face. I have always had a dreadful fear of heights but was equally enthralled with towers, observation decks and city vistas. Here it was, then, the perfect juxtaposition of the sense of infinity provided by the edifice and the vista, and the abandon of her smile and her hand. It is almost an image of someone about to jump to their death.

That sense of open possibility, the one that comes so often in New York, or did at one point is contrasted or abetted by the feeling of despair, or a brilliant death, like the blazing, marvelous, open morning of September 11th. Despair is not the right word. It is more akin to abandon, oblivion, oblivescence, though despair can give birth to abandon in its own right.

The last time—was it the last time?—that I saw my mother, her face and her head were utterly drenched in tears and sweat—the tears of regret and the sweat of the suffocating August New York.

Her body wasted, the cripple was surrounded by photos of herself—not me, not family. Vanity perhaps but we shall not speak ill of the dead. A bit like Candy Darling on her deathbed, and the tears burst out like waterfalls out of each eye socket.

How she wept! It was if rocks fell out of her skull. And I knew the primary feeling was that she "fucked up."

"That's fascinating, Lucky" Betty said dispassionately. "I know you must miss her a lot…" I smiled and nodded, for despite the madness I did miss her greatly.

I began to wonder whether the entire reason for memories was in order to have something to reflect on while you are dying. Pity the one whose memories are utterly pedestrian and pointless but even in the most banal or horrific life there are touching moments—a glass of milk, a piece of bread and jam, a bit of gentle kindness, a sunset, a sunrise…

Be it in the viridian of a hospital room or yellow corridor, only memories sustain the passage from one life to the next, otherwise we would all be screaming in fear.

THIS SPORTING LIFE

Whee whee whee!
We spend our youth in glee!
The beast lurks in the jungle, but we cannot see
when he will pounce and ounce for ounce,
it's better not to know, right?

Wrong. I struggle how to guess which one is
easier but all in all,
it's not a theme park after dark.
Existence's worth its salt and
therefore something much more stark.
Allow me to explain...

Lights do not dim then fade.
They turn from candy colors of the ferris wheel
into fluorescents with a dash of
phosphorescent green, hospital viridescent
or sometimes hospital yellow.

For some the world's a stage, for some
it's nothing but carnival lights.
Performers know how to put on a show
even in the shadow of a crematorium at Belsen.

My mother's mother does this now.
Reads palms and flirts,
she's unaware her daughter's dead
and she can hardly recognize me.
I hardly know if she can see.

And so, with age, the interstellar space
becomes wide open and deranged.

What dark or dusky or maybe
even totally blind future dangles taunting
by our eyes whereas before...

In Buchenwald I danced.
In Belsen I pranced.
I slept in Sobibor

because there were so more, so
many places still to see…
The one place that's too close to me
are the colds isles of Solovki.

I mean no disrespect and hate no
one to such extent, the
weirdness is the truth.

We dance, we prance, we beg
the dance floor not to close,
not to shut down…

It's Shiva's dance, it never ceases.
Kaleidoscope for when we're young,
and neon bulbs and green and blue
and rather childlike you have to wear diapers
until a fat Haitian cleans your ass.
Odd how so quickly that the days and years have
passed, ne c'est pas?

With the development of blindness
(my biggest fear) I'm told the loss of sight
is gradual (although quite real).
Much like a sunset.
That's what I learned from Borges.

Sightless or not, the carousel will never
ever really break.
It's just we're taken
to the kiddie section while we wait as
others buy a fare and
we still wish to jump and
hold the plastic horse, but

we're no longer let to do that and
thus spend our toothless
end in yellow corridors
with our lives
painted on walls
in colors of despair.

A sporting life is what it is, and when
the technicolor canopy is dropped
the ones alive go home,
turn back and wonder
"Did we even see the show?"
We'll have to wait to know.

Deceiving my grandmother seemed atrocious to me but it kept her alive. Everyone needs hope, even if it's a lie. How would I tell her? Why should I?

This is how I remember the last time I saw Tonya, my grandmother, in a semi-coherent state. We were visiting her in the nursing home before she became completely delirious. My grandmother said, "Once upon a time there lived Tonya. And she gave birth to a baby girl named Julia..." The rest was gibberish. Yet the words stabbed my ear while my mother with her brandy in a Poland Spring bottle and decked out in her fur hat and coat also stifled tears. And while everyone has a family story, and every family has its secrets and ghosts, it was only now, now that everyone was dead, that I became so interested in it all, lying awake in the humid Brooklyn night and reflecting on tales of bygone times. It is a terrible thing to bury your children, but luckily Tonya was too far gone to understand. She kept asking where she had gone and why she didn't answer her letters, and even though she had lost her hearing, she still tried to call her daughter. Before she lost her mind entirely, I would pacify her with explanations like

"Julia had to go to Russia for work," or, "She moved to Czechia/Canada/California/France/Mexico..."

I had no idea what was going through her head. Was this why being with Betty, whose feelings I found equally hard to read, brought back memories of my grandmother? And when Betty held my hand and pulled herself closer, despite her chair making it difficult, was it that "touch of a woman"—or, even more basically, the touch of a person—that reminded me so much of my mother, who in her delirium insisted that she missed human contact most of all?

My marriage, sexless at this point as I had mentioned—had made the most basic flirtation or appreciation exciting and titillating. The slightest woman's touch sent millions of blood cells rushing not just into the penis but into the heart as if I had been struck by a gentle Cupid's arrow—at this point it could have come from anyone, and in this respect I understood my mother's sentiment. And yet Betty was utterly elusive. Sometimes I would think she was being coquettish and using her paralysis as a device, and I hated myself for having these thoughts. How could we consummate our love when there are physical barriers? But I did not think of it that way. In truth I equated her with all the other girls who played cat and mouse with my cock and my heart until I would be forced to give up the chase.

So what was happening now? Betty, in her chair, her hand on mine as we sat on the boardwalk in Brighton Beach, gazing at the ocean... We were content to do it... A stupid term, a cliché but my heart would indeed go "aflutter" when she touched my hand, and yet, I had no idea what she was thinking, for her deep blue eyes, deeper than a well, deeper than the sea, deeper than the Mariana Trench held a secret at the bottom of the ocean, and I was afraid, too afraid to enter a bathyscaphe, flood the air tanks with sea water and fall into the abyss.

To her credit, while she kept most details of her life hidden, the upside was that she never mentioned any previous paramours, boyfriends, one-night stands or what not. This in itself, especially in combination with her condition, was so much a comfort and a relief that it almost made up for her opacity, and if it didn't completely prevent me from wondering, it certainly cushioned it. Of course, sometimes, on less fortunate days, it did quite the opposite, and I would imagine the worst possible scenarios. At least she wasn't blinded by acid like Linda Pugach, I would say as an excuse, though my speculation that her paralysis could be traced to a jealous former lover immediately hit the brakes as too sick and frightening of a thought. Nothing she did or said could have formed the seed of such a horrid thought other than my own wicked imagination.

What if it was something unspeakably worse than a so-called indiscretion? Karla Homolka? Bodil Joensen?

Another odd concern that would occasionally creep into my head was that she never asked about my book—the one I was supposed to have been writing. Perhaps if she did, things would have turned out differently... Perhaps I would have been bolder in my desire to make her my actual lover. I imagined the possibilities—forget about her condition—I saw her as not just my muse but my guide, my manager, my motivator. "This is brilliant, Lucky," I pictured her saying as she pored over my manuscript once I finished the first draft. "We need to get this to the right people. I have some names in mind. I'll make some phone calls for you tomorrow. You're going to sell this book!"

What tomfoolery! What flights of fancy! Who would she possibly know that could help me with finding an agent or publisher, not to mention that the manuscript was a blank page at this point? No, this fantasy was just that—fantasy, and it would only surface in deep, unattainable dreams. And yet, this sweet dream would also sometimes be interrupted when I would, bizarrely, think that she had already read my unwritten book, or that she could somehow read my mind and already knew the story from beginning to end. Madness through and through, but the thought would reappear from time to time.

As much as it bothered me that she was so taciturn, I was perhaps equally bothered that we had not yet kissed. The process of kissing and sex without much conversation is easier than the other way around. That was my case with Farrington, with Vainonen, with others. While the sex existed in spades, and the legs were always open, the mouth was relegated mostly to a sexual organ and when not used for that purpose was essentially either silent or spouting inanity of the highest (or lowest) order, so banal that it isn't worth repeating and was never even worth committing to memory.

Betty was different. I could sense her intelligence and her wit, which, though seldom used, was undoubtedly sharp. It was just that she preferred to listen rather than talk, and for a while I had had no issue with such an arrangement. But our meetings were marred by my subconscious pity for her, no matter how strong I saw she was. I had to wait until pity was drowned out by desire. That accursed hypersensitivity that followed me my whole life was once again interfering with action. If watching Dumbo and hearing "When I See an Elephant Fly" could drive me to tears, if video game jingles could remind me of a Fassbinder soundtrack by Peer Raben and throw me into a fit of heartbreak, what was I to do with the sorrowful sight of a beautiful girl confined to a wheelchair? I waited for the right moment when passion would trump compassion and it never seemed to come until finally one evening at the Café Europa when the conversation was at its most pedestrian (something about the slice of cake she ordered), I reached over and kissed her on the mouth. There was no shock on her part and she more than reciprocated by sticking a strong, powerful tongue down my throat. I was surprised by the force of the kiss, the way the tongue thrust itself, and was overcome with a swell of mixed emotions—that it felt like all her strength was concentrated in that one muscle; that she was almost waiting for me to make the move; and last but not least, a certain fear: What now? What next? Yet the awkwardness was fleeting and I could sense that for both of us the kiss was a relief. Vague memories of similar situations popped into my head but I could not place the faces, the names, the mouths...

Neither of us pulled away. We separated locked lips at the same time and she smiled and this time she did not smile sadly. This time, perhaps for the first time, I glimpsed a brief moment joy on her face. She took a bite of her cake and smiled and again. There was an understanding of some sorts that for tonight, at least, this was where it was to begin and end. We went back to banal talk. As the evening went on we became more comfortable, perhaps even "used to" one another the way couples are, and while there was now hope for something the rest of the evening went as usual and there was no talk of going any further than the kiss, although I thought, or hoped, it had sealed something.

After I walked her back to her place and left her at the front door I went back home and was enveloped in frenzy. I stumbled around the apartment, gripped by two conflicting emotions yet again: excitement on the one hand and a sense of shame and guilt on the other. Other than my dream lovers and the occasional lascivious thought about a stranger, I had always been faithful to my wife. Now it seemed too dangerous, that I was ready to cross the line. My hands were shaking and I could barely pour a drink without spilling vodka all over the kitchen counter. The guilt rose steadily and quickly and I had no clue how to stem its tide. My instinct was to call Los Angeles and confess all but after the second drink, reason took over and reminded me that such a confession would in fact make everything worse. My only hope was that alcohol would take care of the problem, although that sparked a new worry—I did not want to black out entirely and make the evening's events too dark and distant in the morning. A "distant episode" minus the cutting out of tongues. I opened a notebook and wrote about it—a brief synopsis. But the next morning I ripped out the page and threw it in the trash. I wanted to keep it solely inside my head and heart.

I prided myself on not overdoing it with the booze the night before. The memory of the kiss was still fresh and clear in my mind, as if I could still somehow taste her. Emotion was recollected in tranquility. The frenzy had stopped, at least temporarily, and I was perfectly content to have at least had that one kiss from her. If nothing more were to ever happen between us, I thought, at least I would always have that.

Emboldened, I was looking forward to the evening's tryst. I skipped my 10 a.m. glass of rosé and decided to go for a swim, a baptismal entrance into a new phase of our "relationship." It was a perfect summer day to immerse myself in the Atlantic. Indeed, the weather—which has such profound effects on me in all her manifestations—was ideal and Madeleine like. I drifted into very distant remembrances of childhood, the end of school, the very beginning of the summer, those first truly warm days before New York becomes oppressively hot and muggy. Odd that the summer was in full swing but the weather and temperature felt as if the season, and all other things to match, were only just beginning. I was forgetting and ignoring my age, my life in California, my family, and did nothing but revel in this strange blast of renewal and rebirth.

The summer nights went on lazily. The book was still a blank page but at the moment I was still too enraptured by Betty to think much of it. I didn't care. The days were spent solely in waiting for the appointed meeting time. Love is strange, and God is odd. How odd it was for Him to give me this little love. Romance can take many forms, and my love was crooked and bent the way I imagined my own soul to be. At times that I feared that my book was like an evil talisman and that I should delay completing it for fear of unlocking a spell to be punished by death.

In between dates, all I had were waking dreams, memories floating through my mind like leaves whipped up during a Listopad. These memories weighed heavily, not because they were sad but because the world they belonged to was lost. Some days were easier than others, but I swung like a pendulum between a torturous yearning for a past that can never be repeated and a desire for something new, with Betty. And in between the two, at night, there were my dreams.

One night we went to the movies. Although there were plenty of excellent films playing in Manhattan, the trek would have been too long so we decided to keep it local and took a cab over to the multiplex at the mall. I don't remember the film at all. I only remember the aftermath, when she turned into a ball of sadness, not unlike when Sandra broke down at the Rainbow Room. I recalled how I went to see Eraserhead with Sandra one winter day. The screening started in late afternoon and the day was cold and dark to begin with, but when we exited the theater it was practically pitch black out and snowing. We walked in silence back to my flat as if we were living in that same black-and-white world of quiet horror. The pure, pure snow fell gently on her fur hat and on her yellow hair and even her bright blue eyes were monochrome on that walk.

I wish I could remember the film Betty and I watched but for some reason I cannot. There was a female protagonist. It was a little bit like Thelma and Louise; there was a tragic ending. Even though I was unable to wrap my arms around Betty I could sense that she was shivering, not from cold but from whatever in the film made her shake. I tried to make a joke about something or other— it was still humid and 90 degrees outside; the end of summer was still to come. And then she darted her eyes at me and with a look of the deepest dejection raised her voice: "It's not funny!"

Our days were not without lumps.

"Look at the stars" Betty would say when the sky was clear, or not tell me, for it is hard for me now to discern what was said and what occurred in my mind; perhaps she saw stars, not just the stars she would see from a fist hitting her head (she would tell me about that later) but the stars she wished to see. On my end, I would see mist and perhaps a faint tail of a comet while I concentrated on the rubbery asphalt of New York City streets melting in the humid darkness of a July evening.

As much as I wanted to know what had happened to her, I also did not want to know. I knew that she would tell me in due time. It would have a gross breach of etiquette, to say the least, were I to broach the subject first. It was either utterly banal (most likely) or something dreadfully spectacular (but what is spectacular?)

And then she said something that struck a chord, something very poetic and cryptic. "You know, Lucky..." she turned to me, looked in my eyes and then looked away into the distance, "Sometimes I feel like my life is a movie that someone wrote but no one's ever seen."

I was afraid to respond. I paused, swallowed, and with the best of courage, and in foolish trepidation, bounced back: "Hit me! Twenty five words or less!"

Her glance then would have pierced any heart.

"It's not a joke," she said and bit her lip until I saw it bleed. There were tears in the corners of her eyes. "It's not a joke, Lucky!"

I grabbed her arm but she continued to stare at the wall, chewing on her lip, and did not notice my gesture.

"It is not a joke," she kept repeating without looking back at me. "Do you ever wonder why your parents created you? Or better yet, why God created you? Do you ever wonder why you were created?"

I had nothing to say. She kept sobbing and repeating variations on the same line: "Why were we created? Why was I created?"

I grabbed her arm at the right moment, just before the sobbing collapsed into hysterics, and kissed her with the utmost passion. I told her firmly, "We're going now."

I spun her around and wheeled her away from her thoughts. I was short of breath, short of time. I pushed her chair onto the boardwalk and ran as fast as I could until she started to laugh from the exhilaration. I ran because I wanted to forget, to forget everything, but mostly to forget everything she had just said... I rushed forward, escaping Betty's past, escaping my past and my present, rushing away from every possible thought until the wheelchair stuck in a broken slat of the boardwalk and I landed face first on the wood and Betty laughed even harder, despite her mode of ambulation stuck in rotten wood. I picked myself up, bruised, bloodied but unbowed. Instinctively, as if seeking a return to the womb, I crawled up to her chair and made the only leap a man would wish to make—to go back to the womb. I intuitively stuck my head in between her legs. She smiled. At least I imagined she had smiled. And then she laughed.

I did not want sex. Not then. I needed to be petted, I needed succor, maybe I needed a mother. I wanted to get inside the uterus again.

She petted me, rubbed her fingers through my hair and her laughter became interspersed with sobs. For some reason I started to cry too.

"Oh, Lucky...." She stifled tears. "It's okay, honey... It will all be okay. Don't cry, Lucky... I'm the one who should be crying. See how I'm holding up? See, I'm not crying anymore..."

She kept stroking my hair until my hysterics passed.

"Come," she said. "You need to order me a cab. Don't worry, I'm not going anywhere. I'll see you soon. But now it's time for us to go to bed. Our separate beds."

I booked a taxi on my phone and it arrived within a few minutes. I put her into the cab and disassembled the chair and took her back to her apartment building. "I'll see you" she winked, and disappeared into the lobby.

I took the taxi to my own flat twenty blocks north. From the window of my apartment I stared at the dying lights, the glimpse of the ocean...It was difficult to summon Morpheus when I was preoccupied with horrible thoughts and fears that made my heart race. What was it that Betty was hiding? What would be the worst thing one can imagine to be in a woman's past? An abortion addiction? Bukkake porn? Eating shit for money? The degradation that Bodil Joensen spoke of—what was it that she had to do that repulsed her—her, who fucked farm animals for fun and profit? Is everyone's idea of horror different? For some it is a sauna filled with spiders... Each of us does indeed have a Room 101. Exhaustion eventually took over and I fell asleep and in my sleep I dreamt that Betty walked.

MAGIC AFTERNOON

One day, when Betty wasn't around (she told me she had a doctor's appointment), I dreamt of a magic afternoon.

The girl's name was Rachel (why Rachel I have no idea, but for some reason I remembered upon waking that that was her name) and she had bright reddish hair, almost dyed but it seemed to be natural since the carpet matched the drapes as I found out later in the dream. I was cleaning out my mom's house in Washington Heights, waiting for the last of the movers to arrive when I saw her through the window, sitting on a fire escape, smoking a cigarette, dangling her legs. She must have been seventeen years old. She looked like what one would call a meretricious "girl from the neighborhood" who was just embarking on a journey of boys and sex. Was she a pass-around girl? I didn't know and didn't care. I knew she was too young and that this was dangerous territory but it was literally "love at first sight." I wooed her, tried to seduce her gently at first and then finally I confessed that I was madly in love with her, to which she admitted that she felt the same way. We kissed. I lifted up her skirt and licked between her thighs. She giggled. How bright, how fiery and wonderful that summer afternoon felt, as if youth in a tidal wave of emotion just dowsed me in fictional memories of the sweetest kind. What a glorious manifestation of summer. My maiden, the princess of summer, rode in on a sorrel horse, guided by the pleasantly scorching sun, kicking away the garbage and debris of ageing thoughts and burdens, all manner of discarded faiths and longings, reigniting long dormant passions with a golden torch. Compared to the grey, cold planet where we "haste upon decay," who wouldn't prefer to spend one's entire life dreaming?

Somehow, I knew or understood, later when I woke up, that Rachel was Betty. They did not look alike but nonetheless I knew it—because my love, the feeling of love that I wore like a hair shirt in my dream was real and comforting, and that feeling stayed with me for a long time until the dream went "whoosh" and disappeared like steam under a door.

Later it dawned on me that the girl in my dream looked a lot like a porno hooker I had seen a few times. First softcore and glamour shoots, she looked like she could have been walking down the catwalk in Milan and then, progressively her "work" became raunchier, ending with an orgy in which dozens of horrible looking men circle jerked and ejaculated into her mouth. That last video was the perfect combination of arousal, disgust and terror. Would I, if the dream were real, be able to "date" her and have a romantic relationship with such a cheap slut? I shuddered and let the dream float away completely. There were always other dreams to be had. My youth was gone but at least I found comfort in the endless variety of dream dates who would continue as long as I could dream, as long as I was alive and perhaps even in the next world.

I used some broom of self-control to sweep away these gnawing images, which were pleasant and frustrating in equal measure. I had lost track of time, the way I did during that seemingly chthonic week in childhood that I spent under black stars. Betty and I often stayed up late into the night. I would walk her home, kiss her goodnight, go back to my apartment to drink and spend much of the day with the curtains closed, gently chopping away at my hangover with rosé or vodka tonics until it was twilight and time to see Betty again. In the process, I had neglected not only my writing but also my daily swims.

One evening Betty told me she could not see me the following day—she had a checkup scheduled with a doctor. I don't know how many days or weeks had passed at that point since we first met and it was only then that I realized that we were seeing each other every single day. I decided that some time apart, even for one day, was positive and resolved to go swimming in the morning the way I used to when I first arrived.

I rose early as I had kept the drinking to a minimum the previous night, and after a bracing shot of vodka after my coffee I took the train down to the beach, ready to rinse my mind in the muddy surf. But my mind did not need rinsing. My head was in the proverbial clouds and I myself was a cloud in trousers. I was ignoring my work, and whatever ideas I tried to sketch were utterly inchoate. But I wasn't worried. I exited onto the filthy platform, dodging dog and human waste, used condoms and broken beer bottles, and as I made my way down and toward the boardwalk and the sand, where salt air pushed away the garbage smells, I once again reflected on how I missed the East Coast beaches and summers. How wonderful it would be, I thought, if I could somehow drop anchor here, acquire a pied-à-terre perhaps, so that at least every summer I could come back and live this other life with Betty, my mistress, my summer girl...

What would poor Betty do without me during the blue and purple winters under the cold yellow moon? Would she shiver alone out on the boardwalk, looking at the horizon and waiting for a ship with scarlet sails to enter the harbor and bring her happiness at last? Would she be an exile without me, and would the cold ocean look like the Sea of Okhotsk and the city like Magadan? Who would push her chair along the boardwalk? Who would wrap her in warm clothes, put a shawl around her shoulders and keep her warm when November comes and strips the trees? Who would carry her to bed in her dark little flat where she would lie alone and look at the beam of the lighthouse in agony of longing? Who would snuff out her candle and give her a warm blanket as she gazed, shivering, at the purple sky? My reveries turned into pathetic, maudlin sniffles, again straight out of Hans Christian Andersen.

The heat roused me from my icy fantasy. The sun was blinding and the humidity was becoming uncomfortable. I stripped to my swim shorts and walked into the water. I submerged and dove under a wave, and for a second I thought I saw Betty swimming alongside me. "Could she swim in her condition?" I wondered. What evil force had bound her so? Perhaps she could swim, and grow scales and a fish tail? Had some wicked enchantress created her human bondage but allowed her life as a mermaid or perhaps a Rusalka? An unquiet spirit? In Slavic folklore the Rusalka is a water nymph, the spirit of a young woman who drowned herself in order to escape an unhappy marriage. In some versions she is pushed into the water and drowns against her will. Was I the one who would eventually break the spell and return her to her previous human form?

I dried off, sat around on the beach observing the New World Odessite lumps of sagging flesh and soon decided that I had had enough. I was bored. A vague unsatisfied feeling began to break through the summer idyll. Superficially, at least, there was nothing to be worried about. I was on a holiday of sorts, and I was in love, although I feared this love... Everything was nearly perfect, especially if I ignored the little problem with my book, not to mention my wife and child, which I had come close to successfully ignoring. If I believed that this was it, this was totality then the ennui would have resulted in the boredom that comes with achieving all of one's goals—non plus ultra. Castles in Spain were built and half the world had been conquered, and yet life had become a dream. The kings and queens reposed in the gloaming, the ladies danced to the Chaconne or promenaded through the gardens of El Escorial, and ages and memories passed alongside them. Everything was occurring all at once, and in the New World, the sea captains were bathing their boots in the same waters I had just emerged from.

I began to feel hungry and walked over to Primorski. I had a strong desire for grilled meat and vodka. I thought that eating and drinking would help to fill the physical and figurative emptiness, but it had the opposite effect. Sitting alone in the place that I now so closely associated with Betty was dreadful. There was something missing from the picture, something dreadfully missing in the picture and it was her... I felt as if she were gone forever, and all I had were memories of a summer long past, memories conjured by the taste of charred lamb and the burn of vodka. After the second shot, I began to feel completely, utterly alone and tears came to my eyes. The wait staff ignored me, which was natural in a Russian establishment. What did they think? Why was a grown man crying over his lamb and grilled tomatoes with rice? Did he get laid off? They weren't the tears of financial distress. Did he lose a love? Was there an accident? Did someone die? I finished the vodka but not the lamb, paid hurriedly and caught the train home. Tears had turned to sweat. The minute I walked through the door the phone rang. It was her.

"Meet me at Café Europa."

Soon there we were there again, at our little safe haven where we looked out upon the sunset, pensioneered and smiled. Europa served alcohol, and Betty liked to drink, even if she always did so with grace and control. What is alcohol, anyway? A diviner. We all die. Let us drink while we can, let us swing low. At the Café Europa we sat and smiled, gazing lovingly into each other's eyes. I put my hand on her leg which couldn't feel a thing and yet she kind of knew it was there. I peered deep into her eyes. I had to hold onto myself so as not to fall in. But I was falling nonetheless... falling... Ich bin von Kopf bis Fuss... I was not thinking about my wife and daughter, I was under the sea. When would I finally rip her out of that ungainly trap and throw her on the bed and make love to her?

It was an awkward date. I was expecting something, anything.

Anything to break the cycle of waiting for some type of resolution to this. To all this. And yet, to my disappointment, there was only idle chit chat. Perhaps we were spending too much time together, always a risk at the beginning of a new relationship. Relationship. Is that what we had? I remembered that years ago I was stalked by that girl Andrea "Andie" Easton who I met outside a movie theater. Though we had a few platonic dates, and talked on the phone a few times—we had a mutual interest in film and I thought she may be of use—we didn't really see each other that much, and I wasn't terribly interested in getting her in the sack. And yet one day she called me out of the blue, yelling: "We really need to talk about our relationship!" "What relationship?" I said and hung up. In order to avoid turning into Andie myself I remained taciturn and we ended the evening rather early.

I decided to spend a bit of time away from Betty, even just a day, but the next day she called me in an excited tone and suggested we go to a free symphony concert in Central Park.

"Come on, we never go anywhere, we just stay here in Brooklyn and do nothing," she said slightly flirtatiously. My heart skipped a beat when she used the plural. We never go anywhere—so there it was in one grammatical nuance, we were a "we," a couple. So now it was she who was being Andie, but an Andie that I actually wanted. Elated, we took the train that early evening into Manhattan. I held her hand in the subway car. She knew how to maintain her chair and I tried my best not to be too doting, letting her dignity and independence ride alongside my insecurities and fears and when the train hit a bump I only reached out to balance her when I saw in her eyes that she needed some help, and when I straightened her out she smiled and looked at me with something that I felt was love.

The train ride took forever. Even without the added problem of us looking for elevators and other handicapped access ramps and tunnels, the process of exiting the underworld added another half hour to our journey until we finally exited from the depths, stepped over a Styx of piss and finally saw the green of Central Park and the windows of the buildings to the north and southeast burning in the evening reflections, jolting me back into the underworld of my own which cannot be seen by the living, only the memories seen by the dead or nearly dead. The twilight over the park was magical. Though many of the buildings past Central Park South were new and obstructed the sky, at least the perspective remained the same as in my youth.

I crossed the Acheron when we passed the stone entrance gates and headed in the direction of the orchestra tuning up, that slightly nauseating cacophony of instruments trying to find their place among each other. Before we made it to the stage, the first violin came out to applause as de rigeur, then the conductor. "Come!" she yelled, "Hurry!" as she wheeled herself furiously and pointlessly— there was no way, at this point, that we could get good seats unless the entire crowd was touched by her incapacitation. We rushed closer to the stage nonetheless and the music came rushing toward us, and within the first few minutes I realized what they were playing. In my excitement over this date I didn't even have a chance to ask Betty what the program was for the evening and in the roar and racket of the subway journey we hardly spoke. But now I heard it: it was Dvořák's Ninth Symphony, "From the New World," the New World Symphony. How did she know—if indeed she knew— that this was my favorite orchestral piece? We made our way to the stage, as close as possible. Again, a burst of timidity struck me when I didn't know what to do with the blanket and the picnic bag we brought with us, I didn't know how to move, how to act, how to make her comfortable. I was reminded for a second about how I had started to act around my wife, that because I had become an economic parasite I had to keep reminding myself that my pitiful life dangled by a thread, that I was a mere economic equation (and a negative one to boot), that at any moment a misstep could cost me my life, that my life would not be missed in the least. But I snapped back. Betty had found a spot. Kindly, or fearfully, people had moved aside and managed to make some space for us. I asked Betty if she was okay and she nodded. And so I sat next to her chair—there was no space for our blanket or for me to lift her out and carry her close to me so I held her hand and sat on the grass and fell into the music. She dug her fingernails into my forearm at the beginning of the first movement. The piece must have been familiar, perhaps all too familiar, to warrant that reaction of pain or delight. Oh, what heights the symphony reached; not the Iowa prairies but the skyscrapers of Manhattan, a journey across the continent like the one Stacy takes, a patchwork of colors, a quilt of misadventures large and small, of loves and tragedies, and then finally release, an apotheosis. During the robust parts, of which there were many, I started to get hard. This was not unusual for me. I had on many occasions experienced a very strong sexual reaction to music, live orchestral music in particular.

Just then my eyes began to fill, and as I surreptitiously wiped away tears Betty banged on the arm rails of her chair, motioning for me to hold her hand. I squeezed her palm and saw that her face was stained with tears and she was shaking. It was the end of the symphony, the Allegro in E Minor; we had already survived the Scherzo. I closed my eyes and pictured us levitating, leaving the world, her drifting up like an angel kicking her miserable chair aside, embracing me and carrying me into the blue atmosphere like a guardian angel ripping me out of hell. The music ended and I opened my eyes. She was smiling, tear-faced but beaming, as if she too had imagined both of us soaring up into the firmament. The concert goers immediately started to disperse at the first sound of applause, so we too pushed ourselves away and onto the path and then out of the park. I pushed her in the direction of Columbus Avenue. We found a café that wasn't too crowded and went in.

The night turned chilly and the café was cold and did not serve alcohol. After a few frustrated minutes I nodded and we left in search of warmth and booze. Down the street, towards the 1 train, there were several pubs that I recognized, including a few Irish pubs with green awnings. In one of these, I seemed to recall, Roseann "Easy to meet, nice to know" Quinn met her Mister Goodbar. We went in. This place was equally cold but they had whiskey to warm us.

After a flight through the country during the concert, I felt odd being snapped back to reality. I tried to recapture the feeling I felt a half hour ago but could not reach that plane again. The bar was unfamiliar yet oddly reminiscent of something. A vague memory of drinking in the afternoon with my dad in that same neighborhood when he worked at Lincoln Center. Memories of youth. The scotch warmed our veins and loosened our lips.

"It was the first time I'd heard that music," she said, "but it felt like the millionth."

We took the train back to Brooklyn in silence, at least at first. I nodded off for a minute, falling into reverie and mumbled: "Well, that went by quickly."

"What?" she asked

"My life," I said, then added, "Never mind."

"You'd like to live forever?" she asked.

"Of course, who wouldn't?"

"What about dying, then coming back and reliving the same life again? Would you like that?"

"I don't know."

"Think about it. Beginning to end, infinitely."

I knew the old trope about how lives, like books and films, need a beginning, middle and end, otherwise one would be bored stiff, or like the jaded undead doomed to walk the earth for infinity, but it offered little consolation. I had never thought about what it would be like to relive my life again and again, to accept all the beauty of childhood, the angst of adolescence, the torture of searching for steadfast love. I had no answer, but I was reminded of a children's song from the USSR and I rocked with the train and the melody in my mind, Betty's hand in my own as I tried vaguely to translate the words into English without falling asleep...

One by one the minutes slowly slip away,
Don't expect to meet them, live or dead.
And although we're sad that our past can't stay,
Better times, of course, still lie ahead.

As a long runner roll
The long path spreads away,
In the end it juts against the sky.
And everyone still believes
In the coming of the day...
As our blue railcar
Sets off to roll and roam.

Maybe we offended someone, hurt for naught,
Calendar will cover this day's sheet.
Paths to new adventures with our friends we plot...
Engine driver, gather some more speed!

Our blue railcar runs forward as it sways,
The express train's speeding up ahead...
Why is this day coming to an end? I'm dazed,
I wish that it would last one year instead...

We always thought that happiness was just ahead of us, but as the song says—and I wonder if others even got the nuance—the horizon is unreachable. And what was there to say as Betty and I sat in our own blue wagon in the darkness, returning to our platonic affair somewhere at the end of Brooklyn, at the end of the continent?

When we returned to the outer borough, we went our separate ways. I took her home, of course, accompanied her back to the door (she never let me inside, though I was always curious about what mystery lay hidden behind those walls), and after a peck on the cheek I took a black cab back to my own flat, filled as I was with anxiety tremors, a longing I could neither shake nor explain, an itch that could not be scratched. She was always almost there— always just a hairsbreadth out of reach, almost like a webcam girl. I tried writing a letter, though I knew that I would throw it in the rubbish in the morning, not out of spite but out of fear of possibility. If I did (I don't remember if I did or not) it would have sounded something like this:

"I don't know why I am writing to you. I see you every day and yet we are not together the way I wish we were, but I don't know what that wish actually is. I see you, I hold your hand and I watch you cry and wipe away your tears and I feel as if we are lovers but on a different level of reality. Perhaps we are lovers in a parallel universe. Maybe I am imagining you, but imagining is better than not having anything at all. Oh Betty, my love. Perhaps you are my false true love. How can I own a bit more of you? How can I get you to give yourself to me just a tiny bit more? I am writing a book, I told you. But I have no one to talk with about it, and I have no one to hold either. I clutch the sweaty sheets in the balmy morning and I wish you were here with me, sweating with me, rolling over gently under the cover, turning to me upon waking and opening your sleepy eyes and mumbling, 'Good morning.' And I hold you tight, so tight, tighter than I have ever held anyone ever in my life and we drift off somewhere together... but that morning never comes. Save me, Betty, and I will do all I can to save you and to hell with everyone else, to hell with rhetoric, to hell the naysayers, to hell with spinal discs and wheelchairs, to hell with past flings, but not to hell with love. Be my lover, Betty, not just my love. "

As I had predicted I knew I would do, in the morning I crumpled up my love letter and threw it in the trash. I was sure I would see Betty again that evening. Our meetings had become almost like clockwork. But that day I felt a particular sense of desperation, perhaps something had happened at the concert, or on the train ride home—her tears, her silence. Something had changed, perhaps something very small but something nonetheless. Perhaps my desire, my longing, had gotten out of control.

Everything I wrote to her then was true. It was the desire, the desire to own her somehow, to own a piece of her that would not let go. I felt like one of the prisoners in the Chinese Torture Garden sticking my neck out to try to grab a bite of a piece of rotting bat flesh that a Russian princess or a German countess stuck onto the pointed tip of her parasol and giggled each time she pulled away just as I strained to take a rancid bite.

The phone rang. It was Charlotte.

"How's the book coming along?" she asked mockingly. I knew it was mockery by the tone. The question was disingenuous and rhetorical.

"It's coming," I lied. I was tongue tied and didn't feel like talking and was terrified of making a slip and saying something about Betty. We stuck to idle banter. "The little one has been learning to swim." "Don't drink too much." "Hurry up and finish your book so you can come home." At least the palaver was performed calmly.

Within a couple hours I was on my way to see my lover, my mistress. I decided to go on foot to the Boardwalk. The early evening was the perfect temperature, and the brisk walk would only take me a bit more than half an hour. It was cold by the time I reached Café Europa and I was chilled.

Some folks like to say "change is good." They say it when someone loses a job, and sometime importunely they say it when someone breaks up with a lover. They even say a variation on theme when they say turning forty, or fifty is "just a number." But I didn't want change—or maybe I did and I didn't, but I knew that something was about to change and that evening at Europa confirmed it. Something in Betty had changed after the concert. I felt like she wasn't quite the same anymore, as if something happened that I wasn't aware of or was unable to decipher. Nothing terrible happened that evening; we ate cake and drank coffee and brandy. But I had never seen her so distracted. I looked into her eyes, trying hard not to stare, trying my best to figure her out, but her expression gave no clue to an answer. After I had walked her home and left her in the lobby, where she waited for the elevator, I felt a shard of ice pierce my heart, my guts, my cock. I kissed her goodnight as the rickety elevator arrived and went home.

On my way back I was even more dreadfully chilled. I was sure I was developing a fever. I thought that vodka or whiskey was the logical way to nip it in the bud, but I resisted the temptation to submerge myself further in alcohol and when I entered my flat, I undressed, pulled the covers over my Italian Guido bed all decked out in white and gold and immediately went to sleep to sweat out all my concerns.

To some extent it worked. I awoke feeling spritely and ready to resume the living dream of mine and Betty's affair. I called her after I had my coffee and vodka and asked her the borderline unthinkable because I wasn't truly thinking: "Do you want to go swimming?"

I bit my tongue the moment I uttered those words. But then Betty laughed and said,

"We could have gone swimming every day, silly! I live next to a beach! What are you talking about?"

"Silly? You're silly!" I laughed. "There's a reason we never swam in that dirty Coney Island beach. It sucks! It's disgusting. Come on, let's go to Long Island, let's go to Jones or Moses. I want to see you in the water."

"I don't have a swimsuit, and besides…" she started to mutter, slightly dejected, "you know it's…"

"I know everything…" I began, but she stopped me immediately.

"You don't know everything. You know nothing."

I was about to drop the phone. The way she spilt "nothing" was brutal. Hurt, I fell silent. But I could tell she was smiling. I could hear it.

"Fine. We can go to Long Island," she said. "But you have to buy me a bathing suit."

Within a few minutes I had a rental car reserved and ready for pick up. All I needed then was a bathing suit for Betty.

Presently we were speeding down the Long Island Expressway. I had disassembled and assembled her chair before but no in nervous excitement I was fumbling until I remembered how to put my fingers on the buttons to release the wheels and finally managed to get the chair in the trunk. Betty was smiling. The moisture of the New York summer was at the perfect level and we careened down the empty expressway, smiling at each other for a good thirty minutes until a monstrous traffic jam interrupted our fine mood. We took it in stride. Betty was wearing her usual outfit: a short black skirt, stockings (why had she worn stockings to the beach?) and shoes that she would never walk in, but I said nothing—we were on a road trip and I had promised to buy her a bathing suit.

We stopped at a surf shop and I said, "Come on, let's pick out a bikini." "Come on!" I kept forgetting that she would need my help not only to help her pick a swimsuit but to enter the tiny shop.

"Oh, for fuck's sake!" she yelled. "Just pick something out and get back in the car!"

I did. I found a black bikini for $50 that I thought would look just right on her. I paid in a hurry and went back in the car where Betty was sweating and waiting for me to return.

When we got to the beach I started to panic. How would I help her with the bikini? Did I make the right choice?

"Just fucking let me do it," she barked when we pulled into the parking lot, and then soon enough, faster than I could have imagined, she had changed into the new bikini I had bought for her and lay there, in the hot back seat, smiling. "I'm ready. Come on!"

What was this "come on"? I helped her out, helped her into her chair. Her day clothes remained on the back seat. She saved me some trouble, I thought. But what if, at other times, she'd need my help? Would I have to dress her, change her? Did she wear adult diapers? I had a flashback of changing my daughter's diapers when she was a baby. How did poor Betty go to the bathroom and clean herself?

"Come on!" she repeated and smiled, this time genuinely, and we walked. I pushed her chair until we reached a concession stand where we rented a beach wheelchair, a ridiculous device that made me cringe. I helped her closer to the surf and saw a couple of other people using the same Flintstones' car. Most of them were retards. I wanted to retch. "Come on, let's go!" she yelled, disregarding the tragicomic situation, and so I pushed her further and quicker, and she laughed loudly, enjoying the day, the salt spray sprinkling and almost showering her as the drooling retards stayed cringing and twisting in the same devices I pushed her in, down to where the sand turned moist and stopped us in our tracks. I lifted her out of her chair and carried her into the waves. She laughed and laughed, and when I was up to my waist in the warm summer waters of the Atlantic I let her go just slightly to bathe her body in the ocean and she held on to my neck almost the way my daughter did when I was teaching her to swim, as a toddler, and she kissed me and said

"Don't let me go… don't let me go yet!"

"But I'll let you go for one minute, so you can swim just for a little bit, no?"

"No!" She held me as tight as my daughter used to hold me the first few times I took her to the beach, when the incoming tide scared her to death. "No! Don't let go of me Lucky! Don't ever let go of me! Not until I tell you!" she grabbed my neck and I held her tighter and tighter and whispered in her ear "I won't, Betty. I will never let you go." And suddenly, she looked at me in hatred and disgust.

In a few more moments it was over. "I want to get out," she said. As much as I had hoped for her to become a mermaid, to break free of her earthly chains, she did not.

She wiggled her arms and her useless legs. I could tell that she felt nothing. "Come on, let's go," she said, "I'm cold." And so I lifted her dripping body out of the sea and lowered her gently onto the dry sand. We lay there together on the beach for some time. She let me touch her skin, even kiss her. I gently licked the salt from her neck while she, languorous, no longer confined to her chair, lay with eyes closed, smiling gently. No sooner had I closed my own eyes, ready to fall into blissful slumber, than she woke me. "I want to go home. Maybe it's time that you do let me go. I am getting tired of all this…" I straightened up and examined her face. She was resolute. She didn't want to stay any longer and I didn't wish to protest. I put her back into the ridiculous clown car for wading invalids and wheeled her toward the parking lot and put her in her normal chair.

We drove back to Brooklyn in silence. She kept fiddling with the radio, trying to find the right song, and nothing seemed to please her or hold her attention for more than a few seconds. It annoyed me to no end. I kept looking at her crotch, to see if there was any hair peeking out from her panties. There is something spectacularly sexy about just a bit of hair that makes the panties or a swimsuit appear as if the gift inside is only a string pull away. But I could not detect one. I used the distraction of pubic hair to stave away my gnawing fear and trepidation, I still knew almost nothing about her.

"Good night. I'll see you soon," she said after I helped her out of the car. She had already changed without my help, handing me her wet bikini nonchalantly. Something about her was different now. When had it happened? Was it after the park and the symphony? Was it today, at the beach? Did I do something wrong, and if I did, what was it? What could it be? I have learned from experience not to push these things, not to push my luck. I accepted the peck on the cheek, drove to the car rental place and took a ca back home.

That night, after the beach date, was among the most restless of the whole summer. Absurd dreams tortured me throughout. Dreams of mermaids and mermen, visions of quicksand, of tidal waves, of unnatural sized eels and worms; and then, in a denouement right before sunrise, the sleep gods threw me a bone and I was able to return to some pleasant thoughts of childhood, of autumn, of warmth; of some type of "full stomach," of my hand around a waist, of a sweaty, freckled back of a girl I loved... For so long, I had forgotten that one time, sex was actually linked to romantic love, and Betty rekindled the original emotion of desire.

I awoke, and while I knew that Betty and I would see each other that day, I had a horrible, unsatisfied feeling, and feared that the meeting later that evening would also end unsatisfactorily. For the first time since I had settled into Brooklyn, and for the first time since I had met Betty, I thought of our quotidian evening trysts as hollow theatrics. But who was I to pick and choose? We met as usual, talked as usual, and the evening ended—with her going back to her mysterious flat—as usual. We did not talk much about the beach; we hardly talked at all. I prayed to god that something had not changed, but I felt as if some shift had taken place.

For sanity's sake I decided to spend the following day alone. I took the train all the way to Washington Heights and revisited my childhood.

It was a moderate mistake, for it did not come out the way it played out in my dreams.

RETURN TO THE HEIGHTS

The train ride to Upper Manhattan seemed never ending. Back when I was first starting to compose Stacy's story, the view across the Manhattan Bridge and the descent down into Chinatown always filled me with emotion. The light, the morning light where she finally decides to come home and leave her misadventures in New York behind, the yellow blinding light illuminating the stacks of garbage, the decaying buildings, the prison barges that were once moored in the East River. But today, travelling from one end of the city to the other, I felt strangely numb. As the D train went over the bridge, everything looked different. I felt no pangs or flutters. All of it was gone in real life, it only remained in my vision and in my unproduced film.

When I exited the 175th Street station, things were a little better—it was mostly the same old slum—but the tears which I expected never came. I walked past the park, green as I remembered it but still filled with the same winos and dealers. I approached my mother's building and vaguely expected to hear some faint laughter coming from within. Somewhere in my mind a song started to play—a very vague melody of something I must have heard one summer when I was young, but probably never had. A lilting melody, one which I probably only imagined. In some ways I was glad this forgotten part of Manhattan had remained its ugly self. There were fewer Dominicans and Cubans sitting on milk cartons playing dominoes and sipping Heinekens, but they were still there, still present, as were the darting eyes and on my end, the perennial feeling of alienation I felt there from day one. Even then, I did not belong.

The blue haze of New York summer blanketed the filthy streets. Across the river, the mild green of the Palisades Parkway beckoned from the river, over the George Washington Bridge, the bridge that I always hoped would take me somewhere. The green leaves whispered something to me in the afternoon breeze but I could not understand their language.

I crossed back from the waterfront and made my way down to Broadway. I needed a drink but there are no bars in that part of town so I entered a bodega, of which there are plenty, in search of an ice-cold beer.

"Buscando algo?" the man behind the counter asked and grinned. I said nothing, paid for my Heineken and carried on my way. Si, estaba buscando algo… Yes, I was looking for something. But what?

I exited onto the broken street. My dream was ruined. I had not noticed until now that I was covered in sweat.

Next, took a train up to Kingsbridge Heights in order to walk those old, familiar streets. The only thing worse than the seemingly endless trip from one end of New York to the other was the prospect of the same journey coming back. I got off at the 231st street station and saw that very little had changed. In some ways it was a relief, preferable to the "Disneyfication" of much of Manhattan and Brooklyn. That sinister feeling that dwells just below the surface was still there. All cities have ghosts, but New York to me, always seemed to possess the most sinister ones.. Behind every snowfall there is a rapist poised to attack. Behind every gorgeous view of the Hudson from the West Side Highway, there is a dead child stuffed into a plastic cooler.

As for Van Cortland Park, that's where my grandmother spent her last years looking through her window when she wasn't looking at the green fluorescent corridors of a nursing home, waiting for her daughter to visit her, wondering why she doesn't come anymore. If I moved to Kingsbridge with Betty, I would be returning to childhood the way my grandmother acquired her second childhood of dementia. No, I had to return to Brooklyn and try to write. I was able to sneak in a few mini bottles of whiskey onto the now cop-infested subway to make the ride tolerable. This was it, I thought. I must somehow finish a draft of the book and return to California as soon as possible. I already felt the pre-autumnal chill that is the harbinger of winter, bringing on the season of death. And yet autumn in New York is inviting, and that brief hint of an Indian Summer was tempting me to stay just a bit longer.

But what really tempted me to stay was Betty. And there she was, popping up like a dream or image each time I thought about returning. So, when I arrived back in Brooklyn, with the sweat stuck to my back from the ridiculously cold subway air conditioning, just as I warming up in the humid night, I broke into shivers of a different kind. Betty was outside the front door to my building, her face wet with tears.

"What is it? What's the matter?"

She motioned with her hand as if to shoo me away, gesturing like a deaf mute between sobs.

"Come. You need a drink," I said.

There was a bar a few blocks around the corner that I had spotted once but had never gone into. It looked seedy, but I needed her to calm down and there was no time now to cab it to Europa or Primorski.

The bar was a relic, an anachronism. With the green awning, the green lights and the geezers sipping their little beers with a shot on the side, it was a throwback to times we only remember from movies. The smell of stale beer was particularly redolent. We sat down and ordered whiskeys on the rocks. They came quick and she bolted down the booze and the tears dried. She started to speak.

"Oh, Lucky. There are so many things to say."

"Everyone has a story, and your stories, they don't compare to mine. Your stories make me feel tiny...But I have a story too..."

I squeezed her hand.

"Betty," I told her, "everyone has a story. And those aren't my stories, they're my parents'. And they're not happy stories. I haven't got much of a story myself, that's why I'm struggling with this book. But, of course, you have a story. Why don't you tell me yours? I still know so little about you."

"There are certain things people should never, ever talk about, Lucky. There are certain things that should never be written about, either. But I will talk about it. I will talk about it briefly, and then you can make up your mind about me and who I am."

"You can tell me anything," I told her, biting my own brain and heart out of fear for something terrifying, but I needed to know.

"Very well, I will tell you a few things. But not everything, and not right now. No, I can't tell you right now. Let's just drink this one and then I want to go home. Anyway, what's up with you? Don't ask about me. What did you do today?"

I told her a bit about my day, my exploration of places haunted by memory. I told her how I felt that although everything changes and the locomotive of time speeds on, the fact that some things like buildings remain made me feel like the past still existed, that time wasn't yet destroyed by Kali. When she asked me about Kali, the black mother goddess, I explained that I hated myself often and that I considered myself an unsuccessful drunk a lot of the time but that at one point I had studied Hindu philosophies. I told her that she, as a jiva, is caught in samsara like all living beings and is waiting to be liberated. This intrigued her but also frightened her though I could sense an oddly hopeful fear in her eyes. I walked her to the train station—she insisted taking the subway home by herself—and went back to my apartment, exhausted but pleasantly tipsy after my voyage to childhood. I also felt something was fomenting. I was not at all sure what it was. Perhaps I was about to break out of my writer's block, I thought, or perhaps something was going to happen with either Betty or Charlotte.

The night after taking Betty to that peculiar old bar, I had the most wonderful "virtual sex." In one especially sweet dream a girl in a red wig came up to me and said, "Come, let's go home and get naked," and gave me the key to her flat. Perhaps keys, apart from their obvious Freudian symbolism, held a special significance for me—perhaps they represented my wish to see where Betty lived, to be invited into her house, whether real or metaphorical.

Back to the redhead: I wait for her in her flat. She lives in a messy apartment on the top floor of a brownstone, in an unnamed town. I know I shouldn't be doing this. I know I shouldn't even be there. And then she comes in, begins to undress slowly, saying, "I haven't had sex in so long..." I reach over when she's down to her bra and panties and kiss her stomach, then I wake up.

But I am still dreaming. I wake up within my dream and run into Betty on the street. I try to tell her what happened in my "dream" without being too explicit, try to apologize and she laughs. Then I woke up for real. I lay there sweating, thinking, "Something has to change. I can't go on. This can't go on."

A few days went by without seeing Betty. There were excuses, doctor's appointments (I never asked for what) and I brushed aside because to paraphrase Swinburne I was hoping that absence would make the tart grow fonder.

I took another excursion. The one place I knew I needed to visit was The Met, but that too, I found, had changed, and not for the better. Like everywhere else in the city, it was too chaotic, too crowded. Even the little things were missing, like the iconic metal admission buttons, or the info desk (now two separate counters). Artworks littered the gallery like city trash, piled up hodgepodge in every available space, a triumph of congestion and wealth over subtlety.

I wandered aimlessly through the galleries, trying to remember what, if anything, would elicit the "saudade" I felt for New York in LA, but which seemed to be missing now that I had arrived. The Egyptology collection remained as stunning and creepy as I remembered it: strange, ancient dreams preserved in stone. It was when I segued into the American Wing, searching for something to help me find me a connection to this America, that I found myself staring at Sargent's Portrait of Madame X. I had read something about the subject, that she was a "professional beauty," and I wondered if that was simply a glamorous term for a high society slut. There was also something about her that vaguely looked like my poor Betty, but standing tall and not confined to sitting. What did this glamorous Madame X do in the bedroom? And then I l also remembered Mlle X: *"French Neurologist Dr. Jules Cotard was surprised and confused by the female patient (known only as Mademoiselle X) brought to his office at the Pitié-Salpêtrière University Hospital in Paris one afternoon in 1882. The 43-year-old described a peculiar set of symptoms: she claimed she had "no brain, no nerves, no chest, no stomach, no bowels — that there was nothing left of her but the skin and bones. Also, she claimed she had no soul, that there was no God and no devil, and that overall she was nothing but "a disorganized body." With no internal organs, she claimed to not need to eat anymore. Further, she expressed her belief in her immortality, noting that she could not die a natural death, but "will live forever unless she is burnt, fire being her only possible end."*

Just as I pondered these awful thoughts, there was a silent rotation of the security guards and, mouth agape and laughing quietly, I was approached by one of the guards who it took me a full minute to recognize. It was my friend Felix, whom I had not seen or talked to since moving to Los Angeles a decade ago. It was his lunch break and he invited me to eat with him at the staff cafeteria, to which I gladly obliged.

Over a lunch of tasteless salmon and ratatouille we did our best to catch up in the little time that we had. I knew Felix when he was a guard and I still worked at the info desk. He had always had talent and ambition, but now, twenty years later, he was sorely lacking in the latter. Felix and I were never terribly close, but he knew Dick and Mike, and would appear at parties of mutual friends and join in for the occasional after work drinks. Never particularly exciting nor a great conversationalist, he was often the "voice of reason" during feuds and a good listener when it came to talking over the girl problems we others all had.

As he talked it became clear that, for reasons he never explained or even hinted at, he had completely given up on any ambition, not only his art career but even to rise up in the ranks of the security department. And while letting him talk in his signature monotone I silently composed a jeremiad of my own failures and about all the things that I too had given up on. Yet Felix, nearly bald now and resigned to mere survival, was a picture of defeat. The only lively thing about him were his cold Putin eyes that shone despite the despair. He was content, or so he told me, but I understood that he envied me despite my own failings, and so he broke out the old trope about writing being the noblest profession. He too had flirted with the idea of writing a novel, but it eventually gave up on that ambition, content with his health insurance and dental plan from the union.

"Write, man! Just do it," he said, unaware that the imperative to "just do it" was the thing that grated me more than possibly anything else. "I can't figure out how to do it anymore, but I still try sometimes. You know that writing is primeval? It's the only thing that gave our ancient relatives the ability to transmit something to the following generation. I mean, look at this place—the pharaohs, the hieroglyphs…"

"For what purpose, though?" I asked. "To keep the human race alive?"

"Yup." Felix smiled and dipped into his slop with a smirk.

"Evolution and all that. I dunno. What do you want from me? I'm just a security guard."

"And I'm nothing," I said and started drifting off while Felix mumbled recycled philosophy and told me about his life. His words faded in and out. He mentioned something about how we live on through our children, which was surprising since he had none. Soon enough his break was over and it was time for him to return to guarding treasures of art.

I gleaned little from that episode. I garnered that he was single, lived alone. Another New York soul lost in the anthill. Before we parted, he went to the vending machine and bought a "Hostess Fruit Pie," proudly joking that these disgusting desserts had "never been touched by human hands." As he headed back to his shift at the American Wing he looked to me like the Black Dahlia, Elizabeth Short, disappearing into the lobby of the Biltmore Hotel never to be seen alive again. The only difference was that Felix would go back to his own Biltmore via the Met until his death. And I emerged from the Met with a taste of death on my tongue, not to mention the man-made salmon. Death is the ultimate certainty. When it will come and in what form is the ultimate uncertainty.

All things must come to an end, and we are supposed to accept that. But I could not. The randomness of whether it will be a happy ending, a tragic ending, a false ending… it drove me crazy. There are platitudes that seek to explain this misery, that without death we would not appreciate life and other such nonsense, but they have never worked for me. A day before my meeting with Felix I dreamt of my father. He was old, as old as he was when he died, but was still making plans for a new choreography. I had just bought him a new iPhone to better stay in touch and was showing him how to use it. In the middle of explaining how to take photos I was struck by the terrible realization that he would be dead soon, and that with his death his work would simply vanish. There was no way

I would be able to continue his work, nor did he pass his knowledge onto anyone who would be able to do so in turn. Conquering death by death only works when you're the Son of God. I resolved, on waking, to finish my book. But when I got home that evening after meeting Felix, all I could think about was Betty. And the pages were still blank.

There was no way to know or tell where Betty would be the next day. I supposed I could walk back to the Boardwalk and wait for her at Café Europa. Eventually sleep won and my eyes closed. I did not shut the blinds before I collapsed and sleep lasted for only an hour or two, at the break of dawn. In my delirium and in my search for a woman, I took the subway to the end of the line and walked to the Café Europa in the vain hope of seeing her.

"Gingerly" is not an adverb one would usually use to describe a person eating a plate of fried eggs, but there she was—gently and, yes, gingerly cutting through the runny sun of the yolk and scooping it up with her toast.

The only thing she said was, "Sit." No hellos, no I missed yous, no where have you beens. I sat down as she gingerly finished her eggs and toast.

"I have to go out of town tonight," she said as I rubbed my eyes in disbelief. "But I'll see you again soon, okay, honey?"

I grinned politely and swallowed bile.

"Can you help me? I'm done."

She threw a banknote on the table and I wheeled her down the boardwalk toward the street. We didn't talk. I had nothing to say. The taxi was already waiting.

"He can do it. I'll see you soon, honey," she said and motioned me over. We kissed on the cheek.

When her car pulled away I hailed another cab, went home, and slept for eighteen hours.

Where had she gone? Why didn't I ask her? Who exactly was she?

The latter question seemed to me less important than the former. Where did she keep on disappearing to all the time?

I too wished to disappear—but with a woman, perhaps even with Betty, despite her immobility. I wanted to sit on a beach in Miami, Palma de Mallorca, Cascais... with a woman. With a woman's waist in easy reach. But Betty's midsection was out of my reach, it was entrenched in her chariot. Perhaps I needed someone else. One of Jim's litany of bimbos. But then I would imagine myself married to one of those strangers, my arm around her waist, mumbling, praying, "Oh my Betty, oh my Betty... it is you that I want, no matter how crooked and crippled you may be, it is you, my Betty..."

I awoke in my sweaty tomb and believed for a moment that she was there. I saw that I was only hugging wet pillows and loneliness broke through me and shattered my heart.

ATLANTIC CITY AND THE END OF SUMMER

As the summer nights went on, I knew that all good things must come to an end—the question was: in what fashion?

Into each life some rain must fall
But too much is falling in mine
Into each heart some tears must fall
But some day the sun will shine...

By now Betty had been to my house a few times. "Don't be mad," she said as we sat one evening on my balcony watching the sky turn orange then black, the stars and the airplane lights flickering overhead. Vol de Nuit. I had always been enthralled by the sight of planes departing for destinations unknown to me apart from their names, exotic and unfamiliar lands and cities. It was a reminder that there were other places to discover, that there is always a journey even if it is just to the edge of the night. The reverie came to a vicious halt when she finally blurted out:

"Don't laugh, but I met this guy..."

Lump in my throat. I had heard that line before, on more than one occasion, but it was the time that Emily Vainonen said it to me in San Francisco that stuck. Et tu, Betty? I was petrified. For some reason I took it for granted that because of her condition I was the only knight in shining polyester for her and that no one else would take an interest. She interrupted herself to put me at ease.

"I was at the bodega the other day buying cigarettes and this guy comes in. He's older and fat and balding, sweating through his suit.

I wondered why he was wearing a suit on a hot day and decided that he must be on his way back from a funeral. Anyway… Total guido, he looked like the guy from The Sopranos, or maybe Harvey Weinstein. And he's staring at me, breathing heavily, sweating…"

My heartbeat slowed ever so slightly. Maybe it wasn't as bad as I feared. She continued.

"So I turn around and make eye contact and he laughs a little, nervously, and I keep staring. He goes, 'I'm sorry, you're gonna think this is weird but, well you're real pretty and I was gonna ask you something—whether you wanted a job.' And I'm thinking, oh fuck, this guy looks sleazy as hell, what kind of job could he possibly offer me? In a whorehouse for people with a cripple fetish? 'C'mon I'll tell you about it outside,' he says, so I go outside. What's he gonna do? Kidnap me?"

I feared what she was going to say next.

"So I go outside with him, he looks even sweatier in the sun, and fatter too, like a bloated toad. He goes up to his car. He drives a big green Cadillac, can you believe it? It's like out of a horror movie of some kind. Anyway, he tells me what he does. He's like a 'professional gambler' and he wants me to go with him to Atlantic City."

To do what? Suck his cock? The bile came rushing back up my esophagus. I had come to believe that people are capable of anything, women especially, even when paralyzed.

"It's not what you're thinking. He told me he's superstitious, something to do with some part of Italy that his family is from where… anyway, he told me crippled people bring him good luck. I was offended at first, and the whole thing sounds completely bizarre—he just wants me to sit next to him at the poker table. I thought about it and when he offered me a thousand dollars, I said yes. I mean, come on, just to go there and do nothing—money doesn't lie on the ground, and I don't get much for disability…"

"When are you going?"

"This weekend. But I'll be back in a few days, don't worry. It's just for a few days…" She smiled.

I could not help but sulk, although I wanted to break her face, and she could see it. Our relationship was chaste, and she could do whatever she wanted to with the rest of her life. I had no power over her, and just as with every other woman, I could not and would not ever truly possess her. I stifled a tear as I went into the kitchen to mix two more vodka tonics and when I returned, morose, she tried to change the subject.

The moon was out now, brighter than usual, and she said, "Look at the moon, spying on us." I felt another shudder—those words reminded of something but I tried to block it from my mind.

"I saw a science show about space the other day," she continued in an attempt to deflect from what she told me about her plans, "and they said that for a commercial jet to orbit the biggest star, flying at 400 miles an hour, would take eleven thousand years. Can you believe it? Isn't that incredible?"

I nodded and replied dispassionately: "Yeah. That's pretty incredible." What did it matter how long it takes to orbit a star millions of light years away? Europe, and all my travels that I wished to pursue, seemed light years away, and so did any hope of writing and finishing my book. So, too, did Betty. How long would it take to peer into her soul, to let her reveal herself to me? I continued to sulk and took huge sips of my drink. She put hers down on the table.

"Well I guess I'd better be going," she finally said and wheeled herself into the living room. I followed her to open the door and she turned back, smiled, and said again, "Don't be mad at me. I'll be back soon." The taxi was waiting outside.

Once she left, I cursed myself for suspecting the worst from her, for being jealous, for acting insecure and being a petty brat. I went back to the balcony and continued to drink, staring at the night sky, looking at infinity and repeating in my head, "It doesn't matter. Nothing matters at all in the end..." A nice, comfortable despair began to set in. I did not finish the bottle as I thought I would. Instead I undressed and covered myself in the sheets and dozed off.

I was terrified that she would not come back from Atlantic City, or that if she did everything would change. What if she didn't return? I had some experience with this, more than once. That fatal brief separation that spells disaster happens too many times and I was engulfed in fear.

A few days prior we sat on the boardwalk again, smoking cigarettes, and the silence and the pauses irritated me until I finally blurted out, "Why don't you tell me more about yourself? I feel like I've known you all my life but don't know anything about you."

"Oh, Lucky," she smiled sadly. "Wouldn't it be better if I told you about all the things I could have been instead of what I am?"

When she uttered such melancholic statements she reminded me of my mother, though without the latter's penchant for melodrama and exaggeration. Betty was earnest in her sweet despair.

"Life doesn't always turn out the way you want it. You probably know this, don't you?"

I nodded. I most certainly did know this. I had always expected something spectacular to happen but, alas, there was no fame or fortune, no walking around stoned on La Croisette in a two-thousand dollar suit, not even white shoes on St. Mark's Place. In fact, now that time had begun to accelerate and the light at the end of the tunnel had grown dimmer and almost sighed out, I actually periodically pined for stability, for a library or teaching job perhaps, for savings, a good used car, a two week vacation each year... But all of these things were unattainable now unless something magnificent happened, something unexpected, the beast in the jungle released at last, if even for a brief time before it's chained and caged again in the form of actual old age, which seemed just around the corner. And that persistent, gnawing feeling that time was running out made my insides bleed...

"You want to know about my accident, don't you?" she said.

I remained silent, did not offer so much as a nod. Of course I wanted to know, but I was also afraid of upsetting the balance of this perverse idyll. Already she had hinted at things I did not wish to hear, the way one doesn't want to know about past lovers, past indiscretions.

"I will tell you about it, one day, just not right now. I will confess everything, but let's just enjoy this moment, every moment. Every day is a gift, you know? Every day we're alive."

I did and didn't want to know. I was enchanted, and despite my yearning and curiosity I had become accustomed, used to this liminal, hypnagogic state of being, with the blank page on the laptop, the evenings spent in quiet, boozy melancholy, the unreturned calls from my wife. Like a hospital stay or a long plane ride, I was carried on, levitating whether by jet or sedatives and felt relieved of all desires and responsibilities. But the fabric of a dream can so easily be torn—I knew this, hence my desire to keep Betty and me in this perfect, or should I say imperfect, equilibrium, Platonic as it was. Fear of upsetting this balance was always somewhere in the back of my mind.

In Bulgakov's Master and Margarita there is a story about a girl in hell. From what I remember, her name is Frieda. She lives in a normal house, in a normal room of her own and probably dreams the sweetest dreams. But every morning when she opens her eyes, on her night table is the red kerchief with which she smothered her newborn child—and that is her eternal punishment, to always be reminded of her crime and her sin.

Was I waiting for a similar kerchief to appear? Was I embarking on a journey leading to the discovery of hell? What was Betty hiding? A stupid question.

Within each person there can be a Mariana Trench of unfathomable darkness, with women doubly so. I knew she was from Upstate New York, that her mother was alive but they did not get along. Nothing about her father. She had a sister who worked for Planned Parenthood, somewhere on the west coast. That she had lived in LA and San Francisco. All very superficial information that told me nothing about who she was, and nothing about what exactly happened to her.

PARTIR C'EST MOURIR UN PEU

We met in the morning for a "farewell breakfast." I hated to think of it as a farewell, but it was to me a separation serious enough to feel semi-tragic, filled with trepidation. I had remembered similar breakfast dates with past girlfriends. The details were hazy but the lump-in-the-throat feeling was still embedded somewhere in my mind.

In LA, not long before leaving for NY, I heard a story on the radio about hyper-sensitive people; the ones who can be driven to tears by ephemeral bursts of sadness from something as trivial as watching Bambi or Dumbo, or hearing a familiar melody that very vaguely reminds them of something, and I realized I fit squarely into that category. As we sat in the diner before Betty was to go to Atlantic City, I felt a horrible tinge of despair that this was farewell forever, that this was the last time I would see her. While this was potentially and hopefully untrue, since she did promise to return in a few days, staring into my greasy omelet I was reminded that this too will come to an end, like all things good and bad. Summer would end, and I would have to return to my life in California. I had barely thought about my wife and child during this journey. What was going to happen between now and the time I had to return? What will happen when I return?

I had always hated diners. Something about that very New York institution revolted me. I don't know whether it is the smell, the geriatric clientele, the meeting place for mobsters or the lighting and crystal chandeliers, or that Burt and Linda Pugach, the crazy love couple who got married after he left her blind in an acid attack loved them, or that they were often part of peoples routine as they sank into more routine and life passed them by... Or perhaps it is the extensive menu, which is absurd and overwhelming even when you know that everything will taste the same. Anyway, it was her idea, so we sat in Park View Diner which was nowhere near a park and did not offer much of a view. I was melancholic, she was distracted and distant. I observed the bulbous, gelatinous hides draped over shrinking skeletons devouring their club sandwiches and patty melts and felt immediately nauseous.

Much of the breakfast was spent in silence, and the day felt like a bleak and boring Sunday, though it was Friday and Betty was leaving in a few hours. Usually our silences were comfortable, the way one can easily be silent together with a spouse or parent or very close friend, but that day the silence was intrusive, as if some "quiet angel"—in Slavic folklore, when people stop talking unexpectedly they say a quiet angel flew past—kept interrupting. For the first time with Betty I felt tongue-tied. It was as if that particular morning, or starting from the night before to be precise, she started to seem different to me, as if she was someone else. Several times I asked her whether she was okay, until she finally snapped and stared at me and said in a hostile voice, "Yes, I'm okay! Why do you keep on asking me that?"

"Bye. I'll see you in a few days," she said as we left the horrific diner. I squinted through the brightness, the sidewalk stained with pigeon and seagull shit. "I can go home by myself." She turned her wheelchair and started to push herself away. "Bye." I said nothing and walked to the subway, not knowing what I should think.

When I came home an odd thing happened. I felt a modicum of freedom and decided to put at least part of her out of my mind and try to write.

On the morning of this farewell breakfast, I awoke without a hangover for a change and felt I now felt that despite the sadness of her departure I could concentrate on the book. The sky was turning grey; a storm was coming in from the ocean and the and the fog and mist of the marine layer chilled and refreshed. I turned on the computer, looked at the blank page I had been staring at for weeks, and miraculously started to write. It started to come automatically as if on autopilot, from some divine or demonic inspiration. And though I cursed myself for writing in verse again, I could not stop, and so I went on.

"It doesn't matter," I kept telling myself when I wanted to slam on the breaks. "Sure, no one reads poetry anymore, but maybe some people still do, and you can be certain that no one reads screenplays, so just keep going. At least you will have completed something, even if it's not what you wanted when first conceived the idea."

Sometimes I would be interrupted by a flash of a thought about Atlantic City, that utterly wretched and blighted excuse for a town. I would wonder what Betty was doing but tried to shoo away that thought. When I did, brief memories popped up of when my mom dropped me off at Atlantic City for the summer, and what a boring and pathetic summer that was for a twelve year old kid to spend in such a hovel. But I'd kick those ugly memories aside and they would scurry away for a while as I returned to the story at hand: the saga of Stacy Fox.

Why Stacy? Why did I devote my life to telling and obsessing about the miserable and tragicomic story of this fictional character? Others have done the same, I suppose: Cervantes with his peabrained knight errant, Petrarch with his Laura... Stacy was my filthy bit of a creation, a Galatea with STDs, and I was a talentless Pygmalion or Geppetto. And in time she became my Laura and my Christ.

I admit it: the reason I didn't want to start typing was because I didn't want it to end. But I had to, I felt like time was running out, desperately. Forget my health, forget my madness, forget it all, I knew that now was the time for me to finish this book. I was determined not to fall into that vague but inextinguishable sadness that would overcome me as a child. That New York feeling, never more pronounced than when I would return; the tears would well up in my eyes the minute I saw the George Washington Bridge and knew I was coming back to a dubious home.

I set out to write, and write I did. Occasionally, over those few days, I would get a phone call from an old friend or acquaintance, once even from someone in high school, but I had no desire to see anyone, much less indulge in gormless juvenilia, reminiscing about the supposed "good times"—I was too busy creating my own past as I revisited it. I didn't need any of Frieda's handkerchiefs, reminding me of how utterly stupid the real past was. How did they manage to track me down? I didn't pursue the question and so I kept going. I wrote like a man possessed, and I suppose I was to some extent, or if not wholly possessed then certainly pursued by some manner of furies. Stacy was the America I could never understand and never hold.

Exhausted, I collapsed and slept fitfully, the book and real life forming a very murky mélange. I had no idea how long I slept for but when I looked at my phone I saw that it was Wednesday. Betty had left on Friday. There were no calls from her, no messages. I started to panic. The satisfaction of finishing the manuscript evaporated.

At first, the New World Symphony seemed to be about three different women, all three of whom suffer the same predicament. They were also all, though unmistakably rotten, possessed of not just a tragic quality but a need for some type of redemption— even, if need be, through death. I considered having them as the saga of a single character or archetype, a theme-and-variation on the Fallen Woman. Finally I decided that the New World Symphony should be a continuation of The Girl from Below (Garbage Dump) and that it should follow the pitifully sordid saga of the protagonist Stacy Fox.

At the same time, I wondered what was the worst thing a woman could do to merit what I put my character through. I was not thinking of Irma Grese, Elizabeth Báthory, Darya Saltykova or Ilse Koch—those were true monsters who should have been shot in the cradle. I was thinking about sleaze, something sexually depraved. But what is depraved these days? Even De Sade is, after all, rather pedestrian; fetishes have been around forever.

One story that came to mind was Jean Lorrain's "The Unknown Woman," about an upper-class female who seduced petty criminals, slept with them and then turned them into the police solely for the ultimate purpose of masturbating and reaching orgasm as they were either sentenced to prison or even guillotined. Or there's the story of Casanova, who fucked a whore in the ass while looking out of the window at the regicide and achieved the most powerful climax as the wretch was dismembered. From Wikipedia I learned:

Fetched from his prison cell on the morning of 28 March 1757, Damiens allegedly said "La journée sera rude" ("The day will be hard"). He was tortured first with red hot pincers; the hand with which he had held the knife during the attempted assassination was burned using sulphur; molten wax, molten lead, and boiling oil were poured into his wounds. He was then remanded to the royal executioner, Charles Henri Sanson, who harnessed horses to his arms and legs to be dismembered. But Damiens' limbs did not separate easily: the officiants ordered Sanson to cut Damiens' joints with an axe. Once Damiens was dismembered, to the applause of the crowd, his reportedly still living torso was burnt at the stake.

But those instances are rare, and there are many more pedestrian ways a woman can create fear and horror in a man. The old ghastly whore who narrates De Sade can be dismissed as apocryphal, a titillating fantasy, but much lesser sins—when they are real—can fill the heart with fear of the unknown, and send the mind reeling. For it is the things we cannot see, or do not know, that are most frightening. And thus I always suspected there were deep and ugly secrets hidden within each person, and particularly within each woman. I have never been able to let go of this fear, this fascination.

The first few days were a blur. I would be overcome by a wave of exhaustion and once as I lay down a bunch of murky lines of verse went floating through my head. I was a poor student in high school and college other than in English literature, or any kind of literature, and in English I had a fine memory for recitation. I lay down on my gaudy "European Furniture" bed and fell asleep mumbling to myself the section of Chaucer's Manciple's Tale that I was still able to remember with clarity:

> Taak any bryd, and put it in a cage,
> And do al thyn entente and thy corage
> To fostre it tendrely with mete and drynke
> Of alle deyntees that thou kanst bithynke,
> And keep it al so clenly as thou may,
> Although his cage of gold be never so gay,
> Yet hath this brid, by twenty thousand foold,
> Levere in a forest that is rude and coold
> Goon ete wormes and swich wrecchednesse.
> For evere this brid wol doon his bisynesse
> To escape out of his cage, yif he may.
> His libertee this brid desireth ay.

To escape out of *her* cage, if she may, is what I was dealing with.

Part III

THE BOOK

THE NEW WORLD SYMPHONY

It all came to me almost automatically. I did not care anymore about form or length. I had no hopes of it being published anymore. I only wanted to capture a feeling and I found my calling in the verse form. I wanted "it" to somehow exist, not as a screenplay for those are impossible to read for pleasure but as something more concrete. And so a poem formed as if Gabriel dictated the Quran to me, the Prophet. But more about Gabriel later. I had wanted to write Stacy's misadventures as a prose novel, but the poetry took over and within a few days I had a verse narrative. I have condensed my long poem for the purpose of this novel.

As a symphony, the story is told in three or four distinct parts: a lento, an allegro, and at least one scherzo before the coda. A scherzo was imperative because that is what god pulls on you: a joke. The symphony could just as well have gone: I. Scherzo II. Scherzo, III. Scherzo and IV. Coda. To make a short, sordid story even shorter, here's what happened in that script, to repeat what I had already written earlier in this book.

Stacy Fox returns home—to Del Mar, Cortland, Albany, New Paltz, Watertown... take your pick—but she doesn't stay long. After a summer spent sleeping on a roof in Queens, in which she did not so much dip her toes in filth as dive head-first into a quagmire, Cortland, Albany or New Paltz just don't pass muster. Frankly, she is bored.

It was no surprise that sooner or later I had to kill her off. But what could I do to her to still warrant that "terrible sympathy" which I thought she possessed? The sympathy lay only in romanticism,

Jose and Carmen, Raskoknikov and Sonia. Before I killed her off I had to give her more life, let her live and fuck and eat for a while. Thus I extended Stacy's life, after she came home to New Paltz with a black eye and Jerry ended up in the slammer.

The blackwalled tires of the Greyhound bus, illuminated by the red taillights and the exhaust smoke, formed a mild kaleidoscope against the humid black of the night and the silhouettes of the green trees. Stacy had come home. The prodigal daughter. But this was not the end of her story… Rather, her life adventure, her "big dramatic moment," was still to come, years later, at the climax of the New World Symphony.

But yet again I get ahead of myself. Here is how I started the poem.

THE NEW WORLD SYMPHONY
1. Lento
2. Allegro
3. Scherzo

Part One: Lento

I write this sober now,
older but not much wiser, though sadder and more numb.
But with what intoxication, in my youth, I slurped up
all the flies that landed in my soup, two decades ago or more,
drunk on whiskey and little loves.

And though my salad days have wilted, she
remains, immortal, and stays with me
even when she sleeps alone.

For my last birthday, my wife bought me
an hourglass. How apropos.
For I've got some cobwebs in my mind now
and my teeth are longer.

Not Stacy, though. No spiders up her fanny.
She still gives to the poor her all, just like the leading
lady of a movie that someone wrote
but no one's ever seen.

Ah, film, the temptress. Arch Priestess Celluloid
of the unholiest of unholies,
inviting us to play God and mold Golems,
turning words into pictures moving.
I did manage to animate poor Stacy in a
short film, but fifteen minutes wasn't enough.
All this was a screenplay once, that someone
wrote but no one's ever filmed.
How I wished to bring her to life eternal.
This poem, then, is the closest we
can come to a realization of her story, something
that someone may actually read and verse be damned.

I did raise you, after all, my darling.
My lovely duckling, my ugly cygnet.
And you still live, my dirty innocent love,
and we meet each other when our dreams
collide from time to time.
You in your gulag of spacetime,
me in my California exile and purgatory
on the isle of Circe, pining for a non-existent Ithaca.
We will be bound together until
we're both forgotten, and hopefully and probably
you will outlive me.

Aeaea, Aeaea, Aeaea
I hear the sound, the fading
echo of times past, loves lost.

St. Stacy of Rivington Street or Red Hook.
How I wanted to throw you under the rails
somewhere in Loisaida: Essex, Attorney, Orchard…
When New York was such a sweet hell. How mother
night would make or break you.
Maybe Delancey, where Hasids from Williamsburg
drive over to get blowjobs from
five dollar crack whores. But it was Rivington Street
that gave me the sweetest pain.
But let me start back in Cortland, New York.

After her summer adventure, Stacy's last
school semester was uneventful, as if nothing had happened.
And while the closets were always ready to swing open
for a skeletal embrace, life went on.

Spring in upstate New York comes in not like a
lamb but like a stoat, doing its weasel war dance before
killing a beast ten times its size. The skies are so cold,
so purple, it might as well be winter.
Stacy's story begins in the purple and black spring
and ends in the red and green of a Greyhound's tail lights
illuminating the trees at the Cortland bus stop.

There was nothing unusual about Stacy.
She sure was good looking, always would be, even much
later when the world would spin out of control.
For now, through the cracks of the cold spring, through the
long, grey line of suburbia stretching from coast to
coast, perfect weather comes, an unseasonably warm night,
moist with the first breath of vernal longing.
Let us follow her on her travels through the spring
exultances, as Stacy walks to her after school waitressing job.

There's Jerry, outside the diner, eating an apple
like Adam as she approaches.
It's hot in the kitchen where he's washing dishes
and he's got his shirt off.
Diner's empty, no one will notice or care—could wring out
his wifebeater from all the sweat.
God, he's handsome, she thinks, and blurts out,
"You're gonna catch cold with your shirt off like that!"
and swiftly enters the diner.
And the moon, peeking through the blinds, was
getting out her binoculars.

"Is it true none of you made it with that girl?"
Jerry asks, sweating again over the dishwasher.

It was too early to guess
what she would become, and her face…
why, there is only one woman with so many faces.
How to describe her? Fleeting, at times icy.
But she would melt when God would stick
razor blades in her candy apple. Blonde hair and
sky-blue eyes, an attitude at times that cloaked
whatever spiny things were hidden in her heart.
So I molded her, before I tried to murder her.
For now, her crimson merrymaking was just
beginning. But imagine her any way you wish,
Put her on autoplay, autoamerican, while I blow
under her sails and gently pull her strings and guide
her to sweet hell in this tears-and-sperm soaked story.
I held her like a dove, not so lightly that she could
fly away, not so tightly that she would die.
But let's go back to the diner, where six men and
a girl are taking up their positions.

She changes into her waitressing skirt but her
head and heart are aflutter: God, he's handsome.
All thoughts of Mike, her boyfriend, are out the window.
Meanwhile don Jerry is making his own inquiry,
which is met by
"Don't even try it" and "She's got a boyfriend."
To these poor devils, she's the zephyr of spring, their
break from the monotony, from the dirty diner, from
their bleak lives. She comes in like tonight's west wind,
breaking a crack of warmth and moisture to signal winter's end.

"They're all the same…" Jerry laughs off her defenders.
"Ain't nothing to it. Take her out, buy her a beer
and lay her down.
Or bend her over a garbage can."
"Wanna make a bet?"
Soon enough the kitty's full and Stacy's shift is over.
Everyone looks on
while Jerry stalks his prey.

Rape! Rape! Rape!
The dirty angels trumpet, but that's not how our
Jerry does it. What words does he use to
enchant her as she's leaving? It's hard to tell—
the others are huddled in the kitchen,
struggling to hear and see the rake's progress.
And that ancient heartbreaker, the moon,
illuminates their tryst.
Right in the fucking mud.

"You bastard… You poor bastards…" she smiles bitterly
"What do you know?" spits Jerry.
Walking home she thinks, "Mike's gonna kill me."

And so the little creatures here they hear
the highway screaming… Awake or
barely dead, they crawl, they learn to crawl
off to the nearby factories, diners, 7-11's
and the spring of green when there's an
itch that you can't scratch, an itch that will
last for decades never leaves. Why should it?
"It's such a small town."
Well, word gets around.

Everyone waiting for that magic moment,
passed out in the bar, with bartender
waking you up and telling you you're the
only one left, tits in your beer, sloshed,
probably pissed your pants, or the magic
moment under the bleachers of the football field
where word gets around quicker than fist
meets nose and produces blood and snot,
where you protest and say
"I didn't do anything" when your football star
boyfriend beats you black and blue,
the same knight or prince valiant who
played a part taking his own turn in the
round table of a daisy chain of gang rape
just the night before. It was all in good fun,
just a kegger, etc etc etc.

"Did you lick his ass too? You got shit in your
    teeth?" He pries her lips and jaw apart and
    spits in her mouth and walks away.

"What do you know?" she thinks,
and bloodied and muddied,

sullied and disgraced, but not as yet
unbound, she walks back home.
Now what to do?

Soon enough she picks up her shoes
and is on the road to nowhere.
She's already kissed her little sister
goodbye.

What a perfect spot to meet,
if not at the railroad yard
then at the Greyhound stop.

"Going somewhere?"
A startled pause. A rush of blood.
"I'm running away from home."

Run, Stacy.
Run, run, run.

"The bus is here," he says. "Looks like we're going together."
"After you."
"No, after you."
He smiles and smacks her ass.
They both laugh.

Well, as your friends, we wanna say,
He'll break your heart one day
So you'd better run, run, run. Yeah yeah yeah.
Oh, but he's such a quiet kind of guy.
How he thrills me, my oh my.
Maybe it isn't true
what they say about him.
Don't be fooled by the shyness in his eyes.

And don't you know he's just a devil in disguise?
You'd better run, run, run. Yeah yeah yeah,

Oh, Stacy, Stacy, you'll be singing
that tune many more times, don't you worry.
That Greyhound Bus is like Al-Buraq, carrying
Stacy and Jerry through the Lincoln Tunnel
toward their own personal New Jerusalem.
Their night journey, their Isra and Mi'raj,
carries them into a little hell while they
are unsure what to do, but fucking hell
they're stuck together at that moment
until the bus exhales its fumes.
Where are they headed, anyway?
Jerry tells her he might have a job with
the Sanitation Department, a friend of his
from Queens was always telling him he
could hook him up.
"And you?"
She can't fully answer. Only been to NYC once on
a school trip…
When the bus doors open the sky is black
and purple. A streak of red light above
the Port Authority Bus Terminal.
"Come on," he says, and she takes his hand
"He took me this far. And I didn't say
anything to my parents. God damn. But what was
I going to do? If word got around that I sucked cock
and fucked around in the mud?
But what do my parents care, or my class mates.
I want to have a little fun without
everyone judging me. Leave me be, I'm on
a journey.

"OK Jerry. You lead the way, you brought me."
"Da fuck? I found you on the bus."
"Not what I mean, I mean we're here now, so
come on, lead the way."
Maybe he's sobered up, or something's changed
over the course of their bus ride from upstate.
Out in the street, the manholes shrouded in white steam
remind her of Santa's hats.
Where to now, prince and princess?

Molto vivace

Avoid the dog shit. Ignore the bums.
Don't buy drugs from strangers.
"Come on, keep up!"
It's all too much for her—the dirty spring,
the bearded plumes of smoke, the itch
in her pussy, the guy she follows without knowing why.
"Come on, keep up…"
"Hey!" she stops and yells. "Hey!"
"Where are you taking me?"

"Come on."
They end up in a shit hotel
with a view of brick on one side
and a view of an alley from the toilet window.
She goes to brush her teeth.
Jerry is asleep.
Abraham slept, Noah too…

Jerry, who had delivered Stacy from Canaan,
presented her then to some fleabag and
an Egyptian falafel stand.

Stacy emerged from the bathroom, saw his paunch
bulging under his wifebeater, traveling
toward his own dreams, passed out, and so she too
closed her eyes and hoped tomorrow would
be the start of something new.

Sometimes she couldn't even contain her
enthusiasm and would wake up
in the middle of the night
and smile.

In the morning, the yolk of the sun
explodes, bleeds out, runs down
her thighs. Hungry, she gets an egg sandwich
on the street, and munches on
the leftover popcorn from
the trip, while Jerry sleeps.
Run, Stacy. Run, run, run.

I would run too, if I were you.
But where is it that you so wish to go?
You made your bed in this flophouse.
Jerry is snoring.
Who is this prick?
Why'd you run away with him
on nothing but a whim?

"Oh, I don't know" you'd tell me
if we could truly talk, but you are
my marionette, so, darling, I'll guide you
back along the string and rails. Go back inside,
my dear. See what Jerry has to say.

He wakes, winces at an empty bottle of Popov.
"God damn, got a little fucked up last night, huh?"
But you hardly drank, Stacy. It's he who's got
the pounding head. Lie down with him, please, my love.
Stroke his chest, rest your head on him and smile.
This is what you wanted.
Soon, soon, my dear.
Wings ripped off flies—that is
your future. But why?
Because I love all my corpses
and all my cripples. But there's still time
for that.

Now, let's go.
It's hot in the city, amid the trash
and broken dreams.

And my dream always comes back
to the same ending, which is also just the beginning:
The Greyhound takes her back
and the green and red tail lights
are a painting across the white
exhaust fumes.
Stacy came home,
but not for long.
God wanted to surprise her.

Thus I would form her, shape her, take a piece of Vainonen, a piece of The Girl from Below, roll around that ball of clay between forefinger and thumb and let my creation sleepwalk. I backtracked as my own world was spinning, the poem kept being rewritten, there is no right way to write it. I keep repeating and

going back because I didn't know how to end it. Repetitions. I'm
only aware of them now but I'm putting it all down as it was written.

The engine spews white smoke,
the harbinger of steamy nights.
But for now, skeletons old and cold or young
sit and wait to sprout their shoots and leaves,
expanding, filling up with shit and fertilizer.
Here on Broadway, it isn't the
flickering lights of strange interludes, it's
RAPE screaming across the violet sky while
secrets are huddled in slums and housing projects
you want to look out for.

Stacy sees an Eraserhead world outside,
the way God sees the world.
A man smashes a man in the face
with fist, with broken beer bottle, fists, bottles...
Crowds gather, ribs are kicked and
teeth are spat. Around the corner in an alley
someone complains that the car smells like cunt.

Jerry complains about the blacks and Stacy
looks at this philosopher and like Xanthippe wants
to empty the chamber pot over his head.
Must wait.
See what he's up to first.
In my mind, the Vltava is turning from a
burbling brook into a swell, soon to pass
a peasant wedding, sifting brutally into C# minor.
Wait until spring, Stacy. Wait until rebirth.
But first some self-immolation.

Oh, I forget. Did I tell you that Stacy ran away
from home again and spent a summer
on a roof in Astoria or Long Island City and
would wake up to the sound of airplanes landing
in La Guardia? But that glorious blue and yellow summer
Was just a blip on the radar. For now, let's deal
with cards. The deck is stacked, the deck is loaded.
So let's get fucked up.
Stacy comes down from the relative north
And other girls come from crisscross applesauce
Down on Minnesota Mile.
Some only have to cross the water on the Staten Island Ferry
to fall, or to become nothing at all.

This loaded deck.
They wake, the dreams of innocents give way
To raging hangover hardon.
"What did I do? Why the fuck am I here?"
She lets Socrates sleep, goes downstairs to
The street
"Orders a coffee and a bun…"
Then what?
Abraham sleeps again
She tries to rouse him
"Get up! Get up you fucker!"
He only snores and rolls over.
And a light comes shining in from
the greasy window.
Shine a light on me…

They're walking like a couple through
the crowds in Times Square

"I've never seen so many people
at once!" She squeezes his arm,
he's wondering what the fuck he's doing
and who he's stuck with.
They dodge the passersby and the cold
air pushes them back. They struggle, pushing on.
Your author here's smug as a bug
in a cunt, but for these two "loss of innocence"
is a loaded term. Let's go deeper for now
into this dark lake. The wind whips up trash,
whistles up filth and whatever else it can
while we huddle.
What's Jerry gonna do?
Where's he gonna take her?
At least buy her a hot dog.
She needs to get away again.
I have to get away.

Jerry's friend who can get him a job
is M.I.A. so they lie around
a lot, sipping from pint bottles watching the news.
God, she's bored.
No calls for Jerry, he fucks her but
it's not the same because it's quite the same in the
faded grey of the hotel room…

Smoking cigarettes, burning holes,
"C'mon let's go to a movie. Get up!"

"A movie!?" Stacy laughs, rolls over
on the bed. She smiles bitterly.
"I really don't care for movies,
they have nothing to do with life."

She's seeing things she's never
seen, for sure. She was always too smart
to end up filling gas, serving burgers
or working the tills, but she was sheltered,
as she herself admitted. Rotary Club took
her to Sweden and her big sister went all the way
to Zimbabwe, but she has only gone as far as
New York (twice) and now she witnesses
how ripe it is with desperation, the rivers of
the Hudson and the East and Harlem heaving,
ready to spill their guts.
A young bum picks through the trash
to reach a hair-encrusted crust.
"Look!" she pulls Jerry close and points,
as though at an animal in a torture garden.
"Look. He's hungry…"

So they walk around for days,
waiting for spring.
Meanwhile Stacy's own spring
is coming.
Oh Stacy, Stacy, let me buy you
a little black house on the edge of
a dark planet, where I can come in
every night and cover you with
a smallpox blanket.

Whose shadows do you see downstairs
when looking down onto the street
from your room in the Hotel Carter?
"Wait, wait… you look like my rape baby,
as if the other man that I despise

is always in your eyes,
You might have his eyes…"

Wait, Stacy, in a week or just a few
days, the trees will look like they're exploding!
And the nights melting with possibility!
But now a storm is brewing inside your
little heart and in between your thighs,
I know, I know…
Soon, when the lime trees are aglow
and blossoms look like pompoms,
you will peek through like a monk
pushing away the branches to see
a pagan orgy, except you'll find
something too horrible to warrant
contemplation: you'll see a slut,
her bloodied panties still around her
ankles while monsters pounce,
won't leave her alone even among the garbage.
Go, see, go see from sea to sea, I will
be waiting, I will be with you always, and I will
dream of holding your hand as we walk along
the sand and smell the sewage from the
water in Santa Monica.
But you still have unfinished business
in New York. Amid the shadows there's
a man or two waiting to truly
seduce you. I watch from side stage and direct
while you oscillate between pain and sleep,
from thinking about dog food to thoughts of God.

Jerry's thoughts are elsewhere too.

"I gotta call Rudy tomorrow"
"What does Rudy do again?"
"Works in sanitation, promised he could
hook me up."
Sanitation. Jerry's dream is garbage.

My ugly cygnet, my beautiful duckling,
you don't know this but I raised you.
You don't know that, how would you?
Even Christ learned too late.
My little gosling, my fragile bird
borne of fever dreams and aborted loves.
I nursed you and gave you duck feet
and flightless wings.
And if it walks like a duck…

Hey Stacy, have you been to the outer
boroughs yet? How about some Harlem projects?
This is before the yuppies moved in,
when fat negroes squatted at their TVs,
sweating out fried foods, drinking Hennessy
in their steaming government apartments,
turning up the set when there's screaming
in the hallway, throwing trash and fetuses
out the window. Have you seen that yet?
Go on, Stacy, explore to your heart's content.
Jerry will be there snoring, waiting for a call
for a garbage man job.

And so we come to the part of the story where Stacy meets
someone we'll call the Underground Man.

Stumbling around Manhattan's west side, Stacy is mistaken for
a streetwalker. And she almost goes for it, but the kindly, romantic

young man named Brian wants instead to show her how she would ruin her life if she went along with it. So he invites her to come see him instead. What a coincidence that he lives in Coney Island.

He confides in her, tells her how miserable he is. She takes pity on him and is rewarded by a date rape, after which as a final insult he throws her a greasy twenty dollar bill. In a perverse way, the lesson he tried to teach her works.

Brian runs after her. "Wait!"
But it's too late and though he runs in circles
around his Coney Island block and the
blue hairs stare and wonder what he's doing
and laughter echoes from his own building,
he's lost now, spinning. Doesn't matter, he'll
be dead soon. Guys like him don't last too long,
they end up in prison over a broken heart.
Meanwhile Stacy's on her way, away away,
in a cab, the windowpanes streaked with tears.
She doesn't want to be there, she closes he eyes.
Wake up, Stacy.

She decides to leave New York, drop Jerry and return home. As a reward, Jerry beats the crap out of her on the street and is promptly arrested while she goes back to Cortland, the way Iris goes back to Pittsburgh.

She climbs up the stairs of the hotel
for one last blinding morning,
just as the garbage smells rise so does the sun
along with the workers and the coffee trucks.

"It's over," she says.
"I'm going home."

In a second she's on her back, Jerry's hands
around her throat, legs kicking
like a child learning to ride a bike.
Spit and blood coming from her nose and mouth.
"I'll kill you! I'll fucking kill you!"
She's struggling to breathe. Eventually
NYPD truncheon puts a stop to it.

Jerry would later send her a
drawing of his cock from prison
by tracing the outline of his hardon
with a prison-regulation golf pencil.

Her story picks up a year later when she's graduating from high
school and getting ready for another journey, this time all the way
to the west coast, the other edge of the continent.

Part Two: Allegro

Shall I talk about my love or
my imaginary mistresses?
Shall I describe the beating of the heart
that is forgotten as quickly as a funeral?
Did my love settle into suburban or rural
mediocrity with just a tingling in between
her thighs to remind her of her lovely, hot
transgressions?
Will she dote on children and be a good mom?
Will her new lover forgive her and forget?
There is still a long road ahead, the highway
is still unfolding, the road to nowhere still being paved
with red adventures.

In Staten Island, or Red Hook, under a purple sky,
the wind howls among the bare trees in the housing projects.
New skeletons awaken from the deep freeze as
the first buds shiver when the dew turns to frost.

All things happen at once, everyone both alive and dead.
Somewhere Oksana Makar and Tralala are princesses
and the cripple dances the jitterbug and the Lindy hop,
and I write songs sitting at an outdoor café,
wearing white shoes.

Oh, Stacy. Don't you know that
on your walk home after your tryst
you were on your way to becoming
the girl who trod on the loaf, and the bread gods
weren't pleased. Jesus wept and snotted in his shroud.
It wasn't too long before that itch
got itchier. Graduation was fast approaching.
Meanwhile, it was time to fuck.
Stacy explores,
while I sit in my uncanny valley
unscathed for now, enjoying
the view, don't let's forget
about the views…
It's okay. We'll grant Stacy all
the views she ever hoped for when
she dreamt of California in a bit.
God is not dead for you yet.
You will ask, "Who's God?" and
laugh in due course. But you can see
him slipping away, you stand on
the edge of the ocean, upon

Homeric shores, feeling the exhilaration
of possibility. Even a little storm
can be monumental in a little life,
a little love. No need to watch Europe burn
from the White Cliffs of Dover
to feel the same profound sense
of openness. This one is just your size,
Stacy. Sized for everyone.

I wrote incessantly and until I passed out. After the morning haze I was about to start writing again when I received a phone call. Stupidly, I picked up without knowing who it was. It was the red-haired demoness, Shelly Farrington. How on earth did she find me?

"I'm outside. Can I come upstairs?" she asked. I don't know why I buzzed her in. Decency perhaps, or curiosity, since I was stealing some of her genes and implanting them into Stacy.

Decked out in red leather pants with the glazed look of a crazy person, she waltzed in as if neither time nor her heinous past mattered one bit. She would do this to me when were a couple and seemed to have not changed. Her ass, that ass… she'd ruined it by tattooing "Chico" or "Tito" or some other spic's name on one of her butt cheeks, which bulged under the beige leather. In a few years she would be grotesque. Just like old times she grabbed the cigarette out of my mouth.

"Can I have this? Thanks."

The immediate desire was to hatefuck the living daylights out of her—emphasis on "hate" rather than "fuck." But the repulsion from all the deceit and nastiness luckily got in the way of what would have been a horrible scenario. She ripped through my morning like a pavement saw. What was there to talk about, anyway?

"Shelly…" I started. "How did you—?"

"I've been stalking you for years. You know that, don't you? How's your wife and daughter?"

She gulped down my glass of vodka and immediately gagged.

"What the fuck is this? Straight vodka? You know, you're gonna fucking die," she smiled.

I stared at her eyes, which had grown heavy and wrinkled. How the fuck did she know about my wife and daughter? I tried to remember her age. She couldn't have been over forty, or not by much. I stared at her and seethed. There was a tickle in my groin because despite the horror she was... if not a good lay, at least a rough and stormy one, something I did enjoy. When we fucked it felt like we were wrestling. I could have easily done it; that is what she wanted me to do. But to my surprise I managed to make my hardon shrink, and the blood cells from the penis rushed back into my brain, which, in the process, made it hard to breathe. I wanted to kick her out at once but I was in a state of paralyzed panic. I stood there looking at her witless face, and it was clear from her dumb expression that she was plotting something. There is nothing in the world so bad that cannot be made worse. I started to seethe. What right did this creature (whose pussy, ass, and mouth I had shoved my cock into without much emotional satisfaction) have to interrupt me, just as I was finally getting to work? For a second it seemed as if her entire face was a swarm of maggots, her too-tight auburn leather jacket bulging from bat wings. If she'd had a car parked outside, it would have been a milk truck made entirely of vultures. I wanted to gag. Each movement of her face threatened to unleash a swarm of bugs into the air. She sneered for no apparent reason. She should have put her goddamn red hair up into a beehive "do" so that all the little insects could have a permanent nest. I tried to think of something nice to say but came up empty handed. All I felt was repulsion, with just a tiny tingling in my groin which was rapidly dissipating. She came here to have sex with me, it was clear, but it was more than the desire to go to bed with me, it was that indescribable something, that evil, that brought her here.

The humane thing to do, if it were possible, would have been simply to "wish her away" by clicking my heels but I felt a mix of passion, hatred and that "terrible sympathy" that had plagued me my entire life.

"One more time, Shelly..." I said as I bit my lip, held my hands in check and struggled not to attempt to choke her. "What are you doing here?"

"I wanted to check up on you," she smirked again, nonchalantly. "To see how you were doing, that's all."

In less than a minute, she was out the door, kicking and screaming with my hand forcing her out by her upper arm. "It hurts! Let go!" she pleaded as I dragged her out of the flat and just like the last time I threw her out all those years ago, I felt absolutely no sympathy for this mendacious wreck of a human being. There was no time to lose in getting rid of her, no time to wait for the elevator to come. I opened the fire door and pushed her down the stairs, saw her fall and I immediately felt fear and regret and a terrific pity for her as she got up and pawed her bruised ass. She might even have whimpered. I wanted only to make sure that she didn't suffer any injury, god forbid to the spine... When I saw her walking I went back up and slammed the door to the stairwell as loudly as possible. It was time to get back to work.

I tried to pick up where I left off.

The second part of the story of Stacy Fox, our lady and savior who died for her creator's sins, sees her back at home in Cortland. It's spring again. It's been over a year since she returned from New York, and though the memory of her summer of love and hate remains fresh, the concerns of the day are elsewhere. Stacy has a boyfriend, Danny, who knows nothing about that summer of sleeping on the rooftop, watching airplanes. She meets him most days after school and they watch porn together at his parents' house. He fucks her regularly in the rec room. I'll spare the other details of Stacy's misery but let's just say she's finally fed up and on impulse she throws off her graduation gown and gets in the "man in the park's" truck and decides to go god knows where. She had dreamt of California, after all.

The next day there was nothing to do other than write although inertia was setting in and it was difficult to fight against it. There was no one I could really call, no one to speak with, no parents or relatives—I wanted Betty, and I wanted a walking Betty. I could not call my wife—that would have been a concession of defeat—so I decided to force myself to write down what I had in mind regarding The New World Symphony and the tragic story of Stacy Fox.

So to pick up where I left odd, back in Cortland, Stacy is fed up. Fed up with the dogs and sprinklers, with the graduation ceremonies, with the cocks that are too big for her to swallow as they're shoved down her throat. She's fed up with mild venereal diseases, with chlamydia, with blackout drunk fucks behind dumpsters. She's fed up of waking up with the same trucker, also known as "the man from the park," lying on top of her semi-raped, semi-innocent body. She's fed up with gazing at the ceiling of the bar through tear-stained eyes, its lights like a kaleidoscope of chandeliers crashing all over her. She's fed up with the bartender's pitying eyes.

The next day is graduation and Stacy, with an itchy pussy, throws on her cap and gown and runs to the stadium while the Bacchanale from Saint-Saëns' Samson and Delilah is blasted across the football field by the high school marching band.

She walks to the graduation
amid dogs and sprinklers yet again
and in the auditorium, the band plays
the Bacchanale from Saint-Saens' Samson and Delilah.

In a dirty hallway with her boyfriend,
she picks herself up and walks
outside to freedom, which came rolling in
on eighteen wheels.

As the poem continues, it turns out the "Man in the Park" has a brother, a trucker. He sees Stacy and she sees him. The "Man in the Park" pins Stacy up against a wall and screams in her face. After that she runs to his brother.

"Where you going?" she shouts.

"What do you care? Get in!" he laughs. She jumps in and says goodbye to upstate New York forever.

But it doesn't turn out all rosy. Somewhere by Kalamazoo or Dubuque they need to take a break. Stacy doesn't even know the name of the man at this point, he's just the brother of the "Man in the Park," and when they check into the motel attached to the truck stop, well, let's say she's not into him but they do it. He pushes her down into the rancid sheets, makes her suck his hoary cock, fucks her and passes out.

It wasn't a big deal for her. She had been raped before.

As the trucker sleeps, covered in sweat and dried semen, Stacy goes outside to look at the night sky. She looks at the trucks—they are disgusting. She looks at the sky and imagines she is on her way to the promised West. She's hungry and has no idea what she's doing, so she goes into the truck stop diner, orders a coffee and a bun. She has no money. There's a greasy guy looking at her, greasy but handsome. He winks. She doesn't know how to wink... He's eating split pea soup. He moves closer.

"Gus," he says. "It's short for Gustav. Part of my family's Swedish." Gus is going to California, and Stacy wants to go to California. "I have an idea," she says. Gus fires up his car while she runs upstairs to the motel room and steals the trucker's wallet. She jumps in and Gus puts the pedal to the metal and they ride into the night, excited as young Turks. She likes Gus.

But what happens later? Oh, well first they drive cross-country, star-crossed, see shooting stars and meteor showers from Gus's car window. They sleep in fleabag motels and make love but Gus keeps popping little pills "to take the edge off" and Stacy starts eating them too. At another shithole motel on Santa Monica Boulevard, Gus—who dreamed of coming here to be a filmmaker—is popping those colorful little pills all day long and they're running out of money and Stacy is sick of it and she wants to make a little money of her own, so she answers an ad in the paper for adult modeling. "Gus doesn't need to know. His dick can't get hard anyway and he's always sleeping." So there goes our Stacy, drives herself to Van Nuys and sucks off a dozen cocks in ninety minutes for five hundred dollars.

Somehow Gus finds about Stacy's little "job" and when he does, he beats her to a bloody pulp, beats her black and blue, gives her shiners and knocks out a tooth. When he passes out, Stacy controls her whimpering enough to do what she was good at before and she steals Gus's wallet and takes the next bus up to San Francisco, where the next stage of her life begins.

And inspects her black eye in the mirror:
all those little red canals of blood breaking
and branching. She keeps hearing
"My name's Gus. Short for Gustav.
Part of my family is Swedish."
"Your name is short for dumbass," she thinks.
Soon she's ready. A little makeup on the shiner and
she's shining again.
A spew of grey smoke from the bus's exhaust
and she's on her way.
"What happened to you?" asks the
young man next to her, grinning.

"I walked into a wall," she says, and blows
smoke in his face and soon the bus rolls up north,
to the city on the bay, another glorious
dead end.

Suddenly the telephone rang with a 212 area code. Without thinking, I picked it up. In LA I would usually avoid answering unfamiliar numbers as they were most likely either spam or creditors. Another unwanted interruption: someone named Deirdre O'Brien, who I apparently went to high school with, inviting me to the 30th reunion of the class of 1987. I had no recollection of this Deirdre person and promptly declined. I needed this, as the Russians say, like I needed a second asshole, or to be less vulgar like a fish needs an umbrella. How had she found my number? Someone must have leaked it, but who? I tried to shoo away my paranoia but it persisted for an hour or so until I realized I needed to get back to work on the book, yet I'd lost my train of thought.

What had thrown me was the notion of a reunion after all these years. Thirty years ago I had looked forward to life with a mix of fatalism, fantasy and genuine excitement. Now I looked on the next thirty years of life with a mix of failure, regret and an extremely vague wonder. A wonder about what else is in store, how it will end, what death will feel like. I did not see much happening except hopefully a peaceful feeling of these little fading photographs and videos stored somewhere within my brain, saved for one final viewing.

For those of us who struggle between hope and regret, between pain and sleep, we oscillate between a tiny bright star at the end of the tunnel and a black hole. We maintain a hope that on our death bed we might just get a glimpse of what it all means. So, Stacy leaves LA. But she doesn't wonder all about that yet.

San Francisco has a blinding white light
that's always cold. But Stacy finds warmth
soon enough. She isn't going back.
And the white days and blue nights pass
so quickly, and past times are forgotten
as best they can be.
The white light suits her and
she slithers in this time, before demons
came barging through.
And up she climbs up on the ladder,
slowly but surely,
and within a few years
we find a different more diffident
Stacy, or should I say Ms Fox.
Or so she'd have us believe.

There are people who claim that it is possible to leave the past
behind. They are liars. And Stacy was just such a liar. For though she
starts a new life in San Francisco, her buried past was always going
to come back to bite her on the ass because she missed what she had
lost, she missed diving into the dumpster, she missed sin. And so
even on her lunch breaks, as she worked herself up to become some
type of financial services professional in the Transamerica Tower,
she would sneak out and give blowjobs to random strangers, would
seek out glory holes, would put ads on Craigslist, would pretend to
be a hooker—during these flings she was, of course, a hooker, but
she wasn't in it for the money but for the thrill. She could not resist.
The fire in her garbage can still burned.

And then, one day, she meets an innocent young man. Perhaps
in a coffee shop or waiting for a bus. Another Gus, perhaps, but
Stacy has been in San Francisco for a dozen years now and this guy
is much, much younger...

In the white city, Stacy gets a job and
in her Maria Braun way quickly moves up the ladder.
But if there's one thing she still can't get enough of
it's cock.
How quickly she applied herself and went from turning tricks
on O'Farrell Street to answering phones in
the Transamerica Pyramid
to having her own corner office overseeing
a gaggle of fresh-faced employees.

And then... something happened to her. Something awful happened to her in San Francisco. I don't remember if I wrote it that night or whether I had to wait for Betty to tell me what actually happened.

I dreamed I finished the book. Or a book. I remember the final line: "as the moths and fireflies danced outside our window in the moonlight." And then I was hit by the horrible realization that I had no one to share this joy with, and that no one was going to read it. That I wouldn't be able to tell my mom about it, or to discuss it with her. And where Charlotte was, I had no idea. I was struck by an intense loneliness, an almost unreal sense of isolation as if I was on a rocky planet of my own, somewhere in the depths of space. In fact, I was sitting in my mom's apartment, now empty, and with no one to call. A friend from long ago, Gregory, knocked at my door and I let him in and let him see myself crying. I told him how I missed speaking Russian; not just speaking it but speaking it with someone I knew and who cared about me. He confirmed. "It's not enough to speak it. You need to speak it to a truly close friend." He left me alone to stare at the empty walls. Then I woke up.

After the accident and being bound to wheels, Stacy's appetite for both sex and degradation reaches its apotheosis. One day she wheels herself into a pub on Market Street, not far from her former office at the Pyramid, and orders a drink. A groups of "bros" are drinking pitchers of Anchor Steam at the other end of the bar. They haven't failed to notice: there is a gorgeous girl sitting alone, drinking by herself... except she's in a wheelchair.

And then the pea brains get to work. Bets were placed—who would approach her first? What reward may be in store?

"She's moving around okay in that chair," says one, snickering. "Who wants to see if her internal organs work?"

One of the bros stands up, winks at his audience, without a word to the others, and stumbles over to Stacy. The other bros fall silent as they watch the sly brown fox pull up a chair.

"She can't feel anything in her pussy!" "Who cares? A cunt's a cunt." "He won't feel anything on his dick either" "Guy can bang a bitch and not even remember the next day" "Hope he sobers up to tell us tomorrow" "Tell us what?" "What it's like to fuck a cripple. You know what we used to say eight to eighty, black crippled or crazy" "Fuck that!" another meathead chimed in. "We used to say if there's grass on the field, play ball!" Everyone laughed.

Meanwhile Bro Gallant stands up and pushes Stacy in her wheelchair right out of the door and into the street, into the blinding white and yellow of the San Francisco afternoon.

It is all done with great precision. Stacy knows how to work the wheelchair to get inside a cab. The bro stands there grinning, excited by his bizarre conquest, by the prospect of unusual sex, and by the thought of telling the other bros about it. He thinks of a stupid joke he made up once "I had a blind date that I took ice skating, but her dog had a hard time on the ice."

In a few minutes they are at Stacy's place, high above the city in Russian Hill. The bro is growing anxious. He's afraid she's about to tell him she actually has no legs, ask him "Do you want the legs on or off?" But it is too late now.

"Come on, come on," says Stacy as they cross from the elevator to her door. The bro follows nervously. The scotch is wearing off and the sheer weirdness of the situation is getting to him. He blacked out for an hour or so and now he is trying to remember how he got here and what he said to her. He somehow recalls that it was she who asked him to come see her place before he had a chance to be a stud and so he went along with it. And now it is all different from how he imagined it. Stacy wheels herself over to the bed and raises herself onto the mattress. "Come here. Fuck me," she says in monotone. Bro is speechless.

"Come, kiss me... And fuck me!"

She pulls his arms around her and sticks her tongue in his mouth and moans.

"Ugh... why does the bed feel moist?"

The bro, now sober and genuinely alarmed, tries to pull away but Stacy only holds him tighter, in search of anybody, any body... When she closes her eyes the whole universe seems to be pulling away from her. She pictures herself lying on the bed, she pictures her street from above, she pictures San Francisco from the air, pictures America from space, pictures the Earth from afar, and then everything goes dark.

Everything went dark for me too. Exhausted, I fell asleep in my clothes and had crazy, disturbing dreams that thankfully were wiped out within minutes of waking.

I woke around noon when a car horn playing the theme from "The Godfather" jerked me out of sleep. I was annoyed and amused in equal measure. I recalled how that car horn was popular in the 90s and wondered just what kind of idiot would still use such a thing. I walked out onto the balcony and my mind was blown. It was Peter Sanchez, a friend from high school who was by all accounts mentally ill. After years of drug and alcohol addiction he turned to evangelical Christianity, only to relapse. It got to the point where it was practically impossible to have a conversation with him as he veered from one topic to another, his mind addled by poison. He was also a bodybuilder. I had once seen him drinking vodka from a half-gallon Tropicana carton of orange juice mixed with weight gain protein powder and exercising on his home weights machine while tripping on LSD. What was this idiot doing here?

What had happened during those twenty plus years since Peter lost his mind for good? Oh, nothing, nothing at all—same as me, I suppose. Those dreadful twenty years, two decades that went by in a snap. Other people our age had accomplished amazing things—became doctors, lawyers, politicians, journalists, artists, scientists… Whereas I, like Peter, squandered all my precious time on trying to get laid. We wasted our time for different reasons—he had gone insane, I had tried to write screenplays. Peter's arrival was like me looking at a funhouse mirror, an even greater distortion of what I felt I had become. He was the last person I wanted to see. How did he know my address? Why hadn't he called ahead?

"Heeeey! Luckyyyyyyyy! It's Peter, man!" I heard him yell from the street below and threw a frisbee up at the balcony. I ducked, ran into the house and hid from him the way Elizabeth hides when she sees Hyacinth approaching. I closed the blinds and prayed he would go away. Eventually he gave up and I returned to my desk. I had half a mind to pick up a bottle and throw on his windshield.

How wonderful would it be if even the most pedestrian lives and littlest of loves could simply be bottled like a little flacon of perfume to be put on a wall shelf for us, the living, to sample at our leisure. And though I never made the film, I put Stacy's ashes in a little perfume bottle on my brain's shelf to sniff whenever I wanted to get a whiff of one my favorite little corpses.

Up on the shelf in LA was the unproduced screenplay, bound in card stock and the requisite brass brads puncturing her story. I felt that at any given moment she might unfold greasy black wings and jump right down from the shelf either to dig talons into my neck or simply to sit on my chest until I was unable to breathe.

So, the book, or a book, was finished. Now what? Sure, I put down her story—but verse, poetry? Who would publish it? Who would read it? Who would read my squalid little Totentanz penned by a middle-aged fuckup such as yours truly, with no connection to any literary worlds?

So I immediately put it aside. Suddenly, the only thing on my mind was a desire to see Betty.

I walked over to the kitchen to pour a glass of water when, out of the blue, the phone rang. Impatient, besotted, I rushed over to pick up without looking at the caller ID. It was my wife.

"Well?"

"Hi."

"Well?"

"What do you mean 'well'?"

"Well, how's the book going? Are you writing? Is that why you haven't been calling? Don't you want to know how your daughter's doing? Or how I'm doing?"

"I've been working. I'm sorry, I…"

"I don't believe you."

"Why not?"

"I just don't. I think you're out there, fucking around with the idea of writing while you're spending my money on alcohol. I think you're too brain damaged to write anything at this point and I wish you'd finish whatever it is you're up to over there and come home, get a job, be normal. Act your age, Lucky. You're not getting any younger."

While the mention of "brain damage" was insulting, I wondered for a second whether she might be right. Then I remembered that I had just managed to write The New World Symphony in a matter of days. I didn't need this shit from anyone.

"Look, I can't talk right now, I'm sorry," I said somewhat sheepishly. I did not wish to engage in conflict. Strangely she must have been thinking the same thing.

"Fine. Call me later," she said and hung up.

It was after that night that the nightmares went on steroids. I started having dreams about shit. Defecation. Mountains of shit was coming out of my ass in my sleep. I wasn't crapping the bed but I started wearing two pairs of underwear at night to be safe.

THE DISCOVERY OF HELL

If there is anything more bizarre than the actual process of death, it is the fact that once there was a human and now he or she is no more. It is the disappearance.

Thus with my mom's death, the rich and queer experience of Russian emigration simply disappeared like falling leaves. With my dad's death, the entire world of ballet disintegrated as if it never existed. Granted, I was peripheral to both these worlds, but these sandcastles did indeed crumble in a nanosecond the moment these people died.

One evening, in a mild stupor, my dad said, "The purpose of life is to die." For some, it is comforting to think of death as the final adventure; no one who died ever came back to tell us what it's like. But that sentiment is only possible when one is not afraid of death. I was, and continue to be, afraid.

Did Betty exist? Yes, she did. She existed like my dead parents, like my dreams, like ballet.

Betty was still gone. After the book was finished, she should have been back in Brooklyn but there were no calls, nothing. Just as I feared and suspected, I knew that the miniscule separation could widen into a chasm and I would be stuck at the bottom, trying to clamber out of this canyon I built with my own mind. But there was no respite. She was nowhere to be found. And so I waited, soaked in drink and sweat, waiting for her return. The "book" was finished, but I felt that I had left something out.

My nightmares became worse and worse. The placid dreams

of a picnic with my dad, fishing in a stream (although I had never fished in my life), or the turquoise water on a trip to Miami Beach were replaced with images of me descending a labyrinthine maze while stepping over crocodiles and lizards. In one dream I was chopping up a live cat, a plump female tabby, with a meat cleaver. The bloody chunks of cat meat parts turned into kittens who hissed at me and bounced away, while their mother meowed horribly. In another horrible nightmare, my father was pregnant with sextuplets and miscarried the entire litter.

I would awake screaming, go to the sink to pour a glass of water with my useless hands—the beautiful trembling, tarantula hands of an alcoholic—and then force myself to go to sleep. But another nightmare would begin the second I dozed off.

My sleeping mind would bring up horrible, nasty little visions. I would be walking through a desert, parched, all bones and rags and would see an oasis up ahead, and when I would reach it I would bend down to drink from a pool I thought would be refreshing and cool but which turned be a green standing pond from which a slithering little imp would rise to the surface and stick his tongue out at me.

Sometimes it was a demon, disguised as a ragged old man who would chortle and remind me of my own impending death, and would pronounce filthy thoughts and tell me I had been, in fact, washing his ass my entire life.

I decided to look for Betty, for I had no other choice. I had only seen her house a few times—a somewhat grimy brick structure a few blocks from the boardwalk. Many of the buildings look identical around there and I made many misses until I entered the lobby of what I thought was the right one, and then it struck me that I didn't know her surname. She was just "Betty G." I looked at the names on the intercom and found only one G—a Gromyko. Russian? Ukrainian? I had entertained her with stories of Russia and she would surely have told me if her background was Slavic.

I pushed the buzzer nonetheless in some vain hope.

"Allo? Da?" the speaker answered in a Slavic accent. I could picture who was behind the buzzer, a typical Brighton Beach resident in her bathrobe, cooking cabbage soup and dumplings. I walked out dejected, then from somewhere in the building I heard mocking laughter. I was sure it wasn't directed at me, someone had probably cracked open the vodka on the early side, and yet as I walked away from the building my dejection turned into fear as the cackling seemed to follow me down the street until it was drowned out by the sound of vehicles and what I believed was the surf of the ocean despite that it was far from earshot.

And so the days went on, in loneliness and emptiness. There were a few torturous times when I felt completely bereft of all sensation, and not even the bottle of Smirnoff helped to relieve me of the pain. The summer was coming to an end.

One night, halfway through a bottle of vodka, the phone rang.

"Betty!"

"I'm coming over. I'll be there in ten." Then she hung up.

I scrambled around furiously, trying to make the place a bit tidier. For some reason it felt like a first date all over again. I put all my nervous energy into putting the empties into a plastic bag, throwing away the leftovers still in their takeaway containers, and emptying the ashtrays. I was going to meet her downstairs, wait for her to call, and hold the door open in the lobby now that the concierge had gone to sleep (it was coming on close to midnight). Then the doorbell rang.

There was something about the light, perhaps my borderline synesthesia, perhaps jaundice from my humors, but she stood out against the green carpet of the flooring, the greenish tinge of the fluorescents in the kitchen, her black hair so striking against it that it took me a moment to notice that her eyes were completely red.

But she wasn't crying. It looked like she had already finished crying, and her look was that of someone who after crying acquires a certain menace. The look of someone who is about to throw the hurt right back at the guilty party.

"Move!" she said, and I moved out of her way as she wheeled herself in. I did not know how to act, what to say. I had never seen her like this before.

"Where were you?" I asked her. "I was…"

"You were what?" she interrupted.

"I was waiting for you to come. I went looking for you and…"

"You went looking for me?" she snorted. "The more you keep looking for me, the more you'll never find me. Why the fuck were you looking for me?"

I was up against a wall. I had seen this behavior before, I had seen women—and to be fair, men too—being irrational, odd, confrontational in the way she barked that sentence at me. But Betty, despite her secrecy, despite the darkness that she never revealed to me, always seemed like a rock. Not anymore.

"I'm back now. Are you happy?"

"I am," I said sheepishly, treading with caution. "I'm happy you're back. I'm very happy, very happy to see you."

"Good. You should be." She winced. "Did you manage to get a lot of work done?"

"Yes" I stuttered. "I managed to…" I didn't know what to tell her but she spoke for me again.

"You managed to write your book. Is that right?"

"Yes. Sort of…"

"Good," she smiled. "I'm excited for you. Seriously, I truly am. I'm going to help you finish it. Because I don't think you're done yet."

Before I could process this, she asked for a drink—vodka, neat. I got up to fetch her one from what was now a full bar in my flat. "Now, sit." she said. I grabbed my drink and plopped myself back down on the ridiculous couch. Of course she wanted me to sit, not only to be eye level but to no longer see things from her perspective, to see the world the way she wanted to.

"It's finally time to talk. What do you want to know?" she asked. But before I had a chance to answer, she interrupted.

"You jealous little shit!" she started, and my ears rang.

It is true that I was jealous, jealous as I had never been in my life—but jealous of whom, of what? I was, as I always had been, not so much jealous as scared of betrayal. I kept quiet, and decided to let her do the talking. I had learned from marital experience not to upset the crockery, not to break my hand against the refrigerator door. Talk, then. So she did.

"You want to know if I fucked him? Of course I did. You knew that. I've fucked the entire planet, Lucky. And not just this planet, but the whole goddamn galaxy."

I downed my glass in one gulp. Why had my dream, my last dream, been ripped from me? I knew nothing about her, and yet she gave me the illusion of love, the mirage of hope.

"What do you want to know about me, Lucky?" she said. I swallowed hard. Why now, I thought.

"I'm a whore from upstate New York, Lucky. I grew up walking past dogs and sprinklers but I was always filthy through and through. I would suck truckers' cocks in parking lots in order to get to California. When I was hungry and no one wanted to fuck me even for five bucks I would eat out of garbage cans, finding a crust that had the least hair and shit on it and bite into it the way I would swallow disgusting pricks so I could live."

I was about to vomit but she kept going.

"You know who I am, Lucky. You know damn well. I am death. I am scum."

"Stop it!" I shook her, bawling uncontrollably, minding to not shake her so hard that she would fall out of her chair. She spat at me.

"Fuck you, Lucky! You don't know the first thing about me! You don't know about Gus—the guy I met on the road, the guy who gave me my first heroin shot, the guy I married. Yes, the guy I married! And we lived together in LA and when I tried to make some extra money, I ended up doing porn and when Gus found out he beat the living shit out of me! And that's when I left him and went up to San Francisco, and I was doing well for a bit and then… It was that motherfucker who pushed me. And that fucking nigger Gabriel also, he was…"

The hair on the back of my neck stood up. Was she fucking with me? How on earth could she have read my poem? She kept going.

"I managed to get a job in San Francisco, you know." She started sobbing. "I had a good job, a really good job, for the first time in my life. And yet…"

"And yet what!?" I yelled.

"Something happened. I had another lover there. It didn't work out."

"And?"

"And this is why I am like I am, Lucky. He pushed me under the trolley. I was wearing a scarf, it snapped my vertebrae. It's a miracle that I lived. But that's why I'm in a wheelchair, honey. Now you know."

"Please. No more." I told her, wiping away tears. "I am sorry. I am truly sorry." She raised her hands from her chair to embrace me. I knelt down. She struggled to lift herself towards me as far as she could and in our crooked embrace she whispered, "Lucky, I do love you. Don't hate me anymore."

"I do love you" she repeated though with reservation, "And I want to you to make love to me" she said.

This was my one chance, my one and only chance to make love to Betty. After some struggling with her vehicle I put the breaks on her chair when we made our way toward the bed and lifted her up out of her phaeton. Betty was crying and smiling at the same time.

I actually picked her up and kicked the chair away and carried her as if over the threshold and I threw her on my sweaty bed. I was terrified. I was worried that taking her to bed and undressing her would be like uncorking a funerary urn and decanting the ashes.

"You people, your species sings songs and write poetry with lines like 'we'll live forever' and bullshit like that." she struggled. "Do you know what it's like to live forever? It's dreadful, Lucky."

And then she said it:

"Moist. The bed feels moist…"

It was when she said the same words I wrote twenty years ago that I tore into her body. With an equal dose of fury and pity—a nauseating emotional cocktail—I ripped off her clothes and penetrated her at once and her response was ecstatic. I was entering another world. My cock raged to both save her and destroy her— Vishnu and Shiva, Brahma and Kalki all entangled in a frightful battle. And just before I came I heard the final lines of the screen direction in my script for The New World Symphony: I actually saw the finished print as the camera cuts from Stacy's bed to the outside of her building, and then pans wider, it dissolves into an aerial shot of Pacific Heights, then San Francisco, then California, then America from space, then Earth from afar… and then I collapsed on top of her. We did not speak. I squeezed her. Then things went black.

When I woke up I could not remember if we actually made love or not. She was gone and so was her chair, which I had kicked away in passion. That morning was the worst morning of my life. Eyes closed, still coming back from a dream, in vain I tried reaching for her, looking for her and just like in those lucid dreams I had no idea where I was. Betty wasn't there. Betty was gone.

THE RETURN OF THE GIRL FROM BELOW

When Betty left without a word, she left a hole in my life. The fact that we had consummated our relationship right here on Ocean Parkway brought back unwelcome memories of Wendy Novak, to whom I had lost my virginity decades earlier on that same stretch of Brooklyn's grand boulevard.

Yes, I was devastated by Betty's sudden departure, but as much as I wished for her to return I knew that it was over. The autumnal chill that hits New York in late August had arrived. Before the glorious orange and yellow of an Indian Summer there is always this blast of cold, a harbinger of the season of death.

I had no more business in Brooklyn, or anywhere in New York for that matter. It was time to pay penance for my folly and return to sunny California, to Charlotte, and after Betty's departure I felt that this whole experiment had been a grave error.

What had Betty meant when she said that she would help me finish my book? The manuscript was complete—or so I thought. But right now the manuscript was the least of my concerns. I had now not just sunk but dived into darkness. With Betty gone, what was left? Somehow I was not yet ready to return to LA. The lease on my rental wasn't up, and though I didn't know precisely what it was that I had to finish, I felt there was something yet to be written.

During these long days I would entertain the idea of visiting a prostitute. Not for sex or companionship or succor—all of which had amused me at some point in the past—but to somehow make the hooker feel like shit, and to drive her to tears, to somehow take revenge at least on someone, even in exchange for money. The very inconceivable thing I had never wished to ever entertain even in my most ugliest thoughts.

I became driven to violent ideas and I realized I wanted to insult someone, a woman. I wanted to make a woman cry. If I could no longer fuck then I could at least resort to petty sadism. I wanted to grab this imaginary hooker by her tiny wrists and force her to shake her tiny fists at a silent sky, to wake up, to stop being a character fucked not just by disgusting hoary cocks but fate itself! To get her to understand her own despair, and then after driving her to hysterics to demean her and to destroy her further, perhaps forever... But I imagined that if I grabbed her little wrists she would look at me with disgust in turn and scream, "So what?! Who are you to talk? So what if I use these hands to pull back pubic hair and foreskins to check for scabs before I suck repulsive little dicks and spit out sperm that I hope isn't diseased? You want me to play a Chopin nocturne instead? Everyone has their lot in life. What do you do? Can you play Chopin?" And my throat would close up and my fantasy would become even sweatier and even more repulsive.

Of course, I didn't do it. I couldn't. I wandered the streets in search of the deepest, sweatiest, most disease-ridden quilombo I could imagine, as if to dive into the same depths as Betty, but it was to no avail. Everything nasty had been sanitized, where a place of despair once stood there was now a pharmacy or coffee shop. And even if the chance had presented itself, even if I had been miraculously transported into that desperate world my poor Stacy inhabited, I would not have had the balls to be unfaithful to my wife. But I had already been unfaithful and my mind battled itself. And despair, once she puts a spell on you is a witch you can never truly get rid of.

These nightmares pushed away the dreams I once had about imaginary lovers or my parents. I stopped hearing the sounds of Slavic voices in my sleep. I knew that in some ways the death of my parents had liberated me as a person, and that I now had time to come into my own as a late bloomer, but there some problems. For starters I was much more than a late bloomer; having squandered my youth, I was now firmly entrenched in middle age. And though I felt as I was shaking off some parental yoke, there was still something else, another rope or oxbow that I was not able to release myself from. I knew what it was but I was not ready to admit it. I sensed that I was approaching something that would make sense of these things, though I did not know yet what it was.

After her disappearance I continued to explore New York and find remnants of my past. And then something very strange happened. She started to come back, but in many different ways.

The first time she reappeared was in the subway. I was returning to Brooklyn from another solitary walk through Washington Heights, going through a literal walk down memory lane and the whole memory game and remembering things from childhood.

The A train was crowded and smelled rank as usual. I could not wait to obtain at least a tiny respite and freedom from the bodies pushing against me when I would change trains at 59th Street. As the train screeched to a halt and the bell sounded and the doors opened—there she was; sitting down, but without wheelchair. As I struggled to push myself out onto the platform she looked up and like the first meeting in Primorski, her laser eyes met mine and she smiled and opened her mouth to say something. I could not hear it precisely but it sounded like "I'll be seeing you again." I wanted to turn around but by this point the doors had already closed and the A train sped away. Where was her chair? Why was she on the A train instead of the D? Was it really her? I felt a sharp pain in my lower back, a spasm I get sometimes when I suffer an extreme shock or fright. The D train was not there and I was too shaken up to endure another forty minute journey so I exited the subway and rushed to the nearest Korean bodega and grabbed a bottle of Grolsch which I promptly pounded down. This was repeated several times. Each time I saw a subway entrance, I opted to keep walking as I felt I was not ready to board yet. My mind and heart were both racing. How could she be there? Was the wheelchair thing some kind of trick? A weird fetish perhaps? Or did I imagine the whole thing? Was the woman on the train really her or just a lookalike, a doppelganger? No, that couldn't be because she looked straight at me and said something. I thought it must have been a hallucination so I decided that the minute I returned home, I would drink myself sober. But currently, the bladder was groaning from however many beers I pounded down on my escape walk and I needed to piss. At this point I was approaching Times Square. All the dive bars were gone of course, so I went into the nearest hotel bar, relieved myself, drank an overpriced martini and only then, I was finally ready to face the agonizing train ride with nothing but my thoughts and paranoia for company.

After the sweaty journey, back in my Ocean Parkway apartment, I poured myself a straight vodka and tried to make sense of what happened. I could not call anyone to discuss it. I had very few friends left in New York or LA, and I could not reveal my infidelity to those that remained. I thought about emailing someone I had not spoken to in years, but that would have been selfish—too many people have come out of the woodwork after not speaking to me for years when they needed something, which I found detestable and I swore I would never do that. Perhaps there was some type of chat room or forum I could anonymously post on to get some advice.

Once, when I was a child, I asked my grandmother, "Do devils exist?" to which she most astutely replied, "They do for those who believe they do."

I suppose the rest was inevitable; once she had materialized there was nothing I could have done to prevent it from happening again.

I did not come to New York to have an affair and I was never one for infidelity, even when circumstances in a troubled relationship would have somehow justified it in the eyes of the cheater. But here there was no justification—and yet while moral principles should have prevailed I could not stop thinking about Betty. I poured a drink and looked over the printout of my manuscript. Sure enough, it was still there. I opened my laptop to check my emails. The one at the top was from Betty G with the subject "MEET SOON." I opened the message hesitantly. It did not name the time and place and nothing else but simply said "I will see you soon." I felt like everything had already been decided for me.

"Meet soon," ha! Soon indeed for she started to appear everywhere—climbing down trees and lampposts, leaping out of magazine pages. She would step out from billboards and paintings, emerge from hidden doorways. One day, to distract myself, I took another trip to the Met Museum. Things began melting as if I was on psychotropic drugs. The Ikebana arrangement at the information desk seemed to flow up to the ceiling, like a tropical jungle, shooting up to the top with pythons and flesh-eating plants, poisonous chameleons and impish looking howler monkeys in between the branches while a foxtrot played in the background. Something was not right. They explained to me later, much later, what was happening, though they couldn't quite pinpoint which part of my brain was responsible for it. That would mean nothing to me anyway. When my dad was told to quit smoking, they told him, "Sir, when they do an autopsy your lungs will be black!" To which he rightly replied, "Sir, when I'm dead I won't care if my lungs are rainbow and polka dot."

I controlled myself and went over to the American Wing and there she was, in a Sargent painting, and she stepped directly out of the canvas and followed me through the galleries. I walked faster and faster until I was almost running and while searching for an exit I encountered her again at the Information Desk, now donned in a conservative brown suit, her hair tied smartly in a bun. I escaped and immediately looked for the nearest bar. Luckily I found one and quaffed vodkas until I felt more sane.

Sometimes she would appear out of thin air and press herself against me while my erect cock almost blew a hole in my pants.

One episode affected me quite badly. She appeared and said, "I thought we were going to fuck, Lucky," and before I could answer she followed up with, "That's okay. I know—your wife and all that. That's fine. I'll just find someone else to fuck tonight. I was invited to a group thing this evening, might do that. You only live once, right?" And at that she turned around and walked away. I told her to wait, to listen to me, but when I tried to grab her and stop her, she vanished.

Was she the devil, I began to wonder? Someone pushing onto me the idea that it is necessary, in my case, to learn how to live without hope? That my book is pointless? Was she trying to prevent me from finishing the book? But I thought my book was finished.

"O what a black, dark hill is yon,
"That looks so dark to me?"
"O it is the hill of hell," she said,
"Where you and I shall be."

Or was she an angel who, to prevent further disappointments, was teaching me, in her own punitive Christian fashion how to abandon all hope, and how to live without it?

As I was entering the last third of my life, perhaps even the last quarter, I became obsessed with leaving something behind—something my father failed to do. Not financially—both of my parents died in penury—but something like a book, a work of art. Yet I was totally unqualified. Gradually I began to lose all interest in the books. Who needs more sordid stories? I would say, and the metaphorical writing pen would turn to lead and drop. But I did see that there was another story forming somewhere beneath the surface of my Brooklyn retreat.

One evening, I remembered that quite some time before her demonic/symphonic unmasking, she would repeat that uncanny statement. I should have paid more attention at the time but I chose to ignore it, just as I ignored so many comments made by past lovers. She said, "You know, Lucky, sometimes I feel like my life is like a movie that someone wrote but no one's ever seen."

Had I not been so willfully blind, had I paid more attention, I would have recognized that those words were from a song I tried writing a number of years ago called "The Road to Hollywood," which had a verse containing those exact words. How had I missed it? I suppose I ignored it because I wanted her, and wanted to forgot that one can never really own a woman. But I never sung that for her.

Everyone dies differently. Some quickly, some slowly, some searching, some hiding. Some even go California, some to New York. Just as many are born in New York in order to die there as well. All cities are graveyards, but each graveyard is different in its own special way. I started to think that the best and possibly only solution was to pack my bags and go back to California immediately. I did not want to die in New York. I did not want to die without seeing my family again. There was no immediate reason for my demise but I felt hovering it at every waking minute.

And yet I could not leave. I was stuck, immobilized by a dread as heavy as eyelids so long they fell to the floor, like those of Gogol's demon. Betty was everywhere. Like a filthy, plague-ridden Laura to my Petrarch she followed me in shadows from behind housing projects, subway passages, trash cans, from underneath the Brighton Beach boardwalk, riding naked on the back of a garbage truck... I began to realize that there was something profoundly wrong with me. Betty was the girl from below. The question was: how to exorcise her, how to get rid of her? Yet I was still uncertain whether her existence was corporeal or not.

And then one evening, as I was escaping these furies came the follow-up on the computer, via a message on the screen. User name: "Betty G." It said "Meet me."

That did it. I now thought I was officially out of my mind. What did she want? Why couldn't she just call me, or come over, after disappearing the way she did? It was too much. I pounded down more scotch and returned to the laptop. Another message popped up on the screen.

"Meet me at pier 45. The pier where the fags used to lie around and fuck all night long. Bring a nail with you, bring rope. The pier where the fags used to spread AIDS, you know the one. I want to see you, Lucky. One hour."

I called her but it went to voicemail like it has been. The bellyful of scotch gave me the courage to reply by text message. I was drawn to the madness.

I texted her back: "One hour."

When my taxi dropped me off by the Christopher Street Pier, now redeveloped with no sign of cruising "fags" she talked about, Betty was waiting right in front as if she knew exactly where the driver would drop me off. Dressed to the nines in a short leather mini skirt with hooker rouge lipstick, she guided me towards the water. We walked hand-in-hand like lovers and it never crossed my mind the very basic and most essential problem and question: "Why is she walking now?"

As she walked, she sang. I listened to her footsteps. High heels on the pavement but it took a minute to make out the words of her song that accompanied a familiar melody, something close to "Hush, Little Baby" but the lyrics… oh her lyrics, her lyrics went like this:

Under the swaying green palm tree
I dumped you and you pushed me
Now you write shit and here I sit
In the black wheelchair you gifted me

I tried ignoring it. I was too obsessed with holding the palm of her hand and feeling her pulse. At times I tried to put my hand across her waist. I was too enthralled, too enchanted with forgiveness. I remembered being young, when holding hands was just what it was. And then everything about her changed. The innocent smile turned first wry then frightening as she waltzed into her Totentanz:

"I saw a slut dangling from a lamppost on my way over here. How I wish that I was her. You forgot the rope didn't you? I wonder what she did to deserve it."

She stopped. I stopped. She grabbed my face with her paw and squeezed my cheeks and screamed "YOU LITTLE SHIT!"

"There was a boy I had once," she laughed. "When I told him how many diseases I had he stabbed himself in the heart with a kitchen knife. You're a boy, too, Lucky. You're not a man if you can't handle what you did to me. Did I tell you about my little sister? Of course I did. I told you how I gave her as a present to my boyfriend so he could fuck her in the ass, didn't I? But I gave her too many drugs to knock her out and the little bitch died that night when I was holding her ass cheeks open for Paul to shove his dick inside. I was proud of what I did for him. I think he had one of the greatest orgasms of his life!"

I wished I could die, right there and then.

"And what about you?" she went on. "How were your orgasms when you wrote all that fucked up shit about me? It definitely gave you a hardon but you wanted to cry into your pillow while stroking your cock and never giving yourself the release. When will you release me?"

I was paralyzed but she kept going.

"Remember how at one point I became an abortion addict? It's hard to explain but it was so thrilling! Oh, the excitement of getting pregnant and knowing that I was going to abort! And it was almost as good as when I would pick up those little spic cunts, fuck them and then turn them in to the cops. Oh you can't imagine what a kick I'd get out of it all. It was like drowning a little nest of rats and hearing their little squeals! If I knew one was actually going to get fried I'd even take a plane down to Texas and jerk off like crazy especially when I'd see the drugs starting to get pumped through that sad sack of shit's veins!"

I was trembling with fear but I tried to think of the situation at hand, that the choice of the Piers that I found odd now that everything in New York had changed so much. I was in the back of my mind expecting a sinister place, given the history of that city, given the history of my life and all I told her about, given the history of Betty and now, when all of New York had become sanitized it was as if she wanted to return to a familiar place, another return as if she wanted to revisit a place that was no more, which made sense as it was precisely the same as what I had embarked on. The piers: a place which at one point was as she correctly pointed out was filled with a hundred homosexuals lying naked on the pier, a place when murder and rape was quotidian and drugs were as easily bought as candy, a place where the warm, eel-like black water of the polluted Hudson stank equally with hope and sleaze and where the future shined through youth while you were sucking cock be it for fun or remuneration. That was in the past, the sleaze had been paved over but not for my Betty. Bereft of any excitement of the above sort, it was as if she wanted to take a trip down memory lane, and was on the verge of getting misty eyed under a strip joint sign. Betty wanted to see her past, a past that remained for me in a deep well, a sticky black pool of women firmly stuck in the molasses of the NYC summer night with one leg in the scum, the other in redemption and the cunt open to the flames of hell. Now she walked down Theresienstadt with bat wings neatly folded. And she terrified me more than anything I had ever known.

"This is your last chance, Lucky," she said. "We're going to do this once and for all."

She dropped her hand from my cheek.

"Let's do it, honey," she told me. "I want you to kill me."

I was ready to shit my pants but my sphincter muscle tightened when she added:

"You've been killing me for thirty years!"

I had no idea what was actually happening. Who was Betty? Where was I? Where was my home?

She pulled me closer.

Why was she walking? Why was I awake?

"Don't do it anymore, Lucky... don't talk about me anymore. Don't write the book that you have in mind. It's not worth it. It hurts too much. You're shoving knitting needles in my heart and cunt. I am filth. Filth through and through and you made me this way. I want you to let me go and..."

"I can't... Stop..."

"You have to stop, Lucky. You have to. I *have* suffered. I have suffered too much. And I have suffered enough."

"I can't!" I pleaded. "I'm in... I'm in love with you, Betty..."

"You're not in love with me, Lucky. You're in love with the idea of a teenage whore with a heart of gold or a heart of shit who somehow flies like a bird right into the sky. A perfect romantic scenario from an underdeveloped virgin. Well here's your answer: I'm a whore, you little shit, and I'm rotten through and through—there are no whores with hearts of gold. There are whores with diseased hearts and there are whores with diseased cunts, that is all of us. Your fantasy hooker, your little Iris or Sonia, is a fiction, Lucky.

Whores are whores and you are still a little boy. We want to fuck. We like money too. We don't care about any of that crap you wrote about, about "art" or "suffering," we take our suffering in stride. When you wrote about me, when you created me, you were lying to yourself. I was never a whore with a heart of gold, I was degradation and you know it. You lied to yourself and you're lying to yourself now, that's why you gave me that goddamn fucking wheelchair, you son of a bitch. What the fuck was that all about? To torture me even more?"

But I couldn't let go, couldn't say anything in defense and that was when the anger erupted further.

"Do you know why I'm walking now? Because I threw you away, Lucky! At least to get to this point, I made myself walk when you were too weak and started to imagine me differently. Maybe it was after you fucked me that I got this strength to do it, to throw away the wheelchair you gave me. You gave me this wheelchair, Lucky. For my birthday. Now it's your turn to throw me away! Dispose of me in the garbage dump, Lucky. I can't take it anymore! All those gangbangs, all those orgies… at the end of the night I'd look like someone vomited on me. All that sperm. I wanted to sew my cunt shut but I kept coming back for more, always returning for more. The parties I would go to, my god! Coming home at dawn, my silk shirt soaked with sperm and piss. I would wake up in the afternoon and would want to slash my wrists over the shame and disgust of what I'd done, but life went on. You know why? Because I can't kill myself, Lucky. You have to do it for me. You have to end this charade now. You have to end it. It was you who made me!"

I could no longer speak a single word.

"You didn't finish your book, did you?" she asked, and her lips formed a smile that was both wincing and bittersweet. How did she know?

"You pushed me under the car, Lucky! Don't you remember? Why did you do it? Why did you cripple me?"

And so she spoke and sang like a siren, reciting the verses that I did not want to write, the verses that I did not include in this book when I inserted The New World Symphony but which I knew I was intentionally leaving out. I did write those lines and she recited them to me, word for word.

"You fucking little shit! You left out the juiciest bits. You didn't tell your readers what you wanted to write, did you? You're just as much scum as I am! Wanna hear it?" And so she orated like a Greek poet, and I had to listen for I was her captive audience.

"Here, Lucky. This is the part you didn't really complete. Now you listen..."

In San Francisco, under the white sky
did she become a whore after all? What is
whoredom anyway? When does pleasure
take over from survival? Can we combine?

The corner office, yes, but something gnawed
between Stacy's thighs no matter how
the days and works, the days and years passed by.
But the itch went past happy hour or
blind drunk on Friday night with co-workers or clients
from out of town.

There were trysts with strangers in the most
  disgusting of places, flophouses on O'Farrell Street,
lunchtimes spent sucking cock, or walking down Broadway
like a stuck-up bitch who needed to suck off
some black dicks even at noon.
Black sperm tasted the best to her because
she found it fucking disgusting.
As with her eating shit, it was a sacrament,

the body, the shit, the taking the blood
of Christ, the mandingo Jesus
spurting down her white throat,
and then with an embroidered napkin
wiping off her mouth.
Then putting on lipstick, making herself prim and
walking proudly back to the hardon
of the Transamerica Tower.

There were some close calls,
when she played cat and mouse
in the sack with her version of "trade."
"Come on, fuck me you spic, you greasy beaner shit!"
(That was on a side street off of Mission).
Sometimes she let them play rough.
"Fucking white bitch, take this in your fucking mouth."
"Give it to me!"
Poor Stacy should have never uttered the word "nigger,"
it led to a fat lip that was hard to disguise
like the black eye Stu gave her back in LA.
It wasn't a nigger who sealed her fate but a little shit
reappearing again.

Even though she loved African sperm down
her white throat, and nigger baby batter sliding down
her legs and into the gutter drain.
The nigger's name was Gabriel, like the Archangel.
And NIGGER! NIGGER! NIGGER!
Started to rhyme with EDEN, EDEN, EDEN!
She met one guy who wanted to shit in her mouth.
"You're kidding," she laughed, but the next day she started
training, first eating a bit of her own shit,

then a bit more…
until she was ready to open her mouth underneath his
stinking asshole and swallow the whole load.
She gagged and puked;
covered in vomit and feces her face was radiant,
magnificent.
They shared a shit-stained kiss before she had to wash up
and return to the office.

But it wasn't only blacks or shit eaters
who sealed her unlucky fate
but a little wooden Pinocchio,
flat, made of plywood, with geek glasses and a skinny frame,
all sensitivity, neuroses and insecurity,
who hid like a plank within the walls of Stacy's secret life.
Within the cracks, within the keyholes,
snug with the wood lice, he lived and eavesdropped.
He waits with the termites and
sees her in her intimate moments
and wants to cut himself, but he refrains,
knows that he's a paper soldier.
And so he grinds his teeth and waits
beneath the wallpaper, sharpening his paper knife.
He's stained with wood glue, his little fingers
sticky with the wrong substance,
not something that he wishes to smell.
He drills keyholes, eyeholes, spy holes into Stacy's life.

He is her boyfriend, so she introduces him to others,
or started to.
And what did poor little Stacy end up as?
Pushed under the streetcar by her Petrushka,

the jealous boyfriend.
And then Stacy loses her legs
and pisses and shits her pants
but she still wants to somehow get laid,
despite her condition.

And the bed feels moist while Dvořák and Stravinski
play in her creator's head while she can't move her legs.

"Who do you think Petrushka is? It's you, you son of a bitch! You created me solely to make me suffer forever!" she screamed. "You killed me once on paper, Lucky. Now have the balls to kill me in real life. Go ahead! Fuck me and kill me!"

"Betty, please, please," I begged. I thought I was about to die.

"WHO THE FUCK IS BETTY?! MY NAME IS STACY!!" she screamed.

I was afraid—afraid of her, afraid of the truth. I had hid behind the bottle so many times so as not to deal with the unknown, with the things that sometimes should never be talked about, just like my mother. But here I was, standing in front of Betty as in front of St. Peter with his keys all bloody, or face to face with the Grand Inquisitor. I was now finally forced to take off the many masks I wore and those I painted on people I knew; forced to admit how like a hare I always ran away from fixing a broken mirror. But I could also sense she held no evil in her, that she only wanted freedom—freedom from this loathsome city, freedom from the purgatory known as life, be it fictional or carbon-based.

The world was spinning: the piers, the lights of New Jersey, the faint sounds of people and taxicabs, the honking of car horns. Queer thoughts were popping into my mind, random memories: my mom making an omelet, me pining for a set of white shoes, Easter bells, "don't skimp on the butter," a brochure for the poor about how to raise a healthy baby, Orthodox cheesecake, blood on the panties, the grotesque cycle of creation and destruction, conception and demise, the image of a she-bear eating her young, Saturn eating his sons, mothers devouring their offspring. My heart was pounding like a subway train. Blood shot up into my nose and throat. I swallowed blood as she spoke.

"Kill me, Lucky," she pleaded. "Kill me and get me out of your mind forever so I can finally sleep! Just promise me one thing. Please don't ever write another screenplay or story about me again. I am so tired. Fuck me for the last time, Lucky. Rapefuck me and then kill me, strangle me, murder me, in the name of Christ murder me, but promise me one thing—do not ever, ever write anything about me again. I want to die, Lucky. Don't do this to me anymore. Murder me..." Her voice rose and wilted and then she put her arms around my neck and in a whisper repeated: "Murder me. Murder me..."

"Betty!" I sobbed, "I want you to live. I want both of us to live and..."

"Shut up and kill me, Lucky" she said. I saw how unimaginably tired she was, how tired she was of existing. "Remember how many times you wanted to kill yourself? If you brought me back then I would have told you 'just do it, what are you waiting for?' But you left me buried in your desk drawer gathering dust and silverfish, and you didn't bring me back until you started thinking about 'the book' and then you woke me up from my sleep when I was suspended at the bottom of the ocean. But you never killed me and now you have put me back into purgatory, wide awake. Oh, to die! I would have done you that favor, I promise, if I was a so-called writer. But you didn't. You crippled me instead. Don't you understand that I can't kill myself? It's you who needs to murder me. Go ahead, finish what you started!"

Reluctantly I reached for her neck, and when I had my hands

around her throat and her big blue eyes looked up at me pleading for me snuff her, I tightened my grip and squeezed harder. The very thought of murder always seemed so alien and so horrifying to me, but at that moment something snapped. I had three conflicting ideas running through my head—I wanted to punish her, I wanted to put her out of her misery as she had begged me to do, and I wanted, by killing her, to finally make her mine.

As my grip tightened I saw the fear in her eyes, her utter terror of everything going black forever but still I kept choking her, watching her spirit leave her body until suddenly everything started turning black for me as well and I collapsed on top of her. I felt her body growing cold underneath me and I drifted off into the dreamless sleep of a horrible sinner.

When I awoke I thought what I was lying on top of was her lifeless corpse, but it was only the Manhattan pavement. Betty was gone, once again. No wheelchair, no crutches, no trails. A light cold drizzle started. I picked myself up and began walking to the nearest subway station.

Inside the subway car I shook and shuddered and though I tried to hold it in, eventually I broke down and started crying like a baby. There never was any Betty. I finally accepted it. Like all writers, I had played God. In creating her I also damned her and I finally saw it.

As I tried desperately to keep sane, the doors opened and in walked a tall black man impeccably dressed in a white suit, red shirt and white hat, carrying a brief case. The subway car was mostly empty. He started to preach.

"It's an abomination—an a-bom-i-nation—to stick your penis in another man's anus. And they call it love!"

Betty melted away for a moment, let loose her sticky grip, and I chuckled to myself: "Something you see every day, a well-dressed NYC lunatic..."

The preacher got off at the next stop and I returned to my crazy thoughts. "When I die, will the world disappear with me? Have I imagined not just Betty but everything around me as well? Did I also dream up continents? Did I create Jesus, Hitler?" There were still too many things for me to come to terms with, not just Betty but also the ghosts of my parents. I had to accept that time was running out, to resign myself to the process of ageing, of dying. To accept that I will die and that everything I have done will be forgotten.

When I arrived home, the pink dawn was also helping me lift my own Veil of Maya. The moist, humid night back at the piers was caking and the cool autumn breeze returned—that breeze, the most melancholy of New York weathers, which signals the end of summer.

The first thing that I did was call Charlotte to tell her I was coming home, and to ask her to order me a plane ticket for the next day. Hesitantly, tremulously, I also asked her to find me a psychiatric facility. I had always feared both therapy and chemical treatments but now I knew I had no choice if I was going to survive, and despite my penchant for tortured writing, survival was now priority, if for nothing else then for the sake of my daughter, so that she could have me around a bit longer.

Charlotte agreed to all of this and was if not particularly elated then at least pleasantly surprised that I had finally decided to seek treatment. I feared, deeply, that I would be lobotomized, but I had no other choice.

Part IV

ACCEPTANCE

THE ETERNAL RETURN

The printers are already halfway through their typesetting of The Goat Song and the author and his true friends walk out of a pub into a wonderful Petersburg spring night. A night that makes souls soar up over the Neva River, above the palaces, the cathedrals, a night rustling like a garden, singing like youth, and shooting past like an arrow, which for them, has already flown.

—Konstantin Vaginov, *The Goat Song*

The end of summer, the first taste of autumn, is the most poignant time of year in New York. The trees explode with color and there is warmth and mist. But there is also, at some point, a bleak, frigid interlude that reminds you that all of this will soon end—even starting in mid-August, the cold wind makes you shudder and you know that soon you will enter what Bill Faulkner called the season of rain and death. On the subways people shiver, sweat turning into icicles on our backs, the AC too much now. Samhain is coming, the end of the bliss and madness. People talk about the end of their holidays, going back to work, back to school, back out onto the cold street, and the days get shorter as we reach November.

The dead technicolor leaves make small tornados in the street, the night wind carries in the final warmth before the cold, before hibernation... It was time for me to leave New York, possibly forever. I understood that this adventure was finally over. A maturing. A little death. I would return to California's "endless summer," where time passes way too quickly and where the days and months and years are a hazy blur. New York's Indian summers were something I had always wished to escape, but whenever I left them behind, I missed them dearly. Here I was, leaving New York yet again. New York of the blue light of possibility. New York of the yellow light of defeat. Secrets and confessions oscillate between shoddy and vile, and in the light of life, we oscillate between pain and sleep.

I surveyed the place, my apartment of dreams. Standing in the center, I turned in circles, waiting for something to come to me, some kind of magical clue. I spun around waiting for the room to start moving, for a vortex to open, for some kind of understanding of what happened to me this summer. But nothing happened, and I only ended up making myself dizzy.

I packed clothes, wrapped my good shoes in a supermarket bag as if they were the white shoes that never arrived and were never purchased and glanced around once more. No, nothing. The whole place felt unlived-in now, as if I had never been there. Or as if I were just passing through another moonlit motel, one guest amid thousands, like Stacy did when she tried to find California and found a dead end. Or was that Betty? I didn't care anymore. She was disappearing, the memory was fading. And I never will be caught. There is no body. Cherchez la femme…

I went out to the balcony and lit a final cigarette. I stared at the perfect row of streetlights stretching down Ocean Parkway. And beyond that was the ocean. I considered going down to the beach one last time to bid farewell to New York and the summer, and I suppose also to Betty herself. But I was frightened. A shiver ran down my spine as I considered the possibility. I knew there were no lighthouses down there by Brighton Beach but I felt that if I went to the boardwalk one would magically appear, tall and erect, casting a beam of light across the water and illuminating Betty's silhouette, perhaps as a mermaid, perhaps a rusalka, diving into the black waters of the night. I put out my cigarette, turned off the lights and sunk into a deep, dark sleep.

In the morning, at the airport, I was mostly hangover free, and so it was a perfect time to replenish all the toxins I lost over the course of non-boozy sleep. First a couple of "Cadillac" Bloody Marys at the sports bar where I carried my McDonalds breakfast, then a pint of horrible beer at another pub closer to the gate until I was sufficiently primed to handle the flight.

The airplane rose gently up into the late afternoon sky, avoided Manhattan and ascended into the pink clouds. I had rough, fleeting flashbacks of other flights I had taken in the past, in my youth. I flipped through magazines, stared at the menagerie of grotesque travelers, but I was focused on only one thing—my hapless Betty, and how by creating her, I simultaneously destroyed her. It did not matter to me at this point that she never "lived." She was more alive than you and I will ever be, even as a paper doll of my imagination. And I wept because I realized I sentenced both myself and Betty to damnation because by writing this book, I lied to her. I did not in fact kill her, but instead kept her alive to live in eternal hell. I created her, and she will always, thanks to me, be sentenced to live her fate over and over again with each reader, just the way we, as living humans, once we expire, will continue to live solely as characters in annals and memories. But while memories fade, we who are written about are doomed to be read and re-read, and thus repeat our lives infinitely. It is the heaviest burden. The eternal return.

I ordered a weak drink and closed my eyes after a few sips. As the plane ascended and circled around old brown New York, I finally saw it for what it is—a sad, vinegary city whose horrors lie under the pavements, under the grass in the parks, in the trash cans, at the bottom of the rivers, in tenements and housing projects, and all with little redemption. Rome may be a graveyard, Toledo may be famous for ripping out tongues, Geneva for live cats scratching you to death as you drown… but there is a particular terror that New York always had and which persists for me. LA has its ghosts and goblins and it terrifies me too, but maybe the atrocities are too recent for the blood to truly seep through and poison the entire water table.

I made some small talk with a French girl to my right. She wanted to know what to see in Los Angeles. I mumbled something—I was beginning to fade—and soon, after a few polite words of broken French, I was asleep.

When I awoke, I thought I was hugging a skeleton but it was only the brittle sheets that they give me in this place, the place where I eat bland food but receive some very delicious drugs. Every morning, after breakfast, we do a little dance. They keep trying to find out why I murdered my wife and I keep telling them that I was in New York when it happened and that I don't know what they're talking about. They keep telling me I never went to New York and that there was a "crime of passion" right here in Pasadena, California, and that I was found not guilty by reason of insanity. I tell them again that I was in New York. They tell me about a strangled body, they say they have no record of me getting on a plane. What can I say? I am trying to prove to them that I'm not a camel. There is comfort here, most of the doctors are nice to me, although the beery California sky breaks my heart. I suppose that this is the end now, that I am indeed king of infinite space.

"Do you know where you are?" someone asks me each morning. It makes the mind reel how they insist on playing this game of checkers with me.

"What day is today?" says another.

"Who is the president of the United States?"

I answer correctly and diligently each time, but every time I have to fight the urge to answer: "Ulaanbaatar. April 6, 1683. I am." Would it have made a difference? Would they increase my medication or give me something new? Perhaps I'll try it sometime soon just to see what would happen. ECT can be a rather euphoric experience and I generally look forward to those treatments. What I don't understand is what exactly they want from me. I don't see things differently than they, or you. And besides, if I did, how would they know?

Since drinking is no longer an option and the drugs have rid me of my sexual desire, instead of looking forward to the female ghosts that filled the night, I would instead go to sleep looking forward to breakfast. A cheese omelet, coffee, followed by a banana muffin took the place of early morning erections and fleeting embraces with liminal beings. At least the eggs and bread were tangible, digestible, something that I could empirically state that I experienced "in real life." And they actually served fresh eggs, too.

Once in blue moon, variations on old dreams still return. In one recent dream I was young, wealthy, and able to drink alcohol. My girlfriend was Isabelle Adjani of the times of The Tenant. This time though the sex was more passive. I performed oral on her and did not have the chance to copulate. I was giving her pleasure as if I was atoning for something. And with all the drugs that were flowing through my body, an erection was only a distant memory. In another I was walking through Hyde Park in London, along the Serpentine. It is the 17th century, perhaps earlier, and the courtly ladies are preparing the gentlemen for a unicorn hunt. The dazzle of the sun and bursting green and yellow wakes me up.

I also still dream of New York often. I still picture myself drinking cold white wine with my dad at an outdoor café on Columbus Avenue in warm, green spring. I have just been accepted to NYU film school and we are celebrating my success. I awake excited only to find myself in a mental hospital. I will never go to film school or make a film and two thirds of my life are gone and I have nothing to show for them.

Perhaps I have always been mad, or at least imbecilic. I have always tried to excuse my failure by blaming the changing times. Truth is, now that I am now re-discovering literature—the library here is wonderful—I wonder why I couldn't have been a better learner in high school or college. If only I could go back in time and devote myself to studies in earnest!

I am in a warm, safe place, back in my adopted hometown of Pasadena. In the winter, I can see a sprinkling of snow on the mountains. In late spring, I can see the marine fog coming in from the ocean. In the summer, I am protected from the blazing heat of the valley through double-glazed windows and I look at those same mountains, now a burnt amber. In the case of an earthquake, I have been told that the building is reinforced and there is nothing to fear.

But one morning something strange happened. I awoke and instinctively reached over for a glass of water on my nightstand, where I found a handkerchief. At first I thought it must have been an old t-shirt that I had thrown off in the middle of the night when breaking into a sweat, but this was a tiny square shape that I did not remember owning. I turned on the bedside lamp to examine it. It was a piece of crimson velvet, and on the corner there was one word embroidered in cursive: "Betty G." I picked up the cloth, crumpled it in my hand, put it next to my cheek and began to cry.

The next night I again woke up in need of water and heard laughter, again a cackling laughter. I reached over to the night stand. There was the same embroidered crimson cloth. It looked as though my water had spilled on it, but when I squeezed the kerchief it dripped blood. Then the rag grew tiny little legs, feet, arms and hands, a little fetus that I squeezed across the midsection, one whose fate and life I held in my hand, and this little piece of hell actually started crying, and the tears were dripping out of this satanic little marmoset, weeping "Don't hurt me, please stop it, you're hurting me, you're hurting me honey!"

This thing couldn't decide whether it was laughing or crying, whether it was asking for pity or asking me to pull its guts out and I threw the piece of shit against the wall as fast and hard as I could. It bounced back, then bounced back again, bouncing like a ping pong back and forth until I could not even keep pace with the movement until it landed right back in my palm and again took the form of a handkerchief carefully folded. I opened up the crimson cloth and again saw the embroidery in the corner of the cloth: "Betty." I crumpled it up and threw against the wall again but the whimpering persisted so I put a pillow over my head to drown it out.

"Something great is going to happen to you this year, I can just feel it!" my mother would say to me each year and nothing of the sort ever occurred. There are no happy endings for most. The best we can hope for is acquiescence or the simple return of the waist—but at least for now, I felt somewhat certain that this time a dream was finally just a dream.

Then I woke up again. I thought I was clutching a skeleton but it was only the arm rest and the fold out tray. My airplane food spilled all over the French girl. I apologized repeatedly and clumsily wiped the crumbs of muffin and cheese from her dress, unsure how to dab the wine stains on her blouse without touching her tits. A stewardess turned up and gave the girl a wet cloth and soon the captain announced that we were starting our descent into Los Angeles International Airport. We sat for the remaining forty-five minutes of the flight in awkward silence and I tried my best to avoid eye contact.

As the plane descended down to LAX I saw the white anthill. Those millions of souls who will soon be dead and forgotten, replaced by another swarm, repeating the process until we finally kill off everything on this planet, including ourselves.

My wife picked me up. I was crying. We drove directly to the psychiatric clinic.

WHEN WE DEAD AWAKEN

I was discharged just over a month later and sent home without having to "betray Julia" or admit that "I love Big Brother." I exited into a warm, banal twilight. The clinic was walking distance from home. I told Charlotte that I wanted to walk home and so I walked.

As I passed Cal Tech—the leafy, placid campus where all manner of things were being studied and researched—subjects and theorems and formulas all beyond my grasp—I made a detour and went into Tournament Park, where I would sometimes take my daughter before this wretched and amazing adventure in Brooklyn. I walked past the orange tennis courts, past the running track, and entered the green playground. I was the only one there and I sat on a bench and immediately burst into tears. What a stupid path of life I had chosen in my youth—the path of no path, the path of no direction. What I wouldn't do, who I wouldn't murder, to go back in time, to be an undergrad once again, to have a goal and at least a modicum of talent, to be healthy, to be sober. Oh, how I pined to be twenty again, attending lectures, composing papers, running the track, playing tennis, looking forward to grad school and a career. How simple it would have been to do that. But there is nothing one can do to alleviate such regret except perhaps believe in parallel universes and accept that one tiny failure can often lead to a whole life of subsequent failures and the subsequent contrition and remorse. I dried my tears and continued walking home.

After the dread subsided, I began to experience a type of calm, something like the blissful feeling one has before an epileptic fit or after an insulin low. I started to feel that in these months of madness, my screenplays somehow came to life, that I lived them, that I lived Stacy, that I lived Betty, and that all was not for naught. For a second I thought that I too had had a "rich life," albeit one compacted into a hallucinatory three months in Brooklyn.

All my dreams and all my fantasies and all my nightmares came alive during that summer. And in the end, "the book" that I was trying to write was not the story of Stacy Fox but rather this very case study you are reading. A case study on the process of giving up, on failure and accomplishment, on the strange mess of memory.

I am forty-nine now, and I lived thirty years in those short three months. Finally, I had accomplished something, and this is the record of that journey. It was as if I had finally taken the proverbial "trip of a lifetime."

In a few years, or hopefully, since I do still wish to live, in a few decades, I will die. I will cease to exist. Those remaining years, be they short or long, all point in one direction—the graveyard. But apart from the dreadful desire to be remembered and the utter fear of oblivion, there is the vulgar reality that it was all for naught, and the question remains: why continue in the face of impending obliteration? That is not for me to ponder if I wish to live out my life without taking it by my own hand.

As I reach the end of my own pathetic odyssey, I recognized those suitors that I need to kill: my youth, my ambitions, my white shoes, Betty, Stacy. It is a relief to bury the dead. A friend of mine called it the "death peace."

Though my life could never come close in stature to the lives of many others, though I could not and never will achieve even the petty bliss and horror of my characters, though my life will never be as stunning as my father's or other friends and relatives who lived through unimaginable times, what I managed to accomplish that summer was, in many ways, enough to put an end to the dream. Dreamers and madmen live the richest of lives.

There is no need for any more poems. Safely wrapped up in memories and in the California yellow, I have my thoughts, my recollections and my madeleines to keep me warm until the curtain falls.

People like to forget. I too will be forgotten, perhaps much sooner than later, even if people read this book. Most of our lives are spent in times of forgetting and laughter in between deaths and funerals, not just the "flashing lights of God the Father." It goes the same for wars and genocides, cataclysms and paroxysms. Those books that were on my shelves, those lives who lived through world wars, through cold wars, they now seem as distant as the notes of Roman soldiers or even memoirs of WW2 despite the latter experiences being not that many decades ago from the present. But like my father—better than nothing as I said before—at least my internment has given me the time to write down this autobiography of sorts, truncated as it is.

There is a branch of Hindu philosophy—Advaita Vedanta— that has a simple and poignant explanation for understanding the worst excesses of mankind. In Vedanta, there is no reason for the existence of good and evil. Since we are part of the universe, and therefore part of God, everything that causes us pain brings pain to God as well. When we seek an understanding of the Holocaust, the Gulags, the Khmer Rouge, so does God. When we weep, scream, cry or bawl, so does God. And so I, too, a petty god in my own right, wept. And I wept when I understood that when I created Betty I also doomed her to her fate, exactly the same way that the Moon, unknowingly, ruined Glasha the Mole's life. I saw Betty departing, ascending into black space, trying to find her way back to her tiny little planet, always eclipsed by some bright and beautiful sun.

Like God, like a parent, by giving her life I also sentenced her to death. And by giving her all the joys that life can hold I also gifted her breathtaking suffering. By lying to her and writing this book, I sentenced her to die each time someone reads this story, and if this book is still around years or decades or centuries from now, she will die again and again and again. Time heals all, they say. Once this book is forgotten, her torturous story will cease to be remembered and Betty will finally find peace.

Soon I started to forget Betty. I let her fade away just as I had let my parents fade away, just as I had my youth and my dreams dissolve. There is much to be said for the "process of giving up"— the toil is worth it at the end. Yes, Betty would still come to me once in a while, with a siren call deep in my dreams, but she was disappearing with each nightly visit as her visitations became less frequent. I saw her pulled away by gravity further and further, and soon even the echo began to fade. And then, out of the ashes of a crippled phoenix, a semblance of love was reborn.

My wife and I finally went on a date. We got a babysitter and walked to the movie theater up the block and I was finally able to put my arm around her waist. And so Charlotte and I walked, towing our memories and broken dreams like tin cans from a marital bumper. I was hoping the movie playing she was taking me to was perhaps "L'Atalante" or "Sunrise: A Song of Two Humans"— something dealing with a reconciliation. Instead we sat in the dark and watched apes taking over the world. I didn't mind.

We walked back home in silence but at least she squeezed my hand, and when we went to bed and got under the covers, I could picture her thinking "It is okay... I will learn to live with you... I have already learned to live with you, for many years..." and so I closed my eyes. My nightmare was over, and so was my dream. Sleep masks on to shield us from the early morning California sunlight, we held each other tight at last.